TRUTH, DARE, KISS OR

WITHDRAWN
from Camden Libraries

Also by Liane Jones

The Dreamstone
Painting the Dark

TRUTH, DARE, KISS OR PROMISE

Liane Jones

Copyright © 1997 Liane Jones

The right of Liane Jones to be identified as the Author of the Work has been asserted by her in accordance with the Copyright, Designs and Patents Act 1988.

First published in 1997
by HEADLINE BOOK PUBLISHING

A REVIEW hardback

10 9 8 7 6 5 4 3 2 1

All rights reserved. No part of this publication may be reproduced, stored in a retrieval system, or transmitted, in any form or by any means without the prior written permission of the publisher, nor be otherwise circulated in any form of binding or cover other than that in which it is published and without a similar condition being imposed on the subsequent purchaser.

All characters in this publication are fictitious and any resemblance to real persons, living or dead, is purely coincidental.

Jones, Liane, 1958-
Truth, dare, kiss or promise
I.Title
823.9'14[F]

ISBN 0 7472 1387 9

Typeset by
Letterpart Limited, Reigate, Surrey

Printed and bound in Great Britain by
Clays Ltd, St Ives plc

HEADLINE BOOK PUBLISHING
A division of Hodder Headline PLC
338 Euston Road
London NW1 3BH

LONDON BOROUGH OF EALING	
10752037	
Library Services UK	15/10/97
	£17.99
AFICT	100

They four set them to feasting, and they hunted and took their pleasure.

(Manawydan, Son of Llyr)
From the *Four Branches of the Mabinogi*.

To Jamie Buxton and
Siobhán Kilfeather

Part One

1

A mile inland from the docks, about halfway up St Beuno's Hill, Nye squinted at the page and lost his place. He looked at his watch: three-fifteen – not worth turning a light on. Outside, the sky was giving out lemon colour. Past the shops and playgrounds and the dark wedge of the rugby ground, lorries drove round the ring road. He'd be on it soon, heading into the wrinkled land that was still visible to the practised eye.

It would be a relief to be on the move after the last two hours. His muscles hurt now he tried to relax them – he'd been hunching again. Frustration with Dictionary and Teach-yourself book. He'd expected to make progress today too, with two hours to kill and this itch to soothe, but it was so bloody difficult.

Tom and Georgie would laugh if they were here. They could afford to. They both had Welsh in the family but saw no reason to use it. These words would make matter-of-fact sense to them. Whereas for Nye, they were at best tricky and today even the look of them had turned mysterious, like map symbols: little forests of *ff*s dotted about the page, gully-like *W*s, the delving *Y* . . .

To be honest, his concentration had been flawed. The other two had intruded from the start. He kept seeing Tom's face, from the night Tom had told him he was getting married. And the tilt of Georgie's head yesterday, when she'd listened to his idea. She'd been watchful, resistant, only pretending to be amused.

Would she come today, after all? He thought he could count on Tom.

Time to put away the books. He'd arranged to meet Tom at four o'clock in Caerfach, on the pavement outside the castle. He mustn't be late: it would be cold on the hillside and Tom would be wearing too-thin clothes as usual, looking surprised and pinched.

Nye changed into his thick sweater and coat. At the last minute he took a scarf as well, so he could throw it to Tom if necessary. Or wind it solicitously round Georgie, if she were there.

★ ★ ★

The bus had filled up with pupils from the secondary school, and the noise and steamed-up windows reminded Tom of swimming sessions. He wiped a hole in the glass and saw that they were swinging round Colliers' Corner. The air outside was bluer than it had been five minutes before; all the cars had turned their head-lamps on. Straight ahead the shopfronts were stuck on to Caerfach hill like Elastoplasts. Rumbelow's Electric, Lo-Cost Food Store, smaller shops selling cardigans and souvenirs and fish and chips; nothing you could go into without your heart sinking.

He hadn't been here for months. Even when he'd lived at home and Caerfach had been the nearest town, he'd hardly ever come into it. He'd preferred to make the longer trip to Bartraeth. But Nye seemed to have an odd affection for this place. He came back to the second-hand bookshop quite regularly and claimed that the Black Lion behind the police station served good ham lunches. But then Nye had a car.

The Triumph Herald was standing alone in the castle car park as the bus lurched by. Nye himself was waiting at the bus stop, reading a paper. He looked twice as big as the woman next to him. He folded the paper when he saw Tom and walked the few paces down to meet him. Tom noticed the woman scurrying behind him to reach the bus and realised that she was using Nye, in his thick black overcoat, as a windshield. His own eyes watered as a gust blew straight into them.

'Shit, what a day.'

'It's February, mon.' Nye tucked the paper into his pocket. 'How was your progress meeting with the principal?'

'Oh, all right. At least he didn't leave the room during it this time. It lasted eight minutes; I timed it. He doesn't know what he's supposed to be asking me any more than I do.'

'Has he ever been to see your work?'

'Not since I won the bursary. And you know what he thought of that.'

'God alive, what's the matter with the man?' Nye laughed. 'Does he think looking at your stuff would contaminate him?'

'Probably,' said Tom shortly and turned to the road; grit swirled up by the traffic stung his face. 'Is that the place over there?'

'Yes, Evan and Crosby.' Nye fell in beside him at once, pacing alongside Tom as he negotiated the cars, moving fractionally away so as not to crowd him. Tom saw Nye's sidelong look and felt himself under observation. He pretended not to notice. It would only irritate him to encounter Nye's humorous sympathy.

And it was hard enough keeping himself good-tempered in this wind-whipped place. He'd only agreed to come out of duty and the sense that Nye deserved a bit of indulgence after the last few weeks. Besides, he could hardly refuse when Nye had gone ahead with the arrangements and even taken an afternoon off work to accompany them.

'Georgie's going to try and meet us there,' he called to Nye as they paused to let a van roar past. 'It depends what time she's free. She said she'd call and leave a message at this place.'

'Good,' said Nye. They hurried across the last few yards of Tarmac together and reached the kerb.

'She's quite keen to see it,' Tom said. 'With it being so close to the school.'

Nye nodded. His strong face looked healthy, almost warm. 'I hope I'm not bringing you both out on a fool's errand.' He opened his coat collar and loosened his scarf, staring back across traffic at the huge building, dim behind its moat. 'The castle looks bigger in the dark, doesn't it? Ah well, you've got nothing to lose by looking. I'll buy us all a whisky afterwards. I tell you what, if you and Georgie hate it, I'll buy you two.'

It was even colder on this side, and Tom hunched his shoulders. 'Come on, let's get in.'

'When are you getting married?' The estate agent stood next to Tom in the doorway and they were both watching Nye and Georgie on the far side of the room. The two of them were tapping the chimney breast, trying to hear where it became hollow. Georgie's face was dubious; she still hadn't decided if she was playing a game here or being serious.

'April,' said Tom.

'Spring, is it? You've left it late to go house-hunting.' The man, Mr Edmunds in his forties or fifties with his mac done up to the neck, seemed only mildly interested. Tom felt that he didn't really take them seriously and was only trying to get the measure of the situation.

'We've already got a flat in Bartraeth,' said Tom. 'A university place. It's not perfect but we can stay there till the end of June if we need to.'

'Oh, I see. So you're still students, then? I thought—'

'Only Georgie. I left college last year. And she won't be there for much longer; she'll be a teacher by September.'

'Ah, yes. I remember your friend saying now. Well that's all right.' Mr Edmunds relaxed. 'Your flat in Bartraeth, in one of those red buildings by the station, are you?'

'That's it.'

'There are nice rooms in some of those.'

'Yes.' Tom looked out of the window at the garden. The moon had come out from behind the clouds and the apple and pear trees cast shadows. 'The thing is, they're very small and we've got no room for a studio. That's why we were so interested in the garage just now. We need somewhere like that to work.'

'Oh yes, well, as you saw there's plenty of room for painting in there. And electric points. I'd have thought it would be on the cold side, though.'

'I could get one of those paraffin heaters.'

Nye turned from the chimney breast. 'It's been bricked up,' he said. 'Filled with builders' rubble, probably. Does this little gas fire work?'

Mr Edmunds took the specifications out of his coat pocket and shuffled through them. 'Yes, apparently. Though the gas is shut off at the moment, of course.'

'Listen,' said Georgie. 'I can hear the television from next door.'

'That's Mrs Davies,' said Mr Edmunds. 'She's lived here for nearly forty years. She's getting hard of hearing. Still,' he tucked the papers back in his pocket, 'it would mean she wouldn't be disturbed by your music.'

Tom caught Nye's look of surprise and smiled at him over the estate agent's bent head. Artists, Mr Edmunds obviously thought; loud music, irregular hours, a commune next to Mrs Davies. But a married commune, and the young woman nice enough, training to be a teacher.

And why not?

Tom suddenly felt cheerful. This was going to take more thinking about than he'd expected. Perhaps it might not be such a stupid idea to leave Bartraeth for a while and settle in here. He'd been in the city three and a half years and he'd got to know the people, had more than his share of ramshackle stairwells and sirens outside Chinese takeaways. He'd been imagining more of the same for the foreseeable future – maybe a flat above a lock-up workshop, or somewhere down near the old docks. But it might be more interesting to move out. It would certainly be less predictable. He had a show to prepare for July. He needed to clear his mind if he was to produce work that lived up to last year's promise.

The Islyn: 'You must be joking,' he'd said to Nye when he'd first mentioned it. 'It's next door to Penllwyn. Why the hell would I want to move there? Would *you* move back?'

'It's not Penllwyn, though,' Nye had argued. 'It's separate. How many times did you go there in the last few years we lived in the village? Went through it on your bike, yes, but how many times did you actually stop there?'

It was true; Tom could think of just one occasion, and that had been to go to a party in the barn, hired out by some girls from Caerfach. What was more, when they'd driven in from the west tonight, Nye's Triumph Herald dutifully following Mr Edmunds's car, Tom had been surprised to find that he barely recognised the landmarks. The angle of approach had disoriented him and they'd arrived sooner than he'd expected, and when he'd got out of the car there'd been only a faint glow from beyond the hill to show him where Penllwyn was.

Nye was right: he didn't really know anything about the Islyn. He couldn't say how many houses it had or whether the nearest pub was the Red Dragon up on the Harborth road or the Griffin towards Penllwyn. That could be a problem. But then it would be spring by the time they moved in and it could be quite pleasant riding bicycles around here. The number sixteen bus would do them both for work, and then again, if the gallery sold Big Orange Triangle, they would be able to get some kind of car.

He looked at Georgie, who was now walking towards him, shaking her head. He realised he was still grinning. 'What do you think, Georgie?'

'Hmm.' She blew on her fingers and wrapped them in the ends of Nye's scarf, which she was now wearing round her neck. 'You like it, don't you?'

'Yes I do.' He flicked a glance of acknowledgement at Nye – better now than later, if Nye was going to make a meal of it. But Nye was watching Georgie. 'What about you?'

'I'm not sure.' She grimaced at Nye. It was a public look, meant for Tom and Nye to understand together: here he goes; you know what it's like. Just as well I'm a match for him. But she wasn't unhappy about the idea; in fact, Tom thought she was quite taken with it. 'I think it's freezing and I want to see it in daylight. I might come out here in my lunch hour tomorrow.'

'How will you get here?' said Nye.

'I'll borrow a bike. Then I'll know what the ride's like as well.'

'I'm afraid I won't be able to meet you tomorrow,' said Mr Edmunds.

'Nor will I,' said Tom.

'That's all right, I just want to look around outside. I've never been here before. I've got no idea where I am.'

'I like the house,' said Tom. 'Could we paint it?'

'I'll have to ask the owner,' said Mr Edmunds. 'The usual arrangement is that tenants need permission to decorate. I expect he'd agree – as long as you sign it, of course!' His smile was startling; he looked from one to another of them, beaming with enjoyment. Georgie laughed. The sound could still move Tom sometimes, especially when it seemed to be surprised out of her.

'You want to be careful saying that to a Williams College man,' she said. 'You could end up with an installation of cow pats and dismembered dolls.'

'Oh Good God.' Mr Edmunds's smile broadened further. 'Is that the kind of thing you make?'

'No.' Nye moved away from the chimney breast at last. He was hunched and looked slightly irritable, though it might have been the effort of ducking to avoid the light fitting. 'It certainly isn't. Tom's a painter. About as traditional as you can get and still win a prize.'

'I'm glad it wasn't a waste of time. But there's no hurry about deciding, is there?' Nye sat forward on the plush red pub bench; with his elbows on the table, he took up almost the same space as both Tom and Georgie, sitting opposite.

'No,' said Georgie. 'But why leave it either? As Tom says, someone else could come along and take it.'

'Well, it's been empty three months . . .' Nye shrugged. Now that they were settled in the pub he'd unbuttoned his coat and colour was coming back into his face. It made him look very young. Under his business suit he was wearing a sweater and it reminded Tom of the way he'd worn his school uniform. Nye had always been so very obviously the youngest in the class then, at least a year younger than anyone else, a difference which was impossible to hide, despite his size.

Nye's cheeks were growing rosy but the bridge of his nose was still pinched white. He must have got chilled through in the cottage. Tom had felt the cold himself but hadn't minded it; not like the bitterness on Castle Hill.

Nye swallowed his mouthful of beer and put the glass down.

He leaned back on the bench and eased his shoulders. He seemed vulnerable, as if he were having to concentrate very hard to keep himself balanced. That was familiar from school, too. So was the sheer force of his attention, which Tom could feel ticking away inside Nye's round, darkly curled head.

'What?' he said in exasperation.

'Hmm?' Nye frowned. 'What do you mean?'

'Come on, what? You took us there; you were all for it this morning. Don't tell me you've changed your mind?'

'You like it, then?' Nye said carefully.

'Yes. It's got its points.'

'You don't think it's a little remote?'

'Sure, that's one of them.'

'And what about the distance from Bartraeth?'

'It's not that bad on the bus, and besides, I hardly ever have to be in before lunchtime. Georgie's the one who has to be on time and she's working in Penllwyn now.'

'You're not full-time in Penllwyn though, are you?' Nye said to Georgie. 'You have days off for study, and what about the evenings and weekends?'

'What about them?' said Georgie, smiling.

'Won't you miss being able to see your friends easily? Going round the corner for a drink and a film?'

'Oh no, I don't think so. I'm a bit tired of it, to be honest. I've got marking to do most evenings and notes to write up. I wouldn't mind the quiet life for a bit.'

Nye nodded. All the muscles in his face were smooth; there was a half-formed smile on his mouth. Tom could almost see the hurt hopping round, trying to find a place to settle. This time Georgie's laugh struck him as rather unkind, especially because it had a note of genuine delight in it.

'You idiot, of course we'd miss you. But we won't lose touch. It's only eight miles away, for God's sake, and you've got the car. If we do live there, you'll come and see us all the time.' Her hair had fallen across her cheek so Tom couldn't see her face, but she reached across the table and flicked Nye's wrist: quite hard, Tom thought.

Nye's colour deepened and he turned to Tom. He always did this when he was self-conscious – presented himself face on to show he wasn't afraid of scrutiny. It could be baffling; tonight it made Tom feel shamefaced. 'Do you want another drink?' Nye said. 'I wouldn't mind the whisky I promised you.'

★ ★ ★

'You could have thanked him.' Georgie put the hairbrush down and shook her head to swing the hair over her shoulders. It fell to the third rib from the bottom – not that Georgie's ribs showed; Tom had counted them with his fingertips one night. Now he turned away and climbed into bed.

'So could you,' he said.

'I did, twice. That shows how much attention you were paying to us.'

'I told him earlier that I appreciated it. When we met up in Caerfach.' Tom lied efficiently. 'Look, Nye and I don't need to go round shaking each other's hand all the time and saying "Thanks, pal!" '

Georgie smiled; in fact, she almost laughed, but he could tell by the way she got into bed and stayed sitting up that she wasn't going to let it drop.

'You're a bastard to him sometimes.' She pulled the bedclothes up over her shoulders.

'At least I don't play with him.'

'What do you mean?'

' "I just want a bit of a quiet life for a while, get away from all my unwanted friends. Oh, not *you*, Nye." ' He mimicked Georgie's intonation well; she stared at him, and for a few seconds both their faces tightened.

'You started that,' Georgie said. 'You start what you want when you want and none of the rest of us are allowed to join in, is that it?'

'It's just that if you're so protective of Nye's feelings, I don't see why you'd want to.'

'Oh shut up.' Georgie lay down violently and turned her back on him.

'Go on then,' Tom said, looking down at her. 'Tell me why it is. Does Nye annoy you secretly? Or do you just enjoy the power?'

'Of cou—' Georgie bit the word off and breathed in noisily. 'You make it impossible just to be his friend.'

Tom watched her jaw stop moving and her left eyelid blink. She must have known he was staring at her but she ignored him. She lay on her side, apparently looking at the stretch of wall between the cupboard and the door.

She was right. There was something in Nye which brought out the bully in him, Tom was well aware of that. He couldn't just be friends with Nye; he never had been able to, and therefore he couldn't stand back and allow other people to do it. He was helped by Nye, of course. Nye had never wanted anything straightforward; he'd made that clear from the start.

'Is Aneurin Mathias your friend now?' Alun had asked, a week or so after Nye had begun to use their bus stop.

'Shit no,' Tom had told his little brother, 'he's just in my class, that's all.' Then had come the bunking off; into Caerfach it had been, the first time. And later – quite a bit later, when Tom had left school and was working at the dairy and studying to retake his exams – there had been the afternoon gaps: those spaces between four-thirty, when they entered the empty bungalow, and a quarter to six, when Mrs Mathias came in from her job at the hospital. Two days each week they had spent that time alone in the house together.

That had stopped before Nye left school. In the holidays Nye had gone abroad to work on a camp site. That should really have been the natural break. But Tom had finally got the exams that meant he could go to art college. So, ten days into his first term in Bartraeth, Tom had been sitting in the bar with a crowd of friends when Nye walked in. He was wearing a university scarf and new trousers and a tweed jacket. His face was pale brown from the sun. He'd looked like a shop dummy, or a model from a bad clothes catalogue, except that he was so densely fleshed; his physical substance was overwhelming. 'Oh Jesus Christ,' Tom heard himself say.

Nye had always had his own friends at the university. Within weeks he'd joined a singing club and was playing for the university rugby team. When Tom went to call on him in his rooms, people dropped by frequently, and the cork tile on his door usually carried at least one cheery message. But Tom was where Nye's real interest lay.

Tom sometimes wondered now about the way he and Georgie had become lovers, towards the end of that first term. It had been an explosion of sexual need. But had Tom's appetite been whetted by the urge to shut Nye out?

If so, it hadn't worked. Nye had simply expanded his concentration to take in Georgie as well. He'd been candidly watchful; he'd asked Georgie about herself and soaked up the information. He'd begun to show signs of liking her; what was more, admiring her. He had been shocked when Georgie left Tom for Lloyd Bannen. It was one of the few times Tom had seen Nye wrongfooted.

They had gone their separate ways more after that. Sometimes they'd kept in touch; at other times not. At one stage two whole terms had passed without contact and then they had met at a party. Tom had been astonished to see Nye with a very tall red-haired woman with a soft round face like a baby's and beautiful thin hands which played with Nye's belt. Nye had been playing in the junior international against England the following weekend and Tom had gone to watch. Nye set up two good tries and Wales nearly won.

After that, they'd begun seeing each other regularly again. Tom's crowd, still much the same as in the first year, had welcomed Nye back. The red-haired woman had never reappeared. Towards Easter Tom had started going out with Georgie again.

And here they were, nearly a year later. They were no longer students. Nye now worked for RCL computers. Georgie was doing teacher training. Tom, having surprised everyone and offended the principal by winning the Welsh newspapers' Young Artist Award, was now halfway through the year's residency which came with the prize, and more than halfway through the £2000 cash.

It was Tom who led the others at the moment. This was his time. The critics had been interested in his work, and in the principal's conceptualist disdain of it. The row had reached the press and rumbled on within the college. When he'd taken up his residency in September, he'd found himself hugely popular among the students.

It had been a turbulent passage in many ways, but he was riding it. He let Nye take the piss out of him. He worked. He held advice sessions for students. He laughed at what the principal said and no one seemed to doubt he thought it was funny. He and Georgie and Nye saw each other all the time. He bought drinks for his friends. He and Georgie decided to get married and threw a party to celebrate. Nye had been as happy as anyone.

Which made Tom edgy. Or was it something else that did that? Why, when his life was full and stimulating and advancing fast, did he have this sense of something closing in on him?

There were days when he was sure it wore Nye's face. Then he was capable of hitting out in self-defence and he knew just where to injure.

Even Alun had been surprised when he'd asked him to be best man. 'But – I took it for granted it would be Nye.' Nye, on the other hand, had nodded readily; only a painful loss of balance in his smile.

'Georgie,' Tom said, watching her open eye.
'What?'
. . . *As traditional as you can get and still win a prize.* Bitter. Nye knew that of all the principal's criticisms, that was the one that unnerved Tom the most.
'He does it too, you know.'
'Oh for God's sake!' There was a flurry of blankets and hair and Georgie covered her face.

2

Nye walked upstairs from the kitchen. The first-floor living room had become more crowded in his absence. He paused on the landing, orientating himself before he went back in. About half the people in the room were new arrivals; the party must now be nearly complete. Dark heads mainly, and more men than women, though not by a big margin. There was an air of shyness about some of the people. He guessed that they must be friends of Dick's, like himself, who knew hardly anyone here.

He didn't usually come so far out for a party, but the weight had lain heavy on him this weekend. Now that the days were growing longer, Nye found it hard to be at a loose end in the city. The light came in at unexpected angles and made a lattice of possibilities. He could look at it only for so long.

It was difficult to be alone but harder to be with Tom and Georgie, especially now that the wedding arrangements were advanced. He had been going to a lot of parties and dinners recently. They were a good way of taking his leave after one of the decorating trips to the Islyn. Georgie always wanted to cook him dinner back at the flat, or carry him off to a pub with them. Tom, he noticed, stayed quiet. 'Ah, let him go, Georgie,' he'd said last week, 'he's got other things to do.'

But Tom had been put out today, all the same, when he'd discovered Nye wasn't going to Chris's party with them. 'I can't,' Nye had argued. 'I've got to go to this one of Dick Taylor's. He's invited a man from Southwest Computers who I really need to meet.' He had promised to try and join them later, if he was back in Bartraeth in time.

The man from Southwest Computers was down in the kitchen now, with Nye's business card in his pocket, saying goodbye to his host. It was ten o'clock and Nye would not be going for some time yet. He filled his glass and looked around. There was a slight, fair girl over by the table. She was very different in stature and features but she had something of the quality of Andrea, the auburn-haired woman he'd gone out with last year. He remembered how Tom had looked at Andrea. There was a laconic girl making people laugh in the next-door group. And several men, one of whom looked a bit like Tom.

Where to start? If he chose well, he could have the next few hours in company. At the end of them he might leave with a telephone number in his pocket and the promise of a game of rugby or a drink in some near-future lunch hour. If it was a woman, he might leave with her. A more immediate comfort, flesh to flesh: that was tempting. In fact, as he thought of it, his arms ached. He wanted to hold another body and feel unfamiliar limbs grow confiding.

He'd learnt to be wary of this longing for tenderness. He turned away from the laconic girl, who'd been watching him, and walked up to the cheerful man called Philip.

It was a quarter to eleven and Philip had been bland, and when the laconic girl had joined them, she and Nye hadn't liked each other. The fair girl, as sometimes happened, seemed to have dulled since he first spotted her, and he couldn't even remember which other men he'd thought interesting.

But for a while now he had been watching someone with medium-brown hair and sharpish features. She had an unsettled look which appealed to him. Besides, she was attractive. He'd watched a couple of men try to move in already.

But Nye had an advantage. Yes, definitely, it was the girl from school: Hazel. Hazel . . . what? No need to wait for that, though. Her glass was emptying and she was starting to look round to see where she could get more wine. Nye leaned across the table and found a bottle. Here you are, Hazel – oh, yes, he had it now, funny really – Hazel Thomas.

Part Two

3

The snow fell more steadily now they were climbing the mountain. Above the road, the common was already dirty white: below them, the fields were losing their green.

Cold air leaked in through the window seals and around the edges of the car's soft roof. Hazel tucked her hair more firmly into her jacket collar.

'Jesus, it's a bloody blizzard.' Nye's teeth showed. 'Trust Tom. A spring wedding and it snows. We'll all freeze our arses off.'

'How much further is it?'

'The other side of the mountain. About ten minutes. Do you want me to slow down? It'll probably be warmer in the car than in the church.' But he pressed down on the accelerator and they went a little faster.

There was a sliding noise and a thump from the back, as the red-wrapped present fetched up against the side of the car.

'What's in there?' Hazel asked.

'A book,' said Nye. 'A little extra. I've already given them my main present. I helped them get their house.'

'You what?' It was startled out of her, even though she'd decided to express no more surprise about what Nye did for his friend.

'Well, I paid their deposit and their first two months' rent. And got a phone put in the place. So that helped them a bit, didn't it?'

'Yes, very generous.'

'Oh no, not really.'

There was no answer to that. Hazel resumed looking out of the window. They were climbing high above the houses and the common stretched out on either side. The contours were heavy; every slope was rounded; every dip and hill bulked out against the sky. They seemed to be travelling a long time on a bulbous summit, unable to see down in any direction. She'd never liked this landscape.

'We used to come up here sometimes,' Nye said. 'Do you remember that school trip we came on, the geography one?'

'That wasn't here, that was by the sea.'

'No, it was here.'

'It wasn't, Nye, it was by the sea. I remember it clearly. There was quicksand and someone lost his shoe in it.'

'Ah well, if you insist. I know I came on a trip up here. The whole class stood on that hillock next to the hut, where the triangulation point is. And Barry Caddick lost his shoe in the marsh.'

Hazel looked at the hut, the gravel patch, the hillock, and was disorientated by recognition. She glanced at Nye, but he was leaning away from her, peering through the crust of snow that stuck to the windscreen.

'Swine of a corner, this.'

Hazel held out her hands to the dashboard heater. Her knuckles caught a trickle of warmth and a pea soup smell wafted up. 'The heater's working again.'

'Good. Let's hope it lasts. Look at your poor hands, they're white.'

'They're OK.' Hazel tucked them into her sleeves.

'I've got a jumper in the back,' Nye said. 'Why don't I get it out for you? You could wrap up warm, tuck it up so it won't show under your jacket.'

'I'm fine.'

She turned to look at him as he shook his head. Ever since he'd picked her up, he'd had this odd mix of protectiveness and detachment. Several times he'd made remarks that might have been jokes but had turned out to be serious. Certainly he wasn't laughing now. When he did laugh, his whole face took part and a line creased his chin.

Hazel was even more aware of him physically than she'd been at the party. It was partly because she was having to reassess: he seemed larger now they were alone together, and she hadn't remembered his features as being so regular. Broad nose, eyes that were set rather flat, close-curling hair – he looked like the bust of some obscure Roman consul, coloured and brought to life. Or not quite to life: there was something in him today that seemed to be waiting to ignite.

He wasn't nearly so relaxed as he'd been at the party – or last week at the film. But then he'd never pretended he was going to be. Hazel remembered Wednesday's phone call when she'd tried to cry off today.

'I've got a lot of packing to do. I didn't realise there'd be so much. And I was thinking that I really should start flat-hunting this Saturday.'

'Oh.' His voice had been dull. 'I see.'

'I know it's short notice. It's just that everything's crept up on me. I've got to be in Bristol in two weeks' time.'

'I could come over this evening and help you pack.'

'Oh, there's no need.' Still, she had paused. The idea of Nye driving all that way to see her in her parents' home was quite tempting. It would surely prove he was attracted to her. 'You're busy, aren't you?'

'No one's fit for anything today, after last night.'

'I'd forgotten. How was it?'

'You know stag nights, or probably you don't. Drunken, a bit frantic. We had fun.' It had sounded satirical. The silence had grown till eventually Nye had spoken again. Formally, with a congestion: 'I was looking forward to taking you.'

So here she was, sitting at Nye's left hand, waiting to be introduced to the people he kept at his right. Tom and Georgie. Nye made no secret of the fact that he was keen to see how they'd take her. He clearly didn't expect her to be offended by it; he even seemed to think she'd be honoured.

Hazel was annoyed with herself for submitting to it, and just as annoyed with herself for minding. The last thing she needed was for Nye to realise she was piqued. She didn't know quite what she wanted to happen between her and Nye – if anything – but she felt it would definitely be as well to stay one step ahead. He was looking at her again now, his left arm loosely braced against the steering wheel. They watched each other for a second like neighbours over a fence.

'You look lovely,' Nye said unexpectedly. 'That brown colour really suits you.' Hazel felt a sharp pleasure and a blush generated itself. It began as a qualm somewhere in her intestines and travelled upwards; she killed it before it reached her neck. 'Suitably uncelebratory too. Though I haven't told Tom your views on young marriage, by the way.'

'For God's sake, I should hope not.'

'He wouldn't mind. He'd think it was funny. You know Tom.'

'Hardly.' Though as a matter of fact, she did know – at least, remembered – Tom a bit better than she'd let on.

'He was tickled to hear you'd be coming,' Nye said. 'He knew your name at once, though I had some trouble convincing him you weren't blonde. To tell you the truth,' he chuckled, 'I think he was mixing you up with Hazel from *Crossroads*!'

They drove over a ridge and a new valley appeared beneath them. Hazel listened to the afternoise of Nye's laugh. No, she hadn't imagined it: that had been meant to cut her down to size. Why? In case she thought Tom wanted to see her? She turned but Nye was leaning forward and his cheek had developed a bloom. 'There it is. See the church, down on the left. And further up on the other side is where we're going for the reception.'

Hazel walked down the aisle with Nye's grey jumper on. The wool scratched her neck and wrists. She hadn't intended to wear it, but when Nye had taken it out of the back of the car and held it against her, saying, 'Ah no, it's too long,' she'd been irritated.

'Yes please,' she'd said, taking hold of it.

'But it'll show under your jacket.'

'It's warm. I'll wear it.'

He hadn't demurred further. He'd held her jacket and moved helpfully to shield her from the wind as she pulled the jumper on. But as she rebuttoned her jacket over it, she'd seen disappointment cross his face.

She no longer looked elegant enough for him. Good. The satisfaction was childish but it soothed her. Nye was beginning to act on her like flies on a horse. Yet as they penetrated deeper into the church, she kept in close step with him. The sweater had his powdery, hot smell and the weight of it was reassuring.

'Let's go in here. They'll move up for us.' He had stopped by the second pew on the groom's side. Three young men and a woman were talking across one another.

'*Bore da*. Mark, let us in, will you?'

The faces turned towards them, all strange to Hazel (no prickles of recognition here then, despite Nye's insistence that she would know people) and the nearest man said, 'Aneurin, where have you been?' and then grinned and put his hand over his mouth.

Mark, Caroline, Iestyn and Chris: they had all been at the art college. They evidently knew not only Tom and Georgie and Nye, but various people from other parts of the congregation. After they'd said hello to her they went on talking and Hazel watched them twist and signal and mouth comments across the pews.

The little church was almost full. Older family were hatted, permed, dark-suited: young family and friends outnumbered them by about two to one. The groom's side was shabbier than the bride's and younger. Looking through the rows, Hazel found it impossible to tell who on this side was related, and who friends. They certainly all seemed well at ease.

It was the festive atmosphere which puzzled her. She hadn't expected it: in fact, now she came to think of it, she had gained the opposite impression from Nye – that something was slightly amiss with the event. As if he and everyone else had to work together to make sure it was a good one. It had been in his tone more than his words. For instance: 'Tom's got a lot going for him now,' he'd said at the party, pouring her another glass of wine. 'He's been bought by the Welsh Arts Council.' And later, on the telephone: 'I'm not best man. I'm his oldest friend but neither of us wanted to hurt his brother.'

Hazel turned to Nye but he was no longer there. He had left the pew and was now a few yards away across the aisle, standing beneath the pulpit in a small group. Hazel saw a girl in her teens, a large boy getting his first bumfluff and, turned away from her, two shorter males whom she'd already spotted and who, judging by the front row places they left empty, must be Tom and his brother.

Nye was standing in her line of sight. So although she saw that he and Tom were talking, and could gauge from their muscle shifts when they began to turn towards her, by the time she could see Tom's face Nye was already watching her.

She recognised Tom quickly. He still looked like his schoolboy self, though less concentrated. Perhaps it was just wedding day gloss – the regulation suit and well-brushed hair. But no, there was something subdued in his face. His features were still crowded together, as she remembered, but they seemed less emphatic, as if they'd had the insistence trained out of them.

Oh well. Hazel registered her disappointment and buried it. It was interesting to see how differently people matured – Nye's light burning more brightly, Tom's fainter . . . assuming this first impression was right. It was hardly a typical moment, for any of them.

What did she look like, sitting here on the edge of Tom's friends, waiting to be presented?

Nye's hand was on Tom's elbow; Nye made a comment. Tom listened and nodded and they both smiled, Tom a second after Nye. Hazel's skin pricked in discomfort. Were they talking about her?

Tom looked directly at her now. She thought he was embarrassed. Or was it just impatient? She found herself measuring the height discrepancy between him and Nye: six inches? Eight inches? Half a head, anyway. She smiled, got rid of the smile when she realised how long she'd have to hold it, and covered the change by sliding along the pew.

The two men stopped just short of her. Nye lounged; his big body gave out messages of protection and ease. Tom stood in what seemed a slightly mocking stance, his face poked forward.

'Here she is then,' said Nye. To Hazel's surprise, his voice was tentative. 'And here you are. Hazel Thomas of two F. Tom Griffiths, bridegroom.'

'Hello, Hazel.' Tom sounded friendly, at least.

'Hello, Tom,' Hazel said. 'It's nice to see you again. I hope you don't mind.'

'No, I'm glad you could make it in the end. It's good to see you. Funny though.'

'Would you have recognised her?' Nye said. Tom glanced at him, a touch suspiciously Hazel thought.

'Oh yes.' He spoke directly to her. 'You look exactly the same. But I probably wouldn't have got your name, I'm not good at remembering things like that.'

'No, it's visual things that matter to you, isn't it?' said Nye. Smiling, quietly, he hummed something. A snatch of the *Crossroads* theme tune.

'Yes, yes, all right,' said Tom. 'Give it a rest. So, you're just passing through, Nye says. On your way to Bristol.'

'Yes, I'm starting a new job there.'

'Congratulations.'

'Congratulations to you.' Hazel realised she should have said it first. She indicated the congregation. 'For this, I mean. And for the award. Nye told me about it.'

'Thanks. Yes, I'm on a run of luck at the moment. Thought I'd take advantage of it, see.' As he smiled, his nose and mouth jumped together and suddenly Hazel was returned to the smell of rubber soles and sweat. 'Got my hands on Georgie while the going was good. What about you?'

'Me?' Was Tom quizzing her about her and Nye?

'What are you doing these days? What's the job in Bristol?'

'I'm a chemist. I'm going into aero-engineering.'

'Avon Aerospace,' Nye added. 'I told you that,' he said to Tom. 'Keep up, boy.'

Tom turned to Nye. Because they were standing so close, he had to peer up at him. 'Yes,' he said, after a few seconds, in a voice that must mean something to him and Nye because it was incomprehensible to Hazel; 'I must try harder. That's what Georgie keeps telling me.'

'Speaking of which . . . ' Nye nodded at a woman beckoning Tom to the front pew. She wore a blue dress and a bun and an anxious face. 'Georgie's mother,' he said to Hazel. 'And the vicar's materialised. I think we might be ready to begin.'

Tom nodded and began to walk up the aisle. Then he stopped and turned. He looked from Nye to Hazel and back to Nye. Because his cheek was turned away from her, Hazel couldn't see his expression as he stared at Nye this last time, but she had the impression of sudden panic. Tom's left arm bent as she watched and he pressed his hand against his side as if to ease a stitch. His jacket puckered beneath his fingers.

Nye moved quickly up to him, squaring his shoulders and smiling reassuringly. He looked emotional and embarrassed. 'Break a leg,' he said, and propelled Tom away with a hand on his back.

Georgie was small and had chestnut hair. It was long and thick and healthy. Her skin was fair. Between the heads of the congregation, that was what Hazel saw; that and the alteration in the bride's rhythm as she came past their pew, which, together with the tiny drawing inwards of Nye's muscles, suggested they'd acknowledged each other.

The snow had stopped falling. The sun was out. People clotted the church path, congratulating one another. Nye's hand was lightly on Hazel's arm, guiding her through the other guests to where Tom and Georgie stood, on a flat tombstone to one side of the path. When they were within a few yards, Georgie caught sight of them. Her face lit up and while they negotiated the final distance, Hazel saw that Georgie kept watching Nye, her eyes happy. When they reached her, she held out her hand to him.

'Lover.' Her voice was deep, as it had been in church; it was natural, then, not just the effect of the vows. 'I missed you in the church. You should have been up there with us.'

'You managed though, Georgie.' Nye took her hand and kissed her. 'This is Hazel.'

'Ah, hello. Tom and Nye's old schoolfriend.' Georgie's smile gathered slowly. It breathed health, like her complexion. She had an oval face, not delicate but with strong curved lines and her eyebrows made a striking arc. Hazel had never envied looks like that but she had always been rather afraid of them. 'I'm really glad you could come. Has Tom seen you yet?'

'We've said hello.'

A step away from Georgie, Tom glanced up from his conversation and nodded at them. He looked more relaxed than before.

'Oh, we've had the official reunion,' said Nye. 'In church, while we were waiting for you.'

'That's the trouble with being the bride, you miss all the best bits.'

Nye pulled away from Georgie – as far as their handclasp would allow – and looked at her. Georgie didn't appear self-conscious; she seemed to enjoy watching Nye's face for his reactions. 'You're beautiful.'

Georgie's eyes dilated. 'You would say that.' She swung gently forward, reached up and kissed Nye's jawbone. Then she looked at Hazel. Her expression was friendly but appraising and – yes, very slightly wary.

Hazel was beginning to feel irritated at being under scrutiny from everyone. But it was her turn to speak.

'That green's gorgeous,' she said, borrowing some of Georgie's rich cadences, not quite unconsciously. 'It looks lovely on you.' She gestured at the velvet on Georgie's arms and breast.

'Thank you.' Georgie smiled back. Despite the cold and the amount of flesh bared by the low-cut dress, she wasn't shivering. In fact, her throat was faintly flushed. Her gaze moved down from Hazel's face and locked. 'Oh. You're wearing Nye's jumper.'

'Old faithful,' said Nye. 'It may be past its best but it's still in service. Georgie bought it for me,' he added to Hazel. 'Two Christmases ago.'

'And you've certainly had your use out of it.' Georgie reached out and touched the fuzzy hem showing below Hazel's jacket. 'Poor you, was it really that cold in church?'

'It wasn't the church.' Through the wool, Hazel felt Georgie's light pressure. 'It was the drive.'

Nye laughed at her. 'You can say that again. I tell you, Georgie, I brought Hazel over the mountain in a blizzard, with snow crystals forming inside the car. The least I could do was offer her some insulation.'

'The very least I'd say.' Georgie was still linking fingers with Nye. Hazel wondered if she even knew she was doing it. Nye, it was clear, was well aware of it: he glanced at Hazel with an amusement that was both self-aware and slightly malicious, and his free hand brushed against her jacket.

'So how long have you two been back in touch?' Georgie was asking.

'A couple of weeks,' said Hazel.

'I suppose you've got a lot of catching up to do. Do you still know people in common?'

'No, not really. I was only at the Traeth a little while, you see; we went west after that.'

'And then she went north to university,' said Nye. 'York. After which she worked in Birmingham and very soon now she'll be leaving for Bristol.'

'Ah, poor Nye,' said Georgie. 'He's finding it hard to cope. He's used to being the high flyer. So where did you two manage to meet, then?'

Hazel waited for Nye to reply but he just smiled at her. 'Llanelli,' she said. 'My parents live there and I've been staying with them. We met at a party.'

'That party you went to instead of Chris's?' Georgie looked up at Nye searchingly. 'I remember that.'

Nye smiled down at her; then he lifted her hand and kissed it, chuckling. 'You're annoyed that I didn't tell you about her, aren't you?' he said. 'If you remember, I did mention that I'd met someone.'

'Yes, but you didn't say it was the same person you were going to ask to the wedding.'

'It would have been jumping the gun. At the time, I didn't know if she'd come.'

'Come on, Mark, you said you'd dance.'

'Yes, sure, in a—'

'I'm sure Hazel will excuse you.' Caroline directed a laugh at her. 'You can tell her more later. Besides, Nye's been looking for her.'

The pair went off into the crowd around the band. Hazel could recognise several people inside it now: Chris, dancing with yet another partner. Alun, Tom's brother. That very pretty teenager called Sian who seemed to have a special affection for Tom and who belonged to his family somehow. And over on the left, Georgie dancing with someone she couldn't see. Tom himself, probably.

Nye was sitting on the edge of the drinks table, waiting for her.

She could see him quite clearly past the heads and shoulders of other people, but she went slowly. When she reached him, she saw that he was smoking. She looked questioning but he just smiled at her.

'Enjoying yourself?' Nye said.

'Yes, Tom's friends are nice.'

'We are, aren't we?'

Hazel missed a beat, then tried to correct it. Why did she keep thinking of Nye as separate from this whole occasion? 'You know what I mean. His college friends. You're different.'

'Greater,' Nye took a drag, 'or lesser?' He wasn't entirely joking.

'Earlier,' said Hazel. She smiled at him – unconvincingly, because she had a bad conscience. She knew she'd disappointed Nye in the last few hours. But then, he shouldn't have had those conversations with Tom and Georgie at the church, offering her up to them as if she were a little novelty present he'd found.

Hazel didn't like being taken for granted. It laid a pain under her skin.

It hadn't been difficult to punish him at the reception. The pub annexe was crowded with people and trestle tables and there were plenty of other guests willing to introduce themselves.

She had concentrated on talking mainly to Tom's friends. She would have liked to talk to Tom himself, but she didn't know how to claim his attention. Everyone wanted a piece of him and Georgie this afternoon. Evening.

It was evening and getting late. No wonder Hazel felt she'd been here hours – she had. Most of the older guests had left a while back, after the speeches and the wedding cake, when the band had set up. Now older family were gone too – into the pub, someone said – and here in the annexe debris was starting to scatter and the air had thickened.

She leaned against the table next to Nye. She was very conscious of her body mimicking his. It gave her a peculiar feeling: half comradely, half sexual. She put on her easygoing voice. 'What about you? Are you enjoying yourself?'

'Oh yes.' It sounded flat. But when Hazel looked at him, his face was amused. 'Oh dear, you haven't been worrying about me, have you?'

'No, why should I? Like you said, you're with your best friends.'

'Oh, absolutely. And now you're here, for however short a period it might be this time, I'm with you.'

'I'm sorry.' Hazel pretended to think his sardonic tone was a joke. 'I haven't been rude, have I?'

'A little bit, yes.'

Hazel looked away. She was irritated with herself for starting to flush and she wanted a few seconds to control it. She always could send the colour back down again, if she collected herself.

Her complexion was pale again and she was about to speak but Nye touched her. On her back, between the shoulder blades. He laid his hand flat and left it there, pressing her shirt against her skin. It was a very deliberate touch and so peculiar that Hazel didn't know whether she was insulted or pleased.

'Perhaps I didn't want to be the optional extra in any more chats with Tom and Georgie.'

'What do you mean?' Nye's face was turned down to her. He lifted his hand from her back and put it on her shoulder.

'You were talking about me as if I wasn't there.'

'Were we?'

'Yes.'

'I'm sorry. That wasn't my intention, you know. It wasn't how it seemed to me. I'm very much aware that you're here.'

Hazel's attraction to Nye was strange. On one level it was very simple: she thought he was good-looking and he appealed to her between the legs. But when he talked, he baffled her. He seemed to tie himself in knots all the time, as if he were always setting off after some interesting idea but never quite getting there. Through caution or sheer inability? Hazel wasn't sure she trusted him. Even as she responded to him now, she had a counter-instinct to push him off.

It wasn't danger or ulterior motives in him that bothered her; more a dead weight. She felt it inch forward behind his eyes.

He leaned down over her further, and they kissed. It was only half a kiss because they were sitting on the table, but it was very good. When Nye's tongue left her mouth, Hazel felt aroused – and uneasy because it had been so public. She looked at the people dancing. Georgie had seen: that was clear from the slow smile she gave them; Tom, who was dancing with her, had just turned away.

'Do you want to dance?' Nye said.

'Yes.'

'I warn you, I'm no good.'

'Neither am I.'

'So—?'

'So what?'

'So, what happened then?' said Iestyn.

'I gave in of course,' said Tom. 'In fact, I knocked off another fiver because the frame was damaged.'

Everyone laughed, Tom too. It made his hand jerk and tobacco spilled off his cigarette paper.

'Not that the buyer could see it, mind,' said Nye. 'Tom just felt it incumbent on him to point it out.'

'It was a moral victory,' said Tom.

Hazel, sitting on a cushion two people away from Tom, watched him pick up tobacco shreds while the rest of them laughed again and wondered if he was always this much at the centre of the group.

Georgie leaned over his shoulder. 'That's going to be a moral joint you're rolling, if you spill much more of it.'

'I always said Georgie'd be a good housekeeper,' said Chris.

Hazel didn't enjoy joints but she took her turn at this, just as she had with the last one. She couldn't work out a way of saying no without sounding prim. Everyone seemed to take it for granted she'd want some, even Nye – who she noticed passed it straight on. 'Nye doesn't smoke,' Georgie had said.

Hazel preferred the sharp impact of alcohol, not this furring of her reactions. Tom and Georgie both smoked as they danced, with casual skill.

Tom was looking at her again; laughing at her in fact, as her eyes watered. 'Careful. You took in a bit much there, didn't you? Well, I did make it a bit strong.' Hazel laughed too, and gusted smoke out prematurely.

It was the second time Tom had made fun of her – he'd already had a dig about her determined socialising earlier. She hadn't minded that, either. She wasn't sure, but she thought that joke had been as much at Nye's expense as at hers; that would explain why she had found it so funny, though it didn't say much for her budding relationship with Nye.

'What's this job, then?' Tom said. 'Your new one. I wasn't really concentrating last time.'

'It's with Avon Aerospace in Bristol. I'll be working on alloys, testing them for strength, flexibility, resistance to fatigue and corrosion.'

'Airborne sculpture,' said Nye.

'No,' said Hazel. 'Working with alloys.'

'Let a scientist be pure, Nye,' said Georgie.

Hazel shrugged. 'It's not sculpture and it's applied science, not pure. It's creating the raw material for an aeroplane. Testing alloys so that when you turn them into wings and carriages and cabins and put them in the air, they stay up.'

'You've annoyed her now,' Tom said with satisfaction. 'Haven't they?' he added to Hazel.

'I apologise,' said Nye, mock solemnly. Hazel saw him exchange an amused look with Georgie.

There was a sudden outbreak of movement as Tom jabbed his foot at Nye and missed. 'And now you're both annoying me.'

The air was muggy and the colours cast by the artificial lights had grown too familiar. The band was playing again and people had got their second dancing wind. Georgie was in the middle of them, moving easily with Nye, talking while she danced, now and again putting her arm round his waist and twisting him in a new direction. She seemed to be talking to Chris, on her other side, at the same time. Chris was laughing. Nye moved conscientiously and every now and then sent a look of self-deprecating humour to Hazel.

She smiled at him and Georgie saw. 'Come and join us,' she called.

'I'm too hot,' Hazel called back. 'I'm going outside for a second.'

'Bring Tom back with you,' said Georgie. 'He's been gone too long. Will you see if he's all right?'

Hazel nodded. As she turned, she saw Nye glance quickly at his watch. Was he timing Tom's absence? Possibly; probably; which meant he would be timing hers too. She wondered how much he had noticed in the last hour. The fact that Tom had talked to her, stayed near her and when the music started up again, not danced with her?

Not that she'd wanted him to; she'd moved away. He danced too well and it was very public.

Tom had danced just once then, rather manically, with Georgie. Soon afterwards, he'd sat down on the cushions near Hazel again. And later, when they were opening the extra case of wine, he'd used her name twice, unnecessarily.

One thing Nye had definitely seen was Tom staring at his arm around Hazel's waist. 'Is it all right with you if I touch her?' he'd said with mocking ceremony.

'You would anyway.'

Now Tom was outside. Where he'd gone eleven minutes ago. What could he be doing out there, in the night-frost?

It was much darker now the pub lights were dimmed. In the car park, all the windscreens were iced over and streaks of new white marked the ground – not snow but hail. It had come down half an hour ago, a sound like gunfire pinging off the annexe roof, just as the band were tuning up again.

Tom was down the bank from the car park, crunching round on the frozen stones. Hazel picked her way down to him.

'Hiya. Aren't you cold?' She went to touch his arm but he pulled away. Then he caught himself and tried to disguise it as a shiver.

'Freezing. It's just, I feel sick.'

'Oh. Should I get someone?'

'No. It's just drink, hash, everything. You know.'

'Sort of. I don't normally smoke.'

'No, I didn't think you did.' Tom's smile was v-shaped and nauseous. 'I'm surprised you're not bad too.'

'I've felt better.'

'Sorry. I overdid that last joint. Getting lazy, I wanted the hit without the bother of rolling any more.'

'That's all right,' said Hazel. 'It's mainly the heat that got me. Everyone else is fine. It's a good wedding. Don't you think?'

'I don't know, I've never had one before.'

'Look.' He was shivering properly now and she was beginning to think she'd been mistaken. She held out Nye's sweater. 'Would you like to put this on?'

'No, better not.' Tom looked at it with aversion. A few seconds went by with her watching him, till he flapped his hand irritably at the wool. Hazel tucked it under her arm and changed gear, masking her disappointment.

'OK. Well, I'm getting cold so—'

'Don't go.' Tom took a backwards step up the slope. 'Stay here. Why don't you put it on? Then you won't get cold.'

Hazel shook out the jumper and slid it over her head. She pulled at it, smelled Nye and at the same time smelled Tom. Had he stepped closer or was his body scent somehow mixed into Nye's?

At least she knew she wasn't imagining his interest now.

When she pushed her head free, Tom was where he'd been before. 'Your hair's gone static,' he said. 'So, you're going out with Nye now.'

'Am I?'

'Aren't you?'

Hazel wondered what would happen if she said no. She could

do, quite easily. Would Tom breathe a sigh of relief? Would his interest in her lapse?

'I suppose I am. For the time being, anyway. I'm going to Bristol soon, you know.'

'That wouldn't get in the way of you and Nye. RCL have big offices in Bristol, he already does a lot of his work over the bridge. I suppose it would mean he'd spend more time there, less here.' Tom sounded like someone making a checklist.

He looked at her as if expecting her to comment.

'Go on,' said Hazel. 'Please. I'm interested.'

'Sorry. It's none of my business, is it? Never mind. Tell me what you've been doing since you left the Traeth. Did you go to a school you liked better after?'

'Yes thanks. Well, I mean, the school seemed to like me better.'

'Yes, you never really fitted in at the Traeth did you? Funny how that happens.'

'Yes, well, I never had anything against the pupils, you know.' Hazel felt a peculiar sensation, as if the blood vessels in her legs were filling up from below. She turned so Tom couldn't see her full-face. 'You were kind to me.'

'Shit, was I?' But he wasn't following up the deadpan voice. On the contrary; he'd followed her down the slope. She could feel him standing behind her, to one side; was she imagining it or was it exactly the same position he'd taken up years before? She almost thought she heard the shuffle of his arm lifting, uncertainly.

How long the impression of the past re-enacted went on, Hazel didn't know. Even after she'd become self-conscious about it, it still seemed to continue. It was ludicrous for them to be there on the hillside, two adults freezing in their party clothes, approximating to a gesture made before their puberty. Just before their puberty. And Tom might not be remembering it at all.

'Did they tell your parents?' Tom's voice was rueful; an adult tone, but it failed to hide the curiosity underneath.

'Yes. They wrote to them. They said they always did when someone got the cane.'

'Yeah, they did. I should have warned you about that.'

In fact, of course, Tom had hardly spoken in the cloakroom. He had chewed and the juicyfruit gum on his breath had forced its way through the smell of socks and damp. Then his hand, very tentative just below her shoulder blade, and his voice, embarrassed: 'I get it lots.'

Hazel knew why she remembered it. The childhood shame ('A girl getting the cane,'; her mother's shocked face; 'a girl.') had never diminished. In a way, sympathy had intensified it; both her mother's, belatedly, and Tom's.

But she was taken aback that it should have stayed with Tom. Unless he'd really felt bad for not mentioning the letter. What was conscience but things that stuck in your throat? Bits of life that tasted wrong and lingered on the palate.

'Never mind,' Hazel said. 'Childhood griefs, and all . . . that.' She turned slowly. Her hesitation had been caused by a warmth travelling across her back; the very near presence of a hand.

Tom was moving away. He hadn't actually touched her. He wasn't even looking at her now. But she didn't think she'd been mistaken. What was he playing at?

Hazel stood waiting for his attention to come back but Tom was suddenly restless. He walked a few yards in the opposite direction, turned and stared at a car's lights on the road. He showed no inclination to meet her eyes. He put his hands in his trouser pockets and felt around, then he fished inside his waistcoat, shoved his fingers into his shirt pocket.

'What's the matter?' she asked.

'No cigarettes,' he said. 'A very grown-up grief. Christ, I really want one.'

'I thought you felt sick.'

'I did. But now I want a cigarette. And it's cold. Better go in. Come on, Hazel.'

4

'Are you ready?' Nye stood in the doorway of the flat, looking up at her. He was wearing a black jacket which suited him and a faded blue sweatshirt which didn't.

'Come in,' Hazel said. 'I've got some real coffee.'

'We haven't got time, if we're going to be in Bristol for twelve.'

'I've cancelled.'

'Why?'

'Oh, did you want to go to Bristol anyway? We could still go.'

Nye stared upwards. He looked humorously exasperated. 'No. What's happened? Have you found somewhere else?'

'I can stay on here another ten days. Catrin goes off on a trip as soon as the flatmate gets back.'

'So?' said Nye, climbing the stairs.

'So.' Hazel shrugged, as he came up level with her. As usual, his closeness made something fall silent inside her. She listened for it as he touched her cheek, and kissed the side of her mouth. 'The rush is off.'

'You'll still need a home in ten days' time.'

'I'll find one.' She thought about saying: As a matter of fact I thought I'd stay here in Bartraeth – but she couldn't trust her voice to be natural. Over the last two weeks Hazel had grown used to moderating her speech. She shrugged. 'They sounded prissy, those two girls, anyway.'

Nye's hand rested on her shoulder as they went into the kitchen. 'Oh, heaven forbid. We've got the day free, then.'

'Yes. What shall we do?'

He sat down at the small table and looked out at the railway tracks.

'What do you suggest? A trip to the castle? A shopping day in Howell's?'

Hazel leaned against the cooker so the metal lip bit into her. He was using that tone again – teasing, slightly querying, the way she'd heard him talk to Tom at the wedding. Over the last two weeks it had been gradually entering their own conversation. She knew it signalled intimacy. It turned her on. Nye's hands lay idle on the table; they were clean and pale, edged with hair at the wrists. Early this morning, when she'd walked out to get the coffee, the fresh air had been expectant. Two weeks felt like a long time to have been seeing Nye without sleeping with him. But they had both been holding off, taking small steps forward and allowing the other one to retreat. Hazel didn't think she could go on with that much longer. She had come to the edge.

Under the fabric of his jacket, Nye's shoulders were relaxed. The coffee began to bubble. Hazel turned to switch off the gas. 'We could drink this and be lazy,' she said. 'Do you know how to do that?'

'Surely. I'm very good at it.'

Nye wasn't unobservant. His voice had slowed slightly and as she poured the coffee she felt him follow her movements. She took the rolls out of the oven. She sat down opposite him and passed him a plate, knife and butter.

He broke up his roll, with some difficulty.

'It's been nice having you in Bartraeth these two weeks,' he said. 'I'm glad you're going to be around a bit longer.'

'So am I.'

Nye reached out then and, slowly, touched her hand. Ah, this was new. They didn't usually touch like this so early on a date. Hazel waited; would he drop his head with the kiss now? Or else carry her fingers to his mouth?

But their hands touched for a couple of seconds then he withdrew.

Nye started spreading his butter. Hazel picked up a roll and broke it. When she looked up again, Nye was eating thoughtfully.

'I'll tell you what we could do,' he said. 'Something I'd like to do with you.'

'Go on.'

'You'll probably think it's a horrible idea.'

He was having a joke now; flirting. Hazel recognised the sexual tease and enjoyed it. She wouldn't have thought this was his style but then, since Tom and Georgie had been away, he'd seemed freer. He sometimes showed this light-hearted streak.

'Go on.'

'I'd like to take you to a rugby match. Show you how I used to play.'

★ ★ ★

The stadium was more than half-empty. They sat near one end, between a group of young boys with two older men and a knot of men and women a little younger than themselves.

'Students,' said Nye. 'You get season tickets cheap through the union.'

'I thought this place was always full.'

'Christ no. Only for the big occasions. It will be next week – it's the Stephens Cup semi-final.'

'Do you miss it?'

'No. It took up too much time. I couldn't have done well in my finals if I'd gone on playing.'

But Nye sat forward, watching the players hard.

'See number eleven there? He was a junior international with me. He's got great pace but a bugger for fumbling the ball. He's always knocking on. It's nerves. Come on, man!

'Run it,' he said a few minutes later. Then: 'Keep your head down, boy. You'll get a broken neck like that.'

Hazel sat in his lee, turning her face where he directed, to follow the game. She was thinking about ways of mentioning Tom.

Each time they met, Tom and Georgie's names came up. Often it was just a passing reference . . . 'I went there once with Tom' . . . 'Tom had a set-to with her last year' . . .

There had been only one time when Nye hadn't mentioned him and by the middle of the evening, Hazel had been very aware of it. She'd decided not to raise the name herself, but the longer she left it, the sharper her awareness grew, until she'd felt fidgety.

And then, as Nye was driving her home he'd said: 'Tom rang up today.'

'From Spain?'

'Yes, he said Georgie's gone the same colour as her hair.'

'Are they having a good time?'

'Fabulous. They've been going up into the hill villages a lot.'

That had been all. Except—

'They both say hello,' Nye had added.

Well, now it wouldn't be long before they said hello in person. They were due back this weekend. Tomorrow, perhaps even today; Nye hadn't specified.

She shifted so she had Nye in view. He had his weight set back on his hips and his hands shoved into his coat. His colour mounted as the Bartraeth backs ran through for a try.

'Yes, mon!' he said quietly.

The players walked back for the conversion.

'Easy,' said Nye. The ball lifted over the crossbar and he turned to her.

Hazel didn't look away quickly enough. Nye registered her attention and his expression held deliberately steady. Almost steady enough to hide his intelligence, and his pleasure.

He had no idea that her scrutiny hadn't been of him alone, but of him as Tom's friend. After these last two weeks of getting close to Nye, padding round him in Tom's absence, Hazel felt that her sexual appetite had twinned.

The suspense of having to wait for Tom fed into the momentum gathering between her and Nye. She couldn't separate them out.

She wanted Nye. She was drawn to him. But the memory of Tom at the wedding was sharp on her palate.

'Bored, are you?' said Nye softly. 'I told you you would be.'

'No. You were wrong.'

'Good. But whenever you want to go, just say.' He turned back to the pitch and at the same time, laid his hand on hers, in her lap.

Nye took off his jacket and dropped it on the chair. The washed-out blue of his sweatshirt made him look more relaxed than usual, as if his defences were down.

'Where's Catrin?'

'Out till late.'

He walked into the middle of the floor and stopped just short of Hazel.

'Good.'

Hazel felt his closeness. He wasn't touching her yet, but he would. Now that it was imminent, she couldn't understand why they'd been putting it off.

Moving smoothly – because she wanted to be the one to close the gap – she leaned against his chest. Her mind was clear. She could feel his erection against her abdomen. She moved her hands down.

'You know, I'm getting very fond of you, *collen*.'

Hazel stopped. Her attention snagged. Fond? It was what you said when you wanted to fob someone off but hearing it in Nye's voice, with his arms round her, it seemed to mean something more.

Hazel listened for another second but there was nothing, so she took hold of his face and kissed him. He kissed well, and she'd already learnt how to get maximum pleasure out of it. But this time her arousal was almost embarrassing.

He either shared it or caught it from her: when they pulled away, his face and throat were clammy.

'Jesus Christ,' he said, sliding his hand over her breasts. 'I want to make love to you.'

'I want you to.'

'Now?'

'Now.'

Hazel pulled his head down to kiss her again. Nye eased her backwards till she felt the edge of the sofa behind her knees. She bent her legs and lay down, while Nye knelt next to her and began taking off her clothes.

Nye kissed her neck and breasts. His tongue outlined her nipples. She helped him take off her jeans and pants, then she sat up and unbuckled his belt. He stopped kissing her and took off his sweatshirt and shirt. Under his clothes he was well muscled and proportioned. For the first time since Hazel had met him, he appeared really at ease. He knelt still as she unzipped his fly and he put his hand over hers when she touched his penis.

'Slowly. Take it slowly. God, I want to spend all night with you.'

'You can. All evening, at least.'

'No.' Nye shook his head. 'I'm not free this evening. I said I'd go and see Tom and Georgie.'

Tom and Georgie. Back. Already. She couldn't think. Why hadn't Nye said something earlier? She sat with her forehead pressed against his shoulder, his penis snug in her hand. It twitched now, ridiculously strongly, and the thick warmth set nerves going all along her arm, into her gut. Excitement or alarm? Nye smiled at her with his mouth pulled down.

'What a bloody stupid thing to arrange. Still, we've got a couple of hours. And we can leave there early.'

'We?'

'You'll come, won't you? You said you weren't doing anything. I want to be with you.'

Hazel said nothing. She wanted to be with him too, and she wanted to be with Tom. She wanted to be fucked, now, and the needing to be fucked was part of it. She saw Tom at the end of the wedding party, being driven away from the pub with his arm round Georgie. She pushed her eyes against Nye's neck to dispel the image.

'Yes, I'll come.'

He nodded and his penis moved again. Hazel leaned into him

and opened her hand to knead him against her stomach. 'Touch me.'

'Christ,' said Nye, pressing his hands between her legs. 'My darling, you really don't need to ask.'

Hazel rolled back on to the sofa cushions; Nye stripped off his trousers and pants. Naked and standing, he was surprisingly magnificent. His weight took her breath away.

5

Nye placed one hand over hers as he swung the car down the lanes. He smelled of her soap and of his own relaxed warmth.

'Have you been down here before?'

'No, never. I've got no idea where we are.'

'We're just below Penllwyn. The village is back up the hill there.'

'Behind us? We didn't go through it?'

'No, because we've approached from the south.'

'I didn't even see the lights. Which direction are we driving in now?'

'South-west, I think,' said Nye. 'We're nearly there. I'll tell you one thing, I wouldn't want to live out here. When I leave town, I'll get a place on the hill where I can see what's going on.'

'I thought you helped them get the cottage.'

'I did. It was what they wanted. Tom will paint, Georgie will draw and they'll make love in the hedgerows.' He hooked his index finger round hers. 'I prefer a sofa. Or even a bed.'

Hazel glanced at him, and failed to hold his gaze.

'What's the matter?'

She didn't speak. The memory of their second love-making, Nye's eyes closed in pleasure as he turned her on the bed, had got stuck in her mind.

'Hazel? Darling, you don't regret it do you?'

She shook her head.

'What, then? Did I hurt you?'

'No, no. Nothing like that. It's just that it was unexpected. So – passionate, I'm not used to it.'

He stared at her, then lifted her hand and kissed it. 'So there's a non-conformist conscience in there.'

'Not really.'

'Don't apologise for it. I'm glad you've got one. They're hard to come by these days.'

He let go of her hand to change gear. They had reached the

lowest part of the valley and were running along the flat. It was very dark down here; their headlamps lit up hedgerows and bushes on either side of the road and they passed beneath the silhouettes of trees, still only half in leaf. They began to slacken speed; Nye tipped the indicator lever and after a few seconds peering out of the window, he turned the car sharp right, into a hidden entrance. Ahead were the lights of a small house.

It was Georgie who greeted them. She stood in the shabby hallway, her face tanned, her feet bare, dressed in jeans and a white shirt. Her hair was tied back in a loose ponytail.

'Nye! How lovely to see you. And not before bloody time.' Georgie reached up and pulled Nye's head down for a kiss; she did it thoroughly, and Nye put his arm round her shoulders and squeezed them. When Georgie turned to Hazel, she was smiling broadly.

'Hello, Hazel, how nice to see you again.'

'And you.' Hazel took a step towards her, meaning to kiss her too, but Georgie moved away.

'Come into the kitchen, it's the only warm room. What do you think?' she added to Nye, gesturing round at the paint-patched hall.

'Well, I don't know much about art.'

'Fool. Which colour do you like?'

They paused just outside the half-open kitchen door. There was a smell of damp paint and Nye stood very straight to keep his clothes from touching the surfaces. He looked at the web of intersecting colours on the stair wall. 'The blue,' he said. 'That mid-blue there. It's like the colour the bedroom was painted in that flat you looked at,' he said to Hazel. 'You remember? The flat in Clifton?'

Hazel saw Georgie's eyes travelling over the two of them.

'You're flat-hunting?' she said. 'And Nye's helping you?'

'I am. Not that she needs help; Hazel makes her decisions based on the sound of people's voices on the telephone.' Nye flicked a strand of Hazel's hair with absent-minded affection.

'Not much room for your skills, then, Nye,' said Georgie. She smiled but her eyelashes quivered as she followed the movements of Nye's hand.

Hazel said nothing.

Georgie turned away rather abruptly and pushed open the door. Hazel noticed that, despite the difference made by her clothes, she walked with the same deep, rolling motion as before.

'Look who's here.'

The kitchen was long and thin and must have been built on to the cottage later. The walls were covered in green and white floral paper, peeling away at the top, and a gateleg table stood in front of a window which looked out into blackness. Sitting on the windowledge was Tom, in a dark blue T shirt. He had an enormous bottle of wine between his knees and a corkscrew stuck into the bottle mouth, but he seemed to have forgotten to twist or pull.

He looked at them: at both of them together, very unemphatically.

'It's Nye, with Hazel,' said Georgie.

'I can see. Hiya.' Still he kept his eyes steady. 'How are you both?'

'Well,' said Nye. 'Extremely. And so are you, by the look of you. Spain was hot, I take it?'

'What? Yes, very.'

'And I expect you did a lot of work, just as you planned?'

Tom looked pleasantly at them and seemed disinclined to answer but Georgie spoke.

'Hardly any.' She smiled slyly and leaned over to pull out a chair for Hazel; her shirt gaped and showed a small breast, a white circle against the tan. 'The siesta is a very good invention.'

'Sleep, sex and sun, was it?' Nye's voice had gone a note deeper to match hers. 'I can just see you two wandering through northern Spain like two libidinous babes in the wood.'

Looking away from Georgie's breast, Hazel saw that Tom was watching her at last – but her body not her face. 'That's the rickety chair, isn't it?' he said, just as she was about to sit down.

'Is it?' Georgie bent down again and twiddled the leg. 'So it is. Sorry, take that one instead.'

Hazel sat down carefully, trying to look relaxed. Suddenly everyone's eyes were on her and she had to look down at her lap to regain composure. When she looked up again, they had all turned away: Tom was bent over his corkscrew, Georgie was hoisting the broken chair over to the far side of the table, Nye leaned against the cooker watching Georgie. No one was taking any notice of her. She was on the outside, like a spectator. And she had a spectator's thought: she understood now why Nye was wearing the old blue sweatshirt – it was perfectly in keeping with the house and might have belonged to Tom or Georgie.

'I've never seen you brown before,' Nye said to Georgie. 'You didn't get a tan in France last year.'

'It wasn't hot enough. Besides, then I really was working. We took a house,' she added to Hazel, as she came back towards her, 'in south-east France, with some of the other art students and Nye. We were supposed to be working, but Nye kept sabotaging us with bottles of pastis and wine.'

'Speaking of which,' said Nye, 'is that Spanish wine you've got there, Tom? In that large flagon you're not opening?'

'Yes.' Tom glanced down at the bottle and turned its label towards Nye. 'It's the local wine from the village we used to go up to. The one I told you about on the phone.'

He looked at Hazel now. It was a brief look.

It wasn't as she'd thought it would be. Tom didn't even look the same. His beaky pallor of the wedding night had disappeared under a light tan. His hair seemed thicker. After his false start, he seemed relaxed, too: he sat on the windowledge pouring glasses of wine with a competent hand.

It was very disappointing. Meanwhile, Nye sat next to Hazel and occasionally touched her arm or the side of her face. It must be very clear to the others that she and Nye had recently made love.

Not that Hazel minded. It was perversely arousing to have Georgie's appraising looks to add to Nye's touch. But she needed to have Tom's reaction too. She hadn't imagined the events of the wedding night. She was puzzled to find that Tom could retreat into himself like this – she'd have thought it was more in Nye's character than Tom's – and it made her uneasy. She sat close to Nye, turning her head repeatedly as the other three caught up on their news.

It was ten o'clock; the evening progressed and inch by inch Hazel was making headway. For one thing, she was on terms with the others' conversation now, thanks to Nye. After that initial half-hour in which she'd hardly said a word, Nye had begun explaining who people were and bringing her into the conversation. Then he'd given Tom and Georgie an account of what it was like to go flat-hunting with Hazel and set her off to tell the anecdotes, so that now, when the kitchen was warm with the fug of cooking and they were all slightly drunk, she had worked her way into the evening.

She'd gained confidence too. Because Tom hadn't been able to go on ignoring her. For the last half-hour he'd been looking at her frequently, when he thought she wouldn't notice. He'd become the quietest of the four, doing a lot of listening and drinking. Hazel saw the stain on the chapped part of his lips. She also saw that when she was talking and he could look at her openly, Tom's eyes flicked rhythmically over her face as if he were taking measurements.

In fact, the last time Hazel had told a story, Tom's observation had been so marked that Georgie had looked curiously at him. Since then, Hazel had grown quieter too.

Now Georgie had just finished talking and Tom was peering at her emptying glass and pushing the bottle towards her. 'Is anybody hungry?' he asked.

'Yes, a little.' Nye had finished all the crisps and peanuts and upended the packets.

'Christ, sorry,' said Tom heavily. Georgie just laughed.

'I wondered when you were going to remember,' she said.

'It's almost all cooked,' Tom said. 'It won't be long.' He got up from the windowledge and went round the table, in the direction that took him away from Hazel. He kneaded Georgie's shoulder as he went past her. 'Sorry, Nye,' he said again. He made for the cooker and switched on the gas under a large pot.

'That's all right,' said Nye, looking amused.

'I'll get some plates together,' said Georgie. 'It's all right,' she added to Hazel as if Hazel had spoken, 'Tom's quite good at cooking.'

Left alone at the table together, Nye and Hazel exchanged a look. He seemed to be inviting her to share a joke; she smiled and settled more comfortably on her hard chair. She spread her fingers out on the table. With Tom avoiding her, she felt exposed and would have liked Nye's appreciative touch back on her, but although he winked at her, he made no move.

Georgie moved round the kitchen collecting plates and cutlery. She came swiftly back to the table, laid the places, put out the bowl of salad and sat down closer to Hazel than before.

'So you were at school with these two?'

'Only for a term.'

'Nye told me you were all pre-pubescent together. What was he like then?'

'I didn't know him very well.'

Hazel glanced at Nye and saw that he was watching her, not quite smiling.

'Oh go on. Was he a little thug? I bet he was.'

'I don't remember him like that.'

'Hmm,' said Nye. 'You don't remember me at all, do you?'

'What?' Georgie's mouth curled. 'Really?'

'I'm afraid so. Very unflattering, isn't it? She's tried to hide it, mind. In fact, it's been touching watching you cover your tracks, *collen*.'

'But Nye remembers you so well,' said Georgie with a touch of relish. 'He told me all about you, at our wedding.'

Nye shrugged. 'Ah, don't embarrass her, Georgie. The poor girl can't manufacture memories if she doesn't have any.'

But the look he gave Hazel had a coolness at its centre. It was odd to think that it must have been there all day, behind the intimate things they'd done. The idea unsettled her and increased her sense of exposure.

'I do have some memories,' she said easily to Nye.

'You see?' said Georgie, as if they'd had a side bet on it.

'Just not of you.'

'Oh,' said Georgie.

'You see?' said Nye to Georgie. Georgie laughed.

'I remember Tom.'

'Oh, God, what a surprise,' said Georgie quietly. She hitched one arm over the back of her chair. 'Did you hear that, Mr Memorable?'

Tom, who was holding plates under a hot tap, nodded. 'Sure.'

'He used to get into trouble a lot,' added Hazel mildly. 'I suppose that's why I remember him.'

'Probably.' Georgie sounded sarcastic.

'An inglorious epitaph,' said Nye after a second. 'But better than none, even so.'

'Tom,' said Georgie, leaning back in her chair. 'Nye's pride is hurt. How can we make it up to him?'

'Feed him,' Tom said curtly. He was spooning food on to a plate; his back was curved, his hands moved swiftly. There was something insulting about the way he piled the stew high and slid it on to the table in front of Nye. 'We'll give him first turn.'

Nye looked discomforted.

'You mannerless swine.' He picked up the loaded plate and gestured it towards Hazel. 'Would you like it, *collen*?'

'Not quite that much for me, thank you.'

Georgie was grinning.

'Does Hazel look as if she'd eat anything that size, Nye? I bet she only eats things in the tiniest portions, don't you, Hazel?'

'Well no, not exactly. In fact I quite like—'

'Hazel.' This time the serving Tom held was medium-sized, completely unexceptional. 'Is that all right for you?'

'Yes, thank you.'

Hazel took it with more care than was necessary, one hand on each side of the plate to give herself an excuse not to look at the others. She felt that she'd been tricked into behaving badly in public.

'Say it again – "*collen*". It sounds more like a swearword than an endearment.'

'It's neither,' said Nye. 'It's the Welsh for hazel. "*Collen*" – hazel, not to be confused with "*colled*" – loss, or "*colyn*" – sting.'

6

Was she wicked? Hazel was walking along Meifi Street. Yes, she had decided only minutes ago as she left the station, stepping out of the doors on to the Bartraeth pavement and seeing the April evening wide and light around her, beckoning her on.

Am I making too much of it? As she joined the queue at the kerb and watched her own reflection with all the others in the shop window, she didn't know.

She thought Georgie had noticed something at their last meeting. But not Nye: he couldn't afford to. Hazel had come to understand more about him since Tom and Georgie had returned. It took a lot out of him, their friendship. He worked at it, especially his bond with Georgie, because he had to. Now they were back, Hazel had been surprised by how often they each called him at work; she would hear about it in passing when she saw him herself, which was most evenings now. The last two times he'd been at the bedsit, she'd noticed the way his face and body had changed, gradually, after he'd closed the door, as if he'd been remembering how to relax.

Nye, she suspected, for all his word play and needling, felt protected by her. So he hadn't heard what had been there in her voice two nights ago, when, in the pub, she had explained to Tom and Georgie about travelling to work.

Georgie, plaiting the loose ends of wool that had strayed from her jumper, had looked up at Hazel when she gave the address of her new bedsit. And Nye had seen the look but misinterpreted it. 'No, it doesn't sound brilliant,' he said. 'But it's got its own sink and cooker, and Hazel likes the way the light comes through the big window.'

Nye had a disconcerting way of remembering Hazel's words and passing them on to other people, inflected with his own wry acceptance. She knew it was a mark of affection.

What would he think of her now, following the railings with her heart thumping, pretending not to see Tom dart behind the post van?

Tom was following her. He had shadowed her all the way from the station, keeping about thirty yards behind her, taking shelter behind other pedestrians. When she dawdled he looked in shop windows. When she quickened her pace he hurried from group to group of homebound strollers, maintaining the same distance.

At first she hadn't been sure. She'd seen the familiar coat on the other side of a telephone box and she'd turned away, sucking the cold evening into her lungs, feeling the sky and the city buildings recede. She'd begun to walk, panic-stricken, afraid that he would approach, afraid that it was coincidence, afraid that he wasn't really there at all. She'd grown so dizzy with concentration as she walked along St Beuno's that she had to hold on to the barrier at the traffic lights. And when a woman had stopped her to ask the way to the bus station, she'd glared at her mutely, refusing to speak.

Tom had come across to this side of the road now and she couldn't see him without turning round; she had no idea whether he was yards behind her or catching up, perhaps weaving fast and quiet through other people to approach and reach out – Hazel moved sharply sideways, into a newspaper-seller's queue. She opened her purse and counted out small change; with her head bent, murmuring civilities to the newspaper seller, she found Tom on her peripheral vision. He had stopped near the kerb, still a long way behind.

When Hazel turned off the main thoroughfare, and paused to glance back, he was closer. When she crossed into her own residential street, his footsteps came steadily behind her. He stopped by the porch stoop of the dentist's surgery across the road, and watched her enter the house.

Hazel shut the door, put down her bag and passed her hands over her face. Her palms tasted grubby. She turned the key in her bedsit door and walked straight to the window. On the other side of the flawed glass the street looked wide and Tom was standing by the porch stoop, his coat drawn up around his neck, looking at her.

They didn't know how to touch. They were self-conscious from staring at one another through the glass. It was difficult to find any expression. Hazel led Tom inside and at first he only stood on the brown carpet, looking from the walls to the wardrobe to her. Then he shut the door.

'I just want to talk,' he said.

Hazel stepped sideways. She walked around the bed and sat down on the end of it. 'Yes, let's talk.'

'I was following you, you know.' Tom said it angrily.

'Yes, I know.'

'Why didn't you say anything?'

Hazel sat silent. How could she respond to that? What did he expect her to do?

While she sat looking at Tom, he stared at her, apparently waiting, then began to unbutton his coat. 'I don't understand what's going on.' His anger was more aggressive now. 'Why are you doing this?'

'I'm not doing anything. You followed me.'

'I had to. I had to talk to you. You know that nothing can happen, don't you?' All the time, he was taking off his heavy black coat, folding it, laying it down in a bundle on the floor. 'For Christ's sake, Hazel, I've just got married.'

He spoke her name accusingly, and completely naturally. He pushed up the sleeves of his jumper and rubbed his forearms, once, twice, as he walked to the window and turned.

'I don't want to hurt anyone,' Hazel said.

'You won't get the chance, I won't let you hurt anyone.' He stood facing her, his body held in check. Hazel stood up and walked across to him. Her hands and knees moved too slowly and the skin on her face felt sore. She had hardly any distance left to go now.

She touched his hands and his flesh felt so immediate that she fumbled. Her fingers prodded his and she felt her nails scratch him. Hazel leant against him for balance and pushed her palms against his; then, thinking that he might try to hold her there, she levered one arm free and put her fingers in his mouth. Tom slid his arms round her. His hand went inside her shirt, and stroked between her ribs. She arched her back and pulled up his jumper.

His bare skin lay on hers; she tried to caress him mouth to mouth but he was kissing her neck. Heat coiled at the base of her throat. Hazel wanted to kiss him. She put her hands round his face and tried to raise it but he stepped backwards and pulled them both down into the chair. Hazel lay sideways across him and as he kissed her breasts, she pulled his sleeve as high as she could and licked his arm, pushing her mouth into the crease of the elbow.

Tom lifted her skirt. 'Close the curtains.' He put his hand between her thighs, rubbed his forehead against her stomach. Hazel stretched out and caught the edge of the curtain between her fingers. She twitched it shut but it swung back and Tom groaned and jack-knifed over her. As they slid to the floor his tongue was at last in her mouth.

The city was pale blue. Tail lights flashed at her, and the sign above the late night supermarket flickered. People were leaving the cinema. A cluster of young people, students probably, came out of the Beuno Arms.

Hazel crossed the road to the supermarket. It was very bright inside and customers' clothes stood out lurid against the shelves. From the delicatessen counter, where a young girl with a love bite on her neck served, Hazel bought smoked mackerel and ham and olives in a vacuum pack; bread to go with them; wine and chocolate.

She stepped back to let the man in the brown coat unload his basket. She knew one or two of these people by sight; they had seen her in here on other evenings, buying milk for the morning or wine for Nye. None of them, looking at her now, knew where her body had been in the last few hours. Tom's touch was all over her. His semen was inside her. His voice was in her throat.

As Hazel moved to the head of the queue, she half smiled at the cashier; she said 'thank you' when the woman helped load her carrier bag, so that she could hear her voice. It was low and quite confident. If someone passed a remark – asked her, say, if she had been working late – then she would be able to lie. But no one spoke, only herself saying 'thank you' to a car that stopped for her as she crossed the road again.

Tom was sitting on the bed smoking when she let herself in. The smell caught in her throat. 'My God, what's that?'

'A cigarette. French cigarettes. You don't mind, do you?'

Hazel looked at the blue packet on the sheets. 'No, I just didn't know you smoked them.'

'I don't normally. We bought a box when we were fogbound at the airport, waiting to come home. We didn't have enough money left to buy English ones.' Tom had put on his trousers and jumper, but no socks or shoes. He'd turned on the gas fire and there was a twist of charred paper on the carpet which he must have used to light his cigarette from the flames. Hazel was reminded of a man in a cell. She'd read an account once of a murderer taken to the guillotine in France: he'd been barefoot, with his shirt pulled open at the neck.

She walked to his side of the bed and sat down next to him. Tom looked down at his hand. 'Do you want one?' She shook her head and got up again, taking the bag into the alcove. She put it down on the small worktop and began unpacking; the acrid smell was less overpowering in here but it still pricked her throat.

Her hand was on the wine bottle when she felt Tom's arms pulling her. She turned and let him clutch her. At first she had to steel herself not to flinch from his mouth, sour with the taste of dark tobacco, but after a few seconds she had it on her own tongue too.

'It's all right,' she said. He slackened his hold and she took the cigarette out of his fingers. 'It's all right.' She took a drag. 'Pass me the corkscrew and I'll get us a drink.'

'I have to go,' said Tom at quarter to one. They were sitting in the window bay, with the lights turned off and the curtains opened several inches to let the streetlight in. The top sash was open too, to clean the air and lift their headaches. Hazel put her face into his hands and nodded.

'How will you get back?'

'Taxi. I can call from that public phone in the hall, can't I?'

'Yes, there are taxi numbers stuck up there. But you can't get a taxi every time, it's too expensive.'

'I know. I'll get a car.'

'What with?'

'I sold a painting last week. And we've saved some money from the bursary. We always knew we'd need a car once we moved to the Islyn.'

Hazel thought of Georgie in the weeks to come, waiting in the cottage for the sound of the engine, and felt a soft qualm. Her body or her conscience? She said: 'You won't tell her, will you?'

Tom pressed his thumbs into her jaw and let go. 'You know I won't. I can't. Hazel, don't you want me to?'

'No. You mustn't tell her, and I won't tell Nye. We mustn't spoil anything.'

He knelt up, then stood, steadying himself against the chair. He had to step carefully over the shards, where the wine glass had smashed.

'Don't talk about Nye. I don't want to think of him coming here. No, don't, Hazel, shut up, shut up.'

7

'Do you like it?'

Nye stood back from the bed, and watched Hazel's reaction. The Indian cotton made a pattern of red and orange and midnight blue against the dull green counterpane. The colours were warm and the geometric shapes interlocked pleasingly. It reminded Hazel of someone.

'It's lovely,' she said. She thought of herself and Tom on the bed, their naked bodies pale against the dark green, the candlewick crumpled beneath them.

'I didn't choose it alone, I confess. Georgie picked it out.'

Georgie; of course. The colours, the big square shape, the texture, it was all Georgie.

'That was clever of her.' Hazel had to struggle to keep her voice casual. She felt a violent repugnance to the fabric which Nye had spread, so contentedly, across her bed. She wanted to snatch it up and throw it out of the door. 'She hasn't even been here.'

'I described it to her. She said orange shades would counteract all this institutional green.' Nye picked up one of the corners trailing on the floor, and examined the pattern. 'It's quite similar to the batiks she used to make.'

'How is she?'

Nye looked surprised.

'Georgie? She seems very well. Why do you ask?'

'Well, last week she wasn't looking forward to going back to school.'

'Oh, that was just the last-night-of-the-holidays syndrome. And the come-down after getting married.' He dropped the corner of his gift and smiled at her. 'And what about you? You look better than you did on Wednesday.'

'I am. I'm sorry about that, I was exhausted.'

Exhausted by Tom: exhausted by his arms, his eyes, his hands on the steering wheel, driving her away from him to Nye.

Wednesday had been the seventh day since they'd first lain naked together in this room. The seventh day of lying with Tom and lying to Nye. She had not seen Georgie, but over and over again she'd sent Tom home to her, while she went to sit in cinemas and restaurants with Nye, and let him touch her.

On Wednesday night it had become too much. Hazel had fled home in a taxi and not let Nye come near her since, keeping herself only for Tom. Yet it was strange how, in these intervening three days, she had missed Nye. Cut off from him she felt that she was somehow losing Tom, even when she had Tom with her. She and Tom had been together for hours yesterday: not here, not in this little room, with Tom's hands on her body and his mouth against hers, but driving from town to town in the noisy little car, because it was Saturday afternoon and Georgie was in Bartraeth and they had been afraid to stay in the flat. And meanwhile Georgie had been shopping with Nye – and talking?

'Thank you for the cover. It's beautiful.'

'I can tuck you up in it next time you're tired.'

Nye's eyes were warm and he caught her round the waist. No, Georgie had not been talking. Yet Hazel believed that she must know.

The friends were gathered on the big platform seat at the far end of the gallery. Georgie was positioned in the middle of them. She wore a long dress and an orange-red shirt. Her face was still suntanned from the honeymoon. She was in conversation.

Tom was not on the seat. Nor was he in any of the scattered groups on the wood block floor. Hazel looked round, at first discreetly, then turning from side to side in her need to find him. She stopped in a panic and plucked at Nye's sleeve.

'What is it?'

'There's Georgie and the others, down there.'

'I know. Let's go and say hello to Chris first. He's over there, by his installation.'

'Oh yes.'

Beyond the large coloured panels suspended from the ceiling and the wood and metal sculptures, past a row of collages made from pottery shards, Chris stood talking to a middle-aged man. His installation was an apparatus of clothes-hangers and chairs, broken up and reassembled from one another's parts. A pair of the cannibalised chairs was set out conventionally at the edge of the installation and two young men were sitting on them; one of them was Tom.

The relief Hazel felt was almost overwhelming. And she also felt a shock of unfamiliarity. She had grown so used to seeing Tom looking straight at her, all his attention on her, his hands never far from her face. But he was turned away from her now and didn't know that she was near. Tom's head was bent casually towards the other man and he fiddled with his watch as he talked.

As they approached the corner, Hazel glanced over at Georgie and saw that she was following their path. Then Tom turned his head.

Tom hadn't wanted her to come tonight. They'd fought about it, with Tom saying that he couldn't stand up to the prospect of it; he'd repeated helplessly that it wasn't possible for him to watch her with Nye, that he wouldn't be able to be with her in Georgie's presence.

'We must be able to be together, the four of us,' Hazel had insisted. 'It's the only way we can do it. It's the only way it will work.' When Tom had protested again, she'd said: 'Do you want me to live in a cage? Do you want me only to be alive in this room, when you're here?'

There had been no answer he could make to that. So she'd come, and in the deepest part of her mind she was afraid of what would happen. The suspicion lodged in her that Tom might abandon her, or else that he might, after all, manage it well. She didn't let herself think of what that would mean.

Hazel looked eagerly, and with a hint of fear, into Tom's face. It was soft and oddly naked. He looked up at her with mild eyes, as if he had taken cover somewhere inside himself.

Tom was here, as she had asked him to be, and he was struggling against panic. She could see how it was hurting him to trust her. She smiled down at him, not caring who watched.

They talked inconsequentialities until Chris was free. The show was a mixed one, and Chris's first since he had left college. There had been more people here earlier, according to Tom's friend, Robert, but it still wasn't a very good turn-out. He said this with a frank grin which struck Hazel as strange until she realised that he was employed by the gallery.

Though they were all standing up now, Robert kept one foot propped up on his chair. 'We're supposed to use the chairs,' he explained. 'Break down the subject-object space.' To Hazel's surprise, Nye at once took his jacket off and dropped it on to the neighbouring seat. Then he picked her bag off her shoulder and set it down on the jacket. 'Thanks,' said Robert.

Tom didn't speak very much. He was obviously concentrating. Hazel's palms ached for a touch of him and she found it hard to drag her eyes away, but at the same time she felt over-excited and alert. She talked just the right amount to Robert and Nye, keeping their conversation moving along.

Chris appeared between her and Nye, tapping Nye's shoulder and kissing her on the cheek. He was grinning inside his short beard.

'Hallo. Hallo. Am I off duty now, Rob?'

'What did he say?'

'He asked me if I was in any permanent collections. What does that mean? Will they buy me only if I'm not in anyone else's, or only if I am?'

'Who knows? Derek likes to think of himself as an innovator; we might be lucky.'

'Was he involved in buying you in?' Chris said to Tom.

'He was on the committee,' said Tom. 'But I don't think he was that keen on me. It was Marie Ward who wanted my work.'

'Who is he?' said Hazel.

'He's on the Arts Council Selection Committee this year,' said Nye. 'They bought two of Tom's paintings in February, after he had his show.'

'He does like you,' Chris said again to Tom. He was enjoying himself and anxious to share it. 'He said a couple of nice things about you.'

Nye moved off to a nearby table and poured out a glass of wine.

'Congratulations,' he said, handing it to Chris. 'It sounds good.'

Chris looked at Nye with pleasure. It was coming home to Hazel tonight that Nye really was a part of this crowd, despite all his differences from them.

'Thanks. He didn't say he'd buy. But it's better than being ignored.'

Chris suddenly put his arm through Hazel's, clinked his glass against hers and drank. It was a clumsy gesture and it threw Hazel off balance. She heard Nye say: 'You're spilling Hazel's drink everywhere,' and unexpectedly she heard Tom laugh. She glanced at him but he'd turned away: the others were coming to join them and the group was breaking up. In passing, she saw Georgie touch Tom's face.

★ ★ ★

All evening, Georgie was in the middle of a knot of people. She managed it quietly, but Hazel continually had the impression that she was bringing an escort with her. She and Tom, Nye and Georgie never made their customary four. At times, Georgie seemed to bask in the company of others. When they left the gallery, Georgie led a clutch of friends across the car park and stood amongst them while they examined the new car.

'It's a very – er – vibrant blue,' said Chris.

'How many miles has it done?' Mark said, peering at the dashboard. 'That's not bad.'

'We do have a bit of a problem with the gears,' said Georgie. 'Tom thinks they vote conservative, they're so resistant to change.'

'But the main thing is, Georgie,' said Nye, 'what colour are you going to paint the hubcaps?'

Hazel kept to the edge of the group and only surreptitiously touched the paintwork on the boot to remind herself that she already knew this car better than any of them.

Because they had three cars between the crowd, Georgie proceeded to organise them across town to a cheap Italian restaurant. It was Sunday quiet in there and they were able to push tables together to accommodate the nine of them. Georgie sat at the centre of one long side, between Tom and Mark. David, Caroline and Iestyn, the artist turned house-painter, sat beyond Tom. Chris, who was in high spirits, gravitated to the place opposite Georgie.

In the general jollity (everyone was buoyed up by Chris's excitement) Hazel became aware of silence between Georgie and Tom. It baffled her, because it seemed to come from Georgie and yet it was not angry nor accusing. There were moments when Tom and Georgie were leaning apart, listening to other people, and yet they seemed bound together in a shared stillness. And although Georgie didn't often look at Tom, she emanated a calm protectiveness towards him.

Hazel watched him acquiesce and tried to understand. She had expected that tonight would hurt and reveal things to her, but she couldn't see what was passing between them. She couldn't relate their behaviour to herself. It was only when Georgie spoke to her, and smiled at her across the table, that she realised her voice was too even, and her smile too open, and felt reassured.

Hazel did not want Georgie consciously to recognise that she and Tom were lovers. But if Georgie didn't know, at some deep inarticulate level, then how could she, Hazel, be sure that it was true?

They'd finished eating and the talk was swirling desultorily when Hazel noticed that Tom was watching Nye. Nye was on her right, at the end of the table and he had spent much of dinner talking across it to Caroline and Mark. Yet he took care not to neglect Hazel, filling her glass and smiling at her with his affectionate, half-teasing note of solicitude. Hazel had registered that the current conversation was about books; now she realised that her name had been spoken.

'Are you coming?' Caroline said. 'Next weekend?'

'I'm sorry?'

'To the book fair,' said Nye, touching her arm. 'The one I told you about on the phone. Caroline's father has a stand there, I said I'd be driving over. Will you be coming?'

Hazel looked at him uncertainly.

'Where is it?'

'Harborth, only ten miles away. There's a good pub where we generally end up, The Prince. Mark and Caroline will both be there.'

The weekend: Hazel's gaze flicked to Tom, round cursorily at the others, and back to Tom. He rocked gently in his chair and listened in to the conversation with an expression of interest.

Nye turned to Caroline.

'Are you going over for both days?'

'As usual. Saturday looks like the best day though – they've got some good people doing readings. David Williams is going to be there in the morning. Have you seen the programme?'

'Oh, I'll be there for that, then,' said Nye.

'What about you, Hazel?'

'I don't know. Is anyone else going?'

She looked at Chris, on her left, and across to Georgie. Georgie turned from David.

'What?' she said. 'Is something being planned?'

'The book fair,' said Tom. 'Nye's trying to organise a party to go to it.'

'Am I?' said Nye.

'We've never been, you know,' Tom said to Georgie. 'Perhaps we should. After all, Nye comes to all our things. We should go and have a look at his, don't you think, Chris?'

'Me? At a book fair?' said Chris. 'What do I have to do?'

'It'll be an education to go with Nye. We'll be able to see him in his element. Quoting from the old books. Some of the most venerable and the most forgotten. A bard among bards.'

It was a very good imitation of Nye being sonorous and Chris cackled. 'He does sound just like you, Nye,' he said. 'Do you really want us to come?'

'Oh, I'm desperate,' said Nye. 'I don't know how I've managed without you being there, all these years.'

'That's settled then,' said Tom. 'We'll go along, shall we, Georgie? Do you remember The Prince? It's that pub by the towpath that we went to last summer.' He looked around mildly. 'Anyone else coming?'

'I will,' said Chris. 'I'll come and be educated, like poor old Hazel.'

'I don't even know if Hazel's coming yet,' said Nye. He turned to her and gave a resigned grin. 'Christ knows how we let ourselves in for this. Do you want to come?'

Hazel hoped that her laugh sounded under control. She was exhilarated by the speed at which Tom had covered the ground. Now they would see each other at the weekend. She didn't dare look at Tom but she touched the back of her hand to Nye's arm, in a gesture meant for him.

'Yes, of course I will.'

'We could have a picnic,' said Caroline. 'That's what a lot of people do, along the towpath. Then we can book some time away from Dad's stall and come and meet you.'

'Time away from the stall,' said Mark. 'You bet.'

'I'll come,' said David, from beyond Georgie. 'I went a couple of years ago, actually. In the evening, to see a jazz band.'

Georgie did not join the chatter. Turning as unobtrusively as she could, Hazel saw that Georgie had drawn her knees up in front of her and sat silently cradling them. Tom was watching her with an expression of defiance. He folded the edge of the tablecloth, leaned forward to try and see Georgie's face, and finally put his hand gently on her knee. 'Would you like to go, Georgie? Don't you think it'll be fun?'

Georgie was obviously thinking. Hazel gazed at her hair and longed to see behind it. She had no emotion left for Georgie; she could only observe and try to read her. What level of knowledge was disclosing itself to Georgie now: was it an intimation of danger, only? Or did she have a real idea of where Tom went when he was not in their honeymoon cottage?

'Yes,' Georgie said, almost distractedly. 'Oh yes, of course.'

She leaned forward and asked Chris if he'd like to go in their car. Tom withdrew his hand with a look that strongly resembled gratitude.

★ ★ ★

'Your quiet day in Harborth has turned into something else.'

They were in Nye's car, driving away from the restaurant. It was a dangerous game, this one of raking over the evening just past, but Hazel needed to take the risk. She was hoping Nye would mention Tom's name.

'Yes, so much for contemplation. It might be fun, though. Tom seemed very determined to come, didn't he? He probably decided that he was being left out, and there's no stopping him when he gets like that.'

'Why should he be left out?'

'Oh, Tom gets the wrong end of the stick sometimes.'

'In what way?'

'He's not as easygoing as he seems.' Nye swerved to avoid an oncoming car, automatically putting his hand out to shield Hazel. He smiled at her. 'Sorry, he came on so fast.

'No, what you must remember about Tom,' he continued, 'is that you've met him at quite an atypical time in his life. He's had the show, won the award and got himself a living through teaching, all in the last twelve months. Not to mention getting married. He's riding high now, but he was alive twenty-three years before this one and he's still Tom.'

'And that is?'

'Well, he's not the world's clearest thinker. He's a moody swine. When he's up, he's up; when he's down he's down and when he's only halfway up he's bloody confused.' Nye laughed a little excitedly.

'You're very close to him, aren't you?'

'Oh yes. Surely. You can't help it when you go back so far together. We're each other's first map, in a way.'

'Was it strange for you when he got married?'

'Not particularly. He's been with Georgie for so long; ever since the end of their first term. We all struggled through the trials of studenthood together. There were periods when I knew Georgie better than Tom did; and at times I still do.' He paused, then reached out and slid his hand beneath her hair. 'Is it confusing for you? You probably didn't realise that you were taking on three of us instead of one.'

Hazel stayed still under his fingers.

'I've taken you on, have I?'

'Oh dear, I have the impression I've been premature.' Nye tickled her neck. 'That will teach me. But out of interest, what would you call it?'

Careful, thought Hazel.

'Oh well. Taking you on, I suppose.'

'Good. Here we are.' Nye pulled the car in to the pavement and switched off the ignition. He turned to her, all shoulders and purposeful arms, and she made her mind blank as their mouths touched and opened and his tongue came into hers. There was no difficulty in disassociating this act from kissing Tom – this was only a sequence of random events involving teeth, tongue and lips.

After the initial instinctive shrinking from it, it was painless. It was even quite comforting. Arousing, as it used to be. So long as she didn't think of Tom, she didn't mind the pressing of his skin against hers nor the heat of his mouth. Yes, she could make love to him tonight.

But not here; he couldn't come into the little room and get into the bed where Tom had been. She had her own private map there now.

'It's good to be with you again,' said Nye. 'I've missed you.'

'And I've missed you.'

'So—?'

'Nye. About tonight . . .' Hazel's voice was wary; she made it deliberately so, hoping to rouse his protectiveness. 'I think I'd rather we went back to your flat.'

He raised his eyebrows.

'If you want. But why?'

'It's difficult in the mornings here – padding up and down the hall to the shared bathroom.'

'You do have that streak of nonconformist respectability in you, don't you? Funny girl. But as a matter of fact, Hazel, I hadn't expected to stay tonight.'

'Oh.' Hazel was nonplussed. 'I see. I'd better withdraw the invitation then, had I?'

Nye nodded. 'Goodnight, my darling. Sleep well.'

'Yes. Goodnight.'

He kissed her again, holding her face lovingly in his hands.

Nye did not get out of the car; he sat behind the wheel and watched her until she had opened the door, then he kissed his hand to her and started the ignition.

Hazel switched on her bedsit light and listened as the noise of the engine grew fainter. Still with her coat on, she pulled the orange-red cotton square from the bed and folded it into a drawer. She didn't understand but she was relieved. She took her clothes off quickly, washed at the tiny basin next to her gas ring, and went naked to bed.

Lying where Tom had lain, she covered her eyes and thought of the strange gratitude in his face when Georgie had spoken and of the touch of his hand outside in the unlit car park.

8

'I've just spoken to Nye. He's asked me to get some food for tomorrow's picnic.'

'I know, I've just spoken to him too. I'll buy some later and bring it round this evening.'

'Good.' Hazel looked over her shoulder at Duncan, who was inspecting the test results she had just drawn up. 'When will you be here?'

'Midday. I've got to be at the college at two. I can't be late again. What's the weather like there?'

'Beautiful.'

'It's raining here.'

'Have you been working?'

'No. I haven't worked for two weeks. I'll meet you downstairs.'

'In an hour.'

The lab was bright and warm with May sunshine. Through the sloping glass the tops of trees were varying shades of green. Duncan's footfalls on the lino and his humming mingled with the distant clamour from the refectory, and in Hazel's bones Tom's voice vibrated.

She moved back to her workbench.

'I'm going out early again today,' she said. 'You don't mind, do you?'

'Nope. Not so long as one of us is here for the school visit at two.'

'I'll do that.'

Duncan nodded. He never made any remark about these telephone calls or Hazel's subsequent departures. He stood back from his graph.

'What do you think of this? Does that look like the right kind of trajectory to you?'

Hazel went to look. Each movement she made was precise. She

felt her muscles working. Her sight was clear. She was aware of the blood flowing round her, feeding her. It was necessary if she were to keep her balance.

The affair had catapulted forward. Sunday had broken a restraint between them. They had seen each other every day since, sometimes twice a day. Tom drove to Bristol at lunchtime, or to meet her from work; in the May heat, they sat on the downs or walked in the gorge. They joined the homebound traffic jams over the bridge at six o'clock, heading into the western hills. Hazel had gone once to meet him at the college, at the end of his afternoon's teaching. She'd telephoned an urgent message through that he should expect her, and he'd been waiting at the place he'd told her about, on the top floor by the cleaner's cupboards and the First Aid room.

Today, hot and bright as they walked out on to the gallery steps together, was the fifth day since Sunday, but it seemed much longer. Hazel couldn't remember everything Tom had said to her; it was often contradictory. Sometimes it was hurtful. 'We won't get away with this, you know,' he'd said. 'We might as well enjoy it because we're sure as hell going to pay.' And then a little while later: 'We could escape. We could just go away together.' And once when they'd just stopped making love he'd looked at her spitefully and said: 'What's in this for you?'

To that, Hazel had answered, just as aggressively: 'You tell me.'

Hazel had seen Nye on Tuesday night. She hadn't known how she was going to behave to him; Tom had refused to help her and by the time she'd arrived at Nye's flat she'd been full of excited anger. In the event, she had talked to Nye, wrangled with him and then slept with him. She'd made no mistakes, even though – or perhaps because – she wasn't trying. She felt reckless but her actions had looked after themselves.

The sex had been good. Making love with Nye was direct and satisfying; it also gave her orgasms, which was something that didn't happen with Tom. All the same, the idea of falling asleep with Nye had disturbed her and soon after they'd finished, she'd sat upright and said she had to leave. Nye hadn't seemed hurt: he'd given her a mocking push to the edge of the bed, then lay and laughed at her as she dressed. 'Go on then. Back to your chaste little cell. Are you sure you don't want a bath before you go?'

Hazel had had a bath at home, of course, infuriating her neighbours by making the pipes boom at one in the morning. Then she'd gone to bed and thought of Tom.

★ ★ ★

Tom was squinting in the sun. He drew her down the steps with him, his hand on her back, hurrying her slightly. In the entrance hall they had exchanged a couple of good-friend kisses, which was all they allowed themselves near Hazel's work, but they would be driving somewhere out of the way, for privacy.

'Let's go to the gorge,' said Tom. 'Into the woods. We can be alone there.'

The May heat had sprung on to the land in the last week, and people and traffic and plants were in its thrall. A stillness hung over Clifton and the suspension bridge was outlined against the blue. In the wood at the top of the gorge it was cool. Hazel and Tom sat shoulder to shoulder on the ground, where a pool of sunlight was filtered through the leaves. Tom was sucking Hazel's fingers too hard and she watched the muscles contract and release in his face.

'How did last night go?' she asked.

'Tricky. Nye talked about you a lot – mainly to Georgie. He's after something. He's picked up that Georgie doesn't like you, you see.'

'What was he saying?'

'He didn't say much *about* you, just kept bringing your name in: "Hazel said this." "Hazel and I ran into David." "I don't know if Hazel will come on Saturday." '

'What? He knew I was coming.'

'Yes. I think that one was to test the water. He was looking for our reactions. Nye's an expert on our reactions; well he would be, he's put in years of study.'

'Tom.' He looked up. 'Do you think he suspects?'

He considered her mockingly. 'Well, he knows something's going on. Georgie usually talks to him non-stop but there she was last night, just nodding and going reserved whenever your name was mentioned. In the end he told her how delighted you were with the bedspread she chose and how it's transformed your room, made it "positively womblike".' He twitched on the last word.

'Christ. What did Georgie say?'

' "Oh good." ' He shrugged. 'Georgie's playing her cards close to her chest.' He let go of Hazel's hands and began pushing back her hair, watching the way it fell against her skin when he let go.

'She must know,' said Hazel. 'By now. You're with me so much of the time, she *must* know.'

Tom stroked her hair across her forehead. It was as if he were trying to smooth the ridges out of his own face.

'I couldn't tell you what she knows. *I* know that she didn't sleep last night. I woke up at four and she was sitting in the kitchen, reading.'

Hazel stared at him: the thought of Georgie abandoned downstairs in their cottage disturbed her. She saw Georgie at the kitchen table, probably dressed in a jumper and jeans against the predawn chill, illuminated by the overhead light. She was a clear figure but removed from Hazel, like an actress on stage.

'It's hurting her, then,' she said.

'Of course it is.' Tom snorted with laughter. 'What did you expect?'

Hazel felt the quick anger, gravelly in her throat, that Tom often provoked. 'You said you wouldn't let me hurt her.'

'Oh yes and you believed me.'

Tom pulled Hazel on top of him and kissed her. The upward probing of his tongue was shocking and made her want to squirm. She tried to get away by opening her mouth wide and grappling him but he was suddenly gentle, holding her fast. She felt saliva pool in the front of her mouth and run into his.

His hands went underneath her clothes and touched her skin. Hazel lay still after a while, feeling piece after piece of her flesh exposed and lifted by him. Each touch travelled inwards, thickening, reddening, liquescing until she could no longer think, only desire; and need.

9

'Delicious pies.' Chris lay on his side and dropped another piece of flan into his mouth. 'Who bought them?'

'Hazel,' said Georgie. She pulled three more out of the basket and looked at the wrappers. 'Yes, I thought they must be Addams pies. Where did you find them?'

Hazel didn't look at her. 'One of my local shops.'

'How lovely,' said Georgie. 'I didn't know they supplied anywhere else. We used to live on them, didn't we, when we were in Mundy Road?' She smiled at Tom.

'Best pies in the world.' Tom leaned over the basket. 'God alive, fuck me, you bought enough, didn't you, Hazel?'

Hazel smiled without looking at him. She could hear the laughter in his voice, and now he was trying to intercept her gaze. She knew what she'd see if she looked at him, because of course he had bought the pies himself. She was perturbed by his crudeness – and his insistence; he was still looking towards her.

The company – Nye, Hazel, Georgie, Tom, Chris, Mark, Caroline and Iestyn – were in a rough circle round the picnic food. A few feet away the bottles of wine stood in the shade of a silver birch. It was a fine afternoon and there were other picnickers on the grass, while the towpath was crowded with walkers and people fishing.

Hazel looked across to Nye, who'd just left her side to go and fetch some wine. He was too busy to notice her but she kept watching him, hoping that Tom would follow her gaze and calm down.

But Tom was in a peculiar mood today. He seemed to be enjoying the falseness of their position. He'd already commented on how good Nye and Hazel looked together, and told a string of anecdotes about things he and Nye and Georgie had done in the past. Beyond him, Georgie held out her plastic cup to Nye's wine bottle.

'Do *you* remember Addams pies, Nye?' Now she was at it. 'Do you remember when we were working for our second-year exams and we used to take it in turns to fetch the food parcel?'

'Vividly. Taste the wine.' Georgie sipped. 'All right?'

'Nice. A bit warm.' Georgie watched Nye take a drink from her cup and grimace. She smiled. 'It's not that bad.'

'It would be better a few degrees colder though. It would make all the difference.'

'It's fine, Nye.'

Hazel removed her eyes from them, with difficulty. She turned to listen to the talk between Iestyn and Caroline but she could still feel Georgie sitting those few feet away.

Within a few seconds, her gaze sneaked back. No, she must stop doing this. It brought no insight anyway: she couldn't begin to imagine what was going on in Georgie's mind. Georgie was separating the stack of paper cups now and holding them out for Nye to fill with wine, then passing them on. They worked together easily and Hazel was suddenly reminded of her parents, putting sandwiches and tomatoes on plastic plates, pouring squash out of the Thermos, while she and her brother waited on the travel rug.

'Thanks,' she said when her turn came. Georgie smiled. Tom made an impatient movement and reached over Georgie's lap for his own cup. When he turned back, he left his hand on Georgie's leg.

'What's your new place like then, Hazel?' he said.

Hazel had to look at both him and Georgie together. 'It's a bedsit,' she said. 'One room with a cupboard-kitchen attached. It's small but it suits me.'

'It's *very* small,' Nye said. 'But light,' he said quickly, winking at Hazel, 'and private. Hazel was put off the idea of sharing by the time we'd answered all those Bristol ads, weren't you?'

'You could say that.'

'Why? What was wrong with them?' That was Caroline.

'Oh, this, that and the other,' said Nye, smiling at Hazel. 'It was the cleaning rota, or the flatmate's boyfriend or the way they drank their coffee.'

Hazel shrugged. 'It's tricky sharing with people you don't know. I'm not very easy to live with – I just like a bit more independence.'

'*Noli me tangere*,' said Nye breathlessly. He quivered his hand around Hazel's face. 'For Caesar's I am, and wild for to hold.'

Georgie laughed. Hazel glanced at her, feeling hunted, and saw that next to her Tom was at last looking uncomfortable.

'*Who's* I am?' said Iestyn.

'Henry the Eighth.' It was Tom who spoke. He sat up straight as he did, and took his hand off Georgie's leg.

'What?'

'Caesar was Henry the Eighth. It's a quote from a poem about Anne Boleyn. Caesar was a code name for Henry and he cut off the poet's head for sleeping with Anne in the end, isn't that right, Nye?'

'No,' said Nye. 'Henry just told him to take a long trip overseas.'

'How the hell did you know that, Tom?' said Chris.

'From exposure to Nye's Tudor period,' said Tom. 'Two years ago he never stopped quoting the bloody thing.' His smile at Nye was slow and slightly antagonistic.

There was a little lull, during which Hazel looked over the heads of the others at the walkers on the towpath. Her face felt as if it had been pinched.

'Time to open another bottle,' said Nye. 'I'll go and chill it in the river.'

'He's a perfectionist about everything, isn't he?' said Chris. 'I'm surprised he's not chilling the cups too.'

'Ah, don't knock him.' Georgie spoke softly. 'You don't know what we'd do without him.' Hazel heard a wistfulness in Georgie's voice and turned: Georgie was staring across the towpath to where Nye squatted at the water's edge, holding the bottle under. After watching Nye for several more seconds, Georgie touched Tom's arm. 'It's his birthday in a couple of weeks. Do you know if he's planning to do anything?'

'No idea,' said Tom. He had his head bent. Georgie looked at Hazel.

'I don't know,' said Hazel. 'He hasn't mentioned it.' Georgie almost imperceptibly raised her eyebrows. Hazel gave a polite look of incomprehension in return.

'How old is he going to be?' Caroline asked Georgie.

'Twenty-three.'

'Is Nye really only twenty-two?' Iestyn said. 'God, he's young. How come he's a year ahead of himself?'

'He's a quick learner,' said Tom. 'He had older parents who pushed him at home. He jumped a year back in primary school somewhere.'

'I never knew that. I always thought he was older than us, if anything. So he's younger than you, Tom?'

'Yep. Younger than all of us. Always has been.'

'He's not younger than Hazel though,' said Georgie. 'Is he,

Hazel?' Hazel stared; how did Georgie know her age?

'No, we're the same age. Or we will be in two weeks' time – my birthday was in February.'

'Two kiddies,' said Chris indulgently; he was the only one of the wider group who seemed to feel affection for her. 'Don't say you're a prodigy too?'

'No, we just moved round a lot when I was young. At one point I went from a good school to a bad school and got put up a class to save embarrassment.'

'*I* think,' Georgie was speaking to Tom, 'it would be nice to have a party for Nye. Don't you? For his birthday.'

Tom stared at her. 'A party? For Nye?'

'Yes, why not? We can have it in the cottage. His birthday's a week Friday.' She turned towards Hazel. 'Hazel will help, won't you?' Hazel said nothing. 'Oh,' said Georgie, 'unless of course you were planning something of your own, were you?'

'No, nothing like that. We hadn't talked about it.'

'Well, let's do it, then. Ssh. He's coming.'

Nye came back, smiling. He moved unhurriedly, like a large horse.

Hazel moved her legs to make room for him and he knelt beside her and took up the corkscrew. The density of his body was reassuring and she sheltered behind it; she felt threatened by Georgie and by whatever was passing now between Georgie and Tom.

Georgie was kneeling behind Tom and rubbing his shoulders. She was talking to him and Tom nodded but his head was averted and Hazel couldn't see his face. Even when she leaned forward and wiped the drips off Nye's bottle, earning his touched 'Thank you,' she still couldn't see Tom's face.

10

'You like him now, don't you?'

Hazel stopped him from playing with her hair.

'When did I say I didn't like him?'

'But you like him more now. You talk about him more. I can tell by seeing you with him.'

'You like Georgie.' They didn't use the word love.

Tom left off touching her. He walked to the curtains and drew them back a few inches: the evening outside had taken on a blue tinge, and the streetlamps were lit. He lowered the top sash and his damp hair stirred in the breeze.

'She's not letting go of this party, you know. She asked me for your number again today, so she could talk to you about it.'

'You didn't give it to her?'

'Of course not. I said I didn't have it.'

'Oh Jesus.' Hazel followed him to the window and stood behind him, straightening his shirt. 'Every time the phone rings I think it's her. When you arrived this evening, I thought it might be – I can't face it, Tom. I don't know what she's going to say.'

'Look. I'll fix it. You and Nye come round this week, and you can talk to her about it then. I'll keep Nye busy and I'll be nearby.' Tom went to sit in the armchair and pulled her down on to his lap. 'I've got to go. I'll ring Nye when I get home and ask you both over.'

He held her so that she couldn't see his face but she could feel his cheek pressed against hers and the spidery touch of his eyelashes.

'Hazel? This isn't getting any easier, is it?'

'I don't care. I don't care.'

'This is as far as we can go.'

They had driven into the village over the mountain road and stopped the car behind the highest cul-de-sac. These houses had been new when Hazel lived in Penllwyn; now their rendered walls had dampened in patches and their window frames had peeled. The gardens were more abundant: yellow laburnum chains hung over fences and snapdragons and silverleaf bushed in some beds, weeds straggled in others.

'Quickly. Down here.' Tom pulled Hazel across the pavement and into an alley. 'This is Top Lane. The only people who come here are kids, and they won't know us.'

Tom's hand was insistent on hers. Hazel let him hurry her between the walls and dark stone and mortar, furred with moss. His urgency was irrational and catching. 'You're going to Penllwyn with him?' he'd said on the phone. 'Come with me first. I want to take you there before he does.' So he'd picked her up from work and driven all the way back here, and now he was shepherding her into this walled lane which ran across the valley side between house gardens.

'There.' Here another lane, wider and broken by gateways, crossed them at right angles. Downhill, several children were playing in it. Tom ignored them. 'Come up here, you can see over.'

They stood on the little gravel bank and rested their elbows on the top of the wall. The village spilled down the hill, showing them ranks of back gardens and lean-tos, and glimpses of cars in drives.

'You see. You can see it all.'

'Yes. I see. It looks different. I never realised there was so much of the village up this hill.'

'No, you can't really tell from the other side. But then it's grown since your day. They put bungalows down by the rugby ground and the estate had only just been started then, hadn't it?'

'Yes, I think so.'

'Nye and I used to come here. We used to watch people and smoke. I bet he brings you here tomorrow, after you've been to his mother's.'

'Let's hope the kids don't recognise me.'

'Kids don't care about people like us.' But as he put his arms round her, he drew her down below the level of the wall. 'When you come here with him, think of this.' He kissed her exhaustively.

The wall dug into Hazel's back and her legs hurt from holding their bent position. She spread her hands against Tom's head and wondered if he would try to make love to her here. The pain in her thighs spread into her vulva and she tried to pull his hands down to touch her. But he stopped at her ribs.

'He's falling in love with you, you know,' he said.

'No, I don't know. I don't think he is, don't say that.'

'It's true. I realised last night, by something he said.'

'What?'

'He said he wished he could be in love with a woman like Georgie.'

Hazel let go of Tom and turned back to the village. On the main road stood the junior school, with its steep roof and railings, where Georgie worked. Further down was the valley floor and the river, where new houses had been built, and across the other bank, behind a screen of trees, was the half-moon of houses where Tom had lived.

'That's where I used to wait for the school bus.' She pointed to the right. 'Over there, by the church hall. Why weren't you there too?'

'We got on the other side of the village. There, by the rugby club. There's the shelter. That's where I got to know Nye.'

'He told me yesterday that you were already friends when I came to the Traeth. But I don't think you were.'

'I don't know, the time gets mixed up. I just seemed to be at that bloody school for ever.' Tom began picking tiny bits of grit from the wall and flicking them into the vegetable garden beyond. 'Nye changes things to suit himself anyway. He tricked me over the bus, in the first place.'

Hazel watched the smile move sarcastically across Tom's face. The heat was fading from her groin now and left her bewildered.

'What do you mean?'

'We became friends because he persuaded me to skip school with him one day. I remember it had been raining for weeks, and we'd all been jammed together in the shelter, every morning, so Nye and I had begun to talk a bit. We didn't have very much in common. He was always having his name read out for coming top in exams, and never seemed to be in trouble. You remember.'

'No. I've told you, I don't remember anything about him.'

'Then one morning it was fine, a lovely day, and he suggested we give school a miss. I thought he never did anything like that. But he just came along the road swinging his briefcase and said that the school bus had broken down and we were all supposed to wait for a minibus, but why didn't we bunk off into Caerfach? Not the kids of course – just him and me.'

'So you went.'

'Yes, of course. He took it for granted I would, so I had to. We started off across the fields and we'd got about a hundred yards when the bus turned up. The usual bus, with nothing wrong with it at all. The driver saw us, of course: we were stuck right in the middle of open fields with our uniforms on.'

'Nye was mistaken then.'

'Oh no, he lied.'

'How do you know? Did he admit it?'

'No, he didn't say anything. I said, "Look, it's the bus," and he just looked at me and went on walking. So I knew he'd lied.'

'What did you do?'

'We spent the day in Caerfach together, on about two and six. It was ball-achingly cold. We put our ties in our pockets and turned our blazers inside out and played the machines in the arcade. It was the perfect disguise. Only a dozen or so people reported us to the school.'

'And after that you were firm friends.'

'No, after that we were caned by the headmaster. He said, "I'm disappointed to have to punish *you* like this, Mathias." Nye winked at me, which was a bit of a mistake. It meant he got it worse.'

'Nye got the cane? I didn't think he'd ever been in trouble at school.'

'He hadn't till then. Not that he seemed bothered. Afterwards he told me he'd done lots of things like that and always got away with them before, so it was time his luck ran out.'

'Did you believe him?'

'Not really. But I thought it was quite cool of him, all the same.'

11

'Thank you.'

'What for?'

'For coming to meet my mother. And carrying all those things, I didn't tell you you'd be moving furniture, did I?' Nye put his arm loosely round her shoulders as he bent to unlock the car door for her.

Hazel hesitated before she got in. She was making the most of the gentle evening, cool now the sun was down and with a breath of moisture in the air. Nye stopped on the driver's side and smiled at her across the roof.

'You look lovely tonight. Shall we go for this drink, then?'

Nye hadn't walked her round the village. He hadn't taken her up the lanes, and they'd passed the bus shelter without a word. Now, as they drove out of the cul-de-sac and turned down the hill, he gave her a complicitous smile. 'My mother liked you.'

'I liked her. She's very friendly – considering how sharp she is. You're very similar, aren't you?'

'I'm somewhat larger.'

Hazel laughed. 'That's true. How old were you when you overtook her?'

'Eleven. Poor woman – I used to tease her about it, so did my father.'

'Oh, I expect she could cope.' Hazel watched him as he turned the car on to the main road and towards the sun. He narrowed his eyes; they were his mother's shape but not her colour. Nye's brown-black irises were much more intense and sometimes these days Hazel looked into them and saw tenderness. Each time, it was a shock.

'Well,' he said, 'isn't it a glorious evening? Let's hope that this pub of Tom's is as good as he says. He was very keen that we go there tonight. It seems that village life has its attractions after all.'

Hazel listened to the vibrations in Nye's voice and held his words at arm's length. 'After all?'

'He hasn't exactly been conspicuous by his absence round Bartraeth, has he? He spends more time at the college now than when he was a student there. Georgie told me he's just taken on a new class.' He shifted his shoulder blades against the seat. 'It makes me wonder.'

Hazel looked at the dashboard. Nye was noticing things. When the clock's second hand had moved three notches she said: 'You think he doesn't like living in the Islyn?'

'I shouldn't be surprised. There's no stopping those two when they want to do something, but this idea of Georgie teaching and drawing and Tom painting and hunter-gathering, and both of them buried out in the hedgerows with home-made wine and their bodies for pleasure always seemed a little idealistic.'

'Perhaps he's just lonely there in the day with Georgie at school.'

'I'm sure you're right. The marital nest isn't so cosy when Mrs Fieldmouse is out all day. The trouble is, Mrs Fieldmouse gets home after a hard day at the blackboard and she's ready for some elderberry wine and a little loving in the long grass, and Tom's off in the city with us.'

Hazel laughed, partly out of shock: it was the first time she'd ever heard Nye make fun of Georgie. There had been a distinct tinge of malice in it too. But 'with us'? What did he mean? Tom surely spent too much time with her to leave room for Nye and the others.

'You're seeing a lot of Tom at the moment then?'

'A fair bit. I don't see him every day like I used to but several times a week, yes. As I said, he's in Bartraeth so much.'

Hazel computed rapidly. Nye must mean that he saw Tom at lunchtimes, and perhaps in the early evenings too. That, together with the communal weekend meetings, would make several times a week. 'If Georgie's lonely,' she said, 'why doesn't she just go into Bartraeth with Tom?'

'That's what I suggested to her. But she says she doesn't usually feel like it in the week. She wants to relax in the homestead, as planned. She says solitude's good for her creativity though: she's been getting down to her drawing again. She's even doing some painting now that she's got the studio to herself most of the time. She tends to be self-conscious about painting in front of Tom, because his work's so much stronger than hers.'

'I thought you liked Georgie's work?'

'I do, especially her drawings, but Tom's a much better painter.

There's no question about it. Though whether Tom's going to do himself justice with this summer show is beginning to look very dubious. He's blocked, you know.'

Of course she knew. Except that 'blocked' wasn't a word she or Tom used, because he said it wasn't how it felt to him. It was more like a falling away: fast, constant, sheets of light dropping away from him each time he tried to settle; an agitation in his vision, quite beautiful in its own right.

'No, I didn't realise. Isn't he able to work at all?'

'Apparently not. He says it's terrible, like losing the power of speech.'

Hazel was silent. She had her own loss, which she couldn't mend. It was right in the depth of her mind, where her conscience moved: a fissure, a little gap, intricate as the air.

'Don't let on I told you though, will you?' said Nye. 'He doesn't want anyone to know.'

The Three Pennies was a small pub on the road leading west of the Islyn. Its garden was bordered by a stream and a ford and Tom and Georgie were sitting at a wooden table under an ash tree. They looked exactly matched in their loose T shirts and jeans and Hazel felt uneasy; she put her hand in Nye's.

When they reached the table, Hazel could see that both Tom and Georgie were exhausted. It had the effect of smoothing out their faces and making them look very young. Tom also had himself well in hand: the smile he gave Hazel was no more or less than that he gave Nye, and he stood up to greet them. 'What do you think of our new place? It's all right, isn't it?'

'Hello,' Georgie said to Nye as he sat down next to her and kissed her.

'You two look miles away,' said Nye. 'How long have you been sitting here?'

'Oh about half an hour,' said Georgie vaguely. 'Another beer please, sweetheart,' she said, looking up at Tom.

Georgie always drank beer in pubs: the glass looked natural in her hands, the liquid wholesome and unpretentious. She drank it in moderation but with enjoyment. Hazel drank beer only when she wanted to drink but needed to stay sober: the bitter, yeasty taste forced her to take small sips. She ordered one now.

When Tom returned with the drinks, Nye was still passing on to Georgie the gobbets of family news his mother had given him. After that was finished, the conversation switched back to the pub.

'It was a drovers' pub,' said Georgie. 'They used to bring their sheep through the ford on the way to new pastures. We have quite a few of these where I used to live.'

'How did you find it?' asked Hazel. 'It's not really local to you, is it?'

'I was out walking,' said Georgie. 'One evening.' Her eyes rested on Hazel's as anyone's might: they conveyed no message at all.

There was an odd concentration in the air. It held Tom and Georgie together. It was as though their dreamy faces and easygoing talk was all they could spare from some great, shared effort. Nye was looking puzzled. And Hazel was at a loss.

It was past time for Hazel to be left alone with Georgie. Her cue had come once already, a good forty-five minutes ago, when Nye had risen to buy another round and Tom had got up with him, saying, 'I'll give you a hand.' Hazel had shot off the bench.

'I'll go.' She had picked up the glasses. 'I need to go in anyway.' Two minutes later she had stared at her face in the small mirror on the cloakroom wall and wondered whether Tom and Georgie were speaking outside. Were they even looking at one another?

Now the air was beginning to fill with shades of violet and Tom and Nye were arguing. 'I don't see why he can't do that if he wants to.'

'Because it's inconsistent with his other positions.'

'It's not a problem to me.'

'As you keep saying. Explain it to me then, show me how he can be right last year, this year *and* if he goes to Llanelli.'

'I just did.'

'I wasn't convinced.'

Tom shrugged. 'Perhaps you didn't try hard enough.'

The give-and-take, outwardly like so many she had listened to, had something wrong in it. There was a ring to the exchange, the words striking and withdrawing swiftly. Now Tom was on his feet again.

'My turn,' he said into the air above her head.

'Let's split it.' Nye got up with a spring.

Hazel watched them go. She was unwilling to meet Georgie's eyes; although she knew that the longer she delayed it now, the more she weakened herself, she had suddenly lost courage.

When she looked, she realised the delay had been pointless. Georgie seemed calm and beyond that, Hazel couldn't read. 'Now,' Georgie said. 'They're gone at last.'

She wasn't sure how long she managed to hold the silence; she thought she breathed in and out at least twice. 'So we can talk about the party,' she said.

'Exactly.'

'What would you like me to do?'

Georgie leaned forward on her elbows. 'I thought we'd have a barbecue. Tom and I did. About twenty people are coming so we'll need at least a case of wine and lots of beer. Could you contribute to that?'

'Yes, of course. We'll go halves, shall we?'

'Thirds. There are three of us giving it.'

'Yes. I see. And what about food?'

'That shouldn't be expensive. It's just hamburgers, sausages, bread and salads. Tom will see to all the ordering and buying – he has more free time than either of us.'

It was too dark to make out Georgie's expression. She was now sitting quietly upright at her side of the table.

'I'll make a sweet,' Hazel said. She felt that she was speaking into the unknown, yielding up a private offering that was nothing to do with Nye or Tom but only for herself and the other woman. 'I can make fruit salad or a fool.'

'That would be nice.'

'How will I get it to you though, without Nye knowing?'

'Tom can pick it up with the other things. If you wouldn't mind leaving him your key.'

Hazel nodded. She was now sitting erect too. Thanks to the dimness, she and Georgie were able to sit on like this for a while, looking at each other without being exposed to sight. Then a light flashed on in the tree above them and they blinked as the bulb strengthened and weakened and then steadied. They both drank and turned their heads away slightly.

'What are you getting Nye as a present?' Georgie said.

'Some records.'

'Oh?'

'Yes, classical records. He's started to build a collection, we listen to them in his flat.'

'Yes, he's always liked music.'

'Especially Bach.'

Suddenly there was a clear look of dislike on Georgie's face. Strange that it should have been Nye rather than Tom who brought it on. 'I wouldn't know,' she said abruptly. 'I'm not musical.'

Neither was Hazel but she had liked the Bach concerto well

enough when Nye had played it to her last Sunday. 'It's terrific, isn't it?' he'd said. 'And they've got all of him in the record library.'

The thought of lounging in Nye's flat, listening to his borrowed records and drinking his real coffee, was all at once vivid to Hazel. She turned away from Georgie and followed the new streak of yellow light to the pub door. Surely soon Nye must come back out with the drinks and rejoin them at the table, make one of his casual, possessive gestures to claim her.

But it was Tom who appeared first in the doorway. He walked quickly, holding three glasses together, and from the way that he peered at them Hazel knew he was anxious. But was it for her or for Georgie? She sat very still as he set down the glasses and swung his legs over the bench next to her. When he looked up, it was to Georgie.

'Hazel's giving Nye records for his birthday,' Georgie said. Hazel wondered at the ache in her voice, but Tom obviously didn't: he glanced at Hazel and touched Georgie's hand.

'And we're giving him a party.'

Georgie turned to Hazel. 'I wanted to buy him a new stereo, to say thank you for the house and everything, but we just can't afford it.' Tom's hand twitched away.

'Ah, for God's sake, Georgie, who's counting? Look, if you want to give him a present as well, give him a drawing. You know how much he'd like one.'

'Another one.'

'He always likes them, doesn't he?' His voice was an odd mixture of brutality and coaxing.

It was gone eleven when they finally said goodbye, Tom and Georgie getting into the blue car, and Hazel and Nye into his dark brown one. They drove one behind the other for a mile and then Tom and Georgie slowed and took the turn-off to the Islyn. Above the hedges Hazel saw their lights recede.

'Well, there was definitely something wrong with those two tonight,' Nye said quietly.

'Yes.' Hazel waited: she didn't dare prompt him, yet she needed to know what he'd perceived. Her mind was full of the timbre of their voices and that atmosphere – strained but tender, like a bruise.

'Georgie said some quite cruel things to him, did you notice? About his work and his students.' Nye's face was very still; only his mouth moved. 'I've never heard her do that before.'

'No, she's usually so proud of him, isn't she?'

'I wonder if that's been going on much? He hasn't mentioned it to me, but then he'd probably consider it disloyal. They keep themselves very close in many ways, Tom and Georgie.'

Hazel heard the explanatory note in his voice, confident but slightly wistful, and turned away. She couldn't bear to see the matching look on his face.

'I'm sorry.' Nye misinterpreted her. 'You're probably sick of me talking about them. I suppose I feel responsible for Tom in some ways.'

'Why? He seems tough enough to look after himself.'

'He isn't, though. He's volatile. He'll start things, then get into a bloody awful mess with them. That's why I helped him with the money for the house. Although now it looks as if I might have done the wrong thing.'

'For God's sake, Nye, you can't feel guilty about giving them an enormous sum of money. When did they ever do anything like that for you?'

'Well, money, no, they can't give me that because they're both so bad at managing it.' Nye shook his head. 'They really are hopeless. But they've done plenty of things for me. They're my friends, they show it in lots of little ways – like this party, for instance.'

Hazel stared at him. He smiled. 'Tom told me about it.'

'But it was supposed to be a secret.'

'Yes, but Tom told me. He said he thought I'd enjoy knowing more than I'd enjoy being kept in the dark, and he was right. But it's all right, I won't tell Georgie. Is there anything I can do to help? I don't want to put any more strain on them at the moment.'

Hazel shut her eyes. It was all closing in on her: her lies and Tom's, Georgie's collusion in them, Nye's terrible eagerness to believe; and, grown stronger than ever, the knowledge that she could not stop.

She heard the rustle a split-second before she felt the warmth of Nye's body. His head rubbed quickly against hers. 'You're not disappointed that I know, are you? It's a lovely idea. Thank you for having it.'

12

They were at the gorge again, in the woods. In the noonday hush, every sound travelled clearly through the air. There was birdsong in the upper branches, stillness between the tall grey-green trunks and, very far away, the hum of a car on the other side of the gorge.

'I go to see him because he's my friend,' said Tom. 'Why do you go? Last Sunday afternoon and Tuesday night and – tomorrow, isn't that the next date?'

'I don't keep it a secret.'

'Neither do I.' Tom lifted her dress. Hazel always wore dresses and skirts to work now, so they could make love in the car or places like this. Tom moved his hands between her legs. 'For fuck's sake, Hazel, nothing's simple. We're all in this.' He slipped his fingers inside her pants and his other hand crawled up her neck, pinching the skin.

She was helpless with wanting him. The need seemed to grow stronger each time. The sexual appetite was disorienting; now it made her clumsy, so that when Tom rolled her on to her side and tried to undress her, she couldn't help him.

'I love you,' said Tom, pulling her pants down over her thighs. 'Can I take off your dress?'

'Completely? What if someone comes?'

'No one's going to come. If they did, we could hear them.'

Tom turned Hazel's face in his cupped hands. She looked across the sloping forest floor, up at the tall trees. They were alone.

'Please,' said Tom. His voice was low and stubborn. 'I need it. Now.'

'Yes, I need you.'

He drew his hands down the length of her legs and dropped her pants in the leaves. He sat back on his haunches and then he pulled off his shoes, crossed his arms over his head to take off his

T shirt, stood up and, his head bent and his hands moving quickly, undid his jeans.

He stepped out of his jeans and pants and for a shocked instant Hazel wanted to laugh. Then, as soon as he had thrown them aside, she was frightened. He looked different, naked in the open. His body was shorter and squatter than before and his legs had a more pronounced curve.

Hazel hurt her feet taking off her shoes. She stood up and turned round: 'Please, undo my dress.' Behind her, he pulled the material down from her shoulders; she saw her breasts appear and felt the fabric fall away from her hips. The air was cool on her skin and a tiny breeze passed through her pubic hair.

For a second Tom's hands were hot against her arms and his penis pressed into her buttocks. Then he let go and moved back. Hazel turned quickly, her hands already grasping for him. But he was out of reach. She tilted: she had to touch him, her whole body was leaning forwards, trying to reach him, but she couldn't move.

'Hazel,' said Tom.

He lurched towards her and grappled, as if he were trying to keep his balance, and from underneath she felt him thrust into her. Her legs locked. For a few seconds they clutched one another, shocked.

'No,' Hazel said. 'Not like this.'

'Ssh. I'm sorry. I know. I know.'

They pulled apart and stumbled down on to their knees. Tom began to fumble their clothes together: he folded them and laid them down on the leaves to make a bed.

This morning, in Nye's bed, Hazel had kept her eyes tight shut and kissed his hands. She often stayed with him now. She didn't like starting the day alone: the loss of Tom weighed on her too heavily. At the moment of waking, she was too aware of the gap in her mind, into which she dare not look. Nye's big body could press it away, for a while, until the guilt came in. But that, she had kept secret from Tom.

Did he suspect it as she reached for him now, pulling him against her to obliterate the touch of Nye? Hazel burrowed into the makeshift bed and tangled her arms and legs round him, locking him against her. She tugged at his hips but he resisted her and came into her slowly, inch by inch. They lay still for a few seconds, whimpering; then Hazel climbed on top of him and, lifting herself almost clear of his body, pinned down his shoulders.

13

It was evening; the sunlight was rich and generous. It spread into each corner of Hazel's room. The big sash window was raised and the little casement in the kitchen alcove stood open; on the gas ring the fruit bubbled in the saucepan and the steam rushed for the window.

Tom sat on the edge of the bed, holding a bowl of cream in one hand, and whisking a fork through the runny liquid. His legs were braced against the floor and jiggled restlessly as he whisked.

Hazel watched him around the column of steam: since his arrival half an hour ago he had been unhappy. He had come unexpectedly and he couldn't settle. The sight of her cooking fruit had seemed to shock him.

'What the hell are you doing?' he'd asked with ill temper.

'Making a gooseberry fool for the party tomorrow.'

'Why? Georgie's doing all the food.'

'I felt like it. I didn't want to just hand over money.'

'Jesus Christ.'

When Hazel had said, 'Nye's coming round,' he hadn't answered. So she had given him the cream to whip.

Hazel watched Tom's right hand circling repeatedly and his head bent down towards his knees, and wondered what had happened.

'My love. You must go soon.' She paused, but he didn't reply. She found she was saying it more urgently. 'You must go. Nye's due in half an hour and he often comes early.'

Tom nodded, but otherwise ignored the remark.

'What's the matter?'

'I don't think I can take much more of this.' Tom's voice was deep with exhaustion. Hazel was used to trepidation but now she felt the first disorienting rush of fear.

'What's happened?'

'It's Georgie. Whenever I go home, she's waiting for me.'

'And?'

He shook his head.

'She waits. She just waits. And every day there's something else to let me know she knows. There are things she says and does, and ways she looks at me.'

'It isn't so very hard, though, is it? It didn't seem too bad in the pub last week.'

'Didn't it? Would you have liked to come home with us that night? Anyway, that was just the beginning.'

Hazel moved out of the kitchen alcove. She eyed the bed next to him; suddenly she was wary of getting too close.

'You can hardly blame her.'

'Christ, Hazel, of course I don't blame her! How could I blame her? But I can't keep going between you.' He straightened slightly and looked up at her. 'It's time to call it a day.'

Hazel dodged back into the alcove.

'What do you mean?'

'I want to leave her and live with you.' Tom stared as if he were only just bringing her into focus. 'Jesus, Hazel, what did you think I meant?'

'But you're married.'

'That's right. We've been married all along, remember? We were getting married the day you met us.'

Tom's face seemed to be gathering emotion, almost as if he were starting to dislike her.

'It wasn't my fault!' said Hazel. 'I couldn't help it.'

Tom got up slowly and joined Hazel in the alcove. He set the bowl of cream down on the tiny work surface, next to the gas ring. The space was barely big enough for two people but he took care not to touch her; he pressed himself into the opposite corner beneath the window.

'I'm yours if you want.' He said it quite defiantly. '*Do* you want?'

'Yes.' Hazel was panicking now. This was going too fast for her and she had no time to think; all she could do was answer him.

'Do you want me to leave Georgie and live with you?'

'Yes.'

'So what are you going to do about it?'

'Me?'

'Yes. Why should I do all the work? You're as involved as we are now. I think Nye loves you. So you'd better think about what the hell you're going to do.'

It was true; it was time for her to act. But Hazel was unprepared and frightened of the responsibility. She had inveigled herself into the relationship with Nye and didn't understand it yet. She didn't know the best way to extricate herself.

Tom was waiting.

'I'll leave him, of course.'

'Tonight?'

'You know it can't be tonight. Oh Tom, how can it be?'

Tom's body was braced as if he were about to spring from the corner, but he wasn't moving. His frustration made Hazel feel frightened. 'We're giving him a party tomorrow. He knows all about it, I told him. We've got to get this over with first.'

'That'll be nice. Then he can be even more humiliated when he realises. He'll be able to enjoy the memory of us singing him "Happy Birthday" for years.'

Tom's face had become more vivid with anger. It solidified him and Hazel had an image of what he would look like in those years to come.

'You'll miss him, won't you?' she said suddenly.

Tom looked at her incredulously. She knew how stupid it had sounded but she was defiant; she wanted to be sure he knew what was at stake. 'I mean,' she went on, but he pushed past her into the bedroom. He said something muffled which she couldn't catch; she could only hear the misery. He stopped at the window.

'He's here,' he said after a couple of seconds. He lifted his hand a few inches in a brief signal to the street. 'He's parking the car, he's seen me.'

Hazel could hardly breathe. She kept her voice very calm, so as not to precipitate anything: 'Are you going to tell him now?'

'It's not for me to tell him, is it?'

Hazel picked up the bowl of cream, looked at it and put it down again. 'I don't want to tell him with you here.'

'You want me to go, then?'

She heard the sound of an engine being extinguished across the street, then the opening and shutting of a door.

'No, don't go. Please don't go like this.'

Tom turned and looked at her. She noticed that the sight of Nye had taken all the colour from his face.

'I don't know what to do.' He sounded almost exhilarated.

'Stay with us.' Nye's footsteps struck the Tarmac outside; she spoke rapidly. 'He knows we're arranging the party for him. Pretend you came to pick up the fool and we ran out of time.'

Tom blinked, then laughed raggedly.

'You always did think fast.' He leaned forward and thrust his head out of the window. 'Hallo, Nye. You're too early, go away.'

Hazel hurried up to him and, out of sight of Nye, pressed her hands against his back. His shirt was damp.

'For God's sake, sit down. You're white as a ghost.'

She made for the door.

'I thought I'd come over and make a threesome,' Tom said into the street. 'See what you like about it so much.'

Hazel reached the hall door and opened it. Nye was standing on the steps, looking at Tom with a thoughtful expression, as though he were just beginning to get hold of an idea.

'Hiya, Nye.' She opened the door wide and stood on the threshold, taking her time. 'Tom's here.'

'I know. I saw his car.' Nye was staring from her to the window.

'Look, you wouldn't like to walk round the block for five minutes, would you? We're preparing for your party.'

'Ah. But why all the secrecy? You both know I know, and I'm more than happy to help.' He cast a last look at Tom and climbed the steps. 'Good evening, *collen*.' He kissed her and laid a hand on her shoulder. He jerked his head towards the bedsit. 'What's the matter with Tom? He looks a bit wound up.'

'I'm not sure. He's been like that ever since he arrived.'

'And *your* heart's beating like a drum.'

'I've been whipping cream,' Hazel said. She slipped her hand lightly into his and pulled him down the hall. 'So has Tom,' she added, as Nye ducked his head through the bedsit doorway. 'And the stuff still won't thicken.'

'I'll have a go, shall I?' Nye threw his jacket on the bed and went into the kitchen alcove. 'Oh yes, I see what you mean.' He came back out with the mixing bowl and sat down on the hard chair opposite Tom, starting to whisk. 'Evening, Tom, my turn I think. I won't tell Georgie if you won't.'

Tom looked pale but calm. He lounged in the chair and gazed at Nye as he often did, with unhurried attention.

'You would turn up now, wouldn't you? Won't tell her what?'

'That I'm making my own pudding here. How's the work been going?'

'All right, thanks.'

'Are you near finishing it?'

Tom seemed uncertain of himself.

'Yes,' he said, glancing from Nye to the bowl of cream to the window. 'I reckon so.'

'What's this?' Hazel sat on the bed next to Nye's jacket.

'Just Tom's painting,' said Nye. 'You know, work. The daily grind. Mine's going quite well too,' he said, and his eyes sought out Hazel's with a glow of triumph. 'I think they'll go for that northern project.'

'Oh, of course,' said Hazel. 'The meeting was today, wasn't it? So you carried them with you?'

Nye lifted his hands in a so-so gesture, but he took such pleasure in the movement that his confidence was evident.

'Who knows? I think perhaps so.'

'That's marvellous,' said Hazel warmly. 'Brilliant. Well done.' But she wondered about this work of Tom's. He'd mentioned nothing to her and she, unwilling to remind him of the studio lying empty, hadn't asked. When had he started working again? And why had he told Nye and not her? She stood up quickly to hide her face. 'Let's have a drink.'

'Is this some new painting project you're working on?' she asked Tom, as she brought the wine out of the fridge. She was careful to sound a little hesitant.

'Oh, you can't ask Tom questions like that,' said Nye. 'He won't answer them.'

'Yes I will,' said Tom. 'This is a myth of yours, that I don't like to talk about my work.'

'Pardon me, I think not. You hate answering questions on it. You pretend you don't understand people half the time they ask you about it.'

'Well, half the time I *don't* understand them. I'm not a critic. I'll get the glasses, Hazel.' Tom was halfway across the room when he added: 'Are they in the kitchen?'

Hazel's head was bent over the corkscrew.

'Yes, on the shelf.'

Tom came back with two glasses and a cup.

'I could only find two.' He sat down quickly on the chair arm and held out the first glass for filling. He watched the mouth of the bottle as Hazel poured.

'So?' she said. 'Your work?'

'Well, I hadn't been doing much for a while. I couldn't seem to get it – too much else going on, I suppose. But in the last ten days I've been doing quite a bit. There you are, Nye.'

Hazel counted ten days back: it was the night they'd all met in The Pennies. The night, by Tom's reckoning, when Georgie had taken up her silent weapons against him.

'What's happened to the bedspread?'

Hazel followed Nye's glance to the bed, covered in dark green candlewick. His Indian print counterpane was still folded in the drawer: she hadn't had time to get it out for him, as she usually did.

'It needs washing. It's got cream on it.'

Nye kinked his eyebrows. He looked annoyed, though he smiled to hide it. 'You really don't like being domestic, do you? Well, I'm very touched you've gone to so much trouble.' He bent over the bowl and whisked vigorously. Hazel watched him; she felt it would be shaming to look at Tom. Nye's hand eventually slowed. 'Look, I've whipped the cream for you. What shall I do with it?'

'Oh, give it to me. I'll put it in the kitchen and make the fool later. You know all about it now anyway. Let's drink to your northern project.'

It was dark and the second bottle of wine was nearly empty. The streetlamp shone in on them where they sat on the floor and its orange glare heightened the tension. Tom and Nye were squabbling.

'You're talking through your arse,' Nye said again. 'You'll never do it; never.'

'I don't see why not. David thinks it's a good idea.'

'He would, and it is. But he'll do it on his own. You'd never be able to see it through with him once you got down to technicalities; he'd annoy you too much.'

'There aren't that many technicalities. We're only talking about publicity stunts, not going into business together.'

'I'll bet you fifty pounds you won't do it. I tell you what, I'll put fifty pounds into it, to help with costs. And if you don't get round to it, I want it back plus another fifty from you.'

'Oh shut up,' said Tom, rolling on to his stomach. 'Why do you have to bring money into everything?'

They finished the third bottle. It was later and Hazel was drunker. They were on the dangerous ground of the past.

'No, not Bryn Morgan – Bryn Robertshall. The one with the red hair,' said Nye. '*He* was the one who broke his arm in the schools' tournament.'

'Was he?' Tom frowned. 'Are you sure? I still can't picture him.'

'Come on, even Hazel remembers Bryn Robertshall. He was the

favourite of whatsisname – that little shit of a physics teacher, Lewis.'

Tom glanced over at her. 'Hmm? Oh, yes, I do remember, I think. All right, so it was him who broke his arm, not Bryn Morgan.'

'I can't believe you've forgotten Robertshall. Six foot, aged fourteen, he was.'

Hazel watched headlights flash on the walls. Of course Tom hadn't forgotten the boy, any more than she had. It had been Tom who noticed Bryn Robertshall going to the teacher with her note book. Afterwards, in the cloakroom, he'd told her: *He's a turd, Bryn Robertshall. Everyone hates him.*

And now here was Nye, puzzled at their hesitation, pressing them to try and remember. He quested eagerly, helpfully, like a blind dog.

Hazel felt again Tom's hand on her back – just as she had before, like a mark of shame.

It came back like a premonition. She closed her eyes.

'Ah, who cares?' said Tom. 'He's probably a physics teacher himself now.'

There was a little silence.

'What's Hazel doing?' said Nye.

'Going to sleep sitting up. We've bored her into a coma.'

Hazel opened her eyes and swayed.

'Come here.' Tom took her shoulders and turned her swiftly, laying her down on her back, with her head resting on Nye's legs. 'There. Comfortable?'

'No,' said Hazel, trying to twist away, but Nye laughed and put his arm across her.

'I'm starving,' he said. 'Is there anything to eat here?'

'Gooseberries,' Hazel said. 'Cream.'

'I'll have a look.' Tom went unsteadily to the alcove.

'We've got cheese,' he said, from the fridge. 'And damp crackers. Half a tin of tomatoes. And one blackcurrant yoghurt. Let's have some more to drink while we think about it.' He came back with the dessert wine Hazel had bought for the fool. 'Christ,' he said, tasting it, 'so sweet.'

Hazel turned on to her stomach and balanced her glass on Nye's leg. Tom bent over her to fill it and someone stroked her hair; she wasn't sure if it was Nye or Tom or both.

The restaurant was wedge-shaped and decorated with travel

posters. It was half-filled with students. They took a table by the wall, and as they read the menus a young woman with tangled, caramel-coloured hair nodded to Tom.

'One of yours?' said Nye.

'Yes, first year.'

She looked familiar to Hazel too; this must be one of the students she had passed on her occasional hurried trips through the college to find Tom. Perhaps she was being recognised in turn.

Nye was reading the copy off the poster nearest him. It made Hazel laugh; she and Tom both leaned over to hear better. The wall-lamp threw tasselled shadows across Nye, and Hazel watched them play around his eyes and deepen the planes of his face. She wished she could spare him pain. She wondered how he would look when she inflicted it.

'What are you doing?' Nye watched with interest as Tom spread Hazel's fingers out on the plastic tablecloth.

'Testing my reflexes,' said Tom. He began tapping the tip of his knife in between each of Hazel's fingers in sequence. He started by moving from the outside of the little finger inwards to the thumb, then took the knife back in the outward direction, faster, then in again, faster still.

'You're mad,' said Nye to Hazel. 'He'll cut you. Why are you letting him do it?'

Hazel laughed. She felt tight-winded and reckless.

'I'm sure he'll be all right.'

She watched Tom's hand moving across hers and back. He was concentrating on the precise jabbing movements and he kept them very regular. Twice Hazel felt the stainless steel graze the inside of her fingers, but it was not close enough to hurt. She was fascinated by his steadiness. The noise of the knife on the table was like spatters of water, coming faster and faster till it drummed like continuous rain.

Tom caught the knife in his left hand and held it still.

'I still think you're mad,' Nye said. 'He could have injured you really badly. Look how his hands are trembling from the momentum.'

'It's all right,' said Tom. He was unfocusing his eyes from Hazel's outspread hand. 'I didn't hurt her.'

'Extraordinary,' said Nye, examining her fingers. 'He didn't, either.' He turned to Tom. 'Do it again,' he said curiously. 'Do it to me.'

'If you want. The odds will be worse, now I've done it successfully once.'

'You don't understand statistics. The odds are the same every time. Granted, you're more tired now, but that'll be offset by the fact that my hands are bigger. Go on, I want you to do it.'

Nye stretched his right hand out on the table.

'Your left,' said Tom. 'I did Hazel's left.'

Nye obediently withdrew his right hand and laid out his left.

Hazel watched Tom gather his concentration and angle his head so that he could see all the interstices of Nye's fingers and palm. He began the jabbing movement again and now she saw that the main impulse was in the upswing, away from the table and the hand.

During the first run, the blade knocked against Nye's middle finger knuckle. Tom had a clean second run; the third was too fast for her to see and then Nye snatched his hand away.

'Oh bloody hell, that hurt.' His voice was low and quick and he sucked at the joint of his last two fingers. When he lowered his hand there was blood on his lips. 'That'll teach me. I should believe myself when I notice that you're drunk and incapable.'

Tom looked shocked: he stared at Nye's mouth and glanced down at the knife. There was a thin smear of blood on it.

The sight of Nye's reddened lips, and his thumb pressing down over the broken skin, frightened Hazel more than was logical.

'You should wash it,' she said to him. 'Quickly.'

'It's all right,' said Tom from across the table. 'The knife was clean.'

'Are you still bleeding? Tom, take him to the toilet and wash his hand.'

'It's all right,' said Nye calmly. 'It's only a tiny cut. Like a paper cut, really. I get them all the time at work.'

'Sorry.' Tom seemed confused; he hunched his shoulders and looked around for inspiration. 'I didn't think I'd touched you. Did you move?' He glanced back at Nye. 'You did move, didn't you? I was going fine, all the time, I didn't make any mistake.'

'Tom,' said Hazel.

'I know, I'll get you a brandy.'

While Tom wandered down the restaurant looking for the waiter, Nye hunched his shoulders and shook. After a second, Hazel put her arm round him.

'What's the matter?' Then she saw that he was laughing.

'He's legless,' said Nye. 'Plastered. What the hell are we going to do with him?'

Hazel looked sharply after Tom. He was leaning against the bar, his head flopping.

'We're all drunk,' she said.

'He's drunker. He'd better stay at my flat tonight.'

Hazel leaned her head against Nye's shoulder. Tom and Nye alone in Nye's room, with all their secrets between them: no.

'Georgie won't like that.'

'Well, he can't drive in that state.'

'Why not put him in a taxi?'

Nye chuckled.

'Good God, girl, you won't find a taxi to take him all the way to the Islyn at this time of night. This isn't Bristol.'

'But—' Hazel turned away, flustered. She watched Tom approach, carrying three brandies. 'Oh nonsense, Nye, we'll find one. There are plenty of numbers in the hall at home.'

'Here you are.' Tom lurched to a stop and sat down. 'Now – one for me, one for you, and a double for you, Nye.'

'Christ, Tom.' Nye's shoulders began to shake again. 'We can hardly stand as it is.'

'I know, but it's too late to change that now, isn't it?'

14

'Is he all right?'

'Bruised and shaken and with a splitting headache. Luckily it happened in the lanes so the police didn't get called.'

'But why was he driving? Nye'd given him the keys to his flat.'

'It seems he wanted to come home.'

Hazel looked at the silver metal box of the payphone and tried to identify the emotion that had momentarily enriched Georgie's voice. Malice? Satisfaction?

'We should have put him in a taxi,' she said.

'Yes,' agreed Georgie. 'It's not as if you don't know where to find one.'

The bathroom door opened and the scent of shaving soap preceded Nye as he came round the corner of the stairs, doing up his shirt.

'What's up?' he said.

'Tom's had an accident. The car went off the road in the lanes.'

'Jesus. Is he all right?'

'Who's that?' said Georgie. 'Nye?'

'Yes.'

'I want to speak to him.'

'Why?' As soon as she said it, Hazel capitulated. She passed the receiver to Nye. 'He's all right,' she told him.

'Tom,' said Nye. 'Oh, Georgie.' His voice took on a rich timbre. 'What the hell's happening? Is everything all right? He what? Oh God, the bloody idiot. Hell, lovely, I'm sorry; we should have stopped him. No, well, that's true, he is, but we could always have tied him to a chair. Thank God the police didn't stop him.' He turned to lean his shoulder against the wall.

Hazel stood by the olive-painted newel post and heard Georgie's words again. It's not as if you don't know where to find one. They'd had a crystalline quality she'd never heard before from Georgie. They hung in her mind, pure and confiding. Was this what it was like for Tom when he said that Georgie had a way of saying things?

Yet Hazel was sure that however Georgie spoke to Tom when they were alone, it wasn't like this. There was something in this last limpidity that was meant just for Hazel.

Meanwhile the telephonic hum of Georgie's voice was speaking to Nye in quite a different way. It had a lively cadence and Nye was dipping in and out of its rhythms.

'How are you going to get to school? Shall I come – oh, I see . . . Yes, of course . . . Thank you. What a time to remember. Yes I will. That is, I'm fairly sure I will. But I can still . . . Ah yes, as a matter of fact she did.' Nye's eyes creased slowly into a smile. 'Well no, it wasn't a complete surprise because – yes, he did too. Ah Georgie, I'm very touched. But you see, you're the only one round here who can keep a secret.'

Hazel went into her room and shut the door. She sat on the unmade bed, next to the pair of records which lay half out of their wrapping paper. Nye had put his birthday card on the chest of drawers, next to the clock.

Hazel began to shake. It wasn't fear for Tom but shock, and the alcohol in her blood. It was ten to eight: too early to hear Georgie's voice in her hallway; too early to disentangle herself from the tendrils of the night. She was still there, rolled up in Nye's flesh, reaching across the city to make love to Tom.

But Tom was long gone. And she did feel fear. Hazel saw the blue car driving through the early hours of this morning, swinging round the lanes and skidding into banks, throwing Tom out on to the road where he stumbled along in the dark to reach the quiet cottage which now held him.

Twelve hours must pass before Hazel could follow him there.

Nye came in, looking guilty.

'Christ, trust Tom,' he said. 'He walked all the way back here and drove off under our noses. I should have taken his keys away. By the way, everything's out in the open about the party now and I told Georgie we'd pick up all the supplies, including the drink.'

Hazel nodded. 'Did she mind that we told you?'

Nye took his tie from the back of the armchair and stood in front of the tiny wall mirror.

'I think she's got more pressing things on her mind.' He knotted his tie quickly. 'I spoke to Tom. He sounded very subdued, as well he might. They can't really afford to repair that car, you know. I said I'd ask around at work, see if I could find them a cheap deal.

Even if I can't, I might slip something towards it myself.'

'Why?'

'Why?' Nye twitched his collar straight, looking surprised.

'Yes,' said Hazel stubbornly. 'You didn't crash the car. It's not your fault. Why pay for it?'

'Well, because I can afford it better than they can. And if I want to, what's the harm?' He took his suit jacket out of her wardrobe and dusted it down. 'I'll ring you as soon as I know what time I can leave. Then we can do all the last-minute preparations together.'

15

The lanes had come into full leaf since Hazel had last been to the Islyn. From the road the verge was a mass of green and it wasn't until they drove round it and pulled up in the siding that she saw the cottages. They were prettier than she remembered and smaller and the windows of the two dwellings weren't quite aligned. The garden of the old lady next door was thistly and full of dandelion clocks; on the right-hand side of the fence the grass was just long enough to be shaggy and the narrow bed along the path was bright with flowers. Some of them Hazel recognised – yellow and red poppies and starry blue campanula, and scabious. A few bluebells remained under the fruit trees where the garden came to its irregular point. In front of the living-room window a table was set out on the grass, covered with a blue cloth and shining with glasses and bottles. By the far corner of the cottage, Tom squatted behind a stack of bricks. Music came from the back.

Hazel had thought so much about this place, and imagined what went on here so vividly. And as she got out of the car and breathed in the early evening air, she realised that she had been waiting to come back. There were many things she needed to see in order to understand – for instance, that Georgie had hung a bird table from the apple tree. That Tom parked the car just there, in the dip below the gate. What the cottage had become inside – which colour paint they'd chosen and how they used the space within the rooms – was still hidden from her. This evening she would get to see it. The prospect made her nervous; it twisted in alongside her nervousness about facing Tom.

'It looks nice, doesn't it?' said Nye. 'Georgie's been working on the garden. Every time I come here she's planted more flowers.' His voice was deep and thrummed with a hint of self-consciousness. The vigorous mood of this morning was still on him. His skin was rosy and his hair was slightly damp from his recent shower. He was wearing a white shirt and faded cotton trousers; Hazel knew with what care he must have selected them. 'Look at that table,' he said. 'How many people did you say were coming?'

'About twenty.' Hazel shut the car door and fixed her attention on Nye as he came to join her. She wanted to put off looking at Tom, who was now walking across the grass.

'Here's Thomas.'

Tom was just the other side of the gate. There was something abrupt in his movements and he looked sickly; his cheeks seemed shadowed.

'Oh dear, oh dear,' said Nye. 'You're still feeling it, then. "Bright mead was their drink and that was their poison." '

Tom grimaced. 'Something like that.' He glanced in Hazel's direction but not at her.

'Christ,' said Nye. 'That looks bad.'

The shadow on Tom's right cheek was a bruise.

'It doesn't feel too great either.'

'Where did it happen?'

'By the cabbage field, a couple of hundred yards away.'

'You were bloody lucky to get that far. Stupid bastard.'

'I know, I know.'

'At least you managed to get the car home.'

'Yes. Look, let's forget it for now, can we? Happy birthday. How are you, Hazel?'

Tom's face was wary as he stood aside for her. So far he had barely glanced at her.

'Fragile,' Hazel said. Tom nodded. There was tension leaking out of him with every jerky movement. Nye opened his mouth to speak but Tom turned away. Nye winked and mouthed 'Ow' at Hazel. He was still grinning when Georgie came round the side of the house.

She was a small figure in a black shirt and blue jeans. Her feet were bare and her hair was newly brushed. She was carrying a flat parcel. She smiled up at Nye all the way across the grass but she didn't look happy. There was such an air of loneliness about her that Hazel thought Nye must see it too. But Nye was smiling and holding out his hands. At the last minute, as if suddenly overcome with pleasure, he went forward and hugged her.

'This is incredible,' he said. 'I knew something was happening but I didn't expect anything like this. Who's coming?'

'Oh, as if you didn't know,' said Georgie. 'You faker. Happy birthday, Nye. Welcome to your party.'

Nye held her against his ribs. 'It's a lovely idea,' he said. 'Thank you.'

'It's not just from me.' Georgie straightened out of his embrace. 'We're all three of us giving it, Tom and Hazel too.'

Nye batted Tom's shoulder and then reached over to kiss Hazel. 'Thank you all,' he said. 'I'm very touched.'

'You're very early,' said Georgie.

'Sorry,' said Hazel. 'Nye was determined not to waste such a nice evening.' Her voice sounded strange to her: over-cool and distant. But then she'd had to make her own opening – no one else had given her a chance to speak. 'At least now we're here, we can help. What shall we do?'

Georgie looked down at her parcel.

'Have a drink,' said Tom. 'That's what we all need, or will do soon.' He turned heavily and was already off towards the drinks table. Georgie and Hazel both hesitated, watching.

'Good idea,' said Nye with relish. 'Libations to propitiate the household gods.'

'This is for you,' Georgie said, catching Nye up. She tucked the parcel hesitantly into his hand. 'It's only a sketch. I just wanted you to have something from me.'

It was hard to define the atmosphere. Evening sun lit the garden and sent strips of gold into the cottage through doorways and windowpanes. The four of them worked steadily, carrying the drink from the car, setting out food, trying to get a fire going in the stack of bricks that served as a barbecue. Nye was the source of energy: he went from one task to another, applying himself to each. And the other three moved around him like players, chatting with him, making an affectionate fuss of him, but inwardly all concentrated on their own concerns. And their concerns were one another, each looking and listening for something distinct.

'What made you decide to drive back?' She spoke low, looking out of the kitchen doorway to check that Nye and Georgie weren't close enough to hear.

'You made love with him last night. In the bedsit.'

Tom's tone was conversational, but his hands moved rapidly as he took the beer cans out of the box and stacked them in the fridge.

'So what?' said Hazel angrily. 'I had no option.'

'I know. I knew last night. That's why I left.'

Hazel went on raggedly slicing oranges for the punchbowl. She was so near Tom – he squatted by the fridge, a bare two feet from her, yet she dared not move across to him. Georgie and Nye could see into the kitchen from outside.

'I don't mind.' Tom straightened up. 'I know I've got no right to mind. It's all right.'

'Why did you say it then?' This was a miserable argument to be having, sniping at each other while Nye and Georgie passed within inches of the open door. Tom followed her gaze outside. They could both see Nye's back as he leaned over the barbecue bricks.

'Christ. He looks so bloody happy tonight. Big and carefree and enjoying himself. It's how he always used to be after he played a good match. He used to come round with some of his awful team-mates and buy us drinks. He looks happy just like that again.'

The surface of his skin was puckered with tension; it was a phenomenon Hazel had noticed before – when he felt trapped, and on occasion, when he reacted badly to Nye's teasing.

'What do you expect?' said Hazel bitterly. 'He's with his two best friends and his girlfriend and they're giving him a birthday party.'

Tom stared, then lifted his hands and wearily pushed his hair back.

'It's a bit late for you to agree with me about that.'

Georgie came in from the garden; they heard her footsteps on the path before she entered.

'How are you doing in here?' She went to stand by Hazel as naturally as if they had been friends. She was so close that Hazel had to bend to look at her.

'Well enough,' Hazel said. 'Shall I put the brandy in the bowl now and soak the fruit?'

'Yes please. Guess what Nye's doing?'

Hazel was startled by the question.

'What?' said Tom, leaning against the fridge.

'He's rebuilding our barbecue.'

'What do you mean, rebuilding? It's only a pile of bricks.'

He reckons he can do it more scientifically. He's working out convector currents and things.' Georgie paused. She made a movement towards Tom, arrested. 'I'd like another drink,' she said. 'Tom, why don't you open more bottles?'

'What would you like?'

'White wine, it's all there in the fridge.' She waited while Tom opened the door and watched him bring three bottles out. She was standing with her back to Hazel; her red-brown hair shimmered slightly as she half turned, as if to ask what Hazel wanted, but, after all, didn't speak. It didn't seem calculated; to Hazel, standing a few inches behind her, it seemed that Georgie hesitated because she didn't know what she was allowed to do.

Hazel felt wonder that she should be here: in Tom and Georgie's narrow kitchen, close enough to Georgie to touch, stopping Georgie from touching her husband. Almost without noticing, she had grown to be powerful.

'A glass for you as well?'

Tom was looking past Georgie to her. Hazel nodded, saw his eyes travel back to Georgie's face, and only then added, 'Yes please.'

'What will Nye want?' Georgie asked it uncertainly, as if Nye's tastes had suddenly become unfamiliar to her.

'Take him a whisky,' said Tom.

Nye stood back from the smoke of his barbecue and waved over the hedge.

'It's Chris and Mark and Caroline,' he said. 'With someone else. First blood.'

From where the small back garden angled round into the front wedge, they could see cars driving down the lane.

Georgie, who was sitting on the kitchen doorstep, got up and walked round to the front of the cottage. As she passed Tom she glanced at him: a few weeks ago she would have slipped her hand through his arm or into his pocket or would have leaned up to kiss him, and perhaps Tom anticipated it, because his shoulders stiffened and for an instant he shrank into himself.

Georgie walked on, round the corner of the cottage.

Shadows were moving in from the hedges and the fruit trees, and pushing the party further across the front of the garden to the path, where the sun lingered. Some people whom Hazel didn't know – friends of Nye's and Tom's from Penllwyn – had colonised the gate.

Nye was basking in the company. He strode round the garden, offering bottles of wine and cans of beer and increasingly leaving his sentences unfinished. His gestures grew more expansive.

Hazel had meant to spend more time with him. But she couldn't bring herself to leave Tom. There were bruises on his arms, as well as that one on the side of his face, and he kept looking at her. They were standing under the wooden porch, where it was difficult for them to talk; the most they could manage were brief interchanges of words as other people moved away, yet Hazel clung to his nearness.

'Why do you keep staring at Georgie?' Tom hid his mouth with his hand.

'I can't help it, she looks paralysed.'

'She is. We both are. For Christ's sake, Hazel, look at her. I can't stand much more of this.'

At the bottom of the path Georgie stood with Chris and Caroline and a man Hazel didn't know. She had her head on one side so her hair screened her face and behind it, she was watching them.

'She thinks it's going to be tonight. She thinks we've planned something.'

'No.' Hazel was revolted. 'She can't think that. She can't believe we'd stage it.'

But of course, they had staged it. Everything here was their creation. Hazel looked down the garden at the people sitting on the grass and leaning against the fence, and thought how fine the balance was. These people had come in response to their invitation, to enjoy themselves in the name of Nye and eat and drink the provisions laid on by his three friends. Yet if any of them knew how to look, what would they see? Tracks in the grass, leading into Georgie's sanctuary.

Hazel had come here as a prowler tonight, stalking, looking for a chance to slip through Georgie's defences. But she'd found Georgie's defences already broken. Hazel was in, and her marks were on everything.

There was Nye, happy because she and Tom had arranged for him to be happy. There were two women she didn't know, laughing with him and picking Georgie's flowers. And there was Georgie, silent at the far end of the path, looking up at Hazel and Tom in the cottage doorway.

It lasted only another second, and then Georgie was walking up towards them. She spoke to a couple of people on her way but she didn't pause. She moved on to the doorstep between them, picked up Tom's hand and said: 'I need you in the kitchen.'

'There's my lover.'

Nye's hand scooped Hazel round the waist. 'What are you doing hiding round here? I've been looking for you.'

He smiled; in the almost-dark, his eyes were softened. He swung her gently against him. 'I've got something I want to show you.'

Hazel kept her eyes on the kitchen. Tom and Georgie had been in there for fifteen minutes and she was no longer capable of staying away. Every sip of wine she took into her throat, every movement of her lips in response to others' words and smiles made her more aware of them. She scanned the windows for a sign; she had stopped hearing the voices of the guests around her and the music coming out of the record player in the hall and was listening under them for other sounds. The steeps and checks in Tom's voice. The rounded lilt of Georgie's. The house kept them at a distance.

And now, Nye was taking her away, tucking her arm under his, leading her around the corner of the house, past the brick barbecue, across the front garden to the far crook of the hedge, between the two apple trees.

'Here,' he said. 'Look up there. Across the valley and to the top of the middle hill. Do you see? Just to the right of the band of trees?'

'Yes. There's a house.'

'Plas Bryn. It was the vicarage once. It's up on the south side of Penllwyn and looks down over the valley. We're looking at the side of it.'

It was a tall house, indistinct among the darkening trees. At that distance it was no bigger than a pebble.

'Who lives there?'

'No one at the moment. It's been empty for years: it's too big for most people to live in and in bad condition. Last year a builder moved his business there for a couple of months, but he's gone now.' Nye let go of her hand and parted the apple boughs to see more clearly. 'One day I'm going to buy it.' He paused. 'I've never told that to anyone before.'

The ring in his voice told Hazel that she was hearing something important, but her mind was inside the walls of the cottage.

'Why not?' she asked.

'Because I want it very much.' Nye was watching for her reactions.

'You want to come back and live here?'

'Not now. Nor in the immediate future. But at some time ahead – say ten, fifteen years. Yes, I'd like to.'

'I hope you do, then.'

'Thank you.' There was a pause. 'And how about you? What do you want for the future?'

Hazel's breath caught and split her voice. 'Oh I don't know. I can't imagine it.'

'Not at all? Not an idea? Not a single, sneaking vision?'

Nye let the apple boughs spring back; the leaves bobbed in front of her face and she stepped away.

Nye reached for her.

'What's the matter?'

His touch pulsated, his face was alive. He was very near to knowing. How could he have followed her so far and be so near to her now, and still not know? Surely the warmth of her skin whispered it to him. Her blood must transmit its message. Her throat ached.

'Are you crying?'

'No.'

'Hazel. You're very dear to me.'

Nye could have no idea how old fashioned he sounded.

He linked his arms round her shoulders and bent his head, and then she saw them coming. Tom and Georgie: the shape of the two of them side by side, with that curious low centre of gravity anchoring them together. Nye's curly hair was under Hazel's hands; she could feel the hardness and roundness of his skull as she cupped his head, pushed her mouth against his opening lips and kissed him.

Nye's smile was still growing as he turned to the interlopers, with a touch of embarrassed triumph.

'Hallo there. Where have you two been? Taking refuge?' He reached for Hazel again with one of his heavy-limbed movements, obviously meaning to take her under his arm. But she stepped back.

'What's the matter?' Nye's hand fell to his side. He looked at the other three. 'What is it? What's going on here?'

Tom and Georgie were each looking at him and not at Hazel. They both stood very still but Tom's face was blank while Georgie's was vital with suppressed feeling. Emotions seemed to be flowering into procession beneath the surface of her skin, casting their shadows upwards.

'What?' said Nye, laughter creeping into his voice. 'I don't understand. What the—? Georgie?'

Tom moved: a slight impulsion, only a few inches, but determined, and Hazel began to move as well, away in a backwards, crablike motion which took her rapidly out of Nye's reach. Nye was watching her in astonishment; Georgie turned, her neck curving gracefully inside the heavy sweep of hair.

'Don't,' she said to both of them.

Hazel opened her mouth to speak but Tom took hold of her hand.

'We're going,' he said.

'Where?' said Hazel.

Tom stared. 'To your place, Hazel, to your place.'

'No.' Georgie's voice was euphonious. Hazel was reminded of the low note of the oboe in school music lessons. 'No. You must stay.'

Hazel gazed at her.

'I told you, no.' Tom's right hand curled round hers, grinding her knuckles painfully, and his left hand began pushing at her shoulder, trying to turn her round. He was almost shoulder-charging her. 'Come on. Hazel, come on.'

She saw his face a few urgent inches away and beyond him stood Nye, very upright like a soldier, and Georgie, watching with fierce eyes. Tom was already walking her away.

'Please, Hazel. Please just come. Stop looking back. We're going.'

There were many people looking at them. First Mark, then a group she didn't know, then Caroline and Chris, on the edge of the path, by the gate. Tom stopped in front of them.

'Chris, will you lend me your car?'

'What do you mean?'

'Your car. I need it, to take Hazel home.'

'Why? Ill, is she? Poor Hazel, are you all—? What's happening? Shall I drive?'

'No, it's fine, Chris, I just need your keys.'

'Are you all right to drive? You've been drinking.' That was Caroline. Heads were turning; Caroline's and Chris's, and those of all the people in the narrow garden: turning to look over at Georgie and Nye, and back to them, and back past them to Nye and Georgie, making connections, seeing the tracks at last and starting to follow them.

16

It was windy in Chris's car with the soft roof down but neither Tom nor Hazel knew how to put it up. Tom drove erratically, bouncing them over bumps in the lane and scraping the hedgerows. It was only when they climbed up on to the Penllwyn road, and were driving through the village, that he steadied. They skirted the side of the mountain and pushed on eastwards.

'We've done it,' Tom said.

'What happened in there?'

'Where?'

'In the house. When you went inside with Georgie. What did you say?'

Tom went on driving. 'You don't need to know that.'

He looked peculiar. Perhaps it was the effect of the wind, but his face looked as if it had been stretched so that everything – nose, lips, the curve from cheek to jawbone – was over-emphasised.

'I do bloody well need to know.'

Tom shivered. All along his arms the skin was raised.

'Later. Please.'

'What if Nye comes after us?'

'He won't. He'll stay with Georgie. For the time being anyway.'

'And you'll come with me; we'll do a swap.'

'Something like that.'

'You should have given me time to speak to him.' Why was she protesting now? She went on, screwing up her eyes against the onrushing air. 'He doesn't know anything.'

'Yes, he does.' Tom's face was despairing in the blue and orange light.

'What do you mean? Did Georgie say he knows?'

'I saw it in the garden. You were looking at Georgie, but I saw Nye's face.'

Hazel hugged herself.

'I don't understand. You mean, he knew when he was with me

in the garden? But he can't have done – he was talking about our future.'

'I don't know.' Tom's head inched forward over the steering wheel. 'For God's sake, Hazel, I don't know the whys and the wherefores. I only know that when Georgie and I turned up, he understood.' His head thrust forward another inch, then another. He was at an angle like an arrowhead. 'I'm so tired. Let's just get home. There'll be tomorrow for all this.'

'Oh God, tomorrow it's Georgie's school fête.'

Tom began to laugh in hiccuping bursts, above the noise of the engine.

Back in Hazel's bedsit, where they had come together for the first time a few weeks before; from where she had so often sent him back to Georgie, Tom pulled on one of Hazel's biggest jumpers and sat quietly in the armchair. Hazel looked at him and saw him again with Georgie in the garden, with Georgie in the tin hut at their wedding. More scenes came:

Tom and Georgie drinking wine in their kitchen.

Arguing in a car park in Bartraeth.

The two of them as she'd never seen them but as Nye had described them to her, naked in Georgie's college room on that first time he'd walked in on them; their bodies looking newly peeled.

The images were at Tom's shoulder like ghosts. Could he feel them? He pulled restlessly at the jumper collar, turned his wallet round where it lay balanced on the chair arm.

'You look tired,' said Hazel.

'I am tired. Come here. Please, Hazel, come here.'

Tom's eyes looked almost as dark as Nye's.

'I can't.'

'Why not?'

'I just don't understand anything. Have you spoken to Georgie or did you just walk out?'

'I just walked out.'

'So what were you talking about in the kitchen?'

'She was talking to me.'

Hazel sat on the end of the bed. All the remaining light was behind Tom, glowing in the white window-frame. Tom's face was an indecipherable pattern of shadows and hollows.

'What did she say?'

'Leave it, Hazel.'

'Well, what are we going to do?' Her voice caught with excitement.

'Whatever we can. Go away. Stay here. At least,' he moved his hands, 'can I stay here?'

The blankness of the question aroused Hazel. She got up from the bed and went to him, folded herself over him.

'Oh God, of course you can. Of course. But what are we going to do?'

Touching reminded them of the answer. Tom clung to Hazel as she closed the curtains. Staggering to the kitchen alcove, they groped for wine, then for each other. They opened their mouths, further and further, until they were sucking tongues.

Love-making pulled them on. Hazel could feel it, tugging her out of her skin, offering dissolution, confirmation, to her flesh. They undressed quickly and climbed on to the bed.

At first Hazel thought the knocking was coming from the flat above, then she sat up and looked at the door which led into the hall. The noise went on, coming from outside the house, at the front door.

Tom was still asleep. 'Tom, Tom. He's here.'

'Hallo?' He opened his eyes, only half-awake. 'Hazel?'

'Nye's here. He's banging on the door.'

'Nye?' he said. He blinked up at her then, and as she began to scramble out of bed, he came to and grabbed her arm. He put his finger to his mouth.

'Don't move. Stay here. Don't answer it.'

'But somebody will let him in.'

'Not us, though. Just stay here.'

'Ssh. He's talking to someone.' Hazel craned her head towards the curtains. It sounded as if Nye had turned away from the door and was speaking to someone on the steps. His words were inaudible but he spoke evenly.

There was a flurry behind her and Tom was squatting on the bed. 'Listen,' he said. His head was tipped, trying to intercept the sounds. 'There's someone else. Do you think it's Georgie?' He climbed down and picked up his clothes, his head turned keenly towards the window. 'I think it is. He's come here with Georgie. It's going to be the four of us, here.'

Hazel watched him closely. He was glad; more, he was relieved. His face was illuminated as he began dressing. 'Hazel love, get some clothes on.' He buttoned his shirt, passed her her dress and gave her a fleeting touch. 'Come on now.' He turned and pulled the eiderdown over the bed and switched on the overhead light. 'Are you ready? I'm going to let them in.'

But Nye was alone. He came in ahead of Tom and his eyes went straight to the bed. He walked to the foot of it and stopped, looking at Hazel. He was pale and the curls rimmed his forehead tightly. His hands were quite steady, though. His left trouser leg was splashed with wine.

He didn't speak. His nostrils flared and he breathed more shallowly; the room, Hazel understood, smelled of sex.

Tom slipped in behind him and then came across the room fast. He'd lost his confidence. He held on to the mantelpiece and began pushing his sleeves up and down. 'Georgie's not here,' he said to Hazel. He sounded downcast. 'It's just Nye. He wants me to go back to the cottage with him, to see Georgie. I've told him, tomorrow. Not tonight. None of us can think straight tonight.'

Hazel glanced at Nye. He met her eyes briefly. 'I can think straight,' he said to the back of Tom's head. 'And so can Georgie. It's you two who seem to be having a problem.'

Tom moved towards Hazel. 'I'm sorry, Nye,' he said, but without looking at him. 'I'm really sorry.'

'That's not good enough.' Nye sounded authoritative and Tom flinched. Hazel took hold of his sleeve. She felt she was facing Nye for both of them. But though he met her gaze, Nye didn't seem to want anything from her; he kept looking at Tom's bent head as if he could will him to raise it. Tom touched her hand.

'Do you want to speak to Hazel?' he said to the floor.

'No.' Nye glanced at her quickly, then back at Tom. 'It's Georgie who needs to see you, Tom. Everyone's gone from the cottage, there's just Georgie there, and she needs you to come back and talk to her.'

' "Come"?' Tom screwed up his eyes and peered at Nye. 'Come with you, is that it?'

'Georgie wants me to drive back with you, yes.'

'No, I've told you, I'll go and see her tomorrow, on my own. But not tonight.'

'Why not?'

'Because I don't feel like it.'

'Jesus, Tom,' said Hazel.

'You're afraid of her, aren't you?' said Nye.

Tom looked at Hazel. He raised his hands and dropped them. 'Look,' he said desperately, 'I've left Georgie. She loves me, she wants me to stay with her but I've left her. In the end, I want you more than I care about her. So what's the point of me going over there now?'

He was pleading as if she'd made the request. He was so close she could see where his bruise was turning green. His supplication was oppressive, and humiliating; she had to stop herself from jerking away. She looked past him to Nye.

'It's not so very much to ask, is it?' Nye spoke distantly. 'If it helps her.'

When Hazel turned back to Tom he was hunched and shaking his head. Then he walked a quick circle and sat down on the arm of the chair. He stared up at Nye as if he couldn't focus on him. 'All right,' he said quickly, 'let's go then. Let's all go and talk about what's happened.'

Was it looking at Nye that made Tom's expression disintegrate and become bland? There was anguish left only in his eyes; the lines of his cheeks and mouth were smoothing out. His chest rose and fell. 'All right,' he said again, turning to Hazel. 'You don't want to come, do you?'

Above Tom's head, Nye was looking at her. He was trying to communicate something. His face was avid and faintly sick. A great effort seemed to be coming off him, but whatever he wanted to convey was falling short. Tom was splintering her concentration. 'Oh, Tom, how can I?' she said angrily.

'Think about it, man.' Nye moved his eyes to Tom. He spoke without any heat. 'Think about Georgie, watching you come up the path with Hazel.'

Tom ignored him. He stood up and rubbed his eyes, then he moved in front of Hazel, cutting off Nye's line of vision. Hazel had a feeling like vertigo. In the shelter of Tom's body she was spiralling downwards and she didn't know if it would be worse to go on falling or to stop.

'I'll go but I won't be long,' said Tom flatly. 'I'll see you later.'

'Come on,' said Nye. He was walking past them, his head thrust forward, his face creamy. 'Let's get this done.'

Did she want them to come back? With the electric bars on and the glass shucking in the window frame with each passing car, Hazel wasn't sure. She was waiting for something, she knew. A knock on the window, the quick ring at the door. But her feelings had detached themselves from her; she didn't know if this lightness in her flesh was anticipation or dread.

Nye had something to tell her. And he wanted something from her. What could it be? Pushed by Tom, she had made the step away from Nye and it should have been decisive, but he was still here, bringing offerings and making claims.

Whereas Tom seemed to have reached an end. There had been senescence in his face when he left. That retreat to blandness frightened her; he hadn't answered any of her questions earlier and she didn't think he would when he returned. He would just want to be held. The thought of his weight and his need made her throat close. She didn't want to fail him but warnings prickled in her mind.

There was no one for her to turn to and ask questions of. They were all in the Islyn, arguing in words she was forbidden to understand. On the mantelpiece the clock sectioned off pieces of time.

It was gone three and the hall was chilly. Hazel used the light from her doorway to guide her to the telephone. The chime of the handset being lifted was obtrusive; the dialling tone sprang into her ear.

The bell at the other end rang once and Hazel hung up. She couldn't be sure she had the right number. She dialled again, carefully. One, two, three, four, five, six rings. Seven, eight – then the pips bleeping and her money going in. She listened. She heard a male intake of breath and the receiver was passed from one person to another. From Nye to Tom? From Tom to Georgie? There was a short, crystalline silence which gave her no clue and the line was cut. She got the engaged tone the next time she dialled, and the next.

Hazel had forgotten the number of the taxi firm and had to read the cards on the message board. The man who answered sounded familiar and she half expected him to say something friendly ('Oh yes, the late night trip to the Islyn. We haven't heard from you for a while.') but he didn't and although it was only a few weeks since his cars had regularly travelled out to the Islyn, Hazel had to explain where it was.

The regular lighting of the main road gave way to the lanes. Behind them, Penllwyn slept. One window shone high up on the far side of the valley.

The car slowed down as the reflectors winked at them from the bends.

'I nearly didn't see that one,' said the driver. 'They should trim the hedges.' He switched to full beam and the green walls leapt closer. 'How much further?'

'Not far.' Hazel heard the energy squeezed from her voice. With each approaching car on the main roads that failed to contain Nye or Tom, she had lost an option. She couldn't signal to this one or that one; she couldn't tell the taxi to turn round and head back into the city.

They were over the cattle grid and passing the junction with the lane up the valley. They were alongside Taplow's greenhouses. Through the trees, a light glimmered.

'Just past this bend.' Hazel's voice was almost extinguished. She moved away from that side of the road, leaning into darkness.

As soon as they were round the corner, she saw the cars: Chris's borrowed one, at a tilt on the verge; Tom and Georgie's still tucked neatly in the dip below the gate. But not Nye's. He was gone. Had he left just minutes ago, driving up the back lanes while her taxi approached along the main road? Terror touched Hazel. She was unsupervised at the Islyn, with Tom and Georgie.

But as the taxi cruised to a halt, she saw a third car further down the lane. All its lights were off but its driver's door was open and a man sat still on the bonnet. It was Nye.

He looked incuriously at the taxi and at Hazel as she got out. The driver watched him: 'Will you be all right, then?'

'Yes thank you. He's a friend.'

Hazel walked down to the car; Nye's face was turned towards her and as she reached him the taxi began manoeuvring, its roar giving them a temporary respite from having to talk.

But Nye showed no inclination to speak anyway. Hazel doubted whether he could have found the words. The sickness – was it shock? – she'd seen earlier was stronger now. It widened the space between his eyes and increased the bulk of his shoulders. Nye sitting there on the car bonnet looked full of flesh.

'What are you doing out here?' The noise of the taxi pulling away swallowed her words and she had to repeat them.

Nye almost smiled. 'Because I'm not wanted inside,' he replied. 'They're back together now.'

'No.' Hazel spoke at once. She was at a disadvantage, arriving in the dark lane to find Nye as gatekeeper, and she knew that she mustn't let him dictate to her. 'They're just talking.'

Nye lifted his feet on to the bumper. He stared down and splayed his fingers on his thighs. 'No. It's over, *collen*. He's staying with Georgie.'

Hazel rubbed her arms. A heaviness seemed to be spreading from Nye, entering her cells. She turned to the house; lights were on in the hall and landing, in the kitchen and the bathroom. They shone like signals. 'I'd better go in there.' Her voice came out loud and aggressive.

'I wouldn't,' said Nye. 'They're going to bed.'

Hazel stared at the pattern of bright and dark. There was half-dark in the sitting room – a single lamp on, or else spill-over radiance from the hall. It dimmed as if someone had passed the doorway.

'They're not going to bed,' she said. 'They're moving round downstairs.' Nye didn't answer. Hazel strained to make sense of the shadow, coming and going. 'Tom's packing!' she said slowly.

Nye went on looking past her, towards the house. Hazel touched his elbow, then jumped away: in her sensitised state, she could feel the vigour pent up in his muscles. She stood a couple of feet from him, not quite close enough to feel his physical pull, but near enough to know it was there. She was reluctant to leave him. The little house looked frightening with its squares of light. The path, running alongside the stretch of grass, offered no cover.

Hazel was afraid to walk up that path with Nye watching. But she would have been afraid to walk up it unobserved too: the terror she'd felt a few minutes ago, when she'd thought she was alone, had weakened her. She didn't know what she expected. She didn't even know what she feared.

She stood watching. The sitting-room glow dimmed and strengthened again and someone moved behind the small hall window. Before she could see who it was, a light came on in the room above.

Hazel flinched. Then she moved away from Nye; she was too close to him, after all. She went up the lane and climbed the bank until she could see into the upstairs window. The room was empty; there was only the glimpse of a hand on the switch, quickly withdrawn, and an impression of movement on the landing. Whoever it was had gone back into the hidden part of the house, leaving her to examine this bedroom, which she'd never seen before.

It was all wrong. She'd always imagined a fresh-looking room, with their own pictures on the wall and a quilt on the bed, white perhaps with squares of blue. A chest of drawers. A jug with flowers in it. A simple space with touches of Georgie. Instead, it was crowded and chaotic. The high double bed was wedged between a chair and a wardrobe. It was unmade and clothes were piled on the blankets. There were plenty of pictures, Georgie's and Tom's and other people's, but only one hung on the wall; the others stood on the surfaces, on the mantelpiece and on the floor, ringing the room, although nails stuck out of every wall ready to take them. There were ornaments – among them she recognised a jug Tom had brought back from the honeymoon and which they'd shown her on her first visit here – but instead of being displayed they were stacked on a crate.

Hazel stared, puzzled. Were they packing up? Was Georgie preparing to leave too? Georgie came back into the room. She looked tired and relaxed. She picked up something from the floor and put it on the chair. Then she sat down on the bed. She put her head on one side and burrowed her hand beneath her hair: Georgie was taking off her earrings. She put them away in a box in the wardrobe. Then she walked across the room, unbuttoning her shirt. Hazel shifted behind the hedgerow and saw that Georgie was looking at the pictures on the mantelpiece. She lifted each one in turn, before hanging the first on a nail. She turned away and dropped her shirt on the floor. Hazel watched her bare back leave the room.

The warnings were pricking strongly; they were vibrations in her mind, almost breaking through into sound. Every one of Georgie's actions just now had been unhurried. She wasn't preparing to leave. She looked more like someone coming home; she'd been moving round the room like a cat quartering her territory, taking her bearings, touching things to see what had changed during her absence.

A light went off downstairs. The kitchen light; Hazel just caught the edge of brightness vanishing from the grass. Only the hall was lit now.

The hall light went off. The ground floor was in darkness as Hazel waited.

After Georgie, Tom looked big in the bedroom doorway. His T shirt was darkened round the neck with sweat or shadows. Or perhaps he'd spilt a drink. Hazel was struck by his masculinity. Earlier in the bedsit when he'd appealed to her for help, she'd felt his emotions leaching into her. It was as if they'd become a joint person. But now, standing alone in his bedroom, he was separate from her. Separate from everyone; an adult male whose experiences she couldn't share.

He looked round him. He appeared defeated but also – relieved? There was a new freedom in his movements.

Georgie must have spoken from out on the landing, because he cocked his head, listening. His lips moved in reply. He turned towards the door a second before Georgie appeared in its frame. Her hair was slicked back by water and she held a towel, but she was still bare above the waist. Tom stood watching her until, as she passed in front of him, he raised his left arm – Hazel saw the dark strap of his watch – and splayed his fingers tentatively on her ribs. Georgie's head bowed. Her face glimmered pale through her hair as she gestured towards the window. Tom moved across the room and pulled the curtains closed.

'I'm going.' Nye spoke distinctly and Hazel turned to see him stand up and stretch his legs. He flexed his hands too, one after the other. At first she thought he hadn't been watching, but then she saw his face.

His features seemed to have edged forward and his skin looked iridescent. It was difficult to see in the moonlight but a reaction was taking place.

Hazel felt her stomach shrink. 'You can't go,' she said quickly. 'Where?'

Nye made for the driver's door, ignoring her. 'Please don't leave me,' she said. Nye laughed. But Hazel was undeterred. The vibrations had left her mind: now it was clear and she knew she had to move fast to outpace Nye. He wanted to get away, but she couldn't let him go. Whatever he'd wanted to tell her in the bedsit wouldn't help him now, so he was leaving, but she still needed to hear it. She must hear it. She had lost, without knowing why; he wasn't to take this away too.

Hazel was shaking and her teeth were chattering: hard little enamel surfaces, clashing together – she ran across the road and grabbed Nye's arm. She caught him off-balance and he swivelled. His shoulder crashed against the car roof. 'Fuck!'

'Don't you dare leave me here,' Hazel said.

'Gone off the idea of going inside, have you?'

She wanted to be angry like some cold, flashing metal – droplets of mercury, changing their shape, refusing to yield their character – but she was crying. Her face had crumpled and her tears were hot.

'Tom's with Georgie. You fixed it. Now you bloody well take me with you because you owe me. You've got things that belong to me!' The sobbing didn't diminish her fury; she heard it hurled outwards, transfigured into snot and despair. Nye was suddenly wary.

'What do you mean?'

'You've played with me. You all have. You knew about Tom and me before tonight, didn't you?'

' "Knew".' Nye considered the word as if it were a weapon he'd picked up. 'No, I can't say I knew. It's hard to be sure about people, don't you find?' The sheen on his face had dulled; for a second Hazel's anger faltered. Perhaps he saw it because he reached out and wiped the snot off her upper lip with his fingers. 'What are you looking for now?' he said wearily. 'You made your choice.'

'It's not me, is it?' Hazel was still crying but it seemed to be with someone else's eyes and mouth. 'It's something to do with Tom and Georgie. That's why you're so upset.'

Nye turned his back on her and opened the car door, forcing her out of the way. It was the first rudeness he'd ever shown her. 'I'm going. I've got things to do.'

'Give me a lift.'

'I'm not going home.'

'Give me a lift anyway, wherever you're going. Please.'

The doors slamming and engine starting brought no one to the bedroom window. The cottage was gone in seconds. The lanes were narrow and the hedgerows high. The car headlights reached only as far as the verges where they spent themselves on tangles of branch and grass. Hazel watched the living walls keep pace with the car as Nye drove, too fast. She'd stopped crying and was only shaking, with a tremor like electric currents.

'Will you tell me what happened in there?'

'Well, *collen,* what can I say?' Nye sounded bitter. 'Georgie got him back. That's all.'

'But how?'

He gave a small laugh. 'Good God alive, were you so sure she couldn't?'

'No. Not sure at all.' She looked at his profile. 'Not once you came to get Tom.'

They were climbing the hillside which lay south of the Islyn. Nye stopped the car on a steep crossroads and peered up and down the gradient as if he expected traffic.

'You were trying to tell me something then,' she said. 'Or find out something. Weren't you?'

Nye looked at her as he put the car in gear. He drove across the junction, further uphill.

'What was it?' she said.

'Can't you just be quiet? I'm tired.' He was exhausted. Hazel was quiet, listening to the lack of momentum in his voice.

He turned the steering wheel right and they went up a smaller lane. In front of them, at the top of a grassy slope, stood a house with too many walls and angles for its size. There were gables and a wooden porch. An ugly bay stuck out at the front, boarded up.

'It's Plas Bryn,' said Hazel in surprise.

Nye drove across the forecourt and stopped at the edge of the grass. He switched off the engine. 'What are we doing here?' Hazel said. She spoke carefully; she wouldn't have thought that she would have room for a new emotion, let alone one as sharp as fear.

'I've got something to do here. You stay in the car; I won't be long.'

The fear changed complexion. Nye was taking a long time to open his door. Hazel was out of her side and waiting by the time he clicked it shut. 'I'll come with you.'

Nye nodded and began walking towards the back of the house. Between the house wall and the bushes it was dark, but behind the house was a semicircle of grass and matted flowerbeds and with the moonlight trapped in high cloud they could see quite well. Nye walked in a diagonal, to a point where the garden straggled off into surrounding trees. Broken pots lay on the earth and what had once been a compost heap was grassing over. Garden rubbish was stacked against it. At first glance Hazel took the flat objects for old fence panels, but as she stopped beside Nye, she saw.

The paintings had been neatly propped on their sides, larger works at the back, smaller in front, and a large sheet of cardboard had been weighted down on top of them as a shelter. In the darkness their colours were barely visible – only the different textures showed, a sheen, a dullness, the new flat surface Tom had been telling her about – and the pale patches where he hadn't painted yet, some marked with the tiny symbols which were his notes to himself.

Hazel had only ever seen Tom's work in his college studio or the gallery. Never so many pieces gathered together. Never the sum of what he'd been doing at home.

'Oh, Jesus. Are these from Tom's studio?'

'Yes.'

'Does he know they're here?'

'No. He knows they're not in his studio, but he doesn't know where they are. Though I think he might have guessed.' Nye stared at the paintings without showing any emotion.

In Hazel, though, a heat was spreading. Not in her mind, but in her guts; it flowed inwards and upwards.

'What are you going to do with them?'

'Restore them to Tom. He's fulfilled his part of the bargain; now we fulfil ours.'

'We?' Hazel looked at him incredulously. 'You and me?'

Nye frowned. 'No, not you. Georgie and I.'

'Georgie agreed to you taking his work?'

'Oh yes.' Nye examined her face for a long time. He seemed to find it fascinating; his muscles approximated the first smile she'd seen since she'd left him. 'Yes, Georgie agreed. After all, why should she let him go without a fight? She's been his lover for three years. He's done all his best work with her. This new stuff' – he nodded towards the unfinished pictures – 'might have been done with you in mind, but it was painted in the house he shares with Georgie, on the food she helps him buy, after sleeping next to her in their bed. Why should she let him walk out and take it all to you?'

Hazel was shaking again. This time it was a different kind of tremor.

'Did Georgie say all that to him,' she said, 'or was it you?'

'It was Georgie, *collen*. Tom's wife doesn't need anyone to do her talking for her.' Nye couldn't quite disguise the heaviness in his voice.

'Left out again, then,' she said quietly.

Nye blew a laugh down his nose. 'You can hardly expect sympathy for that.'

'No, I meant you.' There was a silence.

Then Nye said: 'You really don't want to leave me with anything, do you?'

'I'm sorry.' Hazel put her hand over her mouth; it had begun to taste foul.

Nye looked at her for a while. There was anger in his face again now, the same magnifying glow she had seen after Tom closed the curtains. 'It's what he wants, you know,' he said. 'To be in someone's power like that. Georgie must have known it a long time. There's always been some kind of struggle going on between them. I sensed it but I didn't know quite what it was.'

'But he doesn't want to be in anyone's power. He hates it. That's why he left her for me.'

'Yes, it did look like that, didn't it?' Nye turned and moved slowly to the pictures. He squatted down and separated some of the canvases out. He stared from a large completed one to two that were smaller and unfinished. His eyelids flickered; his fingers touched the paint.

'Would you really have harmed them?' Hazel asked.

'I don't know. I didn't know. At the time, when I brought them up here and then came to find you at the bedsit . . . I think I believed I might.' He spread his fingers out over one of the small paintings and lifted his head, like a blind man reading Braille. 'He's *awenydd*, you know, in my opinion. Touched by the muse. One of the real ones.' He turned his face full on to her, quick and questing, without really seeing her. 'Did you know I feel that?'

'No.' She lied out of decency.

'Well, I do. I didn't used to, not when I first knew him, but I've watched him grow into it. I've seen him become more certain.

'So anyway, I brought them up here, all his best work, before I came to get him. He didn't know I had them, but he knew something was wrong. He knew. He was – excited.'

Nye must be sweating. The side of his face shone. Hazel remembered how shocked he'd seemed in the bedsit; the impression he'd given her of a man in extremity.

'What did he say?'

'Not much.' Nye looked at the painting he held balanced on his knees: it was a metallic grey-red, with black edged down one side. His cheek bulged; he was smiling. 'He asked me if I was all right.'

Nye put the painting down. 'Do you know,' he said, 'you underestimated Georgie. She's been preparing for this you know, fighting back every step of the way. Little things. For instance, she started buying white wine instead of red because white is your drink, and she wanted Tom to be reminded of you all the time. She wasn't going to let home be a refuge. And the day she realised you'd slept together, she stopped decorating their bedroom. Did you see the way it looked tonight? They've been lying down in that every night since. On the days he went with you she didn't even make the bed.' He rocked on his haunches. He looked into Hazel's eyes. 'Imagine it.'

'I am.'

'Did he tell you?'

It was too late to look away. 'No. Not really.'

'You see, Hazel, you didn't know what was happening any more than I did.'

Hazel: that was how Tom addressed her, direct and bare. It

was curious to hear it in Nye's mouth.

'Don't give them back,' she said. Nye creased his brow at her.

'What?'

It was hard to speak. She had a hot pain in her gullet as if she needed to burp. 'Don't give the paintings back.' So few words, but they made the pain ball tighter; across her chest, the skin was wet. 'Don't give them back.'

'Georgie and I made a bargain with Tom. He's left you and gone back to her; now we return his paintings.'

'Don't give them back.' It seemed to be all she could say.

'Hazel.'

'No, why should you? Tom's gone back to Georgie, they're tucked up in the marital bed. Mr and Mrs Fieldmouse. But what about you?'

'I'm touched you care, *collen*.'

Hazel looked back at him without a quiver. She'd always wondered what it would be like to lose all her shame. She'd never expected to know.

'You can't be friends with Tom again like you were. He thought you loved me: he told me you did, and it didn't stop him. He was going to be sorry to lose you as a friend when we ran away together, that's all. You called the Islyn "home" just now but it never will be again, you know.'

'I know.' Nye's neck moved stiffly. His Adam's apple was prominent. 'I know that. But I promised Georgie. This work is for his summer show – it's their future.'

'You don't owe Georgie anything more. You gave Tom back to her. All those weeks when she knew about Tom and me, what did she tell you?'

Nye stood up. His legs cracked and his hands were shaking.

'I know you probably hate me,' Hazel said.

'As a matter of fact, *collen*, I don't.' His mouth spasmed downwards; she saw him grit his teeth to control it.

'Just go to the car. Leave me for five minutes.'

'Why? So that when they call the police I can pretend ignorance?'

'I will do it.' Hazel had to say it to commit herself; she was frightened of the police. She dug her hands into her thighs and ran through permutations: if Nye went away and she damaged some, a third, a quarter, she might make it look accidental; or if she chose what she thought were the best and hid them elsewhere; buried them with a spade. Split the canvases with the spade, then buried them. She went nearer the stack; she knelt down. She put her hand on the small dark canvas, where Nye had spread his.

Touching it made her whole body shake. She felt as if she had twice as much blood in her as normal. She knew now how much she wanted to hurt Tom.

She felt Nye behind her. He bent down and touched her shoulder; his hand was soaking. 'Let me show you,' he said. He knelt down beside her and eased the cardboard sheet from the top of the stack. His voice had a wheeze in it. 'The paintings at the back, on this side, are mainly from last summer. Some of these were in his end of year show, which won him the bursary. They're the blacks and the oranges, with the tension on one side of the canvas only. And do you see here, this is where he started to use the torso shape, in the parts of the composition where you'd expect release from bulk.' His voice was deeper now. 'Look what it does to the balance of this one. Concentration on concentration.'

He leaned forward and pulled out a batch from the middle. His cheeks were flushed. 'These here were experiments for a new way to work with vertical relationships. He abandoned them, but I'm sure he'll use them again. Because look, they're ugly and broken-backed but they're so delicate. This blue. You should have seen it in proper light. You've seen others like these, of course. In the gallery.'

'Yes, and in his college studios. He has a red one there I love.'

'Yes. I love this red one. This large one. Careful. It's called *O Arglwydd*.'

'"O Lord", like in chapel.'

'Yes. But it wasn't from chapel, it was from one of my Welsh-English readers. *Tales from the Mabinogi*. He liked the fact that in those stories people call one another *Arglwydd* as a matter of course. One lord to another.

'And these . . .' Nye faltered. He looked at the remaining canvases but his hand was still curled round *O Arglwydd*. 'These are what he's been doing recently. Many of them unfinished, you see, and perhaps not to be finished. But these here are his very latest. Look. Very alive. Very circumscribed. Beautiful.'

He picked up five small canvases and passed them to her. The brightness of the colours showed, though not the colours themselves; and on the contrasting fields small geometric lines that whirred and buzzed. Hazel could see so little detail in this light; she pored over them, clutching them one on top of the other.

Nye took them off her and tucked them down at the front of the stack. Then he took her elbow and helped her stand. 'Are you ready?' His wheeze was back; it was almost a whine.

'Yes.'

'I'm going to keep one.' He looked slowly from one end of the stack to the other. His eyes were sunken and he seemed to be forcing the lids apart. Hazel found her own eyes going to the big canvas; her lips trying to prompt him: *O Arglwydd*. But Nye looked at it once more and turned away. He went instead to the last little canvases and gazed at them. When he straightened, he was holding one.

'You next,' he said. Hazel looked at the painting in his hand. She would have taken one of these for herself, but not now.

'No.'

Nye nodded. He dug in his pocket. With only one hand free, and shaking, it took him a long time to find the matches. But he withdrew them from the box and struck them one by one, holding them carefully to the cardboard sheet. Only one or two flames stayed alight. 'Can you take the matches? If I fold this into a cylinder, we should get it to light. Then we can put it in the middle of them.'

Hazel took the matches. 'Nye. All the paintings?'

Above the cardboard he turned his head towards her. With difficulty, he made the cylinder. Hazel knelt down and, striking matches two and three at a time, made a circle of flames at the lower rim. She watched Nye lift the cylinder above the stack and guide it down, pulling canvases apart to give it room to breathe, throwing sticks on top to help it catch. The light disappeared, flared and from near the ground a thick smoke rose. Nye hurried round the stack and grabbed the matches from her. He was on his hands and knees at the far edge, lighting a dry branch. Hazel took her cigarette lighter out of her bag. It was a disposable one she had bought in Bristol with Tom and it still had most of its fuel. The flint clicked willingly to the canvases. The smoke ballooned into her face and made it hard to see.

The fire was catching, in small bursts. In the middle of the stack, heat crackled. The canvases were shifting; a blaze was taking hold. Across the bonfire, Hazel saw Nye stand up. He turned his head away and gulped in breaths, open-mouthed. She thought he spoke but it was impossible to hear in the roaring air.

Part Three

17

The lobby of the hotel was crowded with men in suits, wearing badges: the conference had broken for coffee early. There were some women among the delegates, Tom saw, most of them wearing dark blue skirts and jackets with white shirts, as if it were some kind of uniform. They looked completely at home here, in this hotel, and with the men.

Last year Tom had picked Georgie up from a teachers' union meeting and the people there had had the same air of belonging, but it had been less exclusive than this. They'd looked less honed.

He didn't recognise Nye at first; though he'd seen him dressed like this before, often, it had never been in a crowd of his colleagues. And it was nearly a year since their last meeting. Nye looked slimmer than before. Both his suit and his hair were better cut.

'Hallo. Have you been here long?'

'No, only just arrived.'

Nye carried a briefcase and looked distracted.

'Let's get out of here, shall we? We've got twenty minutes before the next session starts.'

They left the hotel for the street, where the sun had gone in and the crocuses in the brick flowerbed looked puny against the earth. The wind made Tom remember why he had worn his thick jumper and he saw Nye tense his shoulders inside his jacket. They went to the pub on the corner where there was a cigarette machine, a woman putting away a vacuum cleaner, and two other customers. Tom bought himself a beer and Nye ordered an orange juice.

'I'm speaking at midday,' he explained. 'Anyway, it wouldn't do to go back smelling of drink.'

'What are you speaking about?'

'Customer support for the smaller company. We need to get together to challenge the big boys.'

'Yes, I heard you'd left RCL.'

'Yes, I know you did.'

It was friendly enough – Nye was laughing at him for stating the obvious, as Nye had always done. Because it had been Tom who telephoned Nye this time, calling the hotel last night when Georgie was watching the news.

'You look well,' said Tom. 'It must suit you, the entrepreneurial thing.'

'It does. I always knew it would.'

'All part of the plan, is it?'

'A plan. Plans change, as you know.'

Tom nodded. 'Yes, I know.'

There was a brightness in the glance Nye gave him and Tom went still. They had never yet spoken about it directly – was Nye going to break the code this time? But nothing.

'Congratulations on your daughter,' said Tom.

A look of bashful pleasure came across Nye's face. 'Thank you.'

'Changes your life a bit, doesn't it?'

Nye's laughter took him by surprise.

'It certainly does. We don't know whether we're coming or going. I went to a meeting with spew on my shoulder the other day. She smiles all the time now, which makes things nice.' There was a pause and then, almost reluctantly, as if he didn't want to contemplate anyone else's child, Nye asked: 'How's Ieuan?'

'Well. He's nearly three now. He's a lively lad, into everything, very sociable. He looks like Georgie, her hair, her eyes.'

'How is Georgie?' Nye always asked this question, immediately after Georgie's name was mentioned, but his tone varied. This time it was even and distant.

'Quite well. Looking forward to going back to work full-time, as soon as Ieuan starts nursery school.'

Tom placed his elbows on the bar. He saw Nye looking at his jumper sleeves, the shetland wool all fuzzed and a hole starting. Nye wouldn't say anything about it; he never did any more.

Just how much did Nye know about the way they lived? He must be aware of their difficulties and disappointments. Surely his mother would have mentioned them once or twice on his visits; or even if not, the absence of Tom's name from any arts pages, the fact that they continued on in the Islyn, that Tom still worked at the college, must suggest to Nye how it was.

But although Nye sometimes talked about money – especially with regard to his business plans – he never asked Tom how he managed. And so far Tom had never discussed it. Sometimes he said that things were tight, or mentioned that he was taking extra classes at the college. That was all. That was all that was allowed; anything further would give Nye a glimpse into Georgie's life, and the rules forbade that, just as they forbade Tom asking about Hazel.

'How's work going?' Nye asked. 'Painting, I mean.'

Work was within the compact; they could ask each other about that. Though Tom always found it odd that Nye seemed to feel no embarrassment in going on asking; especially when, each time, he found it more difficult to answer him.

'Not bad. I've started doing a new series. I'm not really sure where I am with it yet.'

'Anything I'd recognise from the past? Or have you moved on completely?'

Jesus.

'You'd recognise it. I'm using new techniques, but the basic approach is still there. And the same shapes come up.'

Nye nodded.

'Good. Are you still with the same gallery?'

'Yes.'

'Have you got a show on soon?'

'I was in a mixed show this winter.' Tom made no mention of an individual show, and Nye didn't ask.

'If I went along to the gallery, could I see what they've got of yours? I'd like to see what you're doing now.'

'Sure. Just ask them.'

'Because we're moving into new offices in London and we'll be buying some paintings. Would you mind if I bought some of yours?'

Would he mind? Mind Nye buying, not one, but 'some' of his paintings? He wondered just how much of his work Nye's company budget would stretch to – he might be able to buy up the whole lot.

'Oh I don't know, Nye. Not yet. It's too difficult.'

'Ah.' Nye took another drink. He slid a quick sideways glance at Tom, then away. 'I see. Sorry.'

Tom felt exasperated: what did Nye imagine he understood now? 'I don't know how you can see when I don't.'

Nye looked at him and laughed, not completely convincingly.

'Tricky, isn't it? Georgie still hates me then? No, forget I asked. The passage of time doesn't make much difference to Georgie, does it?'

'Well, not four years, no. Looks like we'll have to give it another few.'

'It's just as well I've got no immediate plans to come back.'

'That reminds me, Plas Bryn's been bought.'

'Christ. By whom?'

'Two doctors, apparently. A couple. They're going to convert part of it into their surgery.'

'Ah. Oh well, there's plenty of time yet. Anyway, I can't say I'm feeling drawn back very strongly at the moment. Last time I went to see my mother the village looked half-dead. I suppose Glaister's shutting has been a blow.'

'It hasn't helped. But people were moving out before that anyway, especially the young ones. Graig junior school shut last year.'

'That's not good news for Georgie, is it? Will you think about moving, if she can't get a job?'

'I don't know. If we went too far, I'd have to look for a new job too, and colleges might not be queuing up to have me.' Tom pulled his glass towards him. 'Even the half-dead ones.'

Nye looked away, his right eye squinting slightly. So that hadn't been a jibe about the village, only a slip – which made it even more unforgiveable. Tom shut his teeth hard as he swallowed his beer. 'I sometimes think I wouldn't mind going abroad again,' he said, pretending not to notice the silence. 'It would be a good time to do it from the point of view of Ieuan still being young. And I quite enjoyed teaching the Sunday painters in Cyprus. But it would be hard to earn enough at it to support all of us. Besides, I think Georgie's getting itchy to do something for her own career. It's her turn, now, that's how we arrange it, see.'

Tom looked into Nye's face. His mouth tasted bitter with hops and words; good. Welcome to my half-dead world, Nye; come in and see how we live.

But Nye didn't come in. He didn't respond at all. He looked down at his glass and Tom watched the bend of his neck and the way the flesh on his face looked still but in fact shivered with infinitesimal movements, and wondered how long Nye would stay like that. Until Tom spoke again and released him? Probably – in which case Tom would remain silent and keep him in prison. He stared and enjoyed it; the shivering of the tiny muscles seemed to increase as he watched, and then suddenly he was uncomfortable. His spine began to itch and he jerked his head away and drank some more.

'So, tell me about little Elen. Your choice of name, I bet. Who does she look like?'

Nye straightened up and smiled. Tom watched two tiny diagonal lines strike into the skin under his eyes – those were new since their last meeting. The baby must have put them there; it was a foreign thought, Nye feeling a father's love.

'Me, as a matter of fact,' Nye admitted happily. 'At least, we hope she's going to have Hazel's cheekbones. But at the moment she looks just like me, poor little thing.'

At quarter past eleven, with the glass doors of the hotel falling to behind Tom, the morning felt very wide. The streets were full of the colourless light of March. The car was in the car park by the bus station, and on his way back to it he resisted the temptation to go into another pub for a drink; he stopped in a café and had a cup of coffee and two doughnuts in order to stoke up – if he went home and started straight away, he could get several hours' work in before he had to come back to his class.

The doughnuts were thick and much too sweet. Still, Tom ate steadily, filling up the gap. Sometimes after seeing Nye he felt elated, but today he felt lonely. Too long had passed since their last meeting and this morning's encounter had been too short.

The anger was strong this time. It whirled inside him, a furious little concentrated thing, getting smaller and fiercer. It created a space round itself which he didn't dare touch. Was it because Nye had wanted to leave? He hadn't been able to wait to get away, had he? After everything else Nye had done to him, Tom was now being set aside.

Don't think about it. The empty space will suck you in. You'll slip into the desert. You know what it's like; you'll never reach the anger, you simply vanish in there, flattened, going into white.

If, four years ago, Tom had behaved like Georgie, would this anger still be here? But Georgie had been the one to scream with pain; he'd chosen another way. An instinctive choice it had been: made in front of the bedroom window, with Georgie gasping into her hands behind him and far off, half-hidden among the trees, that light leaping.

A small light burning something big, just as he himself had felt big, like a giant inside Georgie's body a few moments before; and then, naked in the warm room, her juice still wet on him, he had watched the fire and felt himself stretch out across the valley, enter the heat with Nye and Hazel. He'd been certain in that instant that he was losing in order to gain. But Nye had beaten him there, too.

By the time he'd understood Nye's true achievement – Christ, so short a time later – it was too late. All Tom could do was submit. So he had been beaten in every sense. Broken and punished. Defeated. Even hit, by Georgie.

He might have grabbed some of it back for himself, if it hadn't been for the phone calls. They were a subtler kind of punishment. He used to listen to Georgie making them, hearing her voice shake and resonate, go thin, siphon off its inexhaustible rage, while she said the things that rightly belonged to him.

It was always Nye who answered, and listened too. Afterwards Georgie and Tom would fight and make love in a desperate way that aroused and humiliated him. With his arms full of Georgie, he'd had no real choice any more.

In the days, at least, he was free. He spent most of them walking. Around the back streets of Bartraeth, among corner shops and yards full of broken fridges. Up what used to be Colliers' Way to the disused pithead behind Penllwyn. The people he met there didn't look at him penetratingly; they couldn't – they had crooked faces, just as he did now.

It was on these walks that he realised Georgie was wrong. His affair with Hazel hadn't been a fling or a delirium or an act of hatred against the woman he'd just married. He really did love her. The love stayed with him now like a bleeding stump, quite useless for everyday life and he couldn't let himself acknowledge it when he was trying to comfort Georgie and assuage her guilt. But he took it with him on these dingy walks and grew familiar with its weight and the warmth of its torn edges.

Later, he met Nye on the Bartraeth road, just past the roundabout. He didn't hit him or curse him. He didn't spit. Nye didn't say he was sorry.

'Take it,' said Tom, holding out the cheque.

'I can't. It was my wedding present to you.'

'You must. We can't keep it and live there. If you don't take it, we'll move out.'

'But how can you afford it?'

'That's not your problem. Or any of your business.'

'No.' Nye took the cheque, gently. He looked rough. His face was puffy and his eyes shiny and not at peace. 'I'm moving to Bristol,' he said.

'I know. Your mother told me.'

'Hazel's coming with me.'

'I know that too.'

'What about you?'

That was the moment to keep silent. Tom looked at Nye, knee-deep in the cow parsley, holding his cheque.

'We're going away too. Abroad for a year.'

'How come?'

'We're going to Cyprus. Georgie's arranged it all. She's going to teach in an army junior school. I'll teach sketching or drive a taxi, whatever.'

'Oh.' Nye seemed to search for a way to react. Behind his blankness, Tom saw, he was sick. There was contamination in his face. Tom stared at him, repelled but wanting to press himself closer. His own eyeballs burned. 'Well,' Nye said, 'good luck.'

'And you.'

'When you get back – well, who knows?'

'Sure.'

'You can find me through RCL. Or my mother. If you want, that is.' Nye leaned over him, his face white. Tom turned, inch by inch, without dropping his head, and watched the road.

'See you, Nye,' he said.

He had seen Nye; did see him. He could still remember picking up the telephone after their return to Wales and hearing Nye's voice. Tom hadn't been surprised. He hadn't even hesitated long. Four seasons of Cypriot sun had put a red-brown tinge in his skin. There was a baby at the Islyn. He'd driven east across the bridge feeling strong, with magnanimity to spare. Looking back on it now, that confidence seemed more far-fetched than anything.

There had been many encounters since, but the trouble was, he couldn't remember them clearly. Nye, he knew, would have them all stored inviolate, but for Tom there was too much friction; scenes from one transposed themselves to another. Intimacy punched holes.

He remembered a roadside café just off the M4, full of senior citizens. A park in Ealing. Confessing, when tired and battered after many bad months, that Georgie no longer drew; and Nye listening hard, his face still, his eyes guarded. That had been in winter – they had been indoors, a pub or a restaurant with a fire. It had been Tom's turn to listen in warmer weather. He could still hear the lack of resonance in Nye's voice as he talked about Hazel and their marriage. The dark flow of hope and a rage he'd thought was over – yes, they had come back to Tom in spring, out of doors, where there was grass and water and a white building.

What had he got from today? Nothing so vital. The smell of the pub and a mouth sticky with jam. And this small anger that whirled round inside him like grit in a quarry.

Tom pushed his plate away. It was ten to twelve; Nye's mind would be on his speech and it was time Tom paid and got on with his day. There was no one to distract him; no prospect of Nye going to a public telephone after his speech and calling him back. Because he realised now that Nye hadn't wanted to see him. Eight months had gone by since their last meeting and it had been Tom who'd phoned Nye at the hotel. Nye hadn't told him he was coming to Wales. He'd left without mentioning the future.

Tom recognised the signs. Nye was going to vanish again. Now that Tom was beginning to claw back a bit of strength, and get the measure of living like this, Nye was going to remove himself further.

For ever? No: Nye might have new smile lines but he had been in pain this morning. Tom thought of his bent head and the flesh not quite under control. He could still threaten Nye then: he and the ghosts of Bartraeth. Surprised to find you can still hurt, is it?

Well, that was something. But of course Nye could hurt; after what had happened they were all injured and just because they didn't see each other's wounds that didn't mean that they were free from cross-infection.

Tom stood up and dug in his pocket for change; the coins clashed noisily into the saucer. He left the café and turned left, breathed in the petrol-chilled air, walked quickly to where he'd left the car. Once again, it was Nye who had broken away. But he'd be back. In the meantime Tom had things of his own to do. Healings to begin and silences to keep.

Part Four

18

Tom was thinking of nothing much when he stepped out of the car that afternoon. He'd come to the village to get ice creams: Rhyn Row was still in the afternoon sun and the door to the shop stood open. Warmth slid over his face and forearms. He strolled across the road, listening to the yell of a radio down by the river and the clink of someone hammering in a garage. It was May and the leaves were thick on the bushes and trees, disguising the scrubby look the village sometimes had.

Tom's mouth was dry. His tongue felt coated with paint-dust and he looked forward to the taste of the lolly. One of those orange ones, packed with sugar. He picked at the paint under his nails: it was odd how having his fingertips blocked up made him feel that his skin couldn't breathe properly. Or perhaps it had been the sight of Ieuan and the others sprawled bare-chested on the grass. These days he noticed new growth in their bodies almost every time he saw them. Ieuan was bulking out and the Jacob's ladder on his abdomen was darkening. Robbie had grown inches since Christmas. Even skinny Huw was developing prominent sinews.

His eyes were dazzled by the sunshine and when he entered the shop it took him a second to adjust. He saw Mrs Howard's white hair like an aureole and the pale shirt of the woman in front of him. Then he recognised Sandra Vannis, one of the generation who had been coming into the village during the last five years, since they'd built the new houses. She was leaning on the fridge talking and she turned and nodded at him, stepping out of his way without breaking her flow.

'. . . A terrible lot of work,' she was saying. 'She's had to give him a list of builders and decorators to take up there with him. Roy Evans estimates there's three months' work to be done, because all the plumbing will have to be replaced.'

It wasn't a very interesting conversation, and Tom edged round Sandra politely, trying to see into the fridge.

'The window frames have rotted,' said Mrs Howard. 'And the garden – well, it's been neglected that long, it's like a waste-ground.'

Tom leaned over one corner of the fridge, trying to see through the condensation on the cover. Mrs Howard watched him with an interested air. 'Good afternoon, Tom.'

'Good afternoon, Mrs Howard. Can I have a quick look in the fridge?'

'You can, Tom. Ice creams, is it? Can you move your bag, Sandra, then I can open the top for Mr Griffiths.'

He admired the deft assignment of names and positions in the hierarchy.

'Thanks,' he said to Sandra, as she heaved her bag out of his way. He opened the fridge and leaned in, breathing in the frozen steam and the smell of ice as he hunted, and Sandra said something else which he didn't hear.

'Well,' said Mrs Howard. 'I wouldn't want to take it on, but then I haven't got that kind of money. Most people haven't. It's all right for some, isn't it? Fair play, though, he has worked hard for it.' Her voice sounded very clear, as if she were speaking directly down at Tom. There was a little pause, and then in a more distant tone she said: 'Do you want anything else now? No? That's seventy pence then, please.'

Tom's mind had gone still. Mrs Howard's words and Sandra's of a minute earlier suddenly hung round his head, frozen like the small agglomerations of ice in here. He inspected their possible meaning, and failed to know what to think. He picked up the ice creams (an orange lolly for himself, a Mivvi for Georgie, three choc ices for the boys) and straightened. Mrs Howard was giving Sandra her change. He waited while Sandra gathered her purchases, said her goodbyes and left.

'Can you wrap them in newspaper for me, please, Mrs Howard? I've got to drive them back to the Islyn.'

'Been sent out for them, have you?'

'Oh, I offered. Ieuan and his friends have taken over the garden and I can't concentrate on work.'

'It's Saturday.' Mrs Howard glanced at his paint-crusted hands. She pulled a newspaper out from behind the counter and rolled the ice creams into a cylinder, her knuckles bending and springing, her very white hair bobbing against her dark brows.

'There's interesting news about the vicarage,' she said. 'Isn't it?'

'What's that?'

'You haven't heard? Sandra was just telling me. There's a family thinking of buying it.'

'The vicarage? You mean Plas Bryn?' Tom wasn't in doubt, only playing for time.

'Yes, the old vicarage. A car went up there half an hour ago. A big, dark blue car, a Jaguar I think it was.'

Tom felt in his pocket for change.

'How much is that, Mrs Howard?'

'Two pound fifty.'

He counted it out and took the cool package from her. 'Any idea who they are?'

'Oh yes. Sandra's sister works for Evans and Evans, so she has it all first hand. It's Nye Mathias and his family.'

There was a ping from the till, a pause as the drawer slid open and Mrs Howard looked directly at him. 'You were friends,' she said.

'Yes. I remember.'

'It's good for the village that he's coming back.'

'No doubt.'

'If he does come.'

'Yes, if.'

The shopkeeper's eyes were vague.

Tom took his cue and left. Outside, the warmth of Rhyn Row flooded him. He walked steadily across the Tarmac. His car sat by the kerb in full sunlight, its windows open, and he got in, started the engine and performed a lovely three-point turn. Mrs Howard watched him as he drove down to the river and took the road along the bottom of the valley.

So, fourteen years after he'd last seen him, Tom understood that Nye Mathias was coming back. He'd always believed Nye would return. But he'd got out of the habit of expecting it. So it was, of course, inevitable that it should happen like this – undramatically, when Tom was looking the other way.

Nye had already come back. He was up there now, inside the Plas Bryn fences, at the top of the hill. At the thought of the dark blue car standing beneath the trees, Tom was tempted to turn his own battered Metro across the river, to twist up to Plas Bryn by another route and spy on them. He could imagine them all standing in front of the house like little plastic figures used to decorate a cake. The Mathias family: father, mother and their two children.

He didn't succumb to the temptation. Instead he drove straight home, thinking of the ice creams and of what he would say to his wife.

She was where he'd left her. Georgie lay on her stomach a few yards away from Ieuan and his friends. She had her chin on her hands and her eyes were closed. Her pupils, Tom thought, would be surprised to see their head teacher like that: she was very different at school.

The boys had spread themselves further across the grass. Their possessions – folders, personal stereos, drinks – now occupied half the lawn and as he approached, Ieuan and Robbie were already moving restlessly. Knees bent, shoulders now smooth, now jerky; heads turning with no sense of caution. Tom felt the economy of his own movements in comparison. He stopped and laid the package down in front of them.

'Ice creams,' he said, pulling the newspaper so that it unravelled in one movement. He picked up the lollies and went across to Georgie. 'Ice cream,' he said again, touching the red lolly to her bare arm.

The studio was muggy despite the open windows. He opened the skylight and stood beneath it, in the weak current of air. The paintings looked overworked to him now; they lacked vitality. He looked at the colours and tried to blank out the last additions of blue. What had possessed him to try and layer in subtlety like that, as if it was something you could add? It had closed the paintings down. It had – no; he mustn't start that kind of analysis. He mustn't look at the work any more; his eyes were seeing false now.

But he didn't want to go outside either. He couldn't pretend to relax with Georgie in the garden, knowing what he knew. He wasn't ready to tell her yet. It would have to come soon but not quite yet. He could go for a walk or a drive: he had enough errands waiting to be done, the last batch of prints was still waiting at the framer's and the car needed its exhaust replacing. They were his jobs, now he had the extra money coming in from the evening classes. But at the thought of going out through the gate, and crossing the rippling land where roads and lanes intersect, he found himself walking deeper into the studio.

He picked up his brushes in their pots of water and carried them to the sink. He began the methodical business of emptying out and pouring fresh, splaying the bristles beneath the stream of tap water, sponging, humming under his breath.

★ ★ ★

The kitchen was pooled with light and some more of Ieuan's friends had just arrived at the annexe door. Tom could hear his son's voice welcome them and he tried to tell from the sudden increase in bass notes how many there were. Only one or two, he thought. Perhaps Robbie coming back, with a friend. Music was coming from Ieuan's open windows – Huw's choice by the sound of it, ambient stuff. The half-melody pulsed along the side of the house and in through their own open pane.

Georgie was drinking red wine and mixing a mustard and brown sugar paste to paint on the ham. Tom was shelling broad beans. He tried to stop himself looking over the annexe roof to the upper slopes of Penllwyn hill.

It was impossible to give the news well and he didn't try. 'Nye Mathias is coming back,' he said.

Georgie was silent for a while and he thought she might not have caught it.

'Nye's coming—'

'Yes, I heard.'

'He's looking at Plas Bryn. He was there today.'

Georgie was looking past him, towards the window. Involuntarily, she lifted her head towards the hilltop.

'How do you know?'

'Mrs Howard told me. She had it from someone called Sandra, whose sister works with Roy Evans.'

'Sandra Vannis. She's got a daughter in school. Lee Anne.'

'Probably. She's fair-haired, good-looking. In her twenties. I've seen her round a bit.'

'You met her at the fête; she was in charge of the trampoline.'

'If you say so. She seemed very in with Mrs Howard, very up on what's going on.'

'She's a Penllwyn prime mover. I like her but her husband's a pain. He's flashy and callow and works in PR at Oshami.'

'Why are we talking about the Vannises instead of the Mathiases?'

'I don't want to talk about the Mathiases. I've got nothing to say about them, or to them. If they come here,' she turned and looked evenly at him, 'I won't see them.'

'Georgie, we'll have to. They've got children. You'll probably have one of them in school.'

'I'm sure I'm professional enough to manage that.'

'What if they come to school functions? He's rich, he'll probably make donations. What's going to happen when we meet them in the street, for Christ's sake?'

Georgie stared up at him. Her long neck was bent and held peculiarly still. 'You've been to see them.'

'No.'

'Do you swear?'

Tom raised his eyebrows. 'Do I have to?'

She put down the teaspoon she'd been holding, but didn't move towards him. It was as if she wanted to be sure of facing him with no distractions, and nothing to take away from her seriousness. 'Tom, when they come back, I don't want you to see him.'

He laughed. 'You can't ask that.' Even with his mind in disarray, he was astonished.

'I am asking it.'

'You can't. Nye and I had a history before you—'

'But it comes down to you and me now. And I can't stand it if it all starts again. I can't stand it.'

'It won't start again. Even if I see Nye, I won't see her. You don't have to ask me that, I'll promise you.'

'I'm not talking about *her*!' Georgie began to cry, quite silently. The tears slid down her face yet her expression didn't change at all.

Tom couldn't touch her at first. His mind was full of Nye and Hazel. His reactions were snarled up. Then he went and put his arms round her but Georgie had already seen; her hands were up, protecting her face.

19

Work started on Plas Bryn within a week and went on for two months. Tom heard about it from several people in the village, especially the older ones. He saw amusement and a sharpening interest in some of their faces, and resigned himself to their observations.

'Finding out about the vicarage, is it? You'll be wanting to know what your friend's doing with the place.'

'Hazel Mathias has been over several times. She comes in the week, usually.'

'He's a bright spark, that Nye Mathias. Wouldn't you say, Tom? Oh aye, very bright.' That one from Vern Jennings, leaning on his stick in the middle of the pavement, smiling widely.

Tom was never going to be sure how they had got hold of the truth. He and Georgie hadn't told anyone; it wouldn't have come from Nye and Hazel. Yet certain people in Penllwyn had known at once. The morning after the fire, when he'd walked down from Plas Bryn into the village, he'd found the streets and shops unusually full. Faces had been turned to him intently, eyes looking at the flecks of ash that still clung to his clothes. Greetings had been muted.

Later, when the show was cancelled, the same people had asked him careful questions, listened to the story of the burst pipe in the studio and nodded their heads. Then they had gone away, murmuring.

They'd known, all right. Tom had seen the knowledge in the way they'd looked at him, heard it in the trailing ends of their conversations. Phrases which might have belonged to many other topics but which, he felt sure, dealt with him: *a shame. No more than he asked for. All turned to ashes in his mouth now, isn't it?*

The talk had been well guarded. At least, the new people who moved into the village never seemed aware of it. It was only some of the older ones, now and then. Sometimes, when news of Nye or a development in Tom's career revived their interest, Tom would hear the dissonance in their voices again.

And he would almost be able to see them in their houses that night: awake and curious, moving from window to window, knocking on walls, looking up at the hilltop to see what he and Georgie were also seeing – that mad brightness.

The reflection of it could still be glimpsed in their faces. Like now, in Vern Jennings's crafty gaze.

Tom stepped back on his heels and felt his veins lighten.

'He was always clever, Vern,' he said. 'But I don't remember you being a particular fan of his. What's brought on the turnaround?'

'Oh, I give credit where it's due. He might have been a sly little beggar when he was a lad, but he's done well as a man.'

'Yes. He's well respected.'

'And he's made a lot of money for himself.'

'And he's bringing work to the area. The new Meifan factory will be employing over a hundred.'

'None of them union members.'

'I hear the pay's quite good.'

'You've still got a lot of time for him then, have you?' Vern peered up at him; he was taller than Tom really, but his back was bent these days and he had a trick of holding his head on one side as well.

'We grew up together, Vern. Why wouldn't I have time for him?'

'Oh aye. You've been up to have a look around Plas Bryn then, have you?'

'No. I thought it'd be nice if one or two of us waited to be invited.'

'Well, you're missing a treat. They're stripping off the old paper and painting the walls, taking down all the low ceilings Wyn Pritchard spent so much money having put in. They're even opening up the fire places so they can have coal fires – never mind the central heating. When it's finished, it'll look as good as old!' Vern's chuckle made him cough.

'I expect Nye wants it to be like he remembers it.'

'What, draughty and ugly? Oh well, who am I to argue with a young man with money? A regular squire we're getting, if his mother's to be believed. A few crumbs are all we ask, eh, Tom? He might commission you to do a portrait – Aneurin Mathias and family, in Mathias Hall.'

Tom laughed outright. 'Have you ever seen one of my paintings, Vern?'

'Hmmm. Of course I have. But our Nye must like them, mustn't he, because they tell me he's got several in his office over in Bristol. I dare say they'll be coming to Meifan with him. If you play your cards right, boy, you could get yourself a patron.'

Vern's eyes widened, then disappeared among his wrinkles. He jabbed Tom's arm and went off, hawking.

A few days later, Tom met Georgie in Bartraeth. She'd been in an LEA meeting that afternoon and he'd been teaching as usual. She was sitting on the terrace of The Star, her jacket pulled tight against the strong breeze. She was obviously upset. There seemed to be a lot of spare flesh around her mouth.

'What's the matter?' Tom asked, kissing her. She folded her newspaper and put it into her briefcase.

'Good news!' Her voice was false. 'I needn't have worried about having Nye's son in school. I've just heard that they were over at St Joseph's yesterday, enrolling him there. That's good, isn't it? So I don't-have-to-worry.' The last words came out in rhythm with her deft finger movements as she pulled her wine glass towards her and drank.

'No, you don't. So what's up?'

'Nothing. That's what I said. Nothing.'

'That's why you're rigid with fury, is it?'

Georgie gave him an unfriendly look.

'You always exaggerate when you want to belittle me.'

'I'm sorry. But I don't understand. The last I heard,' Tom enunciated clearly, a trick he'd learnt from Georgie, 'you were desperate not to have the boy in school. What's changed?'

Georgie sipped again and replaced her glass on the beer mat. She centred it, angrily. 'I wasn't "desperate". I always knew I could deal with it. True, I didn't enjoy the thought of meeting Nye and Hazel at open evenings, but as I told you, I'm professional enough to handle that.'

'Still, now you won't have to.'

'No, not now that I've been passed over. You see what he's doing, don't you? He's trying to make out that we don't count for anything with him. That's why he's never stopped the car when he's seen us, though he stops it for other people, and that's why a school run by me isn't good enough for his child.'

Tom sat down at the edge of the table. 'Has he seen us in the car? I've never seen him. Or only at a distance.'

'Well, I have. And he's seen me.'

'Oh.' Tom felt a twist of jealousy; he looked for the dark blue car every time he went through. 'Well, he was hardly going to stop and get out in Penllwyn, with everyone looking on, was he?'

'It wasn't in Penllwyn, it was up by the school.'

'Oh.'

'Yes, oh. It was midmorning, last Tuesday, and I wouldn't have seen him if I hadn't gone out to check the nature pond. He was parked up in Hillside; I saw him getting in to his car. He must have been walking round up there, looking.'

'So he is interested in the school.'

Georgie shot him a fierce glance. 'In that case, he'd have got in touch. He'd have come to the school like any prospective parent – with her. They normally come in pairs,' she added, with unnecessary sarcasm. 'But they haven't come at all. They've gone to St Joseph's.'

'Perhaps they prefer private schools. Nye was never exactly a radical.'

'The girl's going to the Traeth.'

Tom looked at Georgie. She sat very upright in her linen suit. Her anger was palpable; it emanated from her in waves.

'Are you angry because the boy's going to St Joseph's or because you think Nye's been spying on you?'

'Oh, I expect Nye to spy on us. I'm sure he'll go spying round all over the place, he always did.'

'So?'

'Jesus, Tom, it's the insult. After what he's done to us, he dares to come back here and play the lord and master. Picking and choosing, turning his back on my school without even the bother of a visit. Everyone knows who he is; it's important where he sends his children. This is so bloody slighting.' She looked back at him. 'Don't you care at all?'

'Yes.'

'You don't show it.'

Tom stood up. 'There's not much room for me to show anything these days. I'm going inside, it's cold.'

He was glad she didn't follow him. The pub lighting was soupy and he sat at the bar and drank a whisky, then a beer. A group of nurses sat at the nearest table, smoking heavily. He wanted a cigarette. There was a machine by the toilets but if he bought a packet and Georgie came in to find him smoking, she'd know how shaken he was.

He kept seeing her as he'd left her, sitting on the iron chair. Her hair was pushed behind her ears and frustrated energy swarmed all over her.

Georgie was in prison again. She put herself there, of course, and he knew better than to try and help her. All he could do was get away. It seemed to get harder to bear as he got older – Georgie's terrible look of paralysed desire. She was like a cat trying to spring, all her muscles taut and extended, unable to leave the ground. It was always the same, no matter what circumstance produced it.

The time he'd nearly been picked for the big British Council show. They'd been so certain, he'd left their restaurant table to make an impulsive phone call. He remembered coming back into the room more slowly, and seeing her bright face change.

There had been the morning she'd told him she wanted to leave him for Martin Heylop – and hadn't.

And there were always those moments, random and unpredictable, when she looked at other people's work and her body seemed to tighten.

Always the same thwarted energy. In the old days when Tom had been more brutal, he'd gone on the attack. 'I'm sick of your fucking self-punishment! It doesn't help you and it certainly doesn't help me. Why should I have to carry you on my back each time I pick up a brush?'

He'd long since abandoned those tactics. Now he encouraged, when encouragement didn't seem too cruel and when he knew that to paint was what she wanted. But often he couldn't tell what she wanted. It seemed inchoate, or hidden.

The clock behind the bar showed twenty past six; Georgie had been alone outside for nearly ten minutes. She must be chilled through. Unless she'd gone home. But as he sat scrunched up on his stool, Tom saw the door open in the bar mirror. Georgie walked up to him and touched his arm. She looked refreshed; there was only a hint of effort in the lift of her head. 'I'm better now. We should be going if we want to catch the early film.'

20

The lorry was diagonally across the road, tail against the hedge, the cab not quite able to make the turn into the quarry lane. A horn sounded from beyond it. Tom switched off his engine and got out.

'What are you trying to do?' he called up into the cab.

'Sorry, mate,' said the driver. He was a young man and looked humiliated. 'But I've got to get up here. If the arsehole in front of me would shut up and reverse I'd have more room.'

'But there's nothing up there, just the old quarry.'

'What? It's a house. I've got it on here.' He jabbed a piece of paper at Tom: a hand-drawn map, with an arrowed line leading to a square, and instructions written alongside it. Hazel's handwriting hadn't changed at all.

'No, you want Plas Bryn. It's a quarter of a mile further on.'

'Shit.'

'I'll get this car to pull back for you. Don't worry, you've got enough room to get free.'

'Thanks. Sorry, mate.'

They went on slowly, in convoy. When they approached the Plas Bryn turn-off, Tom flashed and tooted his horn. The driver gave him the thumbs-up out of the window. Tom kept well back while the driver manoeuvred. A line of trees hid the house and its land from the road. He couldn't see what was happening in the drive, and when the lorry stopped with half its length sticking out he assumed it was a problem with the angle. It was only when he got out of the car to go and help that he saw the gleam of other vehicles parked further up and heard voices.

He stood in the lane, listening intently. Hazel's voice hadn't changed much. It was quick and light, friendlier than he remembered. He'd have recognised it in the street. The wind disturbed the Plas Bryn branches and for a second he saw her, standing by the cab of the lorry. He felt no emotion other than curiosity. He got back into his car as quietly as he could.

Ieuan was waiting for him in Greg's workshop. A radio was playing and Greg was working on a blue van. Ieuan was intent on his bike. He'd taken one of the side panels off and screws and washers were in neat alignment on the floor.

'Sorry I'm late, Ieu.'

'That's all right. Greg says the shaft's gone. He reckons we need to order the exact replacement but that'll take a week. He's got a second-hand one here that's almost the same. I reckon it'll do in the meantime.'

'I wouldn't if I were you,' said Greg from the van bonnet.

'He just has to say that in case I sue him later,' said Ieuan.

'That's right,' said Greg.

'Have a look, Dad.'

Squatting down by Ieu, Tom lined up his eye with the shaft. He had to press against Ieuan's shoulder to do it and that made him realise that not only was Ieuan now half an inch taller than he was, but he would soon be broader too. Ieuan was going to take after Georgie's father. 'It's proud, Ieu. A millimetre or so. You'd do better to get the right part, like Greg says.'

'I can make it fit, though, if I use a smaller washer here.'

'You'd have to knock it with a hammer to get it in, and then you risk damaging it.'

'No, I reckon I can do it.'

Ieuan shifted his fingers around the edge of the shaft, infinitesimally. Bigger and rangier than his parents, he'd inherited their manual confidence. A household full of people who knew how to use their hands. Tom had never bothered to teach Ieu dexterity; nor, as far as he knew, had Georgie; Ieuan had simply picked it up from observation. Tom remembered Nye sitting at the kitchen table in number three Foel Close saying: 'Show me again. You balance the coin like this, on the nails of your index and middle fingers and then you flip, using your thumb as release mechanism.'

The rain fell with concentration, pressing down on them like wands. By the time they reached the back door they were soaked. Ieuan put the takeaway bag inside his jacket while Tom let them in. 'No Mum?' Ieuan said when he'd stripped his jacket off; he began taking the cartons out of the bag and feeling them for warmth. Tom went to the hall and listened to the messages on the answering machine.

'No Georgie till later. She says it's going well so she wants to stay and get as much done as she can.'

'She works harder at half term than on schooldays.'

'I'll see if I can get her to take Friday off at least.'

'These need heating,' said Ieuan.

Tom turned to the cooker and squatted over the dial. 'Shit, I can't see for water in my eyes. Throw me a tea towel.' He wiped his face and lit the oven. At the table Ieuan was prising the lids off the cartons. 'Thanks, pass them over. Jesus, I've even got water down my neck. I'm going to change.'

'Can I pour some beers?'

'Sure.'

Tom felt jittery. When he took his jumper off he saw his excess skin and the downward pull of his muscles. He was older, his face had more planes than it used to have. He smiled: the expression slid behind the surface, quite confident. He put on a T shirt and a shirt and went back to the kitchen. Ieuan had made a symmetrical arrangement of the heated-up cartons and set out two plates. He'd drawn two beers from the barrel, with too much head on as usual.

'Great,' said Tom and sat down. He thought Ieuan looked at him curiously, but he just nodded and gave Tom a spoon. They served themselves and ate with concentration.

Half an hour later the table was covered with near-empty aluminium cartons. There was too much for only two people, but they ate on, picking at the remains. 'Well, there's no point keeping it,' Ieuan said. 'It only sits in odds and ends in the fridge and then I eat it cold for breakfast, and regret it.'

Tom raked the last of the rice out of the carton. 'I regret it too. If you didn't always eat it for breakfast I could have it for lunch sometimes.'

'You have lunch with Mum in the holidays. Usually.' Ieuan inspected the last of the vegetables. 'Is Mum OK?'

Tom swallowed his mouthful of beer. 'Yes and no, I suppose is the honest answer to that. Sorry about the fights.'

'That's all right.' Ieuan shrugged. 'You don't have that many and they're none of my business anyway.' He paused. 'So what was this morning's about?'

'Three guesses. Those people who are coming back to Plas Bryn, the Mathiases.'

'Oh them. Your long lost old friends that you hate.'

'That's them.'

'God, they're not even here yet.' Ieuan pushed his plate away.

'What did you fall out about anyway?'

'The usual things – money, sex, power. Treachery and betrayal. Sometimes all on the same night.'

'Yeah, that's what I'd heard. Only joking,' Ieu added as Tom looked up. 'But Mum'll be all right with them really, won't she? Huw says he'd back her in a fight against anyone. Even Aneurin Mathias.'

'You've been talking about it then?'

'Well, only a bit.' Ieuan looked awkward. 'I didn't need to, anyway. There are bits of talk going round about you and him.'

'Yes, there's bound to be.' Tom drained his beer. 'Do you want another one? So,' he picked up Ieuan's glass and went over to the barrel, 'what are they saying?'

'Mainly that he's a bastard and doesn't care who he steps on, and that you and he hate each other's guts.'

'You don't want to believe all you hear.' Tom drew the beer carefully into Ieuan's glass. 'Look, that's how you get the head right.' He passed it to Ieuan and served himself. But his hand jerked and froth spilled over the rim on to his wrist.

'Whoops,' said Ieuan. Tom grimaced and drank. He could remember the taste of another beer, nineteen years ago. It was nearly seven o'clock and warm. There were forty-eight hours to go before Nye's birthday party. He saw Nye enter the city pub and work his way across. There was the smell of Hazel in Tom's hair, the memory of her in his eyes and there was Nye walking towards him, putting aside the other drinkers with gentle hands.

21

The Mathiases moved in on a Thursday. Two pantechnicons took their belongings up the hill and the family followed in a dark blue car. The men were up there all afternoon. Towards five o'clock, a smaller red car – which no one had seen before – came down the hill. Mrs Mathias and the boy and girl crossed Rhyn Row and went into Lower Shop.

Stopping off for milk on the way home, Tom heard about it. When he went back to the car, he glanced over the bridge at the road rising behind the trees but nothing looked different. 'They're in,' he said to Georgie.

22

He knew who it was at once: the black hair had tufts of white now and the shoulders were thicker. In fact, Nye's upper arms were huge. Tom's hands probably wouldn't meet round them.

Nye paid for his evening paper and turned. He was still half smiling from the pleasantries at the counter when he saw Tom.

'Tom!'

'Hello, Nye.'

'Tom.' Nye's gaze locked on to his. For a second Tom was surprised at how far apart Nye's eyes were – or was it just the effect of his face having broadened? 'Christ,' Nye dropped his voice, 'you startled me. I've been expecting to see you all week. I might have known you'd creep up behind me.' He smiled more fully as he touched Tom's arm. 'It is you. It's good to see you. How are you?'

Tom wished he hadn't had that drink; he must smell of it. 'Very well,' he said. 'Welcome back.'

'Thank you.'

'How does it feel?'

Nye hitched up one side of his mouth. 'Well, it's good not to be living up and down the motorway any more. I'm not sure, to tell you the truth.'

'Too much on?'

'I'm busy, yes. But it's more a question of – how do you measure change? We've been doing business down here for a while now; it's not as though I've just arrived. I've been in the area several times a week, at least, for the last few months.'

'Yes, I'd heard you'd been down a lot.'

'I didn't see you,' Nye said. 'I thought I would; I looked out for you.'

'I'm not often over Meifan way.'

'Neither am I, if I've any say in the matter.' Nye laughed – the small chuckle he used to give for private jokes. 'Oh the business park's all right, but I prefer to do my work in cities.' He paused. It was a friendly pause. Tom looked at him – they were standing very close and he could see the grain of Nye's skin and the long lines round his eyes. Nye's mouth opened in a smile. But so far, his physical presence was muted. Tom held himself tense, waiting for the sense of encroachment. It didn't come. 'You look well,' Nye said.

'I am.'

'And Georgie?'

'Yes, she's well too.'

'I read the reviews of your last show. You must have been pleased.' Ah, there it was. Nye hadn't moved towards him but it was as if he'd laid an imaginary hand on Tom; only a very light one though.

'Yes,' said Tom easily. 'It's nice to get some applause now and again.'

'Some? It was a bit more than that. I wish I could have gone to the show myself, but I was away so much at the time. Hazel went, though.'

Tom nodded. He was puzzled. The imaginary touch was still there, but doing nothing. He couldn't begin to think what he was supposed to say about Hazel. For a second he wondered if Nye was lying, but that would be pointless as well as dangerous, so early in the game.

Nye was watching him. 'I heard you on the radio a while back,' he said. 'You were talking about working on a series. "Sediments", isn't it?'

'That's right.'

'And Hazel said you were mentioned in a piece in the *Independent* last week, on artists tipped to break in America. It's all encouraging stuff, isn't it?'

Tom nodded. He had a sense of over-proximity now, but it was not a physical closeness. He was aware of Greg serving a customer behind them, rather quietly.

'Oh well, the papers,' he said. 'They go in cycles, don't they? We don't take too much notice of them, to be honest.'

'But things are swinging your way now in the market, aren't they? And among the critics. I gather you're almost a certainty for the Reynolds Monette shortlist.'

'Do you?'

'Ah. Sorry. Is it confidential?'

'No, it's just a rumour.' Tom looked blandly into Nye's face. If he went on looking and saying nothing, perhaps his reactions would die down and exactly the right comment would rise to his lips. Something to counteract the proprietorial note in Nye's voice, and take the acuteness from his gaze.

For Nye Mathias bought paintings. He was a collector in a moderate way, and had continued to buy during the recession. Karl had first brought his name up to Tom years ago, when Tom had just joined the gallery and they had sold the acrylic diptych to the Bristol dealer. 'Aneurin Mathias is getting quite a name for himself as a buyer. Perhaps he was your anonymous sale.' Tom had shrugged. Karl had taken the hint and changed the subject.

It had never been put so baldly again, but down the years Karl had continued to feed Nye's name into their conversations. Very little was truly confidential among dealers. Tom had always known that if he pushed, he could find out the identity of his anonymous buyers. Or buyer.

His reaction was under control now. He rolled his shoulders, a casual movement, to show he didn't need to defend himself.

'You're in the swim then, are you, Nye? A serious punter?' It sounded joky and slightly patronising.

'I keep up with artists I'm interested in, of course.' Nye didn't look offended. In fact, understanding gleamed in his eyes. 'And I get news from friends. Too much, by the sound of it. Though as a matter of fact, it was Hazel who told me that.'

'Not to worry.' Tom shrugged; he would not ask how she knew. He couldn't. This was like talking and trying to hold water in his mouth at the same time. 'How is Hazel?'

'She's fine.' Nye paused, smiled, and shifted his weight to the other foot. 'She's extremely busy – well, you can imagine, what with getting the house in order and organising the children. Did you know the house isn't finished yet?'

'I heard you still had plumbers at work.'

'Yes, we have only one semi-functioning bathroom and Elen's in it all the time. Fifteen-year-old girls – I promise you, you don't want to know.' Nye turned at a sound from behind him. 'Oh, excuse me. Are you trying to get through? Tom, we're blocking up the shop.'

Tom stepped back. 'Sorry, Mairwen.'

'Thank you. Excuse me.' Mairwen stared up into Nye's face as she went past. Her curiosity was evident and Nye nodded, with a slight hesitation. Tom could see his mental index flicking.

Mairwen, a little younger than me, don't recognise the face; someone's younger brother or sister; a neighbour of my mother's? Tom watched Nye observe her to the door. He was interested to see if Nye would ask him for information.

'Who's that?' Nye said, as soon as she'd gone out. 'Should I have remembered her?'

'Mairwen Lewis. She moved here after you left.'

'Ah, a newcomer.'

'Hardly, she's been here over ten years.'

'She looked at me pretty sharply, didn't she?'

'She's a friend of mine. She was probably interested to hear your rundown on my career.'

Nye returned his scrutiny to Tom. 'She looked nice,' he said.

'She is.'

There was another pause and Nye stepped away. 'Well, I must go. I've got Elen waiting for me across the road.' He gestured towards the window.

'Yes, I saw her.'

'Hmm, outside the rugby club. I've been over there talking to Phil Lloyd about doing some coaching. She's taken the opportunity to hang round after the school bus and talk to the sixth-form boys. She likes the Traeth, our daughter.' He looked quizzical; it reminded Tom of the old days, except that Nye did it more subtly now. 'She thinks it's a great improvement on Whitereed School for Girls.'

'It's a decent school. Ieuan likes it.'

'Ah yes.' Nye glanced out of the window. 'Is he over there now? I thought I might have seen him – a tallish boy, with Georgie's colour hair?'

'That's him.'

'He looks a nice lad. He plays for the club too, Phil was saying.'

'Yes, he's a winger.'

'I'll meet him then, in training.'

'I'll warn him.'

Nye's smile widened and deepened and Tom realised from the way the lines fell that he was seeing what had become a characteristic expression. 'Do that.' Nye turned as he spoke: despite being heavier, he moved more gracefully than in the past. He'd achieved balance.

'See you, then,' said Tom.

'Of course. You and Georgie must both come to Plas Bryn soon.'

'He asked us? He wasn't being serious. It was an insult.' Georgie sat under the chestnut tree, with a cluster of leaves bobbing above her head like a hat. The dappled light, and rancour, gave her face a greenish tinge. 'You didn't say we would, I hope.'

'I said that would be very nice.'

Georgie looked at him. He saw her struggle, trying to work out if he were joking. 'Did you?'

'Yes.'

'I don't believe you.'

'Well, it's true. I wasn't going to be rude. He extended a polite invitation, I gave a polite reply. What did you want me to do – hit him in the face with a rolled up copy of the *South Wales Echo*?' Tom felt his mouth curl into a smile and quickly picked up his beer glass. From round its edge he could see Georgie's hostile expression. He took a mouthful of beer: if he laughed now, he'd choke.

'It's not funny.'

He had to bang his glass down and put his hand over his mouth to try and keep the beer in.

'I'm not laughing, Tom. If you've agreed to go, you're contemptible. If this is a joke, it's pathetic.'

The urge to laugh vanished. Tom laughed anyway, to annoy her; it gave him a tiny irritable pleasure, like ant bites. He gnashed his teeth at her. 'You're not doing very well.'

'I'm not getting much help.'

'Tch. You'll have to loosen up. What are you going to do when he asks me why you no longer paint?'

'What do you mean?'

'I'll probably have to say "pass". Or lie. I'll need all the practice I can get.'

A second ago Georgie had looked as if she might start shaking, but now she folded her elbows in and watched him, furious and supple. 'Well?' he said.

'If Nye asks you anything about me, I hope you'll refuse to answer.' She was very precise, at her most headteacherly.

'Oh, I see. You're out of bounds in conversation, are you? Fair enough.' Tom felt the ants bite a little harder; the irritability was turning to anger. 'You've only spent twenty years telling me you can't paint because of what you and Nye did. I've only spent twenty years living with it. But I'll just go pretending to him that you're perfectly happy, shall I?'

'I'm sorry it's so painful for you.'

'No that's all right. It's been a barrel of laughs – your end of the studio sitting there bare like the Curse of Cornelian. It makes for a great atmosphere to work in. And when you *have* started on something, I can always ask myself – how long before she abandons this one? And will she white it out and start again or will the whole canvas go? Never mind, at least she pays for them.'

'I apologise. It must have been very hard.' Georgie's voice was contemptuous and she was still tucked into the bench, alert and angry. But she looked vulnerable suddenly. Her face seemed to have lost a layer of skin.

'Ah, Georgie. Shit.' Tom felt the familiar seep of remorse across his tongue, like sugar. 'I know it's been worse for you. A hundred bloody times worse. But can't you—?' His mouth worked, producing no sound.

'What?'

'I don't know. Jesus. You give Nye so much power this way. Stop it. Exorcise him.'

'I am trying.'

'You told me years ago you knew it wasn't really his fault. That it's only you stopping yourself painting.'

'Yes, I know.'

'Why do you do it to yourself? He doesn't. He hasn't been inhibited from building up his business, making himself fucking rich.'

'I know.'

'Well then.'

Georgie placed her hands flat down on the table, on either side of her glass. 'Because I don't want to be like Nye.'

'Well, don't be. Just forget him, wipe him out of the equation.' Georgie glanced up at him with a mixture of contempt and accusation. 'All right,' Tom said quickly. 'Not forget. But why do you still have to hate him so much?'

'Because,' she said steadily, 'he's a bad person.'

'Oh come on.'

Georgie was looking down again now. 'I believe he is.' Expressions Tom couldn't identify moved under her face and failed to come to the surface. It was oddly unpleasant: he didn't want to watch but felt he couldn't look away.

'If you remember,' he said flatly, 'I was the one who did the bad things back then.'

Georgie nodded, and this time she held his eyes for a few seconds. 'I remember,' she said quite humorously. She picked up her beer glass. Tom watched in relief and discomfort as her face went back to normal; the only difference was that now it was tired. She gave a biting smile. 'You and – oh, what's her name?'

He didn't know what to make of it. He was glad to have seen Nye, despite the fact that Nye was playing games; despite the foreboding that edged into him every time he thought about what would happen next.

Georgie was his main worry. He was used to carrying the weight of her guilt, and trying to mitigate her frustration. It was one of the great constants of his life: sticking with her as she tried to paint and failed; refused to try; went back to trying, approaching each attempt with a different kind of rage.

You'd think she would have exhausted them by now. But Tom knew better, just as he knew his own reassurances by heart.

You did not destroy my talent. You did not damage my talent. I lost confidence, sure, but confidence comes from within. Besides, it will return. It is returning.

And recently: *Look, love, look – can you see?*

Tom was worried about Georgie. He dreaded meeting Hazel. He didn't know what to expect next.

But he was pleased Nye was back.

The end of the summer term was always demanding. Georgie was checking reports and preparing next year's staff schedules. Tom was writing assessments, arguing about his own schedules, and in this last week of college, helping the third-year students mount their final shows. He left home before eight every morning and never returned before nine at night – later if he'd gone out for a drink with a colleague, or been taken for one by a grateful, half-mad third year.

It was a good time to be busy. It would have been embarrassing for either of them to be visible around the village while Hazel was settling in. Instead there was an atmosphere of camaraderie at the Islyn, with late-night snacks, showers and mutual end-of-year stories. Sometimes he took home a takeaway meal and served it to Georgie over her reports or in front of late night cop shows on the TV.

He had seen Nye on Monday. On the Wednesday it was Georgie's turn. Apparently she was in Bartraeth, on her way to visit the LEA, when she passed Nye in the street. He was with two other businessmen but he stepped away from them to greet her. Georgie told Tom about it that evening, reciting the stilted hellos with that biting humour again. 'I wasn't rude,' she said, 'because I thought of how you wouldn't like it. I wasn't even frosty.' Tom couldn't tell if she were mocking him or herself, but she seemed more cheerful.

Friday was the last full day of term. Tom's classes had already finished; by lunchtime he'd wound up his supervision interviews. Third-year hysteria was at its peak. He bought a bag full of provisions from the canteen and fought his way back past the offices to the exhibition hall.

At ten to three, he was sitting with a small group eating sandwiches and crisps, when he saw Hazel. She was in the entrance lobby, between the steps and the notice boards. She carried an information folder under one arm and a bag over her shoulder. She had come from the direction of the offices and she was looking for someone.

She was walking slowly, with a self-contained air, and her head moved casually from side to side. Tom shrank into his group. Marc Daniels shielded him unwittingly, and by leaning forward, he could watch Hazel's legs and blue skirt pass the other side of the glass doors and disappear to the left.

He sat for a while, chewing and listening to the others, then he brushed his hands and mouth and stood up. 'Excuse me a minute.' No sign of her. He hadn't imagined it. She had been there; but there would be a reason for it unconnected with him. The college was no longer the narrow arty place it had been; all kinds of courses and conferences took place here now. He walked up the steps and into the crowded lobby to make sure she was gone.

She was sitting on one of the seats by the new lifts, reading her leaflets. She wasn't reading very attentively, but glancing round, and she saw him within seconds. She held herself still, then put her hand on the leaflet, sat up straight and nodded at him.

By the time he was within talking distance, she was standing up. She looked wary, nervous even. Older of course. Her nose seemed longer and her brow bone more prominent.

She was well dressed and carefully – neater than he remembered. Several emotions were present in her face: one of them, he was sure, was anger, but a peculiar openness was imposing itself over it.

'Tom. I thought you might be here.'

'Hello, Hazel.'

'I haven't come to see you. I was picking up some information.' She gestured down at the folder on the seat.

'Yes, I can see. How are you? Welcome back.'

'Thank you.'

She obviously had something else to say. Tom was silent – both to let her say it, and because he felt dumb. He and she were changed people, with twenty years protecting them, but they had the same bodies and the same eyes, and their shared history was more strongly present than he'd expected. Hazel didn't blush but her face seemed to close up slightly.

'Nye said he'd met you the other day,' she said, 'in the village.'

'Yes, in Greg's shop. It was good to see him.'

'He mentioned that you and Georgie might come up to the house for a drink.'

'Yes, he mentioned it to me too. Just a suggestion.'

'Do you think you will?' She spoke quickly and it made the question sound furtive, even though she was looking at him very straight.

Tom shook his head. 'No.'

'I thought not. I told him you probably wouldn't. Well, it was nice to see you.'

'And you.'

'I hope Georgie's meeting with Nye goes well.'

'What?'

'Yes, she'll be seeing him at a meeting today. The Meifan and Harborth Primary Heads Association – Georgie belongs to that, doesn't she? They're in talks with the Wellspring Trust about funding. Nye's recently become a trustee; he's going to be at the board meeting with the teachers today.'

'I see. Georgie doesn't know.'

'No, she wouldn't. He's only recently decided to take it on.'

'I see.' Which he did: he saw Nye, dexterously manoeuvring, his skills increased so that his large body moved with the minimum disturbance; and Hazel, telling him. Her expression had a hollowness that was quite deliberate, he thought. And now he saw that she was picking up her folder.

'I must go. You're obviously very busy today. Give my regards to Georgie, if she asks.'

23

Georgie was dismissive and amused. 'Yes, he did. Can you imagine it? Nye bringing a public affairs strategy to a bunch of primary heads. For God's sake.'

'Was he good?'

'Excellent.' Georgie laughed. It was a lovely July morning and sunlight jigged through the leaves of the hawthorn on to her hair. She put her coffee down on the grass, next to Tom's foot. 'He'll do us a lot of good. It could be worse, couldn't it?'

'It didn't upset you, then?'

'For two minutes, at the beginning. Shaking hands with him was a joy. But then I cancelled him out and started listening to what he said and it was fine. Even rather enjoyable, knowing that Nye will be bringing benefits to all these state schools.' Her smile started off as sharp, then widened. After a second she recalled it. 'Besides, now I know what his strategy is.'

'The good citizen act, you mean.'

'Mmm.' Georgie leaned back in the deckchair and half closed her eyes against the sun. 'Making contact publicly. Offering us of his best. He probably plans to become indispensable. Ah well.' She turned her face and sun pooled on her cheek.

Tom sipped his coffee. Georgie didn't seem inclined to say anything more so he asked, mildly: 'Don't you want to know how I know?'

'Let me guess. It's in there.' She gestured towards the newspapers he was holding. 'Nye told us Wellspring would be putting out a press release.'

'Ah.' Something Greg had said to him in the garage shop suddenly made sense. 'Yes, I dare say it is, but I haven't looked at the papers yet. Hazel told me. I saw her in Bartraeth yesterday.'

Georgie's eyes opened and her hand went up to shade them. For several seconds, she looked at Tom, but she didn't seem worried. 'How was it?' she asked.

'How do you think? Awkward. I think she was embarrassed about it.'

'About what? Nye or you?'

'Both.'

'Yes, I can imagine. It can't be easy being Hazel at the moment.' She paused, as if she expected him to speak. 'And what was it like for you?'

'Embarrassing. Awkward. Pretty crippling.'

I don't know, was the truth. I don't know what it was like. I'm standing here now in front of you, recounting it, because that's the deal between us, but I don't know what I mean.

Tom had spent the night failing. Failing to rest, next to Georgie, who had already been asleep when he came home. Failing to remember properly, or to understand. As the hours went by, he'd passed from relief at being awake alone, to curiosity. And then to wanting her help.

'So.' Georgie was giving him help now. 'What did you and Hazel establish for us? Are we friends? Enemies? Socially functioning?'

'We're acquaintances with a cripplingly embarrassing past. And yes, we can function.'

'If we choose to. What did she say about Nye seeing me?'

' "I think Nye and Georgie are going to a meeting together today." '

'They talk about us then.'

'I'm sure they discussed us in detail before they came back.'

'Are you?'

Tom shrugged. It didn't ease the crowded sensation round his head. He sat down on the grass beside her. 'You're not worried then, by having to work with Nye on these funding things.'

'Not really. At least he can't take me by surprise now. The first contact's over. So. What else did Hazel say?'

'Not much. She seemed to be doing a clearing-up operation after Nye, really. Said she knew Nye had asked us up to the house but she understood if we didn't want to go.'

'Our lady of the insight.'

He shrugged again. 'I told you, it was awkward.'

Georgie smiled: that sharp-toothed smile again. 'You feel sorry for her, don't you?' she asked.

What was the right answer to give to that? Tom looked up at her: half sitting, half lying in the deckchair, Georgie seemed at ease. Almost playful. Whatever had happened with Nye yesterday, she must feel she'd acquitted herself well.

'No, not really,' he said.

24

The summer was heavy and warm. There was often thunder that July: the sky went from blue to grey, the air swelled and then came the downpour. The grass was lush. Loose-strife and nettles grew thickly. Ieuan and his friends were always coming in soaking and drying off in his room with cups of coffee and the blow heater on, and the music turned up louder in competition.

In between the rain were clear spells – bright mornings and blowy afternoons, when the kids would be off meeting in groups.

Tom had a heavy schedule of teaching at the summer school. Georgie usually went visiting in the summer holidays, but not this year. She was busy too. She attended a computing course which lasted two weeks. She still had school business to see to – builders were working on the school roof and upgrading the gym – and she spent her leisure hours seeing exhibitions, films, and friends. She also went to a series of lectures at the college, on Durer's influence in modern figurative art.

They saw hardly anything of Nye and Hazel. With many of the local headteachers away, Wellspring meetings were suspended till the autumn. And Nye and Hazel made little showing in the village. Nor did the suggested invitation arrive.

Perhaps if it had been a dryer summer, Tom reasoned . . . but there was nothing wrong with this weather. In fact, it was like the summer that Tom remembered best from adolescence. Back then, on days that were bright and overcast by turns, the sky would sometimes drizzle for hours, forcing them indoors until sooner or later the sun poured in again and irradiated their cigarette smoke, lit Nye's arm hairs to brown-gold. If Tom had these memories, he knew Nye would too – after all, many of them were located on Plas Bryn ground. The house had been empty then and they'd had to prise boards off the window frames to get in.

But Nye didn't get in touch.

★ ★ ★

It was evening and Tom, having taken a late class, was calling at the rugby club on his way home, to give Ieuan a lift. Training was obviously over and the pitch was empty, except for three men standing on the touchlines. From halfway down the hill, Tom knew Nye was one of them; when he was nearer he recognised the others as Phil Lloyd and Edward Davies. He parked the car in the road and walked round the railings towards them.

Nye saw him as soon as he left the car, and kept half watching him all the way in. He didn't show any particular reaction. As Tom cut across the grass and the other men turned as well, Tom waited for a gleam of acknowledgement, or perhaps surprise, to enter Nye's face, but none came.

'Hello, Tom,' said Phil.

'Evening.' Tom said it to all three.

'Hello there.' Edward's greeting was on the heavy side, but then that was to be expected. He'd been sardonic with Tom for a year now, ever since his near-fling with Georgie last summer. Tom nodded at him pleasantly; he liked being pleasant to Edward.

'Hello,' was all Nye said.

'How's it going?' Tom asked all of them again, and it was Phil who answered.

'Not bad, considering. We're getting a better turn-out at training now. Though we were just saying, what we really need are some decent weights and other training aids, something to make the boys get out of bed for.'

'Nye used to use skipping ropes,' Tom said.

'So he was saying. We still do, when we can persuade the boys.'

'Hurdles are what we could do with, most of all,' said Nye. He didn't address Tom; he seemed to be continuing a former conversation. He nodded down the touchlines, as if he could see the hurdles already lined up there. 'They help with timing and balance. John Ellis was telling me they've been using them for several years over at Harborth.'

'Top of the wish list for the club dance money,' said Edward. He spoke with a smile and didn't look at Tom; mentioning the dance was something he often did, presumably to show he dared. 'We'll have to start selling tickets early this year.'

Phil looked self-conscious. Tom said nothing; he was busy looking unruffled. He was interested to see that Nye was puzzled. So he hadn't heard that piece of gossip yet; well, no doubt Phil would fill him in later.

'Isn't that something the Wellspring fund could help with?' Tom spoke across Edward to Nye.

'Yes, it is. Raising funds for the club as a whole is a project that should interest Wellspring. And the committee will be putting in an application.'

'I'm surprised you have to be so formal.' Tom looked at them all but kept his sharpest attention on Nye. 'Can't you just arrange a meeting and get going?'

'Ridiculous, isn't it?' said Phil. 'If Nye wasn't on the committee, we'd just ask him down, but because he is, we have to go through all the official channels. Make sure no one can accuse us of feathering our own nests.' He cocked his head at the squat club house, with its newly donated plastic furniture stacked outside.

'The perils of public life,' said Tom.

'That's right,' said Edward suddenly. Tom turned to him and Edward looked away; he evidently hadn't meant to sound so jeering, or if he had, he wasn't ready with a follow-up.

Tom had been going to mention Georgie next, but he thought better of it. If Edward used the opportunity to say something about her, Nye would pick up on the antagonism and start devining; and it was squalid to be standing here, four men on a rugby pitch, with Tom and Georgie's marriage flapping between them like an invisible sheet.

No one deserved anyone as stupid as Edward laying a claim to them. It was ludicrous that Edward should think he was important in their lives.

Tom moved abruptly away. 'Well, good luck. I'm off to find Ieuan.'

The move startled Nye. His head shot round and at last Tom had a reaction from him. It wasn't what he expected: Nye stood between his new friends and watched Tom go with sullen anger.

Tom worked out afterwards that Hazel must have told Nye about their meeting. He tried to imagine what she would have said. She could have recited it word for word without being caught out, but he thought she'd edit it.

'I don't think they will come over, Nye. Tom more or less said as much. Let's not push it.'

Tom could hear her saying that, delivering it like a report. It had been the first thing she'd extracted out of their encounter, after all – his and Georgie's refusal to come. And when she'd left, he'd had the impression of her carrying it away.

In its place she'd left the information about Nye meeting Georgie. It was a deft exchange, and the deftest thing was that Hazel had let Tom feel that it was important.

She'd seemed to expect something from him. Not at that moment necessarily, but for the time ahead. And he'd acquiesced; more than that, he'd been excited by it. He'd felt that he was on watch, though God knew what for.

If Nye was angry because he'd heard the news from Hazel, Tom could understand it. He felt annoyed himself now. What had he been doing letting Hazel set the pace like that? He had no reason to be guided by her; every cause to mistrust her, in fact.

Was Hazel trying to keep him apart from Nye? If so, she was managing it well. Tom saw Nye's resentful face: the emotion had snubbed his features and brought out the subcutaneous grey of his evening hair growth. He decided to telephone him at work.

Nye was busy and Tom had to leave a message. The next day, he left another. In the afternoon, Nye called back. He was friendlier than at the club, but sounded distracted. Tom asked him if he wanted to go for a drink that night.

'I can't tonight, I'm at a WDA dinner.'

'Oh well, fair enough. Do you want to do it another night?'

'I'm afraid that will be difficult. I'm tied up almost every night this week.'

'Let's leave it till next week then. Unless you want to do it at lunchtime, at the weekend?'

'Yes, that's possible. Let me see. I'm coaching of course, on Saturday morning, and then I might go to Harborth. Why don't I ring you nearer the time?'

'Sure.' Tom wasn't disheartened. Taking the initiative revived him and made him determined. He worked very well for the rest of the week: he took his classes with a sense of fun and spent productive mornings in the studio. He saw himself and Nye journeying on parallel roads to reach the weekend.

When Nye didn't ring early on Saturday morning, Tom knew he'd have to wait till after training. The session ran from ten to twelve; he'd ascertained that from Ieuan, who went off on his bike while Tom was drinking coffee. Twelve o'clock came, and twelve-thirty. At ten past one Ieuan arrived back and Tom went out to meet him.

'Is Nye Mathias still at the club?' he asked.

'I don't think so,' said Ieuan. 'I didn't see his Jag when I left. Why?'

'I wanted to have a word with him,' said Tom. He didn't add an explanation, but he did say, 'Don't mention it to Georgie.'

'OK.' Ieuan shrugged to himself and the two of them went inside.

'I thought you were going out,' Georgie said to Tom.

'Yeah, I'm just off.'

He drove into Harborth and parked behind the old cinema. As he walked through the town, he looked out for Nye's navy blue car, but couldn't find it. He walked down the street where all the bookshops were; it had been pedestrianised several years ago and the Tarmac was covered up with fancy cobbles. He went right down the middle of the street, looking in through windows, but he didn't go into any of the shops. They all had back sections and many of them had rooms upstairs, and he wasn't going to track Nye through old stone warrens.

Much later, as Tom came back along the quay, he saw Nye at a fish stall. He had a large square parcel under his arm – books, judging by the way he carried it. Nye was wearing a grey jumper which looked expensive and immaculate pale summer trousers. The sun had come out and he looked warm.

Tom was fairly sure Nye saw him, but he didn't try to claim Nye's attention. He just walked past him, about ten feet away, and went on to his car.

He didn't know why he'd been warned off, and there was nothing he could do about it. He could hardly discuss it with Georgie. So the summer went on its mild way and he and Georgie barely saw Nye and Hazel.

Tom had a feeling of impermanence. He thought Georgie did too – she was going about her relaxing with too much relish. 'It's a funny summer, isn't it?' he said to her one afternoon in August when she was gardening and he was preparing for his four o'clock class.

'The weather you mean?' Georgie answered, her hands full of the feverfew that was growing rampant. 'Yes, it is. Or did you mean that lot up in Plas Bryn?'

'Perhaps they do just want to ignore us?' said Tom.

'Hmm,' said Georgie. 'That's not really what you think.' There was no edge on her voice. 'You're really wondering when they're going to make a move – which is probably just what they want you to be wondering.' She put the clump down and sniffed her hands. 'God, it's so dank.'

'They're only our neighbours, not a bunch of terrorists. Besides, everything's settled now. You and Hazel are polite when you run into each other, aren't you?'

'Oh yes, we're polite. Not chummy like you and Nye, but polite.'

'Well then.'

'I tell you what, though. Have you noticed who Ieuan and Huw are talking to outside the club more often than not these days? Elen Mathias and Miv Price.'

'That's hardly Nye and Hazel's doing.'

'Oh no, of course not. It's just something that's happening anyway. We could do without it, though. Let's hope it's Myfanwy that Ieuan's interested in.' Georgie sounded vigorous. She reached in between the cornflowers to pull up the bindweed. Tom wondered if Nye hadn't made a mistake by manoeuvring Georgie into the Wellspring meeting. It had broken the tension for her and pushed her into practical mode. Georgie was at her best when she was practical.

But that was to assume that Nye was looking for an advantage over them. Tom wasn't going to assume that. He didn't need to buy into Georgie's attitude, no matter how well it suited her.

He'd noticed the boys hanging round with Miv and Elen, of course. Like Georgie, he couldn't be sure if a pairing off was imminent, nor which way it would go. 'We'd better talk to Ieuan before we go on holiday,' he said. 'Elen's very young. I don't want to come home to find Nye waiting with a shotgun.'

Anger flashed out on Georgie's face – at Tom? At Nye? Or at the idea of Ieuan having sex? It was instantly controlled. 'I've already told him,' she said. She sounded strong, very matter of fact. 'No girls here while we're away. None at all, over-age or under. He's agreed. When we're back, he can invite round who he likes but it's male only while we're gone.'

In fact, by the time Tom and Georgie were due to leave for Crete, the boys' interest seemed to have cooled. They were spending most of their time with friends in Bartraeth who were forming a band. Still, Tom reiterated Georgie's rules to Ieuan, for solidarity. 'And, Ieu,' he said, 'especially not Elen Mathias, all right?'

Ieuan looked at him. 'A bit obsessed are you, you and Mum? Elen's never even been here.'

'I know, but she's one of your friends. We just have to be careful, with Georgie being a headteacher.' He paused. 'Why did you say that? Has Georgie mentioned Elen?'

'No, but her face goes all careful whenever she sees me talking to her down the club.' Ieuan chopped at the air. 'She's on my bus,' he said in exasperation. 'She's in my crowd.'

'Sorry, Ieu. We'll be off your back for two weeks soon, anyway.'

That was two days before they went away. On their last evening, they went to a party. They stood in the Edwardian drawing room on the leafy edge of Bartraeth and chatted to the other guests of Richard Wyn Ellis, banker, MP and owner of three of Tom's paintings. They had come early, meaning to go early, so they were well ensconced when Nye and Hazel arrived. Nye was in a suit; Hazel wore a silk dress and long earrings. She looked odd to Tom's eyes: poised and elegant and yet, inside her delicate outfit, her body was very noticeable. Tom found the physicality shocking, as if he'd caught her being dishonest.

For the first twenty minutes, Nye and Hazel were busy meeting people and accepting drinks. Then Nye noticed Tom. He hesitated, turning his body subtly away as if to organise himself; he smiled at Tom with the lower part of his face and spoke to Hazel. She lifted her head and looked across – Tom could have sworn it was a practised movement – but just then Georgie finished her conversation and moved back to his side and her gaze met Hazel's first.

Hazel lost her nerve. Her eyes slid over both of them. She nodded, though no one had spoken. With a look of false eagerness, she turned back into the group.

Tom watched Nye watch her. Nye spoke again; he touched her arm. She nodded. She was standing stiff-backed, her head angled away from them, looking at the floor. Nye's hand dropped – Tom thought he touched Hazel in the small of her back – then he left her and came towards them.

'What a nice surprise, I hadn't expected you to be here.'

'No?' Georgie was polite. 'Why not?'

'I didn't know you knew Richard.'

'Oh.' She managed to sound both contemptuous and unsurprised. Nye glanced at Tom and smiled.

'Oh dear, that was dull of me, wasn't it? Of course, you know almost everyone round here.' He spoke to Tom, but it seemed directed at Georgie. And Tom was handicapped in how he could answer. With Georgie listening, he couldn't pick up on Nye's provoking note and play him at his own game. But he mustn't show resentment either.

'Not quite,' he said, imitating Georgie's tone.

'Hazel wants to come and say hello too, but she's in the middle of a conversation just now.' Tom was aware that he and Georgie turned their heads together, as if Nye were manipulating them. By the time he wished he could resist, he and Georgie were already staring at Hazel who stood isolated in the group, while on either side of her people talked in pairs.

'Difficult for her,' said Georgie, giving Nye an angry look.

'Yes, it is.' Nye nodded down at her in agreement. His face was loosening. 'Shall I bring her over?'

Tom was caught between nausea and a desire to laugh, almost a reflex, like a sneeze. He kept very still; he was pinned back tonight, between what Nye knew and what Georgie allowed.

Georgie's face had gone into a perfect oval. It would have been like a mask if it weren't for the vigilance in her eyes.

It was Nye who laughed, and glanced at Tom as he did. 'Ah Georgie,' he said in a voice that took them back twenty years. 'I want to—'

'No, Nye.' Georgie interrupted calmly. She had a resonance in her voice too, but while Nye's drew them closer, hers pushed him away. 'We'll have nothing like that.'

Nye's smile went slowly downwards, grooving his face. 'You don't know what I was going to say.'

'I don't need to.'

'I see.' Nye persisted in sounding good-humoured, but Tom thought a shade of authority had left him. He looked past Nye's shoulder. A small, dark woman – Marie Tonkin, wasn't it, from the health centre – had been working her way towards Hazel and was now introducing herself.

Look, Nye, he thought of saying, as the two women settled into a talk, Hazel's free now. But the sarcasm would have drawn more attention to Hazel and he was glad to see her finding cover.

He turned away and knocked into Georgie's arm. His hand closed on her wrist and he converted it into a look at her watch.

'Yes, we should go,' she said.

It was a strange memory to have in his mind while they were in Crete. He saw it in the evenings, as the sea changed colour beneath the reflecting sky and the stars arranged themselves above and below the telegraph wires. He saw it in the Minoan villa near Phaistos. It was caught in the perspiration on Georgie's upper lip and in the crease on her neck, when they had sex in the afternoons.

Georgie had always preferred daytime fucking. It was one

reason she insisted they went to warm places for their holidays.

In the nights, they often went out; in the second week especially, when they became friends with Jane and Morten. Morten and Jane were in their early thirties; they hadn't long since left their marriages for one another, and they took a fancy to Tom and Georgie. So they all followed their own plans during the day, but by sundown Tom and Georgie had usually dropped in at the others' hotel, or Jane and Morten would come by their villa, and later they would go out together, as a four. Then the memory of the non-meeting with Nye and Hazel became most compelling, just before it died.

25

'You're in.'

'What?'

'You're on the shortlist. Kathleen Moran just called me. They'll be announcing it next week. Congratulations.' Karl sounded very businesslike.

'Thanks.'

'Meanwhile, they want slides and a recently completed painting to hang at the press conference. Before the weekend, wouldn't you know it. When can you come in?'

'Tomorrow,' said Tom.

'Good. It'll have to be the afternoon for me. Is that OK?'

'Fine.'

'I was thinking about this new diptych of yours. It's looking very strong; how about giving them that for the press conference?'

'It's not dry.'

'Shame, it would reproduce well. Still, there are several more we can use.'

Sitting on the windowsill, Tom was pierced by a spear of light. The hall was busy with diagonal rays; the late September sun had driven him out of his studio an hour ago. 'Who else is on the list?'

'Liz Tuchman, Asaf Mistry, Hannah Gardiner, she's the photographer who works with steel plates, and Iain Bonetti.'

Through the gaps in the hedgerow, figures moved and Ieuan and Elen turned the corner. Ieuan had his arm round her neck. He was playing with a strand of her hair. Elen's body was jammed against his at an uncomfortable angle.

'All first timers,' said Tom.

'Yes, which is good. It's a thought-out list, too, with a certain feel to it: you and Asaf have been working on extended series recently; you and Liz and Hannah have each gone in for technical development.'

Ieuan spotted Tom through the window; he looked surprised,

then waved. Elen's head twisted and she smiled, above Ieuan's toying fingers. Her face muscles moved fast, in the same way as Nye's, but they produced a different effect.

Tom opened the door for them.

'Hiya, Dad.'

'Hello Mr Griffiths.'

He nodded; Karl talked.

'This is confidential until the press conference, of course. We're not allowed to put out any announcements and we're not supposed to go telling clients either.'

'Sure.'

'But there's no harm having a few quiet words.'

'Who were you thinking of telling?' A few feet away, Ieuan and Elen were breaking apart. They left their school bags on the floor, re-entangled their fingers and went into the kitchen.

'Mark Westing and the Chandlers. And perhaps Susan Blacker, now that she's started that art investment group.' Karl paused. Tom heard it clearly: a hiatus on the line. 'David Olone, that Bristol dealer, hasn't been in touch for a while.'

Tom let go of the front door and kicked it gently. As it closed, the scent of gravel and moistening air gusted in; a scent sharper than the playful light, a reminder that progress brought change. 'Don't take the initiative. But tell him if he calls.'

Tom was drunk. He hadn't noticed it happening; he didn't think he'd drunk very much but here it was. The definition had gone out of his thoughts and his senses had taken over.

Through the kitchen smells, he could feel the evening. An early autumnal evening, the air wet and complicated, with a mineral hardness at its centre. A stream of it poured in through the open top window and – when he raised his nose – travelled into him.

It seemed to connect him with an alternative self; a possible Tom from the past. He had often wondered about this other person, especially at the changeover of seasons, when he would seem to draw close.

Might-have-been Tom was very near this evening. Tom could almost see him standing out there; on the grass just beyond the lip of light, looking at the Tom and Georgie in the kitchen.

He wore a grey jumper and a beard; or half a beard. The bare patches on his cheeks didn't look foolish as Tom's own had done. The man outside had dark brown hair, no thread of white, and his face was subtly angled, finer. The cool air filled his lungs: every now and then he caught a whiff of cooking from the window.

Inside, Georgie was stirring mushrooms and onions in the frying pan. She had a big glass of red wine beside her too, but she seemed to have forgotten to drink it. She was humming 'He Who Would Valiant Be'.

> No Lion shall him fright,
> He'll with a Giant fight,
> He'll labour day and night . . .

She'd asked him very intelligent questions when he'd told her the news. Who were the others listed? What was his opinion of their work? Was he surprised by the selection? Then she had put her arms round him for a long time.

Not a clinging embrace but steady. Measured in triumph.

She'd gone upstairs and changed. For a moment, he'd wondered if she were going out and he'd forgotten. But she came back down in jeans and a big shirt. They were scruffy clothes, worn soft with use. They followed the line of her body and emphasised the sloping ribcage, the strong swell of her hips.

She had stopped humming now and was listening. Beyond the sizzling of the meat and Ieuan's distant music was an engine's thrum. Tom glanced out of the window and saw brightness in the lane.

'Hazel doing her invisible coachman act,' said Georgie. 'I wish she'd just come and knock at the door.'

'She does sometimes.'

'Does she?' Georgie turned. And Tom remembered that he'd decided not to mention it. He couldn't recall his reasons now. Anyhow, it was too late to retrench: he wasn't responsible for protecting each of them against the others.

'Yes. Only Ieuan's door though.' Tom looked at Georgie's face – a question mark, open, puzzling. 'I see her from the studio.'

The engine switched off. They heard Ieuan's front door open.

'I'm surprised they let Elen come here in the week,' said Georgie.

'It's only six-thirty,' said Tom. But he was quite surprised too. He and Georgie had taken the advent of Elen differently but one thing they shared was curiosity about Nye and Hazel's feelings.

The Mathiases were showing nothing. Nye went on coaching Ieuan at the club. Hazel ferried Elen and her friend Myfanwy up and down. They'd had Ieuan to meals at Plas Bryn. When they saw Tom and Georgie they were polite but their encounters were very brief or, in Georgie's case with the Wellspring meeting at school, public.

Last week Tom and Nye had met outside Lower Shop. Nye had been subdued and slightly impatient to get away. Tom had heard him flexing his voice to make it friendly, as he put the usual questions; Nye was so disciplined that his cadences had done their work on Tom, even while Tom could feel the effort going into them. It had made him angry; though afterwards, when he'd been walking away, Tom had wondered if he were feeling his own anger or Nye's.

A door shut. Another opened. The music was much louder. Georgie looked out into the hall and said, 'Good,' with great relish.

'What?' Tom heard Ieuan say.

'We've been waiting for you. Come in here, Ieu, we've got something to tell you.'

These days Bartraeth was like a castle. The new buildings on the approach roads were tall, with humorous roofs and pediments. You drove in between them, were ushered by arrows and emblems into your appointed route, and filed into the city through one of many gates: Docks Cargo, City Centre, Through Traffic, Trading Estate.

Nye had the heavy lorries for the docks on his right, a caravan of buses on his left. He accelerated away from the lights and reached the roundabout first, switched lanes and began the descent down St Beuno's Hill.

The church was the beginning of the true city. And its end, of course. From here Nye had looked out on different kinds of extremity.

He was impatient, stuck in the traffic, and hungry. He didn't want to eat but he could taste his gastric juices and he knew they would be on his breath. He would have to stop in the centre and buy a sandwich. Better be vigorously late for the meeting than arrive punctually, with the smell of ruin.

His first instinct, when he saw Tom in Trisant Street, was to step back into the sandwich bar. But Tom hadn't seen him and wasn't likely to look in his direction: he was taken up with two men – one was Karl Rogers. The other was young and well dressed. Karl and the young man were doing most of the talking, but it was obviously focused on Tom. They spoke to him or through him, and

Tom was standing with his body weight set back on his pelvis, his shoulders relaxed inside his very painterly jumper.

Nye had seen this before, a long time ago: people making patterns around his friend.

The young man shook hands with Tom and Karl, and walked away. Nye bent down and unlocked his car door, watching through the windows. Tom and Karl were speaking and looking at their watches. They walked back towards the gallery door side by side; Nye saw Tom look at whatever was on show in the window. He stopped and stared, and turned to speak to Karl, but he'd already opened the door. Tom said something, laughed, and almost sauntered in.

When Nye had finished his sandwich, he brushed the crumbs out of the car door, ate a mint and drove slowly past the gallery. The painting in the window was Tom's, one he'd never seen before.

Had the young man just bought it? Inside the gallery he could see Tom sitting on the client's chair by Karl's desk, his legs stretched out in front of him.

A quarter to six and Tom was exhausted. Last night's drinking had caught up with him, and Karl had kept him hard at work all afternoon. Besides going through his paintings in the back room, choosing which to put forward for the shortlist show in London, they'd selected slides for the Reynolds Monette press pack, drafted an artist's statement, and worked through an invitations list for the London show.

But more tiring than all that was the waking of his appetite. Halfway through talking to Adrian Speed – a useful meeting, Karl was right about young lawyers – Tom had felt the desire for what was on offer flood through him. Thirty thousand pounds and six months as artist-in-residence in London. Clangour and rapid footsteps; that huge river. A single bedroom and trains to board and disembark from.

And more people looking at him as Adrian Speed had done: not so much with respect – Tom was used to that – but with that hunter's alertness, that excitement, both impersonal and shaming, with which the world responds to success.

He wanted it. In the four hours he'd spent with Karl since Adrian's departure, he'd begun to feel a craving for it. He looked in Karl's eyes for it but Karl knew him too well, and anyway, Karl was taking his own share of the recognition. Tom had seen it in

Maggie, though, when he walked in, and he found several excuses to invite the assistant's opinion.

The wind was getting up now; it skimmed litter out of bins along Market Street but took none of the pressure out of the atmosphere. The air felt full, as if it had some soft animal rolled up in it.

Tom was unlocking his car door when he saw the Jaguar. It was parked on the opposite side of the car park, facing away from him, and inside it Nye was talking on his car phone. He appeared to have been at it for some time: he was resting his arm on the steering wheel and propped up on the dashboard was a document he kept jabbing with his pen. Tom leant on the roof of his own car and watched.

Nye was busy: so busy that he'd resent being interrupted? A week ago Tom wouldn't have taken the risk. But a week ago he hadn't regained his confidence.

This would be a good time to meet Nye again.

He pushed himself away from his car and began to stroll towards the Jaguar. He stopped to let a woman wheel a pushchair by, and as he waited he saw Nye's posture change, the Jaguar's engine came on and Nye reversed out of his space.

Tom knew he couldn't get across the car park in time, so he rushed back to his own car and concentrated on following Nye. The Jaguar was already turning into Market Street when Tom reached the exit, but he was able to keep it in sight. Nye turned left at the top and at the next junction, where the road split into lanes, Tom manoeuvred alongside him. Nye didn't notice him at first; when he did, Tom thought his first impulse was to turn away. Tom started winding down his passenger window but before Nye could respond, the lights changed. Nye pulled a face, signalled apology and accelerated.

It took some doing to keep up with him along the dual carriageway and then on the first stretch of the Penllwyn road, Tom got stuck behind a couple of lorries. Two miles outside the village, though, he saw the Jaguar up ahead, climbing the hill in single file. Its indicator was flashing; Nye intended to take the back route home. Tom turned left into the old quarry tracks, drove fast between the fields and caught up with Nye on the top lane. Nye was driving without haste. When he saw Tom in his rearview mirror, he slowed further, lowered his window and pointed ahead. A couple of minutes later Tom followed him into the gravelled yard of The Hollybush.

'Well?' said Nye.

'Fine,' said Tom, deliberately misunderstanding him.

Nye changed his car keys from one hand to another and laughed. It was like a concession, forced from him against his will, but which he couldn't help enjoying. It lit up his face. 'I take it you want to talk to me?'

'I want a drink with you. Marvellous how you seem to know that as well.'

'Shall we go in then?'

If anything, it was heavier up here than in Bartraeth. The air stroked them like water. The pub door had been wedged open, so that when they went into the public bar the smells of earth and stone followed them and mingled with the beer.

'Have you been teaching?' Nye asked.

'No, I've been at the gallery. Planning various campaigns with Karl.'

'Various?'

'To take advantage of the Reynolds Monette publicity. We've just heard I'm on the shortlist.'

Nye was standing very close to the bar but not touching it, watching Tom. His expression changed. Tom saw satisfaction in it; it spread outwards, yet somehow Nye's face didn't relax.

'Good. Congratulations.' Nye spoke quietly, as Tom had done. 'Jesus, Tom, that's good.'

'Yes.' Tom found he rather liked this intentness of Nye's. 'It is, isn't it?'

'It's about bloody time.'

'I'm not going to argue with that, either.'

'It had to happen sooner or later.' Nye had hardly moved a muscle since he'd heard the news. Tom wondered what he was feeling; his eyes were glowing but the energy was fastened down.

'So I'm celebrating,' Tom said more slowly. He wanted Nye to know that he, Tom, was alive to the complexities of this. Tom Griffiths was free; he'd come in search of Nye to tell him so. He put his hand in his jacket and pulled out his wallet. 'What can I get you?'

'Whisky.'

'With a beer chaser?'

Nye's smile was the brother of the one he'd given outside – spontaneous despite himself. 'I suppose so.' He didn't withdraw when Tom moved next to him at the bar but he turned sideways and put his foot on the bar rail; his leg made a barrier between them. 'So, whose company are you in?'

'Asaf Mistry, Tuchman, Bonetti and Hannah Gardiner.'

'Interesting. A more coherent line-up than usual. I thought they were wrong to overlook you last year, but this will stand you in better stead.'

'We hope so. Though we've got to expect a certain amount of rubbishing when it's announced – that's traditional.'

'When's that going to be?'

'Tuesday. Reynolds Monette are holding a press conference. Till then we're all sworn to silence.'

'I'll be discreet.' Nye watched the barman drawing whisky from the optic. 'How's Georgie taking it?'

'Quietly. I get the feeling she's pacing herself. She wants me to win, you see.'

'Christ.' Nye turned to scrutinise Tom as he opened his wallet; Tom could see his head moving from side to side. 'And you don't, I suppose?'

'Oh sure, I do. But I've wanted a lot of things that haven't come off. I'm experienced.'

'This is different, though. Being on the shortlist is a breakthrough in itself: no one's ever doubted your skill, but now people will have to look again at your originality.'

'Yes.' Tom handed over the money; divided up the drinks. 'In fact, Karl's going to take your "About Bloody Time" approach with the journalists and hope they run with it.'

'Very shrewd,' said Nye. ' "The spell is lifted at last. Look around thee upon the land and thou wilt see the seven cantrefs as they were at their best." '

It was years since Tom had heard Nye quote. The sound of it plucked at his skin.

'What's that?' said Tom.

'The story of the vanishing cantrefs. Don't you remember? The Mabinogion tells it under the name of Manawydan, but it's both Pryderi's story and Manawydan's. The rash prince who gets banished and the cunning prince who bargains for his return.'

'I'll look it up. In the meantime . . .' Tom pushed Nye's whisky towards him. 'Cheers.'

'To your success.'

'Thanks. By the way, don't go mentioning it to Georgie till after Tuesday,' Tom said. 'I won't be telling her I've told you.'

26

Georgie watched Hazel come in through the Taf Street entrance. Choosing that exposed doorway under the clock had put her at a disadvantage, though she didn't seem to know it. Georgie, who was waiting to buy fruit at one of the central stalls, moved instinctively deeper into the queue. Peering over the shoulder of the woman in front, she waited for Hazel to walk towards this section, or the butchers' stalls, or the dairy produce. She was irritated to see Hazel in here at all. The covered market, with its concrete floor and pigeons flapping in the roof, belonged to local life. It would be more fitting for Hazel to buy her food in the specialist shops on Mount Street.

But Hazel carried a shapeless bag that went oddly with her good clothes and hair. Watching her through the Saturday crowd, Georgie saw that she walked flatly, with one foot splayed outwards. The recognition shocked her. She had forgotten that characteristic step, almost a limp.

Hazel browsed at a jewellery stall and a clothes stall. She did not even glance towards the food; she walked into a warren of trestles bearing cardboard boxes. It must have been the context, seeing her with bent head among the old record sleeves and the students, that made her seem so much younger.

Georgie's turn having arrived, she swivelled her shoulders to block Hazel out. She bought oranges and plums and was reaching over the stall to pay when on the edge of her vision she saw Hazel stand still.

Her face was a pale blur, but Georgie could tell it was pointing in her direction. Hazel stood like that for several seconds, obviously thinking she was the first of them to see the other; then she moved quickly to the end of the trestles and slipped into the crowd.

Georgie's relief snagged on frustration: she should have watched the woman more closely. Hazel had been off-duty and she wouldn't get another such sight of her in a hurry. There had been a candour in the way Hazel rooted through the record boxes. Unburdened of her usual poise, she'd been down-to-earth, almost clumsy.

Georgie didn't like it. She felt she'd missed something. She scanned the crowded aisle for a brown head, silky among the others, or for slim grey shoulders working a path. No sign.

When she looked again, however, she could see Hazel clearly. And she was not moving away but coming straight towards Georgie. She had that vulnerable look she so often had, her body tipped forward like a tree before the wind, but her route was unwavering and her face determined and pleasant.

A warning noise came out of Georgie's throat, meant for herself.

'Hallo.' Hazel stopped a few feet away. 'I saw it was you and I thought I'd come and say hallo.'

Well, she was equal to this. 'Hallo.'

'I thought, as we're seeing so much of each other's children now . . .' Hazel was nervous. She didn't try to disguise it. In her face was anxiety and – not exactly an apology but certainly an acknowledgement of what was past. I know you're not going to be pleased to see me, her expression seemed to say; you know and I know that this is really impossible, but with things being as they are, what else can we do?

'Yes?' Georgie's breath was in short supply.

Hazel smiled. 'Oh I'm not saying I mind. Ieuan's a nice boy.'

'Really.'

'He and Elen seem to be getting very fond of each other, don't they?'

'Ieuan's always had a lot of friends. He's popular, people find it easy to like him.'

'Yes, of course.' Hazel's glance of dubiety was swiftly covered up.

Georgie could feel Hazel coming in at an angle, and didn't know what it was. She knew it was working, though; Hazel had always been dangerous like that. If she wasn't careful, while she stared and returned cool answers, Hazel would be managing her. She gathered her strength. She transferred both her heavy carrier bags to her right hand. She lifted them on to her hip, balancing her weight, deliberately opposing her curved, earthbound grace to Hazel's slimness. Her body moved insolently and comfortingly.

Hazel didn't quail but her eyes took on a non-commital look.

'What do you want, Hazel Mathias?'

'Just to say hallo. And to feel that if we meet with Ieuan or Elen, we can be reasonably friendly.'

'I know how to behave in front of my son.'

'And I'd like to be able to give you my good wishes. Like Nye gives you his.'

Georgie bent her knee and swung it back and forth, moving her bags of fruit gently.

Hazel went on talking, courteously, obdurately.

'We were both very pleased to hear about your news.'

'News?'

'Tom being shortlisted for the Reynolds Monette. It's excellent and on such a strong shortlist too. You must be delighted.'

Ieuan: so he had told Elen. The flash of anger was like a little black starfish in front of Georgie's eyes. She waited for it to go. Of course he'd told; she couldn't seriously have expected him not to.

'Elen shared the secret then, did she?' Georgie spoke with rich humour.

'Elen? No. I'm sorry, I'm not with you.'

'Elen didn't tell you about it? Nor Ieuan?'

'No.'

'So how did you know about it?'

'I—' Hazel's smile changed. It became lighter and more mobile, as if an element had been subtracted from it. 'Nye told me. I think he read it in a newspaper.'

'He can't have done. The information's confidential until Tuesday.'

'Oh. Well, I don't know. Perhaps Nye heard it rather than read it. He buys a lot of art you know, Georgie, and these things get around.'

There was a hint of persuasion in Hazel's voice. Georgie logged it and pressed on. 'When did he tell you?'

'A couple of days ago. Thursday, or was it earlier? I can't remember.'

'I see. And what else did he tell you exactly?'

'Nothing. That's all.' Hazel sounded patient and very slightly reproachful. A good mix, for putting someone off the track. 'I wouldn't worry, Georgie. Wherever Nye got it from, I'm sure it's gone no further. He's used to hearing confidential information; he's very discreet.'

'He forgot to mention anything about discretion to you.'

'Yes. He did.' Hazel made a rueful bob. She was definitely acting now. Her smile faded; her shrug combined apology with a wry dignity. Behind the surface expressions, she had snatched her intelligence away, to guard its thoughts from Georgie.

She was much more effective at this than she'd been in the past.

There was a pain in Georgie's arm muscles like cracking wire, and an ache in her hip. She swung the bags down into her hands and flexed her forearms to take the weight, and put all her energies into her voice. 'Thank you for your congratulations,' she said deliberately. 'And for your "good wishes".' She heard the different notes sound satisfyingly: irony, amusement, contempt and binding them all up together, a certain rich confidence. It was very good – it almost convinced Georgie herself; her voice had this wonderful power to conjure with possibilities and make them seem real.

It had carried her through many bad moments; shown her the way across a number of nasty little gaps. Now it made Hazel falter. Her expression shivered, just as it had done the night of Richard's party, and she stepped sideways and hit her hip on a trestle.

Georgie laughed. 'Shall I pass your good wishes on to Tom?'

Hazel didn't exactly blush – she had never blushed in the past; it was one of the things Georgie remembered about her most clearly – but the skin around her eyes seemed to darken. It made her look bewildered and unwell.

'Oh, whatever you want,' she said angrily. 'I'm sorry I tried. Goodbye.'

And she turned and walked away. She went quickly at first but once she'd put a block of stalls between them she slowed; she lifted her bag on to her shoulder and began looking from side to side.

Now, Georgie asked herself; why was Hazel choosing to do this now?

While Georgie watched, Hazel came to a standstill in front of a second-hand clothes stall. Her hand went up as she moved in among the racks. Georgie understood. She might still be able to dismiss Hazel but Hazel was showing that she would not be driven away.

Georgie stopped the car by the railings and looked across the ditch to the playing field. About a dozen boys were on it, practising moves, and a middle-aged man was jogging along the touchlines calling to them. She could see Ieuan on the field, his hair standing up in the wind and his jersey torn. But no Nye. Yet his car was still here, parked next to the old bench where she had noticed it on her way into Bartraeth.

Georgie walked alongside the railings until she reached the gateway, climbed the steps and went in.

As she walked along the corridor, John Vickers said hallo to her. 'Looking for Ieuan? Still on the field, I think he is. Won't be long now.'

'Thanks, I'll wait.'

Next she passed two girls who used to come round to the house last year. They were both wearing boys' cricket sweaters, one with sleeves rolled up and one with sleeves hanging down. Roz and someone. They smiled at her and the one whose name she couldn't remember said hallo.

'Georgie.' Ed Davies came out of the bar – or the room they called a bar, with its crate of beer and bottles of wine locked safely away in the wall cupboard and got out only for committee members and their guests. 'It's some time since you've been down here. Looking for someone? Or have you come to sign on for the sponsored run?'

'I'm waiting for Ieuan.'

'Oh yes. He's on the field.'

'Yes, I know.'

Through the doorway Georgie could see someone else in the bar, leaning against the windowsill looking out. Ed followed her eyes.

'How is the new term?'

As always since the incident last year, Ed spoke with an edge of irony. I will never be less than courteous to you, his tone seemed to imply, but of course I don't really care.

'Not so bad,' said Georgie. She moved across him while he was opening his mouth to continue, and pushed the door. 'I'm going in here. I want a word with Nye.'

She pulled the door to and was alone in the shabby cream-painted room with Nye.

The room was small and he had, of course, heard her voice. He didn't turn at once. He was wearing a black and white tweed jacket with the old-fashioned leather buttons and a pair of nondescript trousers. When he turned, Georgie saw that his jumper was blue-grey, the kind of subtle shade he had never been capable of choosing. He looked at her and waited.

She had meant to be brisk and speak out at once, in clipped tones, but now she was alone with him that urge seemed to have faded and when she finally spoke, she heard herself sounding uncertain.

'Hello, Nye.'

'Hello, Georgie.'

'You look well.'

'Yes, I am.'

'You're watching my son.'

'Among others, yes.' He glanced out at the field and smiled, shaking his large head. 'I fancy myself as a coach but they manage to keep me away from the touchlines more often than not. Really, you see, I'm only wanted here on the money side.'

'I wouldn't have thought the club has any money.'

'That's it. I'm supposed to raise it.'

Nye stood quietly looking at Georgie. It was like it had often been in the past: he was touching base with her, letting her see him without the public trappings. She tried to resist for a second but there was no point. Georgie wasn't even sure she wanted to resist – this recognition had something to offer her as well. It made it unexpectedly easy for her to speak; ridiculously easy when you considered their last few encounters.

'I've just seen Hazel in Bartraeth market,' she said.

'Yes, she likes it there. She goes most weekends.'

'I've never seen her there before. I spotted her looking round at odds and ends. Second-hand clothes and records, home-made jewellery – seventies stuff it was, mostly. Very like what we all used to wear.'

Nye's face was noncommital. Perhaps it was in response to the fearful note which Georgie herself could hear in her voice. But did he understand what she meant by it?

'Hazel spoke to me. She congratulated me on Tom being up for the award.'

Georgie held her breath. Outside the boys had finished practice and were walking towards the window. If Nye looked puzzled, or said 'What award?' she would know that she was right; she was back in that world of truths glimpsed much too late, of suspicion and loss.

She could feel the tide pressing against her already. She could feel the water threatening to fill up her lungs.

'Ah,' said Nye, and a half-proud, half-sheepish expression took shape on his face. 'I gather she jumped the gun?'

Georgie stared at him. Had Hazel told her the truth then? 'She said you'd told her about it.'

'I did. We were both pleased – whatever you might think.'

'But how did you know about it? Hazel said you read it in the papers but there's a strict press embargo till next week.'

'The papers? No, I didn't see it in the press. One of the Reynolds Monette directors told me. Michael Trewin; I was having lunch with him last week.'

Georgie let the air empty slowly from her chest. The muscles of her breastbone, her shoulders, her throat, were relaxing. She wasn't sure exactly what she felt: relief, a quite terrible relief, but there was something else too which continued the disturbance rather than promised to end it.

'I see. That seems a little cavalier of him, when all the artists and their galleries are sworn to secrecy. Reynolds Monette have been very fierce about not letting it leak.'

'It won't leak. There was no one there but me and Reynolds Monette people.'

'Who have you told, besides Hazel?'

'No one.' Nye's voice had been losing its reassuring note. Now it had a roughened sound, as if her question had grazed him. 'I wouldn't want to upset Tom's chances. You might at least do me the justice of believing that.'

Georgie walked slowly round the table till she was standing on the other side of the sash window with the light flooding Nye's face. It was very important that she could see every nuance of his expression. 'What about Hazel?'

'What do you mean?'

'Does Hazel want to hurt Tom's chances?'

'No.'

'How can you be sure?'

Nye lifted his right hand – very pale, very scrubbed – and rested it against the window catch.

'Because Hazel's not like that. Besides, Georgie, think about it. Poor Hazel carries a monkey on her back. When is she going to be able to mention Tom's name to anyone round here, except to you and me?'

Georgie sat in the car and waited for Ieuan to appear. She had the window open and the damp came through it: the air was heavy with autumn. The trees on the far side of the pitch were brown and russet and leaves had been swept into piles in the car park. The season was further advanced than she'd realised.

Ieuan had asked her to give him five minutes for a shower.

She'd been waiting longer than that already. What impression had he gained from seeing her with Nye, she wondered; he'd looked from one to the other of them in the corridor, and hadn't known whether to speak just to her or to them both.

'He's a nice boy.' Nye had said it judiciously, as a statement of fact, and quite unlike Hazel's over-eager assertion. It had pleased Georgie despite herself. For a moment, watching Ieuan go to the changing room, she'd forgotten that there was any reason to resist this simple pleasure.

She had said goodbye then.

The door opened and three boys came out on the steps, Ieuan among them. He paused to exchange some parting shot with the others then loped towards her, knocking his bag against the fence. His hair was wet, all its red notes extinguished.

Georgie moved to open the door for him and as he got in, it occurred to her that perhaps he was too old to be accepting gestures like this from her. As soon as she thought it, she felt a stab of indignant anger against it, as if the idea might have been put into her mind by someone else. She glanced up at the club house, half expecting to see Nye at one of the windows, but there was no one.

27

'Georgie, when are they coming?'

Tom walked into the bedroom but she wasn't there. He had expected to find her at the dressing table or sitting on the end of the bed drying her hair; some time ago he'd looked up from the hall and seen her leaving the bathroom, wrapped in a towel. Now the towel hung neatly over the radiator and the hairdryer, when he touched it, was still warm.

He hurried out of the room and back downstairs. Harry and Alan would be here soon. She wasn't in the living room, nor in the kitchen. But through the kitchen window he saw an oblong of light. She was in the studio.

His stomach shrank and seemed to fall. It was the quality of the light that troubled him: it wasn't bright enough to be the main overhead light, nor even the desk lamp. It was muted and oblique, coming from some source out of range of the window, and it moved. Someone was in there with a torch.

Someone: Tom was at the back door before he knew how he got there. But he could see Georgie now, her shoulder and one side of her head just visible inside the studio. Of course; who else would it be? Not that it diminished his apprehension.

Georgie moved along his workbench and out of sight. The torchbeam was directed low; she was looking for something among his work in progress. He didn't know what it could be but he feared the worst.

Hazel had been very formal when she stopped him this afternoon, and faintly ashamed. She'd stood at an angle to him, as if the width of the Penllwyn pavement might be a witness for her scrupulousness. 'I'm afraid I worried Georgie by bringing it up. I didn't realise it was confidential, you see. But we haven't mentioned it to anyone else.'

'It's not really important,' Tom had said. 'We're not supposed to talk to the press before the official announcement, that's all.'

'Well, we certainly haven't done that.' There had been a peculiar inflection to the way she said that. It had bothered him. Afterwards he'd wondered: was it just the 'we'? Or had he caught an echo of how he was discussed up in Plas Bryn, his name comfortable in Nye and Hazel's mouths as if he were once again their good friend?

Tom thought Hazel had seen his discomfort too, and had deliberately used the same tone of voice to say goodbye. She'd looked self-conscious as she spoke but there, unmistakeably, had sounded the friendliness again. Completely unwarranted after these months of nothing.

Unless she knew that he and Nye had drunk together in The Hollybush. At the time Nye had said he probably wouldn't tell her. Probably.

'Why did you go off to Harborth on your own, last time I asked you?' Tom had said, while Nye was ordering the second round.

Nye looked down at him, across his shoulder, his face giving nothing away. 'I didn't know why you'd rung.' And then: 'I thought we should steer clear of each other for a while.'

Tom hadn't pressed it. A boy came in and fed fifty pence pieces into the cigarette machine, while outside his girlfriend, even younger, waited for him.

Tom, fitting his hand round his new glass of whisky, had liked accepting it from Nye; it was possible to enjoy receiving once you had things to give again.

But now someone was making trouble.

When he'd come back from Penllwyn this afternoon, Tom had looked carefully into Georgie's face. There were signs of disturbance that he'd missed at lunchtime. A quickness to her step. Her mouth redder than usual and her eyes darker: all her features were more clearly defined. Yet she said nothing about meeting Hazel. Tom had even given her some cues, mentioning the Reynolds Monette and next week's announcement, but she'd answered only the surface of his remarks. She hadn't even seemed preoccupied. She'd been energetic, seeing to all the preparations for supper in good time; taking herself off for a shower when she discovered she'd finished early.

The light had retreated from the studio window. It was now in the front half of the room, by his stacks of drawers. Tom opened the door and went quietly out. He crossed the strip of grass and walked carefully next to the wall, keeping in the shadows, ducking below the level of the windowsill till he reached the door.

Georgie stood at the long table, with her back to him. The torch rested on its side nearby, lighting whatever was in front of her. It was where Tom kept his drawing supplies. Sometimes he left sketches there or studies, but he hadn't done any recently. There was only clean paper, pens, charcoals.

Could it be—? Now he came to think of it, Georgie's pose was relaxed, surely more relaxed than it would be if she was spying. Her head was bent in concentration; her shoulders were supple. She looked as if she had no thought of being interrupted; as if she had every right to be there. Which of course she had.

Tom couldn't analyse the throb of dismay that he felt, mixed in with the rising hope. He only registered it, along with the dew seeping into his ankles and the rustle of grass, the trickle of water, the passing of a car high on the hill road.

He'd been listening to the engine for some seconds before he thought: Harry and Alan. Then he realised Georgie could hear it too and was having the same thought. Her head had lifted and she was starting to turn. Tom stepped back round the corner.

'Georgie?' he said, and shushed his feet in the grass. By the time he opened the door, she had turned away from the table and was standing with her hands in her pockets.

'Come to get me?' she said quizzically. Her mouth turned up at the corners and her cheeks were rounded; in the murk, that was all the impression he had of her smile.

'That's right. What are you doing in here, in the cold?'

'Having a think.'

Tom leant against the door jamb. He didn't want to step into the studio; he didn't want to seem to encroach. He pretended to rub his head so he could drop his eyes to table level. All the paper looked clean and the charcoals were in their usual place.

'Having a think about drawing? I'm sorry if I interrupted.'

'You didn't. I wasn't. I was just having a think.'

Tom tried to focus on her.

'What are you looking at me like that for?' said Georgie.

'I can hardly see you.'

She was looking back at Tom steadily. She could obviously see him all right – and so she should: most of the light fell in his direction now. She must have moved the torch.

What was she thinking? Did she suspect that he'd given the news to Nye himself?

'Are you all right?' he asked.

'Fine.' Her voice was absolutely clear.

'You look a bit ghostly in this light. It's in my eyes, can you turn it off?'

Georgie scooped up the torch so quickly he was startled. The motion shone the beam straight into his eyes and he was still blinking when the studio went dark.

'Whoops, sorry.' Georgie laughed.

28

'I'll take her. You rest, you look tired.'

Hazel turned in surprise from the flowerbed. 'I'm fine. I don't mind taking her. I just didn't realise it was that time already.'

The sky was powdery blue and the sun neat and round above the chestnut tree.

'It's deceptive,' said Nye. 'There's going to be a glorious sunset in a while. Stay here and enjoy it.'

She nodded. 'Thanks.'

Nye collected Elen from the hall. Did Hazel know he had misled her? He would have given her the sunset if he could, but of course he would be getting the best of it as he drove through the lanes or walked the path to Fearson's Meadow and watched the river answer light with light. Inside the Plas Bryn garden the brightness would deepen domestically and swiftly, and would probably be gone by the time Hazel put away her gardening tools.

As he emerged from the drive, the land's beauty surprised even him. It was orange and brown and green, and there was a fire behind everything which spoke of how nothing ever died, only changed.

Nye slid down the window as they drove between the pasture fields. Elen screwed up her nose.

'Foul. All I can smell is your petrol. Does the exhaust need fixing?'

'It'll disperse in a second. It's just the engine starting up.'

'Perhaps the mixture's too rich.'

She murmured it casually; she was quoting Ieuan again. Nye's first instinct was to mimic her, but he suppressed it out of respect for Hazel. Last night she'd said he teased Elen too much and that if he went on he'd make her self-conscious. Nye knew very well that Elen was already self-conscious; she was like him. And he teased her to warn her, in a way she imperfectly understood.

'It's the correct mixture, all right. No doubt about that. Powerful cars are pollutants, I'm afraid. I should really use your mother's for short trips like this.'

But he wasn't using Hazel's car. He had never intended to bring it out this afternoon. He was driving down through the valley in his long blue Jaguar; it would make a distinctive shape cruising through the lanes, if anyone cared to raise their eyes from the Islyn and look.

Since yesterday, Nye had been scrupulous in interpretation. He had laid out Georgie's words and actions, atomised them. There had been many small observations to encourage him. The first and greatest was of course that she had come. But there had been others too: the absence of outright hostility. Her failure to leave after he had answered her initial question. The searching way she had looked at him when she asked him about Tom and Hazel – that last most of all.

It showed that some shift had taken place in her mind. Nye knew she would have been thinking hard, all summer. Where had it led her?

They drove across the foot of the valley and through the lanes to the Islyn, chatting amicably about Elen's current history project. Nye had been right about the light changing: in the short time they had been out the sun had slipped downwards and as they entered the Islyn, diagonals of light bounced off Taplow's greenhouses.

'It's just along here, on the right,' said Elen, as they came past the Islyn signpost. 'Up beyond that telegraph pole. There's a sort of lay-by . . .'

'I know. I've been here plenty of times before.'

Elen looked at him curiously. He slowed the car and swung it to the right, on to the familiar stretch of gravel, through the widened gate and up the dirt track that had been Mrs Davies's last time he visited and was now a short driveway along one side of the front garden.

He switched off the engine, unclicked his safety belt and looked out at the house. 'That's good; they're in.'

'Are you coming in too?' Elen sounded astonished and faintly alarmed.

'I'm going to say hallo. Don't worry, I shan't embarrass you.'

Nye got out of the car. After a second, Elen went hastily out of her side too. She looked at him across the roof. 'I usually go straight in through Ieuan's door.' She gestured to a blue-painted door over to the right: it was where Tom and Georgie's little cottage had once ended and where a single-storey extension now stuck out.

'Go on then.'

'OK.' She began walking off at a sideways saunter. 'Thanks for the lift.' She covered a few more yards. 'What about getting home?'

'Nine o'clock, as we agreed. Either your mother or I will be here to pick you up. Be ready for us – we don't want to interrupt the Griffithses' evening.'

'Oh, Mum usually just parks in the lay-by, she doesn't come in.' When he didn't reply, Elen rounded her shoulders and headed quickly away to the blue door. She gave a funny knock: two bangs with the flat of her hand before she pushed it and went straight in.

Nye turned his own steps towards the central, black-painted door. This had been the entrance to their cottage, when they'd had only half the house. To the left was the ghost of another doorway, blocked out in bricks. If he stretched out his arm, he'd be able to touch where Mrs Davies's door-knocker had been. A question occurred to him. He stepped back and looked across to Ieuan's annexe: yes, they had given him Mrs Davies's old door. Of course they would. They hadn't so much rebuilt the cottages as reassembled them.

It was a different kind of alteration from that which Nye had bestowed on Plas Bryn. Georgie and Tom had worked with what they had. Opened and closed angles. Realigned the shelter. From here he could see through the windows of what was now a wide sitting room and lighter hall: inside the familiar cottage walls, the space of the house ran lengthways.

Nye rang the bell. It jangled loudly; the summons to a busy household with adolescents at large.

Tom or Georgie? It was impossible to tell from the footsteps. And whichever one it was, did they know it was him?

Georgie wore jeans and a heavy jumper. She had known. Her face was pristine – it didn't look as if bone lay under her skin; more that her face was moulded out of one pure substance.

'Hallo, Nye. What can I do for you?'

'I gave Elen a lift down to see your son. So I thought I'd take a chance and call on his parents.' He studied her: there was no indication in her face that they had spoken yesterday. 'Is this a bad time? Are you busy?'

'We are quite, yes. Nothing important but yes, we're busy.'

'I won't keep you then.'

'It's all right, I can spare a few minutes.' Georgie sounded alert. It was the tone she'd used yesterday at the club, once the first tense questions were past.

She was angry, he thought, and busy trying to keep it from people to whom it did not belong.

'Quite a few changes you've made,' Nye said. He looked from side to side, then close up at the door which stood open next to Georgie. He placed the flat of his hand on it. 'I'm trying to remember what colour this used to be.'

'And can you?'

'It was brown.' Until she asked, he hadn't been able to, but now he saw it – a fudge colour with rainlight on it.

Georgie nodded. 'It was. A very brown brown.'

'We've done a lot to Plas Bryn, too. You should come and see it.'

He had said it earlier than he'd intended and much too commandingly. Georgie's eyes dwelt on his for a second. 'I know what you've done. I've already seen the photographs.'

'The photographs?'

'When you were having the work done on it, before you moved in, the contractors took a lot of before and after shots. The foreman was Gerry Morgan's brother, and he took the film into Mrs Howard's shop.'

'I see.'

'The befores were no great shakes, but there was a fair old demand to look at the afters.'

'Christ. I'm surprised she didn't mount them on boards and charge for viewing.'

Georgie shrugged. 'This is a village. Perhaps you'd forgotten that? Surely you didn't expect to come back unnoticed?'

Nye shook his head, warily. There was a dissonance in the way she was speaking to him; he could feel her concentration but he wasn't sure it was directed at him.

'I don't think I expected anything in particular,' he said. 'I just wanted to come home.'

A sound came from the kitchen – a chair scraping. That was it: Tom could hear them. He was an unseen party to this meeting.

'How's Tom?' he asked.

'Very well. Very busy.'

'That's good.' He looked into Georgie's face. Her eyes were wide open: was she daring him to mention the Reynolds Monette? 'He's busy painting, I hope.'

'Not at the moment, no. But in general, yes.'

Nye stepped backwards. 'Well, give him my regards, won't you?'

Instantly Georgie's face became self-consciously social. And the constriction eased from the back of Nye's neck. He had not been mistaken; Georgie did want this approach. He stopped moving at once.

'It would be nice to see you both at Plas Bryn,' he said. 'For a drink, or for dinner, when you've got the time.'

'Thank you.'

'Is that thank you, no thank you, or thank you, you'd like to come?'

'I didn't mean to be rude.'

'You weren't, Georgie.' Nye let his voice relax. Just for a phrase or two; the broad, deep-dredging sound of Georgie being named. 'You weren't and you aren't. Please come to Plas Bryn.'

Georgie's pupils contracted as she focused on him, across a stretch of sunshine. 'We'd like to,' she said in a very formal voice. 'Thank you.'

'What about Friday?' said Nye. 'Come to dinner on Friday.'

'Oh, well, why not just for a drink? It's easier.'

'No, if you're going to come, you might as well come and eat. Break bread with us. You know I've always liked cooking.'

'Yes. It sounds very nice. I'll have to check with Tom, though.'

'Yes. Speak to Tom, that's the best thing. About coming to dinner on Friday. And then, shall I call you?'

Nye drove steadily across the valley floor to Fearson's Meadow. He was filled with the desire to go fast, and yet the peculiar colours of the evening checked him, like a hand laid across his chest. The sky was pink and blue. The hills were powdered with gold. Shadows lay confidingly in the ridges of earth and swelled the hedgerows between the fields.

He left the car by the sheep grid and climbed the stile.

The grass was wet with evening dew and on the far side of the meadow, the low rocks by the river were already in shadow. As he walked, Nye could hear the letter rustling in his breast pocket. It was a gentle noise: the paper had softened over the years, with frequent handling. He had brought it with him as a talisman; he'd thought that whatever the outcome of his visit he might want to come down here afterwards and read the letter again, in recognition or in leave-taking. But when he reached the river bank he simply stood beneath the hawthorn and watched the shallow waters flow.

The letter stayed in his breast pocket. The Georgie he had just seen was a long way from the young woman who had written it. So he had no need of looking back at the well-known lines of script. There was no need to hurt himself any more by tracing the flow of the turquoise letters, finding it broken again and again by that one name – its initial rearing up like a Stop sign.

29

Rain fell outside the window of Radio Wales; shiny drops making an agreement in grey between sky, pavement and road. In here the lights were on. White-yellow panel lights, they were, friendly to the eyes of receptionists and visitors, and Tom had no headache.

But he was bothered by the shadow of what was to come. Soon, he knew, he was going to experience discomfort. There would be a procedure like at the doctor's, and a pain would arrive.

Georgie refused to acknowledge it. But then Georgie was deceiving him. She had still said nothing about meeting Hazel in Bartraeth; and on Sunday when the front door had closed she'd come back into the kitchen and spoken dismissively. 'You heard that?'

'Yes.'

'So? Don't pretend you're shocked.'

'I'm not shocked. I knew you were going to accept.'

'Well, then.'

'Why the fuck—?'

She'd twisted her hair up. Was she consciously imitating Hazel? 'Because he asked and he's going to go on asking. Now he's come to the house, there'll be no way of stopping him. So why not say yes straight away? It's only food and drink.'

He had looked hard, but she'd been completely equal to it; in fact she'd leant over a corner of the table and cupped his cheek. 'Ah, lover. I thought you'd be pleased.'

'I am.' If there had been a little shard of truth in her assertion, there was in his too.

He felt crowded. He had his own secrets to set against Georgie's but they didn't buy him the space hers seemed to. Tom didn't think she could fake the zest that attended many of her actions this week, or the sudden, slight unpredictability of her moods.

On Monday, after school, she'd been in the studio and hadn't come out till he arrived home. On Tuesday he'd refused to let himself search the drawers and cupboards. Then he hadn't been able to paint.

He'd searched today but found nothing; he'd known before he started that he wouldn't. Last night he'd made love with a special attention. Her muscles were at their springiest, holding him away, clamping him close.

'I'm going to ask Hazel to marry me.'

'When?'

'God, I don't know.' Nye's face was sweating gently. He looked content and implacable. 'Soon.'

'Are you sure?'

'No. Were you sure when you asked Georgie?'

'It's been very quick.'

'Not really. Do you think she'll say yes?'

'I don't know.' There was a little space around them. It meant Tom could see passages through the seven o'clock drinkers; paths that jinked and wavered but stayed remarkably stable. 'If she does, will you do it?'

'What are you talking about?' Nye's humour was incredulous. He foraged in Tom's face and appeared to find nothing satisfying. 'Why would I ask her if I didn't want her to say yes?' He went on looking at Tom with this dazzle of moisture on his skin, as if his concentration was making the sweat.

So he'd looked in the school corridor when they were fourteen. Sick in his stomach from the caning, Tom had wondered if Nye was going to throw up. The pale face had edged forward from the damp fringe of hair and the eyes held Tom's, confidently.

'Sorry,' said Tom. 'Take no notice, I've been working my arse off.'

'I can tell. You're punch-drunk, aren't you? Still there in your head.'

'No, I'm listening.'

Nye sucked air in through his nose; it made a buzzing sound. 'It's a big week for me, too. I'm doing a major presentation tomorrow. If they OK it, it's the next step achieved.'

'It's all coming together then.'

'Things do, don't they? If they give it the go ahead – well, who knows? A good week for a surprise party.'

'Oh yes.'

'Don't worry, once tomorrow's out of the way I'll help you with it. Discreetly, of course.' Nye leaned across Tom to put his empty glass down. Balanced between the bar and Tom, he twisted to catch the server's eye. His nostrils were open again and Tom watched his head lift, so slightly he didn't think Nye was aware of it. All Nye's intuitions were cerebral; he might be thinking of Hazel now but he wouldn't understand it was because he smelled her.

Tom left Nye at eight-thirty and went into college. He didn't dare go to Hazel's. He was afraid to go home.

It was impossible to know what Nye meant. It was impossible to know if Nye knew what he meant. Tom had eyes and Nye was blind, but then Tom put out his hand to guide Nye and Nye took it, and which one was the leader, which the follower?

He sat in his studio in the dark, imagining Georgie. She would be preparing for Friday's party. It would be hours yet before she would fall asleep and the house would become safe for him to enter.

'You bastard. You bastard.' Georgie had cried, her arms hugging her naked breasts. They were still round but looser since Ieuan, and crimped at the nipples. Tears fell on the fold of her stomach and on the tufty hair at the top of her thighs. 'You bastard.' She was crying because he had just asked her not to leave him; and because she knew she wouldn't.

And because he had told her what she wanted to know about his infatuation of two years before, with his most talented student.

She couldn't stop crying. Her thumbs left white marks wherever they touched. She cradled her feet and placed her open mouth on her knees. She had turned all to water and her skin was reacting, mottling on her body as well as her face, puckering into goose-bumps. She kept asking about the girl's painting: 'You bastard, you bastard.'

Georgie was late home, from a governors' meeting. She arrived just before seven, tired and exhilarated. She took off her shoes and walked around the kitchen, relating details of who'd said what about publishing SAT results. She had a glass of lemon barley water while she talked, to moisten her dry throat, then opened a bottle of red wine.

'How was the radio?'

'All right. It was Paul Henries doing it, so it was light on background.'

'I suppose you can't expect so much depth from the news people. That's not their job. Were you on television news as well?'

'Yes. Only the regional round up though.'

Georgie laughed; she answered his deadpan note with her own. 'I wouldn't expect it to make the national headlines. You must be realistic.'

'At least it's official now and Karl can go to work.'

'It leaked anyway. Hazel congratulated me on it at the week-end.' Georgie looked at him with a flush of belated candour, like someone presenting a gift.

'You didn't say anything.'

'I did to Hazel.' Georgie sounded tough and playful; and oddly sleek. 'I told her it was confidential. But I didn't want to get you involved, in case Nye tried to play one of his games.'

'How do you know he didn't?'

'He might have done. But nothing bad's happened and it's beyond him now.'

Tom went on stacking plates from the draining board. 'Is that why we're going to dinner there?'

'I thought it was best to keep on the safe side.'

It wasn't quite right. Underneath Georgie's well-being, he sensed energy coiled up. Meanwhile, he saw nothing of Nye in the village, nor Hazel. On Friday, at lunchtime, he walked from college to the park near the medical centre, where, last month, he'd seen Hazel eating her sandwiches. She wasn't there. She probably ate with colleagues, now she'd had time to settle in to the job; besides, the day was cold.

Tom walked round shopping streets: the warehouse units near the docks and Mount Street. He was glad not to see her. He wished he didn't have to see her tonight. His cones and rods didn't have room for her and Nye and Georgie at once.

30

It wasn't exactly what he had imagined. It was more informal, and brighter. The Plas Bryn sitting room was cheerful with light; neat piles of books stood on different surfaces among ornaments and framed photographs, and Nye sat on a wide stool, cracking nuts and throwing the shells into the fire. His red v-neck jumper and the flames combined to throw a hint of colour into his pale face.

'I'll do it,' Hazel had said a minute ago, when he'd offered them more drinks; and he'd handed her his glass gratefully, as if they both knew how tired he was.

But he was talking easily enough now, to Georgie. 'I tell you who I saw the other day – in Birmingham airport of all places. Steve Garrett. He lives near Warwick now and works for a regional off-licence chain.'

'No, you're kidding.'

'Can you credit it? He looked very bullish when he told me, I think he was daring me to say anything.'

Georgie was smiling. 'And did you?'

'If the bar had been open I'd have invited him for a drink, but it was seven in the morning.'

'Well, well. What about his politics?'

'Neither of us mentioned them. I had a plane to catch.' Nye's smile broadened into a grimace as he cracked another nut. 'Brazil nut?' He held it towards Georgie. She shook her head.

'Who's Steve Garrett?' said Tom. The name meant something.

'He lived in Mabon Street with me in my last year at university,' said Nye. 'Short man, very thickset. He was a teetotaller and a devolutionist.'

Tom saw him suddenly, Nye's neighbour that he passed on the landing with its orange carpet and smell of toast. 'Oh yes. I didn't realise you knew him,' he said to Georgie.

She was sitting slightly sideways in her chair; she curled one calf round another. 'I chatted to him a few times.'

'He used to come into my room and talk,' remembered Nye. 'Rehearse his arguments for the long-awaited referendum. Sometimes he'd bring his own coffee. And once, do you remember, he presented us with a little box of Milk Tray? We assumed he'd been given it himself, and then I discovered he'd bought it from the newsagents especially for us.'

Georgie nodded. She was half smiling and not looking at Tom. 'I must have managed to miss all that,' he said.

'Oh he was very good,' said Nye. 'He convinced us didn't he, Georgie?'

'Yes, at the time.' Georgie reached out with both hands to take her new gin and tonic from Hazel. 'Thanks.' A second later, Tom sat forward to accept his. He found it difficult to remain seated while Hazel was on her feet. He felt a persistent impulse to stand and move away, just as he did when he saw nuns on the train.

It wasn't Hazel's fault; she wasn't inviting him to feel guilty. She looked restrained and secure in a green outfit that didn't really suit her, and the air of damage he'd spotted once or twice on other sightings wasn't present tonight. Her hair was tied in a loose ponytail, similar to the kind Georgie used to wear, and there was a pleasant give-and-take between her and Nye. Nye touched her hand with his forefinger now as he took his glass. 'Would you like this Brazil nut, Hazel?'

'No thank you.'

'Then it's yours, Tom.' And Tom only just had time to catch the little missile as it flew towards him.

Nye looked broadly at him for an instant and mock-applauded his catch. Then he turned to Hazel.

'You know, I was thinking: I expect you're right and Steve Garrett is still an abstainer. I can just see him walking the moral tightrope within Collins and Shepherd. The Conscience of the firm, at work in the free market.'

'Do you know Steve as well?' Georgie's surprise wasn't polite. Tom tensed but neither Hazel nor Nye seemed to react; perhaps the incivility clanged only in his own ears.

'He looked us up in Ealing once,' said Hazel.

'In seventy-nine.' Nye smiled asymmetrically at Georgie. 'Referendum year. He thought – two more for the cause.'

'Did he get you?' said Tom. He was trying to take attention away from Georgie.

'No, man. Not with the proposal the way it was. We stood to

carry too much expense, and we hadn't got the benefits flowing from the EC yet.'

'Besides,' said Hazel quietly. 'We weren't eligible to vote.'

'And what about now?' Tom asked.

'There's no need for a parliament now.' Nye glanced at Hazel; they must have discussed this together. The thought struck Tom as bizarre. 'Though we need some sort of administrative reform.'

'Who's we?' said Tom. 'Wales or England?'

They both looked at him. Nye put his hand on his heart.

'Ow, there's a shaft.'

'You have been away a long time,' said Tom.

'But we're back now,' said Nye. 'And let's be honest, we're bringing in more than we took out. Hazel's just been asked to sit on a quango, for God's sake. Anyway, since when were you a nationalist?'

'I'm not. I just wondered.'

'I remember you didn't even vote in the referendum.'

Tom stared at Nye; why was he saying this so openly, when Hazel and Georgie sat between them? They must know the referendum was years after they'd all parted; the obvious question was there for them to ask. But instead Georgie was asking Hazel 'Which quango?' with a note of incredulity, and he looked away from Nye's face, which seemed to be nothing but a needling dazzle, and leaned into the women's conversation.

'It's a committee to monitor science and technology training schemes for school-leavers.'

'Did you get that through your job?'

'Partly, but more because of a research project I did in Bristol a couple of years ago.'

'I didn't know you'd been working there.'

'I did an MSc.'

'Oh.' Georgie and Hazel exchanged a look – their first that evening; until now they had been just meeting one another's eyes. Georgie's expression was suspicious, Hazel's guarded; and yet Tom thought they touched shared ground.

'Where did you do that?' Georgie asked.

'At Bristol University.'

Tom turned to Nye. But though Nye was looking at him, and smiling, he wasn't inviting Tom to share anything. The intimacy in his eyes was combative and Tom watched his mouth open, and wasn't surprised to hear the old, robustly teasing voice come out. 'Dear, dear, so you're a political Welshman now, are you? Proper

Welshie, as your Nan would have said.'

'Give it a rest.'

Being rude to Nye on the quiet was as close as Tom was going to get to him tonight. And even that wasn't very close, as both the women heard what he said and Nye made no response. A tiny silence occurred. Georgie watched him sidelong. Tom wouldn't meet her eye, because he refused to take that steadying look. He was here to keep watch on her tonight; he wasn't going to let those positions be overturned. After a couple of seconds, Georgie unwound her legs from one another and made a gesture towards Nye. 'I like that, above the fireplace. Whose is it?'

'She's a young artist, Lilian Berry, who does commercial work for a living. She did the cover of our annual report last year and I was very struck with it; the designer arranged for me to view her paintings. She had to bring them to his studio as she doesn't have one; she works in her flat.'

Tom's jealousy zig-zagged inwards; after the first pain, the sensation was predictable, like the working of a tin opener. It was shaming, too: now he had the Reynolds Monette nomination, he'd hoped to get rid of this reaction to hearing praise of other artists – especially young artists. He had thought he'd be able to encourage, not resent. But it was hard to hear Nye doing the praising and Georgie agreeing, her face lively, as if looking at the girl's work made her refreshed.

It was a good painting too: confident, funny, with an instinctive handling of paint. Most of the pictures in the room were strong, except for the Lucien Freud; had Nye chosen them all himself? Or was he guided by his dealer?

'Ah, this is one of Hazel's,' Nye was saying about the picture directly opposite Tom, one of John di Pradano's tree-bark men. 'She saw him when we were in Paris and said we should buy one. I wasn't sure at the time it should be this particular one, but she was quite right.' So he was guided by Hazel too. Tom looked at the di Pradano and shared Nye's doubts. But now he suspected his view of being corrupted. He stared and tried to clean the grudgingness away.

None of Tom's own paintings could be seen on the well-studded walls. He had looked out for them, sharp-eyed, as Nye had ushered them in, along the corridor, through the square hall with the big acrylic and the bank of prints, into the sitting room. But so far there was no sign; and no indication, either, that any pictures had been moved for this evening. The hanging looked very thought out.

Did Nye keep them all in his office then?

'I didn't realise you were so interested,' said Georgie. 'Do you buy every year?'

'When we see something we like.'

'We'll have to get you on Karl's mailing list.' Georgie laughed. Tom wondered if Nye heard the little breath of openness inside it, and if he understood that she was relaxing.

Nye did. He laughed back at once, exactly the same quality of sound, and when he turned from her to Tom, his eyes had kindled. 'Oh yes. I'll be investing in him now, all right. With your permission, Tom.'

Tom shrugged. 'I don't have a veto over who buys my stuff.' It didn't sound as humorous as he'd intended, because his chest had tightened. 'Buy a big one,' he said. 'They're more expensive.' That was worse.

He could feel Georgie's eyes on him, so he kept looking at Nye.

'Yes, I've noticed your canvas sizes are growing. I think my own favourites are your two-foot-sixers; I love their concentration. I particularly liked the pair of ice paintings in your last show.'

'You said you didn't see that show.'

'Did I?' Nye looked imperturbable. 'I must have made a mistake. I definitely saw those paintings. Did they sell?'

'Yes.' Tom glanced at Georgie, plaintive expression ready, but she had transferred her attention to Nye. She was listening to them with a slight frown.

'As a pair, I hope?' said Nye.

'Yes.'

'Good. Someone's got a good investment there. Of course, the really clever thing to do would have been to buy you from the beginning.'

Nye was leaning forward, his elbows on his legs. Hazel had become less noticeable in her chair. Tom nerved himself to meet Georgie's eyes but when she eventually turned towards him, he twitched his head away.

'Yeah.' He slurred his speech defensively. 'A missed opportunity there. Me and Van Gogh.'

Nye and Georgie stood side by side in the dining-room doorway; over their shoulders Tom could see the ceiling and the tops of some of the paintings in the hall. When he leaned to the left he could see the walnut desk on the right-hand wall. Nye was explaining how he'd bought the desk without seating himself at it.

'It was on a little platform in the antiques shop and I could look at anything, squat down, open things, peer underneath, but there wasn't room to put a chair and sit. It's Chinese, eighteenth century. It wasn't till it was delivered that I realised how small eighteenth-century Chinese were. The kids can use it, Hazel can just sit at it, but me – forget it!'

'It's beautifully solid,' said Georgie. She moved across to touch it. Tom slipped into the space she vacated, but Nye stepped out after her at once.

'That's one of the reasons I love it – it's so workmanlike. And the wood is gorgeous – look how they've selected pieces with the grain running the same way.' Nye's big hand followed hers on to the polished surface.

Georgie's face was interested again. Tom didn't think she was faking, either: after a few minutes' neutrality back there in the sitting room, during which he'd taken the focus off her by talking about the Reynolds Monette, she'd resumed her part in the conversation. She'd shown no sign of what she'd been thinking. When she'd first opened her mouth to speak, Tom had had to pause and consciously push his shoulders down and lean his head against one hand, to control his anxiety.

He had the answer to one question now, at least. She really didn't know that Nye had been buying him all along. The thing was, how much had she just tumbled to? A suspicion? Sudden complete understanding? He'd waited to hear the sentence.

But she'd only made a remark about one of his shortlist companions, and the work he was submitting for the show. It had turned into a question. Tom had been clumsy in answering and when he finished, Georgie had rippled her brows at him quizzically, slightly mockingly, making him realise that his eyes were fixed on hers.

Now they were accompanying Nye on a tour of the house; except that it seemed to be Tom doing the accompanying and Nye and Georgie forming a unit. They walked slightly ahead of him and Nye kept pointing things out to Georgie and saying to Tom, 'Do you see?' without moving, so that Tom had to crane over their shoulders.

Hazel had stayed in the kitchen, a surprisingly bare room without the Welsh dresser Tom and Georgie had bet one another they'd find. Tom could see her now as he followed the others back past the little three-sided opening in the top corner of the hall. She was placing pans on the gas hob and looked flustered; he realised that Nye and Georgie must have been standing in full view of her for the last couple of minutes, as they discussed the history of this inner porch, but neither of them had offered to help her.

Tom hurried to catch them up as they went down the corridor. They saw a big games room with a table tennis table, and a small second sitting room. At the end of the passage, Nye paused and grew self-conscious. 'Now this,' he said, turning the doorknob and inserting himself into the opening, as if he wanted to make them see it with his eyes, 'is where I show my pretensions, according to Elen. It used to be a laundry room; I've made it into my library.'

The room was sudden in the electric light. And odd.

Unlike the rest of the house, which felt comfortably occupied, it had an air of waiting. The walls were lined with green hessian and bookshelves ran floor to ceiling on two walls and around the doorway in which they stood. The fourth wall had a high window, and below it a glass-fronted bookcase packed with matching spines. A set of library steps stood in one corner, and on the unpolished wood floor were two disintegrating armchairs and a small rug.

'Jesus Christ,' said Tom.

'It's only private,' Nye said quickly. 'I don't bring people here. I don't expect anyone else to like it.'

'They certainly couldn't mistake it,' said Tom. 'It's like a time warp.'

'I suppose it seems affected to you.' Nye spoke stubbornly. He moved slowly out of Georgie's way as she came further in, and Tom, entering with her, saw that the skin round Nye's ears had reddened. He felt glad and at the same time, obscurely angry.

'I didn't say that,' he said, keeping the broad edge in his voice. 'Why throw away Illtyd Gooding's old chairs, once you've got them?'

'You recognise them then?'

'Shit yes. I stored them in my studio when your mother chucked them out, remember? Don't say you've had them in your house ever since?'

Tom looked at Nye, who was watching him with his face slightly averted. The question made sense but Nye wasn't answering it. He knew Tom hadn't finished his sentence.

'Since . . .' It was there on Tom's tongue, waiting to be spoken. In every contact he'd had with Nye for nineteen years, they'd avoided mentioning it; it had seemed to be a shared instinct; but suddenly, with Georgie in between them, he was ready to say it.

'Since you burned my pictures.'

There was a little movement from Georgie and then Nye was looking at him, quite normally.

'Yes, they've lived in my studies most of the time. Though they were in storage while we were in Paris.'

'That must have cost you,' said Georgie.

'It did.'

'But then I suppose, when someone leaves you something, you don't like to get rid of it. Especially when it's from an old teacher.'

Tom looked at Georgie. Hadn't she heard what he'd said?

'He didn't exactly leave them to me,' Nye said. 'I bought them from his sister.'

'Oh but, I thought – I'm sure I remember—'

'He told his sister he wanted me to have something, and I chose the chairs. I gave his sister money though; I didn't like not to. She said she was going to give it to a charity, didn't she?' He turned to Tom.

'Yes,' said Tom.

'Do you remember moving them to your place in the back of my Herald?'

'God, I remember them arriving,' said Georgie.

'And leaving,' said Tom. He couldn't believe they were doing this, reaching back over the fire to talk about things that happened during *that* time, as if it hadn't been a passage which snared them all together and set them rubbing and cutting, creating these wounds which they all still carried.

So: 'Leaving,' he said in his ugliest voice, to remind Nye of those screaming telephone calls, and Georgie of her own sordid rage. Nothing glamorous about a midweek morning, the biggest, blue chair stuck in the doorway, half in the rain where Georgie had tried to put it, and the two boys from the van inspecting the red chair, curious about its splintered arm and paint smears; and Georgie watching from the kitchen window, her face exhausted.

'I appreciated your sending them back,' Nye said. He spoke to both of them. The texture of his skin looked suddenly rough, as if honesty was pushing to the surface. 'It meant a lot to me to keep hold of them. It was like an earnest of my coming home one day.'

'I think that's why Tom sent them to you,' said Georgie. 'I wanted to chop them up.' Like Nye, she was speaking candidly; but, also like Nye, she didn't seem to be hurt by the violence of that remembered scene.

Nye nodded. 'To stop me coming back,' he said; it was one of those statement-questions.

Georgie stared up at him: she seemed to be wondering if he was serious. He was; Tom could tell from the stillness of his face and the way he'd shifted his weight to try not to impinge on the two of them. Georgie shook her head. She turned to Tom, smiling incredulously, and teasingly as well: 'God, Tom, did you hear that? He must think we don't know him at all.'

The champagne came out as soon as they went back downstairs. Nye left Tom and Georgie in the dining room while he went to fetch it. Georgie stood by the window, in front of the dark orange curtains; Tom waited beyond the table, by the mantelpiece. On top of it was a Chinese bowl, a clock and three little cast-iron mice he recognised from Nye's Bartraeth days. He'd bought them in his last year at university, from a shop near the art college. On the shelves, too, were other familiar objects: a miniature brass globe on a stand and a pony carved from coal. Tom was surprised Nye didn't keep them in his library or in the study he'd shown them upstairs, where he obviously often worked into the night at his workstation and modem and fax – and where there were, Tom had noticed, bare patches on the walls, where pictures had been removed from their hooks.

It was as if he chose certain areas of the house in which to let the past through; an exercise in love or control?

'You've forgiven him then?' Tom said unpleasantly.

Georgie turned on him, not particularly quickly, but with heat. 'We're here. They're here. Our children are probably having sex right now. What would you prefer me to do?'

'What are you angry with me for?'

'I'm not.'

'No wonder he's celebrating.'

'For fuck's sake, Tom.' Georgie rarely swore; when she did, as now, the words flowered out of her mouth. 'Don't be so pathetic. I think you'll find the champagne's for you.'

Champagne and seafood arranged in a shell and served tepid (prepared by Nye); strips of lamb in red sauce on rice, with roasted peppers and aubergines that had too much oil on them; and red wine; curly salad; cheese; a rich, rich blackberry mousse – made by Hazel with their own blackberries, picked by the children and Hazel in the summer.

Hazel seemed muted, as though she'd put herself in abeyance. But perhaps she simply couldn't get into the current of the evening, which was flowing fast now. You could see it moving over the table like a V in the water, Nye and Georgie its twin leaders. Tom was swirled along in it, without having any control. He could see enjoyment in the faces of his wife and his friend, and he tried to reach some of it for himself, but Georgie refused to pause to let him in and while Nye smiled at him and offered him the words he needed for joining them, Tom could keep up only for a few moments at a time.

He was experienced enough at drinking and listening. Once he tuned in to Hazel, he could see that she too was busy charting the flow. At first she had alternated glasses of wine and water, but now she was drinking calvados steadily. At one stage she'd gone into the kitchen to make more coffee. When she'd come back it was with a packet of cigarettes.

She'd just reached for her second cigarette and flipped the packet round the table. Georgie took another one too, and lit it from a candle. For the last few minutes, she and Nye had been discussing the sister of Marie Tonkin, Hazel's colleague at the health centre. Now, as Georgie asked her a question about Marie, Hazel lifted her head from lighting her own cigarette. 'Two years,' she said rapidly, still on the inhale, and twisted in her chair, dropping the lighter on the table, raising the cigarette to her mouth again. It was a swift movement, careless of Georgie; careless of all the others round the table. 'Or is it three?'

31

Georgie was humming; Ieuan was eating his breakfast slowly. Georgie checked through her briefcase: stapled papers, blue folder, yellow folder, handwritten notes for assembly. Tom, heavy-eyed, watched her. He would start work early today – now, in fact, as soon as Georgie left. This morning he wouldn't wait for Ieuan's shambolic departure.

Instead he'd accompany Georgie out of the back door and turn left across the grass to his studio while she turned right to the car. He would be inside and switching on the electric fire, settling in to his working day, before she had even left the drive.

It was odd to be in competition with Georgie. It reminded him distantly of mornings in their student life, when he and she would leave their shared bed and set off for separate lectures in college. And later times when, not having seen each other for several days, they would meet up in a class, both with the consciousness of a different bed and a different companion on them, always unsure of how to address one another now things had changed.

He had tried and failed to address her all this last weekend. 'Oh, for God's sake, Tom,' she'd said at first, with exasperated good nature. 'I'm just tired.'

Though later, when she was in energetic mood, she'd had less goodwill. 'Yes, a walk sounds nice,' she'd said politely, with burning eyes. 'I'd just like to finish this, and get some letters ready for posting. Three quarters of an hour?' The words had come out with fierce precision, and an hour later she had still been busy and Tom had gone into his studio instead.

Then yesterday, he had been forestalled in the studio.

'I'm thinking. If you want to work just say and I'll go and think somewhere else.'

'No, no, of course not.'

He'd hovered in different rooms, especially those with an east window. Raked leaves in the garden. Watched a science fiction epic on the television with Ieuan and Elen and Robbie.

What was she doing? She had no paints mixed, that he could see. And she was moving about more than was compatible with drawing, or even sketching.

But he didn't think she was just tidying or escaping. There was something creative in her actions. As if she was preparing for something.

It made Tom go very still. He was trying to catch a noise within himself as much as one from the studio. What had it been, that whisper of dismay when he'd looked in at Georgie from the night, last week?

Oh my God, he kept thinking now; I knew it. But knew what? That she was ready to start work again? That she would have less time for him from now on?

It was what he'd longed for, often enough. Release from her expectations; from all that high-tension encouragement. Well, now it had started to happen.

Last night he'd lain curled round her, his stomach warm and growing faintly sticky against her back. It's the Reynolds Monette, he'd realised, it's given her the freedom to start again. It had been like a starburst; for a while he'd been covered in happiness.

Today though, he could see Georgie's eyes again.

She was getting ready to go. She shut her briefcase and stood up. Tom ducked out of his chair, just saved Ieuan's coffee from being knocked over, and picked up his own cup. 'I'll come out with you. I'm all ready. I want to get started early today.'

Georgie nodded. 'Fine. Goodbye, Ieu, have a good day.'

'God, what a beautiful morning,' Tom said as they closed the door. The sky was shot with pink and lemon remnants of sunrise and the air was thin.

'The first frost,' said Georgie. Patches of white lay on either side of her path like tributes. Tom touched her arm.

'Goodbye. I hope your day goes well.'

'And yours.' She began to walk away.

'Will you be home at the usual time?'

'Yes.'

The studio was much colder than outside, so he lit the gas heater and the electric fire. Georgie was sitting in the car running the engine; after a minute he heard her reverse out, carefully keeping the revs up. He put his coffee mug down and began an erratic search.

At eleven-fifteen, Georgie made the phone call. She stood up; it felt wrong to sit at her desk for it. She stood between desk and window and looked out at the playground, empty now except for a chalk drawing of a figure, probably herself.

'Can I tell him who's calling?'

'Yes, it's Georgie Griffiths.'

Then a wait, not long at all.

'Hello, Georgie.'

'Hello, Nye. Is this a good time for me to be calling you?'

'It's not bad.'

'I'd like us to meet.'

'Surely.'

'Can you make it within office hours?'

'Naturally.' There was a tiny pause. Was he registering amusement? Then came a rustle and Georgie realised that he was looking in a diary. 'Very well. Let me see . . . I could do it midafternoon today or tomorrow morning. If you'd like to wait till Wednesday I can give you lunch.' His voice had become more expansive; this time he was smiling.

'No, I'd like to see you today.'

'In that case, does half past three suit you?'

'Yes, thank you.'

'Where shall we meet?'

He knew she didn't want to go to CWM. Appreciation slid through her, warm like whisky. And volatile: she spoke more easily into the phone. 'Do you know the old castle on the Meifan to Penygroes road?'

'Cilfa's Castle? Yes, I remember.'

'There's a car park behind it now. I'll meet you there.'

There were questions Georgie wasn't going to ask, one in particular. She knew that all weekend Tom had expected to be challenged with it, and she had nearly put it, many times; but she'd managed not to.

The bread she, Tom and Ieuan had eaten during the difficult years was gone. Passed through and shat out to clay. What good would it do to know how much of it Nye had paid for?

All the same, it had been a struggle. Tom had hovered round her all weekend, his face pale and filmed with sweat from time to time. He wanted her to take issue with him. He sensed her anger – she saw it in the flinching, insistent way he looked at her – and he was waiting for her to turn it on him.

She wouldn't. She knew she wouldn't get the truth anyway; only a partial revelation, calibrated to what Tom thought she knew. She didn't mean to get embroiled in that kind of fight again.

Groping for the shape and weight within his words.

'I only suspected, I didn't know. I can't police who buys my stuff.'

'Yes, I thought it might be him.'

'Sure I knew, so what?'

She could hear the different tones, see the alternating expressions on his face. The thought of him doing that intensified her anger, and adulterated it so she began to lose clarity.

Which was why she wasn't going to ask that question, of either of them.

Nye was standing at the far side of the car park, where the hill broke into boulders. Theirs weren't the only cars: there was a Dormobile and a smart blue saloon with Raine Motors of Surrey written in raised chrome script on its boot. Georgie walked round it to reach him.

'Thank you for coming.'

He bent and kissed her cheek. Until then she'd been thinking he looked slighter out of doors, but the movement dispelled the illusion. 'This place has been cleaned up,' he said.

'It's owned by Cadw now. They invest for tourism.'

'Can we go up?'

'Oh yes, perhaps even in.'

They walked round the foot of the hill to the kiosk. It was closed but the barrier was low and they stepped over it, as the middle-aged couple and the young family had done. Nye's coin fell into the honesty box with a hollow clunk; it was one of those clear days when sound travels upwards and the father of the young children turned and stared.

Nye's heavy black coat was buttoned and disguised the movement of his muscles.

'Thank you for Friday,' Georgie said. 'It was a good idea.'

'Yes, I enjoyed it.'

On the steep of the hill, moisture breathed up at them. It had a disinfectant tang – the residue of last night's frost was cooling again in preparation for evening. They skirted the children balancing on the earthwork and headed for the nearest corner of the ruin. Over the broken walls they could see the middle-aged couple from Surrey in the far chamber, and the main rise of the western hills beyond.

'I don't want to hear about you and Tom,' Georgie said.

Nye nodded. He didn't answer: he seemed to be digesting, and expecting more. The desire to know pulled at her. She wasn't strong enough to leave it at that.

'Is there much to know?'

His head lifted and turned slightly away from her, but he met her eyes. 'No.' He'd often looked at her like this when he was being honest with her; as if the truth put pressure on his neck and forced his chin upwards. 'The minimum. The minimum that's possible for me.'

She nodded. She didn't want to look into his eyes with the squeezed expression. It told her more than she wanted to know; besides, she hadn't come here to trap him. 'What about Hazel?'

'What do you mean? Is *she* seeing Tom? I don't think so.'

'Does she want to?'

'Not as far as I can tell. We don't discuss it, of course. But I don't think she'd have been able to come back like this, if she did.'

Georgie turned to look south over the vale. From beyond the ridge came the roar of the motorway's flow. 'So it was her decision to come back then, was it?'

'Yes, in fact.' Nye picked up her half-smile. 'More than you're willing to believe. Oh, it was my impetus and I was the one who asked, but she's always had the power to say no. She's said no in the past.'

'I'm willing to believe anything about Hazel.' Georgie wasn't being vehement; she heard her own caution and hoped Nye did too. It had the beginnings of respect in it.

'She doesn't wish you any harm you know.' Nye hadn't turned to look full south; he was sideways on to her, with one hand on the wall; she didn't know if he was watching her or stopping himself from slipping.

'How much does she know?' Georgie said.

'That we were good friends. That I loved you, and missed you when we left.'

'But she doesn't know why you left.'

'Yes, she knows. She knows her own reasons for going, and the reasons she shared with me.'

'But not our reasons.'

'She might have guessed. We went through a lot in the years immediately afterwards.'

'So I heard.' They were in Georgie's mind like her own memories: voices, party chatter, phrases in letters. Hazel in a lilac dress.

'Drunk, apparently, at five.' 'He's got another woman now.'

'We all heard about Paris,' she said, with a touch of spite.

'Yes, everyone did. I certainly made an exhibition of us there, didn't I? Well, it was my turn to be indiscreet and I took it.'

'You make it sound like a competition.'

'Oh no. It wasn't like that.' Nye's features had lost their normal set and he looked young and disturbing. 'I just couldn't help it. I behaved like a swine, I was past reason.'

'You didn't want Hazel to leave though. You followed her home, didn't you?'

'After a few more weeks of doing damage, yes. I'm not proud of it, Georgie. It's not something I intend to do again.'

'No, I didn't think that was what you'd come back for.'

The Surrey couple were coming diagonally across the great hall, stepping on the dressed stones. Georgie and Nye moved along the front wall. They came to a metal gate and climbed over, first Georgie then Nye. The castle floor was lower than the hilltop.

'Did it make things more equal between you?' she said. Even if there hadn't been a hiatus between her last words and these, her voice would have given her away.

Nye's eyes rested on her very lightly. 'Yes, it's fair to say that. In a sense it gave Hazel her freedom back.'

'And what about you?'

'I didn't have to be so careful of her any more. After Paris, we each had a disfigurement. It was easier once she had something to forgive as well.'

'Didn't she always?'

'Something public, which I could admit to.'

Georgie walked round the enclosure, pacing it. It would have been the kitchen once, but it was hard to imagine it filled with people and steaming fat.

'I wish I could admit to something,' she said. Nye didn't comment for a while. He was watching her measure the ground. Georgie wished she could stand still but her legs carried her on and her hands were stretched out to encounter the stones and feel along the lintel above the fireplace, as if she were doing something useful.

'What are you going to do?' Nye said.

The lintel was one handspan thick. 'I'd like to see you,' she said. 'Away from Tom.'

'Good.'

'On one condition. You don't tell Tom about it.'

Nye stood with his hands folded in front of him. Georgie sat down on the edge of the fireplace and looked at his wrists. They were thick and the backs of his hands were fleshy; the hairs which crept down them were grey next to his dark coat.

'I won't tell him. I'll hardly be seeing him now.'

32

'I don't understand.' Tom played with his watch – not unstrapping it but repeatedly checking the time. He wished he hadn't taken his clothes off. He felt at a disadvantage, naked and unable to grasp what Georgie was saying.

Perhaps he'd had too long to anticipate it. All evening it had been clear to him that Georgie was making up her mind whether or not to say something.

But it escaped him. He tried again. 'You've arranged for us to see Nye again, but you don't know exactly when?'

'No,' said Georgie. 'Listen, Tom. I'm going to be seeing Nye on my own now.' She stood by the wardrobe, folding her skirt over a hanger. She did it quickly and familiarly, almost with affection.

'Why?' was all he could say.

'Because I want to. I've missed him.'

'You've missed him?' But of course he could see the truth of it in her face. It was the same candid expression he'd seen on Friday at Plas Bryn. 'Jesus, this is a bit of a turnaround. One evening in his company and you're old friends again.'

'You're right, we are old friends.'

'You've hated his guts for nineteen years.'

Georgie unbuttoned her shirt. The pale fabric fell away and she slid her arms out and dropped it in the linen basket. 'I had some good reasons to hate him.'

'And now you don't?'

She was wearing a white bra and black tights, as if she were dressed for some domestic sport. 'Quite a lot of it was guilt,' she said. She put her arms behind her back and began unhooking her bra. 'And fear. And anger, that he went away like that.'

'Jesus Christ, Georgie, he could hardly stay with things the way they were.'

She took her bra off. Her breasts settled gently. 'Oh, he could have done.'

'Well, he didn't.' Tom stared at her. She seemed completely occupied in what she was doing, putting her thumbs inside her pants and tights, peeling them off one leg, then the other. Her body jack-knifed and straightened and was bare. 'Look, Georgie, what are you saying? Hating him was all a mistake? You're glad to see him back? What?'

'I'm just saying that now he's back, I want to see him again on my own. Like you do.'

Tom stopped in midmovement. He stood between the bed and the chest of drawers, half turned away from her, only his penis belatedly in motion as it swung against his thigh.

'Tom, I've got eyes. And a sense of smell – and seeing him usually involves you drinking.' Georgie was looking at him with an unrelenting kind of sympathy.

'It's only been once or twice. I didn't want you to know in case it upset you.'

'Well, now I want to do the same. Only I do want you to know. I'm telling you in advance because Nye is Nye and I don't want to give him room to play games.'

For a naked man, Tom felt very hemmed in. He straightened up and finally undid his watch-strap. 'So you still don't trust him.'

'Nye is Nye.' Georgie gave a very little smile.

'And is Nye going to tell Hazel about this arrangement?' He heard the rasping note in his voice.

'I don't know, I didn't ask.'

'Georgie, are you doing this for revenge?'

'No.' She looked straight at him, her naked body upright like a sentry, then unexpectedly she giggled. The giggle went on. 'I'm just doing it. I've been seeing him anyway, you idiot, for Wellspring. There's not really any bloody difference at all except that I'm choosing the terms this time.'

She put her hand over her mouth and, chuckling, went out to the bathroom.

33

It was mouse weather: grey with mist in the morning, while thin sun filtered over the afternoons. Things gathered below eye level: leaves, brown bracken, newspaper cuttings that Karl sent him. Tom was third favourite with the bookies, or last but two.

He painted. He would have rested now, normally, but the BBC wanted to film him at work. Putting paint on – that was the quote that got attached to his name most often in the round of publicity interviews: 'I put paint on.'

O Arglwydd. A base of blue. It had been red in the first one, when he was young; he'd laid the foundations with cadmium, the most expensive colour, despite his shortage of money. Red and then orange and black; much later he'd added the isolated lozenges of yellow and blue, with their melting edges to worry perspective.

Tom couldn't remember all of the original, by any means. Nor did he want to; this was no loving re-creation. He painted *O Arglwydd Two* with his usual spasmodic discipline, giving it turns alongside two other paintings. One of them was on a five-foot canvas and this was the one the BBC were interested in filming. Tom wasn't very fond of it but he could see why it appealed to the producer – it had an energy and sense of release that was unusual in his work. It was going quickly too; in fact he was rationing the time he gave it now, to avoid finishing it before filming. Meanwhile he pursued *O Arglwydd Two* privately, using colours and spatial relationships that were the opposite of its former self, a dedicated and bitter approach.

Georgie had seen it and commented with passing interest, 'Blue? Is this a new departure for you?' These days Georgie was being brisk and slightly mischievous. Her eyes acknowledged that she was taking unfair advantage, but she couldn't help enjoying it.

Tom didn't draw her attention to the details of the painting. The mice among the stalks of barley. The bishop's colours. They were there for him, not his wife. A tribute to seeing clearly; since Nye had wiped his eyes for him.

It had been the iron mice in Nye's dining room that had sent him back to the book. Nye had put them out on purpose of course: a Nye-joke, to jog Tom's memory. So Tom had climbed up into the loft and hunted through boxes till he found the old wedding present Mabinogion, and looked it up.

Manawydan and Pryderi, as Nye had said in the pub: one cautious and self-serving prince, one bold and generous. A wedding, a gift of land and an idyllic four-way friendship. A partner swap too, so that when Pryderi is magicked into banishment, his friend's new wife goes with him and Manawydan is left to look after Pryderi's woman. Nye was enjoying himself drawing parallels all right.

What had he said in The Hollybush? 'The spell is lifted at last. The seven cantrefs are as they were at their best.'

In the story, the seven cantrefs were Pryderi's gift to Manawydan, plentiful lands where in the beginning the four had feasted and hunted and learnt to grow close. What exactly was Nye laying claim to now?

Tom painted them in: Nye's claims. Nye's work. The mouse-path eating through the crops. The figure on the hill road, come to strike a bargain. Their coded forms were exact, with a reduced beauty.

Georgie's movements, on the other hand, were confusing. He couldn't tell how often she was seeing Nye. In the ten days since she'd made the announcement, she'd been out more often than usual in the evenings and she didn't tell him where she was going. Each time, the possibility was there. Afterwards, though, when names came up in conversation they were frequently those of her women friends. It was Georgie's way of being kind. Or of throwing up a smokescreen.

Tom had tried to find out from Nye but so far Nye had refused to see him. 'I'm very busy,' he'd said on the second phone call. 'I'll ring you next week.' Georgie, it seemed, had known about that almost at once; that evening she had been very bright and tender with him and when he grew sick of it and sat down to watch television, blanking her out, he caught her looking at him with a new, confused passion.

Was she sleeping with Nye? If it had been himself or Hazel, he'd have been sure of the answer, but with Georgie he didn't know. He couldn't even be sure it was only a matter of time. The subtleties were at work already: every so often, when they were alone together, Georgie's face would go out of kilter. She would come and touch him and hold him too tight. She would press the flat of her cheek against him, a contact that he couldn't shake off.

Sometimes, he let himself fuck her on these occasions; not often, because while it was going on, he always found it hard not to cry.

Tom didn't know if he was being badly treated. He saw Hazel in Bartraeth and in the village; she was friendly and hard to talk to. There was no sign of her wanting to tell him anything now, and he couldn't make up his mind whether he'd imagined it in their early meetings.

He knew he hadn't imagined her panic at Richard Wyn Ellis's party, nor her sudden carelessness late at night at Plas Bryn. But the meaning of them was beyond him.

When he stared at her too openly during their short encounters, she would register first caution, then discomfort, and pretty soon would take her leave. Sometimes she did it with a tinge of reproach; last time he thought he'd seen haste, her spirit tacking inwards from her smile.

He didn't know what to do. He didn't know who to be angry with, if anybody.

Georgie had been angry in Cyprus. She had hung above the wheatfield like a small sun. Tom was well used to her rages but this was different.

When, pressed into the corner of their balcony, she finally said, 'How can he?' her voice was small and distinct. She seemed to have shrunk too. She had carried the newspaper all the way home from the party, holding it across her knees as she sat in the passenger seat and stared out of the window at the dirt roads and white houses and telegraph poles. Now she stood in the furthest angle of the balcony wall, the paper in her hand.

Tom ran the tap. Georgie's lips were bleached and she still looked shocked. 'Here, have this.'

She took the glass obediently. 'Did you know?' she said when she'd drunk nearly half of it.

'No, how could I?'

'You don't seem surprised.'

'I'm not. Nye's in love with her. He told me back in Wales he was going to marry her; you knew that.'

Georgie nodded. She looked at him. He could see she was putting together the facts with impressions she'd carried in her own mind; belatedly making adjustments. It obviously hurt.

Tom took the newspaper from her; she held on to it for a second before letting go. It left ink on her hands. She must have been holding it for almost an hour, ever since she'd found the notice. Tom had missed that moment. He'd been busy drinking retsina when Elena had said, 'Is Georgie ill? She's gone white.'

Hazel Thomas and Aneurin Mathias were married on Saturday 23rd May, at St Peter's Church, Llanelli.

Georgie drank from the water glass again. Behind her, the sun was travelling rapidly down the sky, but it was still so hot that it scorched Tom's skin. Georgie's hair burned orange round the edges.

She looked grief-stricken – literally, physically. Understanding rolled through Tom like a wave. 'You still want him back, don't you?' he said.

'Not any more.'

'But you did. You didn't think it was over yet.'

Tom stared avidly; he couldn't stop himself. His face was hot under the eyes, but his tongue felt cool. At the far end of the balcony, Georgie's body was dark against the sky, bright against the balcony wall.

'I don't know.' Georgie had begun to move her head fast from side to side. 'I don't know what I thought. He owed us more than this though, he shouldn't have done this.'

'He's married the person he loves.'

'No.'

He hadn't believed it either, of course. But he hadn't expected Georgie's confident denial. That evening, sitting inside beneath the ceiling fan while Georgie stayed out in the bruising air, he had begun questioning.

What did Georgie and Nye share? Tom had always known they had their own secrets; you couldn't get close to Nye without them. He had accepted the fact and never before felt threatened by it.

34

On the outskirts of Harborth, in the pub by the level crossing, Nye and Georgie wrangled. This evening Georgie was beautiful in a very characteristic way: her hair was brushed back behind her ears and her face had a bare, lunar quality. When he'd first known her, Nye had found this off-putting. He'd wondered how Tom could kiss such a large expanse of skin.

'But why didn't you see *me*, like you saw Tom?'

'You didn't ask me to,' Nye said.

Georgie rolled her eyes between heavy lids. 'Oh, and you waited for Tom to ask you, I suppose?'

'That was different. I had amends to make to Tom back then. And you'd told me to keep away, very vigorously. Those phone calls, Georgie, and that letter you wrote.'

'I'd been in touch since then. I wrote to you when we came back from Cyprus.'

'Not with words.' Though that wasn't entirely true; Nye remembered the line of Georgie's handwriting on the back of a drawing in that first consignment she'd sent: *I don't draw any more.* He'd discovered it some time after he'd pulled the sheets out of the envelope, when he'd already been studying them five, ten minutes.

'You didn't reply because you can only see one of us at a time. And you were already seeing Tom.'

Nye listened to the taunt in her voice. Her jumper sleeves were pushed up to show her wrists and a slender gold watch.

'Yes, there's something in that. Although I wasn't aware of it at the time.'

'When did you become aware of it, as a matter of interest?'

'Very recently. In the last few weeks.' Nye looked into her eyes, which were shining with a headlong light. 'What are you trying to make me say?'

'I'm not asking you whether you're seeing Tom.'

'You are, though, in a manner of speaking.'

'Well, don't answer me.'

'I think you already have your answer.' Nye found laughter beginning to rise in him. A minute ago he'd felt tense and almost oppressed, but Georgie's quick changes were infectious.

There was danger in it. He didn't think Georgie was completely in control. Yet he felt it was wilful, in part at any rate; she was choosing to take risks with him. He was fairly sure that when she went home, she slipped discretion back on.

She would need to. Tom must soon begin to suspect that they were meeting, if he didn't know already. Then they would have to find a way to contain him, because Tom was creative.

'You have such beautiful grammar,' said Georgie musingly. Nye laid his hands on the table, opposite hers. The commitment must come soon; he did and he didn't want his to be the fingers to cross the gap and make the crucial touch.

Georgie was right: growing close to Tom carried too much possible pain for him. Nye didn't know how Georgie could have understood this before he did. She was ahead of him now; it was enrapturing and irritating, and Nye scrambled to catch up.

'What are you doing with your hands these days, Georgie?'

'What do you mean?'

'Are you painting?'

Nye entered the house with his coat folded over his arm. Beer had been spilt on it in the pub and it still smelled; while he didn't lie to Hazel, and barely even dissembled, he didn't want to rub her face in his activities.

She was in the sitting room, clearing away Davy's possessions from one end of the table. Elen's homework was spread over the other.

'Hello, you're earlier than I expected.' Hazel's voice had no edge to it. She straightened up, holding Davy's football cards.

'Yes, it was only a quick drink.'

'Are you hungry? I don't have any food ready yet.' She had a pile of her own papers waiting to one side, with a notepad and pen balanced on the top.

'I'll get myself a snack; you're working by the look of it.'

'I haven't started yet. Davy's only just getting out of the bath.'

'Where's Elen?'

'Gone to look for a book.'

There was a pleasant atmosphere in the room. Nye was

reminded of work sessions with fellow students when he'd been at university. Tom had always been impatient when he'd come round to find someone else in Nye's room, reading or taking notes.

'Don't let me interrupt you. I thought you'd finished that report.'

'Oh I have. This is background for next week's project. I just wanted to have an early look because next week is half term, so I'll be working from home.'

Nye nodded. Hazel looked tired but freer than she often did. She worked too hard at the new job, especially given that it was part-time, and the sight of her bent assiduously over files late at night aggravated him, but he had made a bargain with himself not to complain. He tried not even to pass comment.

'Is it interesting?' He looked over her shoulder at the pile of laser-printed documents. SOURCING – COMMUNICATION – MULTI-SKILLING – PARTNERSHIP.

'Yes. More than it looks,' Hazel said briskly, and with a trace of warning.

'Good.' Nye had been going to ask if she'd made up her mind yet about joining the quango, but refrained. 'Is there any news? Apart from work, that is.'

'Tom called. They've asked us down on Sunday, for a lunch party.'

Nye stared for a second before he recovered himself. 'Oh. Did you accept?'

'Yes, of course.' Hazel's eyes settled on his. She looked alert and slightly intrigued; she didn't bother to hide these reactions nowadays – they were her reward for behaving so gracefully. 'Didn't you want me to?'

'No, that's fine. It's for all of us, I take it: Davy and Elen too?'

'Yes, I think it's going to be quite big, with some of Ieuan's friends as well. Tom said everybody wanted to make the most of half term.'

So Tom had discovered them. Well, it wasn't unexpected; though Nye thought it would be a shock for Georgie when she got home. Unless she already knew, had hatched the idea with Tom, and simply not troubled to mention it to him. Nye wouldn't be astonished to learn that that was the case. Georgie seemed to be experimenting with strength and her own ability to bend the rules.

If Georgie knew, it was probably safer. For Tom to have taken the step on his own meant that he was trying to discomfit her, and Nye. His tactics were good: an invitation to a party at the Islyn set up ripples in all four of them. It would probably be hardest for Hazel; had Tom taken that into consideration?

Looking at Hazel, who was now setting Davy's belongings next to his satchel, refusing to lose her balance or drop the intelligence from her eyes, Nye felt angry that Tom should subject her to this; and puzzled because he didn't know how she really felt. That ignorance carried its own fear, too.

It was a debilitating fear, which made him want to hold on to her. There were gaps in his love for Hazel and they were crucial to both of them. They couldn't have survived the early months if she hadn't been able to slip sideways and elude him; the blizzard of anger and punishment and grief would have been too intense. And too relentless, because it had continued so long; much longer than a loving couple could have stood.

Hazel had saved them by learning how to hide. Nye could still remember the first time she'd done it. It had been about six months after they'd left Wales, early morning after a party, and he woke with the usual headache. He'd heard the floorboards creak and he turned cautiously, remembering the journey home and Hazel crying. But she was facing away from him, taking a shirt from the wardrobe, and something in her movements and the set of her head alerted him.

'Hazel?'

When she turned, her hair was slicked back, her eyes mild.

Those hiatuses; those periods of absence – they were the secret place in which their marriage grew. Nye couldn't look into them, but he knew that things of his own as well as Hazel's lived there. Sometimes the gaps had a glassy surface; at others they were thin as air; recently he'd felt them disclose a new nature – warm and soft, sprinkling their absence on him like coal dust.

Naturally, now, he was vulnerable. He could hardly ask to be exempt from that, given what he was doing, but when the fear came it reached so far in, it took his words away.

The children's voices sounded in the hall.

'I'm going to see *Aladdin* next week,' Davy was saying. 'With Simon. And swimming.'

'Are you?' Elen was leafing through her book. She glanced up. 'Hello, Dad.'

'Hello. Hello, Davy.'

'Hiya. Yes, you see, Mum's taking me and Simon. To the Metro in Bartraeth.'

'Lucky old Mum.' Elen looked across at Hazel. It was a sardonic, easygoing look. Hazel smiled back, amused, and changed the smile to affectionate for Davy. Her relationship with each child was different and changed as they grew; she and Elen had more of a comradeship now than they used to have. Nye liked observing the two of them; he knew that he and Elen were alike in an essential, instinctual way, whereas her relationship with Hazel was subtler. He was less at ease contemplating Davy, because the points of contact between him and the boy were so volatile. Nye loved him with a passion which sometimes seemed to vaporise to nothing at all. He needed Hazel's help to sustain it, as he needed her help with so much else.

35

'Georgie.'

'Mmm.' She didn't look up from her drawing. Tom could see it clearly from where he stood: on a large sheet of their most expensive paper, she had drawn a big figure balancing a tiny counterpart in its hand. The charcoal had been used swiftly – the outlines looked to be almost one continuous stroke, and the blank-faced figures had their own dynamic, as if energy had obliterated their features. A lucky chance, which would spoil when she added more detail? As Tom watched, Georgie turned the stick on its side and put slashes across each corner of the paper. Suddenly the image had the emblematic quality of a playing card.

She had been in here for nearly two hours, ever since she'd come home. Tom put down the plate with the tomato sandwich on it.

'I've made you this.'

'Thank you.'

'Has it been going well?'

Georgie picked up the sandwich and sat down in a chair. 'You tell me,' she said, taking a bite. Her face was dewy; she looked as if she would smile, but was too preoccupied to disturb her muscles.

'I don't need to, do I?' His tone went wrong; it sounded bleak rather than affirmative. Tom had sworn to himself that when Georgie began painting again – as he suspected she would soon, despite his not having found anything in his last search – he would encourage her. But already he was slipping, and she was only drawing. But then, her drawing had always been her most original work, and this time she was starting strongly. The image that looked up from the paper seemed to threaten him. He smiled and struggled to relax. 'I've invited some people over on Sunday.'

'Oh yes? Who?' Georgie munched her sandwich. Her face conveyed enjoyment of it, and interest.

'Judy Morgan, Harry and Alan, Nye and Hazel and their kids, from the village; and the art crowd – Karl and Iestyn and Nia

Jenkins and the others. A lunch party, really. Would you like to ask your staff? With it being the start of half term, they'll be feeling good.'

'Mm, but quite a few are going away.'

'I know, but that's a good thing isn't it? You don't want the whole staff room.'

'No, it's a bit awkward. The ones who are going away have already mentioned it to me. It would look as though I'd timed it so they couldn't come. It would be better to leave the teachers out of it, I think.'

'OK, if you want.' Good: that was what he'd banked on. 'In that case I'll add in some of the art writers I've been talking to – David Price and Ceridwen. Oh, and Beth Chadwick from the BBC. I'd forgotten how much I liked them.'

Georgie nodded and took another bite.

'It's all right with you, is it?'

'Fine.'

'Is there anybody else you'd like me to ask?' Tom couldn't help pressing it. He had expected more of a reaction than this: a clicking on to guard, a protest of some sort in her eyes, if not aloud, because she must realise that he was fighting back.

'No, I don't think so. Just go ahead.'

'Good, I think it should be fun. It will be good to have the painting and writing crowd again' – he felt the need to return to it; emphasise his new status, remind her of his success – 'and I thought it would be a good way of having Nye and Hazel over. Nye probably knows half of them anyway.'

Georgie smiled at last, her face lighting up with inward laughter. She brushed crumbs off her hands and stood up to touch Tom, but he moved away.

'Tom, I've never tried to shut you out. Yes, let's have Nye and Hazel here. Again.' She leaned past him for the charcoal, turned quickly and kissed his shoulder, and her hair brushed his face as she went back to her drawing.

Tom watched her hands moving speculatively through the air, shaping what might or might not belong on the paper below.

'You've really started again now, haven't you?' he said.

'Yes, I think so.'

36

Now that the leaves were thinning, they could see much more of the village from the house. Hazel no longer had to go right into the corner of the window bay to see the houses tripping down Gwern hill. And though the valley bottom was hidden by the bulge in contours and the alders clustering round the river, on the far slope the main road through the village was visible now, and growing clearer every day.

Today the sun slipped in and out of high cloud. The pale yellow light made the weather seem fine, but when she'd opened the windows the air had been cold and damp. Hazel was ready; Nye was in the bedroom, still changing.

Last time Hazel had been in there, he'd had his red sweater on. 'That's got a mark on it,' she'd said. 'A faint one, on the front. I meant to tell you.' It wasn't true, but she didn't want him to be conspicuous in scarlet, announcing his position with every move he made round the Islyn.

Nye would have worn the red, v-necked sweater, she guessed, as a mark of belonging. He'd bought it soon after their return to Wales, once he'd seen other men wearing them, and for him the colour meant homecoming. 'Joining the ranks of the red men,' Elen had said sardonically and Nye had stared at his daughter in exasperation, recognising his own ability to coin a phrase, not enjoying having it turned on himself.

His footsteps were on the stairs and he came through the doorway, wearing dark grey. It suited him much better than the red, but he still looked very noticeable.

'I feel like the vicar,' he said. And he did resemble someone come to perform a ministry.

'You look fine.'

'So do you. You look lovely.' Nye spoke with that hesitant intensity again.

'Thank you.' Hazel glanced down at herself; for form's sake, she pretended surprise. *I haven't bothered to dress up*, her look said; but she knew very well that her tension had translated into an air of expectancy, darkening her eyes, emphasising her mouth. She had watched her appearance come together in the mirror and wondered if she had willed it.

She was wearing a brown jumper and black trousers, because they were the most unobtrusive things she possessed. She had just tied her hair back and put a faint dusting of rouge on her cheeks – faint in case it grew hot at the party and she began to flush; though she had slipped the make-up into her bag to take with her, so that she could add it later if she remained too pale. Her instinct was to blend with the others as much as she could.

Nye walked up to her. He seemed about to touch her and Hazel had to control the impulse of her flesh to shiver and rise up to meet his hands. In the last few days, every physical contact between them had been charged with a burning gentleness.

It reminded her of other points of departure in their life. Nye's touch always altered at these times. Was it a good thing that it was gentle now, or was that just the way she was receiving it?

'Are the children ready?'

'Davy is. He doesn't want to come though,' she added. Nye looked impatient and Hazel made a quick gesture, which would have cupped Davy's shoulder if he'd been there. 'You can't blame him, he won't know anyone.'

'All the more reason for him to come and meet someone. Georgie said Joe Llewellyn's son will be there.'

'He wanted to go to Bryn's.'

'He needs another friend besides Bryn. What's going to happen if they fall out? It's all well and good not subjecting the boy to pressure, but we can't leave him to his own devices for ever. I think—'

The spatter of light footsteps descending the stairs stopped Nye talking. He turned.

'Mum.' Davy's hair was wet from his face-washing and he hugged his chest resentfully.

'What have you got there, son?' said Nye.

'My remote control car.' Davy looked at him briefly then back to Hazel. 'It won't go in reverse.'

'Won't it? What happens then, lad? Show me.'

Davy looked past his father at Hazel, although Nye was already walking towards him. Nye was going slowly, with his head tilted forward in the way he thought was casual. Hazel could see the patience in his movements; she knew it represented hours of thought about his son and a certain resignation he had never voiced to her.

She watched Nye squat down, straight-backed. 'Let me see.' He held out his hand and Davy reluctantly gave him the car.

The first time she'd come back here with Nye, in January, he'd stood in this room and talked about Davy. 'It might give him confidence, having this as his home. I'd have loved it. Loved it. I used to imagine it when I came up here – these partitions weren't here then, of course.'

Now the partitions were gone once more. They'd had them knocked down, the rooms picked clean and mended. But on that first visit she'd stood on dirty lino and damp carpet and watched Nye walk through the tunnel-like corridors, his arms stretched out to knock on plasterboard, his feet measuring the distances eagerly, always carrying him to a window.

The house hadn't looked as she imagined it. It didn't fit into her past at all, and the garden was different too. They'd walked all around it, several yards apart and not saying much, and she'd walked right across the site of the fire, still looking for it, before Nye had remarked: 'That's where we did it.'

Since they'd lived here, she'd got to know that corner of the garden for herself. She usually went up there when Nye was out. She felt embarrassed to be there in front of him, not so much because of the fire as because from the site, you could see the Islyn. It was the only part of the garden from which Tom and Georgie's house was visible. She'd noticed that back in January – it had seemed appropriate then, like a function of memory. It was only quite recently, a month or so ago, that she'd become aware of another logic to it. If they could see, they could be seen. Nineteen years ago, Nye must have chosen that piece of ground deliberately, so that Tom might watch his work burn.

She made small discoveries like that. They came out of living with these constant, discreet movements. She was growing skilled at navigating, manoeuvring out of people's way. She kept her eyes open to avoid collisions, not really to seek information, but every now and then she would make a turn and find herself staring at something that had been hidden from her till now.

Sometimes they were important, sometimes not. They always increased the subtlety, rather than cleared it up.

'Turn it clockwise. You know which way clockwise is, don't you? That's right, now . . . what's this?'

'It's mended. It came off but we mended it.'

'I can see that.' Nye was peering at the tiny lever mechanism, wedged with a matchstick. 'It's good. Did you do it?'

'Ieuan.'

'Ah.' Nye looked up at Hazel. His face showed several shades of humour, and a withdrawal. 'I can't compete then. Shall we go? You can bring the car with you, can't you, Davy? Let Ieuan have another look at it.'

He stood up and touched the boy's back, lifted his hand off immediately, so that Hazel wondered if Davy had even felt it. 'Where the hell's Elen?'

Nye often joked about Ieuan's prowess at fixing things; about Ieuan's bike; about Ieuan in general. Today, though, he'd cut himself short. He was thoughtful and receptive; he was exercising control.

As they drove down past the houses – Davy craning to see into Bryn's front garden, sun flashing off a car windscreen across the valley – Hazel felt free. This defiant energy came to her quite often. It forced its way out through the other considerations. Despite you, I'm happy.

'You're well, aren't you?' Nye had said in September, during her first week at the health centre. She'd realised then that coming back here had been a bigger gamble for him than for her. She knew what she could stand whereas Nye, for all his assiduousness, could only take her word for it.

Hazel had paused and watched Nye wait for her answer. She'd wanted to put her hand up to his face and say, 'Yes. Yes,' clenching her teeth as she often felt the urge to do when she was emphatic, but she'd been afraid Nye would feel her vitality and be suspicious. Besides, the hiatus was real. She'd let it continue, and tried to measure the distance between his meaning and hers, before she smiled and said yes.

They crossed the river and drove past a group of kids on bikes and two old women coming back from church. Elen was humming a complicated tune which required her to interrupt herself. Hazel wondered if Nye was going this way to spare her the more intimate approach of the lanes. It didn't matter to her which route they took; she was in a public mood now and she didn't intend to take any part in the private drama.

Since the dinner, Nye had been in touch with both Tom and Georgie; she could tell as much from the look on his face and the absences in his conversation. That evening, his concentration had been on Georgie. He'd been trying to turn something round. Hazel had helped him, to the extent of effacing herself and allowing him to slight her with neglect. She had seen Tom notice, and look away.

Perhaps Tom thought that was how she and Nye lived together. Her subservience in return for his forgiveness. Sometimes in the past she'd wondered if Tom grasped the complexities of Nye, or of her. He'd seemed to have a vanity now and then that made him stupid, simply unable to see. Could he really think they had settled for that kind of petty bargain?

Hazel could show Tom what true humiliation looked like.

Nye and she naked on the hotel bed; his face a curious mixture of yearning and self-disgust, his hands hovering, bubbled across the knuckles with burn blisters, reluctant to touch her.

Nye coming home ten months ago and asking her the question.

Various acts of forgiveness and generosity in between, from him and from her.

Hazel's contempt for Tom could turn to anger when she thought about this, and that was dangerous. Nye was glancing at her. She looked back at him but no, he was checking the mirror as he turned off the main road again and took them down Deryn's Lane; and though she was used to coming on this route to pick up Elen, Hazel felt the narrowing of the hedgerow like a hood going over her head, and put her hand up against it, tapping the beat to Elen's tune on the window.

'Did you join the quango, by the way?' Georgie paused by her elbow, with a bottle of wine. It was a friendly enquiry, just loud enough for the man on Hazel's right to overhear, and he looked duly interested.

'Yes, I've just accepted.'

'You'll be busy. It's an interesting area.'

'Which quango is this?' the man asked. Hazel had forgotten his name.

'One of the ones we actually need,' said Georgie.

'It'll assess science and technology training schemes for school-leavers.'

'Those schemes have been invented and re-invented for over ten years now,' said Georgie. 'In the usual a-wish-and-a-prayer way. It's about time they were evaluated.'

'What's your background?' asked the man. Georgie smiled and disappeared.

The party was crowded and people rubbed up against each other easily. There was usually someone to provide an introduction; Hazel had been without anyone to speak to only once, and then Georgie had materialised and opened up a new group for her.

There was quite a strong art contingent. Nye seemed to know several of them; at any rate, he was talking to them as if they were on easy terms. His relaxed air was emphasised by the fact that he was usually holding a plate of food, or filling up guests' glasses. Half an hour ago Hazel had watched him go into the kitchen with Tom, the grey back and the white back slanting at exactly the same angle as they passed through the doorway. They had come out five minutes later, Tom with a tray of pizza, Nye with two bottles; Tom's shirt had a grease stain on it.

Nye was helping, but he was not taking over. He managed to give the impression of being in the background. But Hazel thought that he was continually and unobtrusively disrupting Tom's rhythm. Tom was kept very busy – busier than it was necessary to be, at a casual party. A few times Hazel had seen him slow down and relax, usually when he had fellow painters and art journalists around him; but then, when he looked round for Nye and Georgie, they would always be settled elsewhere, out of his reach.

Tom was beginning to look frustrated. Hazel wondered if he'd planned this party as a way of putting himself centre stage again, among the four of them. Did he really think that just by getting them all in a room in public, he was going to pin Nye and Georgie down?

He wasn't looking at Hazel very much. When he did come face to face with her, his eyes were cautious, almost resentful. It reminded her of the days of their affair; he'd been afraid to meet her eyes in the presence of the others then, too.

This time, of course, the fear was different – perhaps Tom thought that she would tell him things he didn't want to know. Perhaps he believed she was ignorant of what went on, and was afraid of being the one to enlighten her.

It made her impatient. She wanted to shake off Tom's wary looks and walk across the room, start talking to that man in the blue shirt, or Catrin, the actress with long grey hair. Make her own connections, as she did when Tom and Georgie weren't present.

Nye had always acknowledged her right to keep clear of Tom and Georgie. She had come back here for his sake, not theirs. But now that she was here, she had to face their claim on her. Which was why she stayed on the margins and allowed herself to be blended by Georgie's skilful hands.

Tom detached himself from one knot of people and walked to another. A man whose back looked familiar turned and spoke to him. The man was still wearing a jacket; he'd obviously only just arrived. Hazel saw his profile: it was Chris, the installation artist, who had been with them in the past.

He hadn't changed much at all. His eyes lit on Nye and she watched him straighten in surprise. He spoke again, Tom answered with a gesture and by the time Chris glanced at Hazel, his face was a mix of curiosity and embarrassment.

Hazel nodded and smiled at him, as Jack talked. She allowed herself a lively smile, more than just social. Chris had always seemed to like her then. Enjoy her company. In fact, he was the only one of that group who hadn't treated her as if she was somehow spoken for. It would be good to talk to him again. It would also be funny if she could do it before the others stage-managed it.

Hazel gave herself a treat. 'Excuse me,' she said as Jack hesitated. 'I've just seen an old friend. Do you know each other or can I introduce you?'

'Oh no, you go ahead.'

Taking no notice of Georgie, who was watching from the left, and Tom, who was disappearing, she walked over to Chris.

37

It had been raining again. Bright orange leaves, freshly fallen from the chestnut trees, were churned up with the mud; they reminded Georgie of the cornflake-chocolate crunch her infants made.

'Another evening with the shoe polish,' Nye said, knocking a thick pat of mud off his sole.

'What does Hazel say when she sees you come home like that?'

'Nothing. I scrape the worst off first.' Nye looked down at her. 'You don't think I ask her to clean my shoes, do you?'

'No,' said Georgie defensively. Then she added: 'How should I know?'

'What about you? Does Tom interrogate you every day? Is that why you've changed into walking boots?'

'Tom sometimes asks me where I've been.'

'And what do you say?'

'Out for a walk. Seeing this friend or that.'

'He never questions it?'

'Why should he? He's used to my going out at half term.' It was true, but this half term Tom must know very well where she went, because Georgie didn't discuss it with him as usual. On the few occasions he asked, she offered a lie, but it was only for form's sake and Tom seemed to accept it because he never pressed matters. 'He's in London today, anyway. He's gone to look over the Reynolds Monette show and to be interviewed on television.'

'It's all happening for him, isn't it? When is the prize announced?'

'Next week.'

'Is there a ceremony?'

'No, there used to be, but they could never get all the artists to attend. People who'd been shortlisted once and not won, tended not to come the second time.' Georgie felt her smile broaden derisively. 'Too damn humiliating for them, you see.'

'Well, I can see it must be hard.' Nye wasn't joking with her.

'Some of us work year in, year out without being garlanded with praise. Anyway, now the artists hear by phone, then it's announced. The winner goes to a ceremony later on, at the institute, when Reynolds Monette give out all their prizes and grants in one go.'

'Two lots of coverage,' said Nye. 'I suppose it's quite a good deal from the RM point of view.'

They'd been talking like this ever since they'd left the car – on shared subjects, but diverging all the time. There was an edge to the conversation too.

The wood gave way abruptly to common land. The grass was bright green, striped with broad channels of mud where bikes had torn up the turf. 'Yours?' said Nye mock-ceremoniously, looking at the tyremarks.

'Yours too, if it is. They're together.'

'Not at your house?'

'No, they've gone into Bartraeth.'

Nye nodded and turned to look out at the view. They were standing very close but not touching; less than a hand's width separated them. The common sloped down the cutting to the road, then up again on the far side, covering the hilltop. Further down were the roofs of Caerfach – they could see only the outlying houses, though; the huge castle and most of the shops were concealed by the turn of the hill. Beyond the immediate hill, and as far as they could see to the west, more hills ran, round and regular, crazed with roads and towns and estates.

'Does Tom want this prize very much?' Nye asked.

'I don't know. I think he must. He's trying very hard to make the most of being on the shortlist. A kind of insurance for if he fails.'

'What will happen if he wins?'

'I've no idea.' Georgie had no idea what would happen if he didn't win, either. Everything was moving ahead of itself.

Since the party, Tom had been withdrawn in a stubborn, sweated way. He'd been working long hours in his studio, Monday and Tuesday. On Wednesday the BBC crew had arrived to film him at work. Today was Thursday.

Georgie had seen Nye every day this week. She was certain that he couldn't be seeing Tom at the same time and if she hadn't been, his face as he asked about Tom and the prize would have told her.

Tom and Nye were apart and she and Nye were together instead. They were in unknown territory.

A car sounded, accelerating up the hill, and without speaking they both turned their backs on the road and began walking across the turf. They stopped by the bench and picnic table.

'Tom and I got married down there.' They could just see the edge of the church tower through the trees.

'And I brought Hazel.'

Nye's voice was heavily inflected. When Georgie turned, he was looking at her.

'Yes,' she said. 'I didn't go on believing it was accidental.'

'Oh, it was very much on purpose. Except that I didn't know what my purpose was.'

Nye showed no sign of apologising. After a second, Georgie wondered why she should have expected him to. It had long become irrelevant.

'Nye, how well did you know Tom and Hazel at school?'

'I didn't know Hazel at all. At that stage, I wasn't friends with Tom either. But I noticed what he did and I saw that he liked Hazel.'

'Did they go out together?' Georgie heard the curiosity curling through her voice.

'Oh no, they were too young for that. They weren't even friends. But I could tell that Tom liked her from the way he helped her out with teachers. She got into trouble like him, you see.'

Georgie felt the familiar irritation, petty but unbeatable. 'Hazel the bad girl,' she said sarcastically. 'God, that's a useful reputation to have.'

'She wasn't bad, though,' Nye said. 'Neither of them were. That's the joke.'

'It's a joke, is it? Remind me.'

'Ah, Georgie. There are ways and ways of breaking the rules, you know that. People like you and me do it all the time, successfully. Hazel and Tom just don't have the knack of getting away with it. They never did have.'

Georgie laughed. The truth of what Nye said burrowed into her unexpectedly.

It touched on a warmth that was already inside her; a scooped out, tenderised area. She had been carrying this gap around for days now. It was a space which defined itself further with each meeting between her and Nye; each step they took into that rebarbative closeness.

'Georgie.' Nye sounded matter of fact.

'Yes.'

'I want you.'

She was looking at his coat button as he said it. She lifted her head and saw that his face was smoothed flat. 'Do you really?'

A light shone in his guarded eyes. An energy he couldn't repress – triumphant? Or desperate?

'I do.'

'Then let's find a hotel.'

Nye stood by the bathroom door, undressing himself. The last time he'd offered himself to her, he'd needed her help.

Georgie remembered the noise of the car driving fast down the lane, stopping. She'd known from the engine that it was Nye and she didn't understand how he could have got back so soon.

She had been watching the clock; she knew. It was forty-eight minutes since Nye had driven out of the lay-by, his boot wedged open by the paintings, his back seat stacked with them. He'd had smears of paint on his shirt and all down his sides the fabric had been wet. He had been working fast, but then he had a lot to do.

He couldn't have done it all yet – not hide the paintings, drive to Bartraeth and return with Tom. Georgie ran to the hall and peered through the window. The car was parked neatly by the gate: its boot was closed and the paintings were gone. But though Nye had sworn he would bring her Tom, he was alone.

He didn't see her through the window; he walked across the grass looking at the side of the house and Georgie startled him when she pulled open the door.

'What is it? Has something gone wrong?'

'No. I've got rid of the paintings.'

'Got rid of—?'

'Hidden them.'

'Well, then, what about Tom?'

'I haven't been to Bartraeth.' Nye looked big in the night but his words seemed to float.

'Why not?'

Nye walked towards the door. He had the manner of someone come to deliver bad news. 'Let me come in a minute.'

'What is it?' Georgie retreated from the door; she went to stand by the stairs. The fury which, for the last few hours, had widened her veins and kept her blood speeding, threatened to leave her. She put distance between herself and Nye as if she could safeguard it.

Nye followed her. He held on to the newel post. He was keyed up, to the point where he almost couldn't speak. Georgie could see that he was struggling with some deep-held intention, but whether he wanted to force it out or hold it back, she couldn't tell.

'We don't have to do this,' he said, in a rush. He stopped and closed his mouth to breathe in, then out. 'We don't have to. There is another way.'

'What?'

'We could let them go. I could stay here with you.' He was gaining confidence now, although his speech was still jerky. 'I don't mean just tonight. Afterwards, I could stay here, or you could come with me. Tom and Hazel have done something too bad for us to put it together again.'

'No,' said Georgie. 'I'm going to get him back.'

Something kindled in Nye's eyes – was it a reflection of her own anger?

'Listen. This is the second time Tom and you have split up. What kind of future do you think you'll have? I can't be your friend any more.'

'Yes you can.'

'Oh no. I'm not doing that, joining in on the edges again. If I do this for you tonight, that's the end. You'll never see me again afterwards.'

'Why?'

'Because I'll be going away to make my own life. Then you'll be left here to try and hold on to Tom on your own. Or. Or we could do something else. There is the other way.'

They looked at each other in silence for a second. Nye's skin glowed.

He let go of the newel post and stood alone. 'We can let them go. We can take each other instead.'

Nye walked towards her. He took two steps, facing straight on to her, and stopped within arm's length. He reached out and put one hand on her shoulder, the other on her cheek. Georgie recoiled. With one quick convulsion she moved out of his touch and kept on moving. 'No, no, no.'

'Georgie.'

'Yes?'

'Aren't you going to undress too?' Nye stood bare-chested, holding his shirt in front of him. He seemed uncertain. His body was looser than it had been, and there was a ridge of flesh around the top of his trousers. The hair which had covered his chest and stomach now spread across his shoulders and into the v of his throat, and it was no longer all black.

He wasn't sure of himself. Georgie stared. 'Yes, of course.' She sat down on the bed and took off her shoes and socks. Next she unbuttoned her jeans: the sight of Nye had made her realise that they would leave marks on her and she wanted to give them time to fade. She did not want to be crumple-fleshed for him.

Nye sat down on the opposite corner of the bed and followed her lead, untying his shoes. When he stood up again barefoot, he carried his socks and shoes to the chest of drawers and slotted them underneath, folded his shirt and laid it on the top. His back and upper arms were solid and huge. He'd grown some moles like large dark freckles.

Georgie took off her jumper, slowly, then her bra. She stood up to take off her jeans. When she straightened up, Nye was bent over, stripping his trousers and underpants off, watching her. He released himself from his clothes and squatted on the floor, holding them. The intentness of his face, and his reluctance to stand up, disturbed Georgie.

She took off her pants, quickly. 'What are you doing?' she asked.

'Looking at you.' Nye stayed squatting. Georgie wondered if he would be able to say anything else: he appeared speechless. It was almost as if he wanted to hide from her.

'Well?'

'Ah, you're so bloody beautiful, Georgie.'

'Get up.'

Nye rocked slightly, then stood up. He put his clothes aside and revealed his penis, erect, pointing up at her. Despite the purpling, it seemed very pale inside his black hair.

'Oh, Jesus.' Georgie's sigh untied the tension in her lungs.

'What is it?'

'I thought you couldn't get an erection.'

'No.' Nye tried to smile, but it ended up being just a gesture with his eyes. 'You underestimate us both. I do want you; I have wanted you.'

Naked, their bodies seemed more of a size than before. Georgie didn't feel overpowered. She moved towards Nye carefully and touched his hipbones; the flesh over them was firm. She lifted her arms so that he could slide his beneath them. Their bodies were touching in many different places at once, startling her with heat, hair and bulk.

In the middle of one night, Nye had snatched Tom back from

Hazel and delivered him to Georgie's door. Then he had left and lit a fire.

Last Sunday, he had brought Hazel to their home again. That had been another gift for Georgie. Though she had seen how, at one moment, Hazel had cast out a line for independence.

Nye must have seen it too but he had said nothing and Georgie didn't ask. Nor did they discuss whether Tom had seen. These days Hazel and Tom were too dangerous to be named.

On the hotel bed, Georgie fucked Nye.

38

Tom knocked on Ieuan's hallway door and waited. There was a long pause and he wondered if they'd heard him over the music. Then Ieuan opened the door. 'Oh, hiya.'

'Do you want some tea? I've made toast and things.'

'Brilliant.' Ieuan's head turned back to the room. 'Tea and toast's ready.'

Tom heard sounds of appreciation from inside, then the rustles and muffled thumps of teenagers moving themselves. Just in time, he realised he was hovering, eagerness and relief probably evident on his face. He turned away, saying, 'I'll see you in there,' over his shoulder.

In the kitchen he counted out plates and knives and spooned tea into the teapot. He'd even remembered to warm it. He had an instinct to create comfort. Attend to the small needs, make things as nice as possible.

It was humiliating to be lonely in his own home. The place was full of activity, with Ieuan's friends around and Georgie working in the studio. Tom had tried to make himself stay in there but it was no good: every quiet movement of hers, whether she was drawing or just looking out of the window, drinking coffee, threw a shadow across his vision. As he'd packed up and left, keeping his face preoccupied, Tom had wondered if Georgie enjoyed the reversal.

She was showing no obvious sign of doing so, but then he would not be caught watching her.

Tom knew she had slept with Nye. He had known it last night, when he came into the bedroom still carrying his London case and found her in bed. Her hair was clean; she smelled of soap and softness. She was wearing a warm nightshirt and reading. She put the book down and propped herself on her elbow to ask him questions, as if she'd been waiting for him.

Tom knew. He could almost see Nye in her skin, as if she'd

internalised him. Even when he went into the bathroom and found it steamy and the big bath-towel damp, and a curling paperback on the laundry basket – all the signs of a lazy evening at home – he had no doubts. Georgie was just creating an alibi.

He said nothing about it at all. He washed and brushed his teeth, returned to the bedroom, talked to her about the show and the interview. He joined her in bed and leant over and kissed her.

For a second then, he contemplated trying to make love to her, but with the idea came a surge of ugly laughter that alarmed him. He turned on his side, away from her, and pillowed his cheek.

This morning he had overslept. When he'd come downstairs Georgie was already at her desk, listening to the radio and sorting out bills. All day they had each been busy at their own pursuits, round the house.

He didn't know what to do. It wasn't a shock; he'd been very well prepared for this eventuality, since Georgie's announcement that she was going to see Nye. Sunday had brought it closer, of course, and now it was here.

He felt trapped, not by what the others were doing to him, but by how they behaved together. Georgie and Nye were fucking, making a rope of flesh. Hazel was complaisant, or at least not protesting. They were all looking steadfastly inwards, not at him and he had no opportunity to pull at their shoulders, interrupt their concentration, although there was as much space as he wanted to run around in – alone.

He had been fenced off: with a fleshy, Nye-and-Georgie mesh, and Hazel's thin hands helping weave it.

No one had touched him in the process. If they had, he wouldn't be so desolate.

Huw came in first, with his soft half-stubble now trained into something like a goatee. Then Miv, who had grown in the last few weeks; and Elen, Ieuan and Robbie, back on the scene after an absence of a month or so.

They ambled round the table and took up varying positions. Miv tucked herself into the window-seat: she was feeling quiet today. Robbie stood up, passing butter and jam and letting his leather jacket hang at a bandit's angle.

'Shall I give Mum a call?' Ieuan asked a bit later, when they were all sitting down and well into the toast and crumpets.

'She's working,' said Tom. 'I shouldn't think she'd want to be disturbed.'

'What, working working? In the studio?'

'Yep.' Tom looked at Ieu just long enough to remind him that they were with other people.

'That's great,' Ieu said quietly. He picked up his cup. Both Elen and Huw were listening, Tom saw: Elen glanced from Ieuan to Tom; Huw's eyes meandered round in the air and made contact as if accidentally with Ieuan's.

Tom guessed that Ieuan told his friends about Georgie's block and Tom's problems; he was bound to, given how much they affected his life. But they didn't need to be blatant about it. Tom liked to give Georgie a measure of protection, even now; especially now. She was drawing again and she might soon be showing again; she was meeting Nye in secret. How soon before people started to talk?

'I could take her some tea and crumpets through,' said Elen. 'Shall I?'

'Don't worry,' said Tom. 'I'll make her some fresh when we've finished.'

'Oh. Pity.' Elen giggled into her toast. 'I'd like to see in the studio.'

'Would you? I didn't know you were interested.'

'Oh yes, we all are. Mum and I watched you on the BBC last night and we taped it for Dad. I didn't realise you painted like that, using wires and planks.'

'That painting isn't very typical. And even with that, the wires and planks are only a small part of it; there's much more brush-work and knife-work, but that looks less spectacular on film.' Tom spoke easily but he was watching her. 'I didn't know anyone taped those things – even my mother doesn't bother.'

'Dad always likes to see when his friends are on TV or in the papers. He gets some agency to send him press cuttings. He's collected all your catalogues, for instance, and Georgie's.'

'Mum's catalogues?' said Ieuan. 'She hasn't got any. She can't have – she hasn't been in any shows since she left college.'

'Oh well, maybe it's just the cuttings and letters then. The stuff that used to come in the post.'

'In the post?' said Tom.

'Yes, along with the drawings.'

The kitchen was empty of people. Plates and mugs kept Tom

company; crumbs and smears of jam were convivial; he sat among them, not wanting to clear them up.

Outside, in the window square, the studio shone, converting the afternoon into evening. The light had come on in here too and various objects – an apron, a clock, pictures, the fridge – distributed their shadows.

Georgie was not coming in. Georgie must not come in. Not yet. Tom was thinking. Tom was wondering.

39

'Take your keys,' Georgie said to Ieuan. 'I'm out for the evening and I don't know what Dad's doing.'

'All right.'

'Your helmet's under the window, by the way.'

'Oh, thanks.'

'Be careful. Have a good time.'

From the top of the stairs, Tom watched their newly washed hair catch in the hall light. With the bloom of hurry and anticipation on their faces and Georgie's scarf hanging loosely round her shoulders, they might have been friends rather than mother and son.

'Don't drink and ride your bike back. I mean it.'

'Sure, Mum.'

Tom started to walk down quickly. He needed to know a little bit more before Georgie left. 'Are you both off? Have a good time. Can you do me a favour, Georgie?'

'If it's quick.'

'Are you going into Bartraeth?'

'Harborth.'

'Either will do. Take my card and get me some cash from the machines.'

Georgie's expression stalled. 'Yes, fine,' she said a second later. 'Thanks.'

So she wasn't planning to stay in the public parts of the town. Perhaps she didn't intend to go into it at all. Did Nye take her to country house hotels? Or had he rented somewhere? A small house down a lane, or near the quay.

Tom could see it: a nondescript cottage in one of the terraces, with two upstairs windows and one downstairs, looking at the channel; net curtains for screens in the daytime, thick green and red curtains closing the rooms off at night. They would open the upstairs curtains eventually, having switched off the lamps, and watch the aeroplane lights move across the water.

Or at least, they could do that in winter. Nye wouldn't have had time to get everything in place yet.

Tom tugged his wallet out of his pocket as he reached the hall, and found the cashpoint card for Georgie.

'How much?'

'Eighty.' She would have to make a detour now; even Nye wouldn't carry enough cash to spare him that. He watched her slip the card into her bag, and felt like chuckling. It might be demeaning himself to act like this, but he was certainly prepared to do it.

Then the motion of Georgie's head as she looked up at him, self-possessed, lucid, pulled shutters down against his eyes.

Twenty minutes after they had gone, Tom left the house. He did not expect to meet Nye on the road. He was fairly sure Nye would already be in Harborth; he wouldn't make Georgie wait for him.

The night was clear. The space between hills which the Islyn occupied – the valley that wasn't a valley – seemed wider than usual. Tom drove steadily along the lanes. There was still a doubt in his mind. He could have called, of course, to make sure he wasn't mistaken, but he hadn't been able to think of what to say. 'I'm coming. I need to talk to you.'

40

Hazel was in the kitchen when she heard the car engine; it drew her into the scullery, to look. She stayed there at the bare window, watching Tom turn the car and point it into a corner of the drive. He put it on the very edge of the Tarmac and when he got out he had to walk on the grass.

Tom walked slowly, and the long way round, staring at the house; he must be trying to work out who was in. His eyes moved from room to room and passed over Hazel's face: there was no light on in the scullery and she was invisible to him.

She rested behind the pane of glass, tracking him, and then when he was within a few yards of the porch, she realised that the doorbell would fetch Davy. Too late; by the time she was level with the kitchen table, the sound shrilled through the house.

41

Hazel looked guarded when she opened the door, but not wary. She was wearing a black jumper that hugged her throat and wrists, even though the hall was warm. Tom could smell soap and towels.

'Hello, Tom, come in.' As if he were expected. Hazel stood back and Tom moved past her, and then he saw the boy standing just above him on the stairs, wearing pyjamas, his hair wet. He retreated a step when he saw Tom, and sat down.

'Davy love, if you're going to come downstairs, finish drying your hair.'

Davy shook his head. 'I'm in my bedroom,' he said indignantly.

'OK. You can come down if you like, though. And rub your hair anyway.'

'All right.' Davy stared at his mother and didn't move. She turned back to Tom. 'Shall we go in the sitting room? Nye's not in.'

Tom followed her. He could feel Davy's eyes on him, but when he glanced back at the boy, he dropped his head with a spiderlike movement. Once Tom had gone into the sitting room, he heard a scuffle and the noise of bare feet trotting back upstairs.

'He's shy,' Hazel said, and then she seemed to regret it because before Tom could answer she walked over to the tray of drinks and said, with a peremptory inflection, 'would you like one?'

'Yes please. Whisky.'

The bottles were thick on the tray, long necks glinting like a mini-Manhattan. Tom watched Hazel's hand go to the back. He saw two labels – a Famous Grouse and a Talisker. Famous Grouse had been Tom's drink when he had been sleeping with Hazel and could only afford a blend. Without hesitating, Hazel picked out the Talisker and poured him a glass.

'Soda?'

'Not with that.'

Hazel carried the glass not to him but to the low table, and set it down near a chair. She returned to the tray and began making herself a gin and tonic. Her absence of ceremony was disorienting; it brought their familiarity suddenly, startlingly back to life, as if it had been there all along, only disguised for the benefit of others.

Yet the familiarity wasn't erotic or even affectionate. It was more like two officers meeting during a lull in a military campaign. These paintings on the wall could be maps of terrain; Hazel's black outfit a uniform.

Hazel turned round. 'Tom, sit down. I'm just going to get some ice.'

It was cooler in this room than in the hall; Tom understood Hazel's jumper now. The hearth was empty, although there were ashes in it which suggested a fire yesterday or the night before. Perhaps it was lit only when Nye and both children were home.

Hazel came back in. Her glass was very full and she was wiping her hand on her trousers. A sign of nervousness, or just of that carelessness Tom had seen in her before?

She sat down on the very edge of a deep chair, looked at him and took a drink. She glanced at him again and took another. 'How are you?' It was very sardonic.

'I don't know, to be honest.' Tom picked his own glass up and took a generous mouthful – at least he didn't have to pretend to be nonchalant. 'Am I imagining this or were you expecting me?'

'You or Georgie or someone. It was going to be my turn for a visit sooner or later.'

'You thought you might see Georgie tonight?'

'Well. Not tonight perhaps.'

'Ah.' Since they'd started talking, they hadn't lost eye contact. Tom felt as if they were engaged in some sort of face dance, manoeuvring through tiny sequences of muscle tension and release. 'Where is Nye tonight?'

Hazel rose, walked to the hall door and pushed it gently closed, and sat down again.

'He's with Georgie somewhere, I expect. I don't know where. Do you?' She sounded facetious.

'No.' Tom retaliated by sounding cold; at which another small chain of reactions went across Hazel's face and settled into an expression that didn't seem to belong to her.

'Would you like a cigarette?' she said. She was already reaching for the box, one slim arm stretched over the glass table; the gesture both an excuse to turn away and a defiance.

'Not with the malt.'

'You don't have to be so respectful of the whisky. It comes in a bottle, not a grail.' Hazel said it without looking at him, her head bent to the cigarette and the lighter. When she sat back, her hair flapped over her face and she breathed out a long line of smoke.

'I like good whisky. Should I give that up, as well?'

There was silence. From upstairs, they could suddenly hear Davy singing. Hazel took a careful drag on her cigarette.

'Look, I need to ask you some things,' Tom said.

'Go on then.' It came out very glibly. Tom stared at her while she reached for her glass.

'Are you going to answer me honestly?'

'Oh yes.'

'After you and Nye left Wales' – he articulated with great care; he felt that he was piecing together a vital formula – 'how soon did Georgie get in touch?'

Hazel watched the far corner of the table. 'Just after we were married.' She said it obligingly, like someone taking part in a game.

'And *how* did she get in touch?'

'She wrote to Nye.'

'Do you know what she said?'

'Not in the first letter, no. I never saw it.' Hazel shifted position: she picked up an ashtray from the table and put it on her chair arm, then she folded her legs up beside her. 'He didn't tell me about it, you know.' She looked impatient. 'I saw the package arrive – it came to our house one morning with a Cyprus postmark. Nye opened it in front of me – I think he thought it would be something sarcastic and angry like the phone calls. I saw that there were drawings inside, but that was all. I was standing behind Nye at the time, so I couldn't really see. He put them back in the envelope and didn't say anything. Then he went out to work.'

'And?'

'And nothing. I didn't ask him about it. He didn't say anything.'

'Didn't you want to find out what was going on?'

Hazel gave him a strange look. It was self-deprecating and slightly scornful. 'Yes, and I thought I would.'

'How?'

'By keeping quiet and waiting. You see, I thought it would be my turn next.'

'What do you mean?'

'I thought I'd hear from you.'

Tom stared. Hazel raised her eyebrows and tucked in one side of her mouth. 'I know.' Her voice had a little tinny resonance. 'Anyway. A year later, another package came from Georgie, which surprised me, because I'd assumed she and Nye were communicating through work. It had a Welsh postmark,' she glanced at him, 'but I knew you were back anyway.'

'What was in it?'

'I don't know – more drawings, I presume. Nye took it off and opened it in private.'

There was a silence in which Hazel put out her cigarette and drank some more gin. She looked shadowed and sharp-faced, as if she'd turned into a negative of herself.

Tom realised that he had no right to be here asking questions. He'd forfeited it, along with his ability to understand. He couldn't give up, though; he had shrunk in the last few minutes – he could feel his intestines thinning, his muscles become of less consequence – but he sat forward and pressed his finger pads against the tumbler.

'Hazel,' he said incontinently. 'The drawings. Did Georgie go on sending them?'

Hazel finished her gin and set the glass down. 'I'll get some more in a minute,' she said, then she nodded. 'She did send more. But not for a long time, and the next ones she sent came to me.'

'To you?'

'Yes, just one batch. They came to the house in Ealing after I moved back from Paris. I thought at the time it was a gesture of solidarity. But actually I think it was an initiation.'

Tom blinked at her. She was using Nye's language but she sounded just like herself, flippant, with an edge of self-hatred. She moved suddenly. 'Oh Christ. Look, come with me, and I'll show you.'

Tom followed Hazel upstairs. The pictures on the way up struck him more forcibly than they'd done the night of the dinner: they were very mixed – some woodcuts, a silk-screen print and a small oil. He couldn't make sense of the assortment, nor the odd way they studded the expanse of wall.

Everything was foreign. Hazel had gone on waiting to hear from him for years after they'd parted; Georgie had never really lost her talent. Tom had been unsighted, somehow. And now, although things were being shown to him, he missed the perspective to make them fit.

Where was Nye tonight?

'You don't have to look as though you're going to your execution,' said Hazel. 'It's a few pictures, that's all.'

'I don't know what I'm going to see,' said Tom. His chest and throat were tight; he was almost panicking. An idea had risen like a wall in front of him: the blank spaces of wall he'd noticed in Nye's study.

Hazel paused at the top and pointed to the right, towards the study door. 'Along here.'

'That's not what I mean,' he tried to say. But he padded along the carpet after Hazel. *What am I going to see?*

Paintings Georgie had sworn she could not do. Drawings, bold of line; prints, even – from the lino cuts and steel plate engravings that had once been her pleasure. Colours he had once watched her make flashed on to his eyes and hurt them.

Hazel opened the door and switched on the light. 'Over there.'

They were not paintings. They were only drawings, six of them, in frames. Three were charcoal; one was pen and ink; two were charcoal with coloured chalk.

Tom stood in front of them and looked carefully. He was in almost all of them. In a couple he was a humunculus; in another he recognised his body without a head. They were all scenes, with buildings and plants and an action or two, not necessarily human.

Nye's face flowered on a bush in the pen and ink. In a charcoal and chalk he was a small dragon, a spot of fiery pink over his belly.

Each drawing had a building of some sort, the parallels and angles all mixed up. Tom recognised their apartment in Cyprus. And a sketch of the architect's plans for their extension, the perpendiculars converging like a wigwam. Hazel's features, without a defining outline, ran round the crazy walls like a frieze.

Georgie had put herself in too, and in one she whirled, tiny, like a miniature moon orbiting Nye, and at her heel was an even tinier sphere, just recognisable as Ieuan.

'Those aren't all of them,' said Hazel. She was sitting on a corner of Nye's desk; with her foot she opened one of the drawers; she leaned down and scooped out a file. Her movements were disrespectful. 'These are the others. They're not so good.'

She spread them on the desk. There were five of them and they were similar to the framed drawings but weaker. One or two were very botched, and had images redrawn and scribbled out.

'She got worse as she went on, actually,' said Hazel. 'I think this couple here are the last she sent us. That must have been—'

'—don't tell me.' Tom put his hand up to block her out. He was scrutinising the five. His throat was knotted up, but with relief rather than dread, a desperate relief that he wanted to hold on to. She hadn't been able to draw all along. It had come in spurts, and after the earlier phases, she had lost it. The images were like a calendar, helping him to orientate himself.

She had drawn in Cyprus, after they'd heard about the marriage. She had drawn well back in Wales, soon after Ieuan's birth. Then later – some years later, the primary school in Bartraeth was in this one – she had faltered. Struggled again soon afterwards – and these, these last ones that Hazel had indicated. Had Nye known what to make of these faces, too fussily drawn – Melanie, his best student and his lover; Martin who had packed up and moved away and waited in vain for Georgie to join him?

'Four years ago,' he said. 'Four years ago to three.'

Georgie taking sleeping pills at night; Georgie giving her easel to the charity shop. Georgie getting promoted.

'That's right.'

'So you and Nye look at these together, do you?' he asked.

Hazel stood up. 'No.' She suddenly sounded exhausted. 'We don't. Any more than you and Georgie did.' She faced him as if her vision had blurred and she was waiting for it to clear. 'Look, I'm going to go and tuck Davy up. When you've finished, leave the drawings on the desk. I know the order he keeps them in.'

When Hazel came out of the bedroom, the house was very quiet. The stairs had creaked some time ago and she had heard a door open and close. She went along the landing to Nye's study.

The door was ajar and she could see the loose papers still on the desk. She crossed the room quickly, tensed, but when she reached them, she saw that the drawings were unharmed. And all six were still on the walls, in their frames.

She leaved the loose sheets together in Nye's preferred order and replaced them in the folder, in the drawer. She looked around the room: nothing was unusual.

As she went downstairs, she heard a sound from the sitting room. He hadn't gone after all.

He was sitting on the stool by the empty fireplace and he'd refilled his glass. The colour had come back into his face but divided, so that the skin was flushed in patches on his nose, forehead and cheeks. 'Is he asleep?' he asked.

'Probably, by now.' Hazel took her glass to the tray. She reached for the gin, but the thought of it suddenly made her feel sick. She gave herself a new glass and a whisky instead.

'Was the drawing Georgie sent you one of those?'

'Yes, the pen and ink with the spinning plates and Nye's face on a bush.'

'So you did show it to him.'

'No.' Hazel walked past the chair she'd been using before and which was too close to Tom now; she chose his old chair, on the other side of the glass table. 'I was back in Ealing but Nye was still in Paris at the time. I put the drawing in a new envelope, typed his work address, drove over the Severn bridge and sent it to him.'

Her hand hovered over the cigarette packet, but she realised suddenly that she didn't really want one. She sipped the whisky instead.

'Why?' Tom's face was grooved with suspicion.

'Because I didn't want to share a secret with Georgie. And I didn't want to confide in Nye, or hand it meekly over, thank you. "Oh look, Nye, it's from Georgie, what can it mean?" ' Hazel heard herself sounding cool and derisive – it was the only way she could stop the anger from snapping out at Tom. He didn't deserve it; or at least, not all of it.

He was crowded and jostled by late discoveries. He was naturally suspicious. Hazel took another quick mouthful. 'I just did a switch. Took advantage of their secrets. It was really quite nice to know more than other people for once.'

Hazel had searched Nye's face the night he came back, mining it for knowledge as he sat on the stairs in the hall of their Ealing house. His overnight case was at his feet, still zipped and strapped shut.

'I'm not interested in going back to Paris,' she'd said. They were quiet, because Elen was playing in the living room. 'You'll have to come here.'

'I know that.' Nye was sweating. 'I'll arrange it. I'm sorry.'

'You're in love with Veronique, aren't you?'

'I'm desperate about her. It will pass.'

Hazel had looked at her husband and wondered what had made him pack his case and come after her. It was just six days since she had posted Georgie's drawing on; before that, she and Elen had been in England three weeks. Georgie would have known she'd walked out. Had that been why Georgie got in touch: in order to affect the outcome?

Hazel reached for a cigarette now; a quick snap of fingers and filter tip and lips.

'Look, Tom, I'm not an oracle. I can't sit here and tell you what's going on. She never sent me anything again, by the way.'

'Fair enough.' Tom sat forward, his back bent, and stared into his whisky. After a while he looked up (it was an economical movement – just a contraction of the muscles in his shoulder and neck) and said: 'Did you know that for twenty years Georgie's been unable to finish a single piece of work?'

He obviously wanted an answer but as Hazel wasn't sure she understood him, she kept quiet.

'She used to spend hours in the studio sweating it out.' Tom's eyes were piggy and supplicating. 'She wouldn't work in front of me. She destroyed all her attempts at painting. I used to try and get her to draw or make prints, but she wouldn't. She said she wasn't interested in second best, it was only painting that mattered.'

Jesus. So that was what Georgie had been doing to Tom. Hazel had no idea what she was meant to say.

'Yes well, it looks like it doesn't it?' She inhaled and felt the nicotine bless her bloodstream.

'Jesus,' said Tom. He made a laughing sound, like an animal spitting out a furball. 'Jesus.'

'Why don't you sit back?' She hadn't meant to say it so abruptly, but Tom was cramped up on the stool like someone who was expecting to go through a tunnel. He stared at her, uncomprehending. 'You're hunched up like that,' she added. 'It makes me uncomfortable to look at you.'

It made her more than uncomfortable. The sight of him huddled opened up physical memories. Hazel could feel the angles of his body as if they were pressed into hers. She sensed the tension in his limbs.

She didn't want to be tipped back into that kind of familiarity. It was treacherous and she'd drunk enough from that cup anyway; she'd drunk until she was nauseous and she'd still been thirsty. And Tom, she could remember very well, had been parched.

Tom straightened up. He looked miserable and slightly angry; he must think she was laughing at him. He thrust his legs out in front of him, held up his hands. 'Is that better?'

'Yes.'

'Oh good. Is there anything else you want me to do? Any other way I can make you more comfortable?' He was trying to be scathing but he couldn't hold the tone; he'd never been any good at that. He looked away and focused on his glass; she saw him notice the amount of whisky in there and surprise, then greed, entered his face. He brought the glass to his mouth, and checked. He looked at her thoughtfully and when he laughed, it was like an experiment. 'Except leave,' he said. 'I don't want to do that.'

He couldn't say he understood. Hazel was tightly wound, her black arms and legs precariously anchored by drinks and cigarettes and cushions. She seemed to want to look at him but she kept changing her expression. Protective camouflage, but for whose benefit?

Georgie had tied him up very bitterly. Nye had helped. And Hazel. But then, Tom had let himself be tied. He knew very well he wasn't exempt. He drank another mouthful of Nye's malt: it covered his tongue beautifully, he was glad she'd chosen the Talisker. He'd pour some more in a minute.

'Did you know Georgie told me she couldn't paint?' He asked it quickly.

Hazel hesitated. 'I knew she didn't have shows. Someone told me once, when I was here on a visit to Nye's mother, that it was a shame she didn't paint any more.'

'But you didn't know what was going on at home in the studio?'

'No, how could I?'

She seemed irritated. Though God knew why she thought she had the right to be. Perhaps she followed his reaction because having glanced at him, she put out her cigarette and said: 'I did once ask Nye why she never sent him paintings, only drawings. He said she'd never been any good as a painter and she knew it.'

For an instant Tom was looking down a tunnel of glass and at the end of it stood Georgie and Nye, reduced in size and absolutely clear. In each other's confidence; isolated from the rest by the hard light.

'Do you think it's true?' said Hazel.

'God knows.'

'Perhaps she was glad of an excuse to give up painting.'

Tom thought of Georgie in the studio, her face twisted with wretchedness. Nothing had been clear then, and as he thought of it now, the confusion came rolling back in. 'Perhaps.'

What made Georgie glad? Happiness? Freedom? The weight of Tom's dependency? The dangerous pursuit of Nye?

Georgie's lies and truths overlapped, as did Tom's. They bent and kinked into one another. What made him happy with Georgie didn't make him happy with Nye, or with Hazel. Because Tom, Nye, Georgie and Hazel had splintered one another's vision. They saw more than they understood and felt more than they saw.

There were no steady lines to follow; no authentic symbols. You could only be guided by what you found beneath your hands; the edges of shapes that other people were busy making.

Between them they had made a hole, an invisible O. They had come to the edge of it on the night of the fire and had been moving round it ever since. In the transparency, exchanges had taken place. Something had been sacrificed; something of Tom's, but also something that had belonged to the others. And he, as much as the others, had reached out for the recompense. He was still reaching.

Hazel's hands were linked on her knees now: very loosely, an intermediate resting place. Tom wouldn't be surprised if they suddenly pointed to the door, or pushed her out of the chair to turn music on. What were Georgie's and Nye's hands doing now?

But though he tried, he couldn't see them. Instead, incredibly clearly, he was back with Nye in Caerfach on the first day they'd missed school. Nye sat on the wall behind the bus station, and grit blew in his face. 'See if you can stand dead still for five minutes without asking me the time.' And Tom had done it, for much, much longer than five minutes, the muscles knotting at the base of his spine, while Nye watched him.

'What is it?'

'I'm just standing up. I wasn't very comfortable.' His tongue slipped on the words. His stomach was empty; the gap inside him seemed to grow bigger as he stood, elbow wedged against the mantelpiece. 'I'm very hungry. Can you give me something to eat?'

Georgie measured the distance between her body and Nye's. The room was warm but now that she'd rolled over, she was in a draught. She watched the skin on her arms pucker and the hairs stand up. She moved her arm, inch by inch, and stretched it out against Nye's side. Her shoulder nestled his buttock; her fingers just grazed his armpit.

'We weren't going to make love,' she said.

'I know.' Nye didn't seem completely at ease. Inside the humour, his voice was off-balance.

She stroked the muscle that led from his armpit to his chest.

'We can't go on like this,' she said. 'We'll have to ration ourselves unless we want to burn up.'

'Like Tom and Hazel did, you mean.'

There was definitely something wrong. At first she'd thought it was because they were trying to forgo sex, and sure enough when they had made love he'd pressed his face against her body with such yearning that she'd been startled. Georgie had fed on his need with her own curious surge of restive pleasure.

But they'd finished and Nye was still tense.

'Please tell me.'

'What?'

'Whatever it is. I can feel you thinking about it.' She walked her hand down his flank, spider-fashion, wanting him to feel her insistence, yet also wanting to keep the matter light.

She heard the swish of his arm moving across the sheet towards her head; his fingers found her scalp and moved over it gently at first, but with tension, and then with a questing pressure.

'I talked to Michael Trewin today. The Reynolds Monette director.'

Georgie's breathing stopped. Nye's fingertips scraped loudly next to her ears. 'And?'

'He's not going to get it. It's between two of the others.'

Georgie's heart went on thumping. It was as if she still waited in suspense. She pushed herself away, into a sitting position. The disappointment was immediately familiar; it closed in at the well-known angles while she tried to push it away with words. 'No, not again,' she said. 'Oh Jesus, not this time. Are you sure?'

'I am.' Nye looked back at her with a steadiness that made her want to shout at him.

'How can they? He deserves it. I thought the judges were – oh hell.' The breath caught on the back of her tongue. 'Oh fucking hell.'

'I'm sorry. I didn't know whether I should tell you.' Nye sat up too. Outlined against the hotel headboard, he looked disproportionately strong.

Georgie stared at his broad neck with the red band where his shirt collar chafed. She should go home and find Tom and tell him. She should get out of bed at once and hurry off, so that even if she didn't tell him straight away, when he heard at least he would have had her under his eye for a few days; he wouldn't have to wonder about her absence as well.

But she wanted to stay. She needed to stay. She crossed her arms over herself.

'You made love with me, knowing that.' She turned away slightly as she said it; she was beginning to feel angry and afraid and she didn't want Nye to see it. 'You didn't tell me first.'

'No, I'm sorry. I didn't want you to know. I wanted to have you again, one more time, before we go back to thinking about him.' Nye leant his head back against the wall; then he put his hand on her leg. It was an odd gesture – complete in itself, deeply sexual. 'What will happen now?'

'What do you mean?'

'You'll have to tell him, won't you?'

Georgie was already scrambling among the options. If she waited till tomorrow, she could say she'd met Nye in the street. Perhaps she might say she'd run into Michael Trewin tonight. Or, looking at Nye, feeling anger swell inside her – Nye had found out; Nye could tell him.

'I'm not sure I'll tell him.' She grasped her left thumb and pulled.

'It'll be hard living with him between now and the letter.'

'It'll be hard after the letter too,' Georgie said bitterly. The familiar walls were closing in over her, some steep, some oblique, all bringing duty and responsibility with them. She was in the wrong again. It was the place she most hated to be. Christ, Christ.

She pressed her hands into her belly, rejecting the pain. But she couldn't reject it without lessening the tie between her and Tom.

'I'm not going to stop seeing you,' she said defiantly.

Nye's hand shifted on her leg but stayed there.

'Ah, Georgie. Don't you think we should stop for a while – for a month or two? While he comes to grips with this.'

'No. Why?' Georgie reached out for Nye. He let her touch him; his head turned in her palms. She felt his hands move up from her leg to her waist; they lifted her, brought her next to his body.

There was no reassurance in his touch. He pressed and delved and his appetite seemed to slip by her. Georgie felt herself come apart and reassemble under his hands and she moved hers over him in answer, trying to read the memory stored in his muscles and skin, the energy they hadn't yet turned into action. She was afraid.

'Cutting towards you.'

'What?' Hazel glanced up but her hand continued to saw lightly at the bread.

'You're cutting the bread towards you,' Tom said. 'I haven't seen anyone do that since my grandmother. It's an old Welsh habit, Nye told me.'

'Nye would, he told me too. I've always done it.'

'Have you?' Tom tried to get a picture of Hazel in the past, cutting bread for him; he knew she must have done it, all those scratch meals at the bedsit, but no picture came. He had watched her obsessively then, but he hadn't noticed which way she cut. He had noticed other things, and left that to Nye.

'Mustard?' Hazel said.

'Yes please. Not too much.' He watched her butter and stack the ham. 'Are you going to tell Nye I came?'

Hazel opened the mustard pot; her eyelashes held still as she did it; she was thinking. 'Yes. I think I am.'

'What'll you tell him?'

'That you came up on the off-chance of seeing him and stayed to talk to me.'

'Will you tell him I saw Georgie's drawings?'

She put the top slice on the sandwich and cut it across. 'Do you want me to?'

'No. Christ.' He said it so vehemently he had to catch his lip to stop spit coming out.

Hazel glanced at him and suddenly he had another memory: Hazel among some trees, saying, 'It's hurting her,' and Georgie standing in the hall of the cottage, her white shirt the only bright thing in the moonlight, letting him see her face.

Hazel had caught something in his face. She pushed the bread-board towards him and sat down. She did it very lightly, folding her legs back as if in readiness. 'Will you be telling her?'

'No-o.' Tom sent the word across his tongue slowly. It was a betrayal of Georgie; though it was a betrayal he now wanted to make. 'I won't be telling anyone.' As soon as he'd spoken the words, his diaphragm gathered up, as though someone had drawn a fingernail along it. Getting the wind up, they had called it in the war; the invasive lightness you feel before a battle.

Easy. Balance. It was hard, sustaining the counterpoise between denial and intemperance. Defiance and control. Hazel had paid, and paid, for her past transgressions. She had learnt to enjoy paying.

It had taught her delicacy. She brought that to Nye and he knew it; he was generous in acknowledging it.

Tom ate quickly. His Adam's apple moved up and down. Hazel

felt it – and the noise of his swallowing – on the skin of her arms: a response between excitement and oppression.

'Are you going to ask me questions now?' Tom said, his eyes sly, his hands already lifting the second wedge of bread and ham.

'About what?'

'There's one you must want to ask.' He bit into the sandwich, held it in front of his mouth as he chewed, bit into it again. 'About the night of the fire. Don't you want to ask why I didn't come back? No? You don't? Well,' he laughed, and chewed fast, 'get this. The truth is I don't know. I still don't know. You were there, weren't you?' Tom said. 'At the Islyn that night.'

I was there; out in the darkness with Nye, looking up at the room. Georgie shaking out her hair. Tom pressing his face into her shoulder.

'Yes.'

Tom ate the last piece of crust. 'Will you let me see you again?'

Nye lay on Georgie, hunting. His mouth was full of her fingers. With one hand he cupped her head; he slid the other beneath her back, to hold her up.

He felt her effort and her fear; he joined them with his own. He needed to cling on to stop himself falling. They were travelling fast towards the others again.

It wasn't enough. It was never enough.